Carol Marinelli ... asked for her job ... years, to be able to ... it asked what Carol ... pen for a moment Ca... third question asked— ... Well, not wanting to look obsesse... ...m, boring, she crossed the fingers on her free h... and answered 'swimming and tennis'. But, given that the chlorine in the pool does terrible things to her highlights, and the closest she's got to a tennis racket in the last couple of years is watching the Australian Open, I'm sure you can guess the real answer!

Sadly, **Margaret McDonagh** has passed away since the writing of this book. She will be remembered as an author who lived for her writing and who brought joy to readers everywhere.

Anne Fraser was born in Scotland, but brought up in South Africa. After she left school she returned to the birthplace of her parents, the remote Western Islands of Scotland. She left there to train as a nurse before going on to university to study English Literature. After the birth of her first child, she and her doctor husband travelled the world, working in rural Africa, Australia and Northern Canada. Anne still works in the health sector. To relax, she enjoys spending time with her family, reading, walking and travelling.

Hot Single Docs
COLLECTION

July 2018

August 2018

September 2018

October 2018

November 2018

December 2018

January 2019

February 2019

Hot Single Docs: The Playboy's Redemption

CAROL MARINELLI

MARGARET McDONAGH

ANNE FRASER

MILLS & BOON

Published in Great Britain 2018
by Mills & Boon, an imprint of HarperCollins*Publishers*
1 London Bridge Street, London, SE1 9GF

HOT SINGLE DOCS: THE PLAYBOY'S REDEMPTION © 2018
Harlequin Books S.A.

St. Piran's: Rescuing Pregnant Cinderella © 2010 Harlequin Books S.A
Special thanks and acknowledgement are given to Carol Marinelli for her contribution to the *St.Piran's Hospital* series.

St.Piran's: Italian Surgeon, Forbidden Bride © 2011 Harlequin Books S.A
Special thanks and acknowledgement are given to Margaret McDonagh for her contribution to *the St.Piran's Hospital* series

St. Piran's: Daredevil, Doctor...Dad! © 2012 Harlequin Books S.A
Special thanks and acknowledgement are given to Anne Fraser for her contribution to the *St. Piran's Hospital* series

ISBN: 978-0-263-26830-0

09-1018

MIX
Paper from
responsible sources
FSC™ C007454

ST. PIRAN'S: RESCUING PREGNANT CINDERELLA

CAROL MARINELLI

CHAPTER ONE

'I'M READY to come back to St Piran's.'

No words filled the silence, there was no quick response to her statement, so Izzy ploughed on, determined to make a good impression with Jess, the hospital counsellor. 'I'm really looking forward to being back at work.' Izzy's voice was upbeat. 'I know that a few people have suggested that I wait till the baby is born, I mean, given that I can only work for a couple of months, but I really think that this is the right thing for me.'

Still Jess said nothing, still Izzy argued to the silence. 'I'm ready to move on with my life. I've put the house on the market....' She felt as if she were at an interview, effectively she *was* at an interview. After the terrible events of four months ago, Ben Carter, the senior consultant in A and E, had told her to take all the time she needed before she came back to the unit where she worked as an emergency registrar.

It would have been far easier to not come back, and at nearly twenty-eight weeks pregnant she'd had every reason to put it off, but Izzy had finally taken the plunge, and instead of ringing Ben to tell him her decision, she had dropped by unannounced. But to her surprise, instead of welcoming her back with open arms, Ben had gently but firmly informed her that it would be *preferable* if she see one of the hospital counsellors.

'I'm fine!' Izzy had said. 'I don't need to see a counsellor.'

'You are seeing someone, though?' Ben had correctly interpreted the beat of silence.

'I was.' Izzy had swallowed. 'But I'm fine now.'

'Good!' Ben had clipped. 'Then you won't have a problem speaking with someone else.'

'Ben!' Izzy had hardly been able to contain her fury. 'It's been four months! You know me—'

'Izzy!' Ben had interrupted, refusing to be manipulated. 'I worked with you daily, I've been to your home, I got on well with Henry and yet I had no idea what you were going through, so, no, I'm not convinced I do know you or that you'd come to me if you had a problem.'

Izzy had sat with pursed lips. Ben could be so incredibly kind yet so incredibly tough too—he would let nothing jeopardise the safety of his patients or his staff and he was also completely honest and open, so open it actually hurt to hear it sometimes. 'I've spoken with my senior colleagues...'

'You've discussed me?'

'Of course,' Ben had replied. 'And we all agree that coming back to A and E after all you've been through is going to be tough, that we need to look out for you, and rather than us asking every five minutes if you're okay, which I know will drive you crazy, I'm going to insist that you see someone. I can page Jess Carmichael—she's good, all very informal, you can go for a walk, have a coffee...'

'I'm not sitting in the canteen, chatting about my life!' Izzy had bristled. 'I'll see her in her office.'

'Fine,' Ben had responded, and then his voice had softened. 'We want what's best for you Izzy.'

So here she was, on a Friday lunchtime, just before her first shift back, *again* sitting in a counsellor's office, telling the same thing to Jess that she had to Ben, to her mother, to her friends, that she was fine.

Fine!

'It's often suggested,' Jess said, when Izzy had told her that her house was on the market, 'that people wait twelve months after a bereavement before making any major life changes.'

'I'm twenty-eight weeks pregnant!' Izzy gave a tight smile. 'I'd suggest that change is coming whether I'm ready or not. Look…' She relented a touch because Jess was nothing other than nice. 'I don't want to bring the baby home to that house—there are just too many memories. I really want a new home by the time the baby comes.'

'I can understand that,' Jess said. 'Have you people to help you with moving?'

'Plenty,' Izzy said, 'Now I just need someone to make a half-decent offer on the house.'

'How will you feel—' Jess had a lovely soft Scottish accent, but her direct words hit a very raw spot '—when a domestic abuse case comes into the department?'

Izzy paused for a moment to show she was giving the question due thought then gave her carefully prepared answer, because she'd known this would be asked. 'The same as I'll feel if a pregnant woman comes into the department or a widow—I'll have empathy for them, but I'm certainly not going to be relating everything to myself.'

'How can you not? Izzy, you've been through the

most awful experience,' Jess said and even her lilting voice couldn't soften the brutal facts. 'You tried to end a violent, abusive relationship to protect the child you are carrying, and your husband beat you and in his temper drove off and was killed. It's natural to feel—'

'You have no idea how I feel,' Izzy interrupted, doing her best to keep her voice even, a trip down memory lane was the last thing she needed today. 'I don't want the "poor Izzy" line and I don't want your absolution and for you to tell me that none of this was my fault.'

'I'm not trying to.'

'I've dealt with it,' Izzy said firmly. 'Yes, it was awful, yes, it's going to be hard facing everyone, but I'm ready for it. I'm ready to resume my life.'

Only Jess didn't seem so sure, Izzy could tell. She had made such an effort for this day—she was immaculately dressed in a grey shift dress with black leggings and black ballet pumps, her blonde short hair, teased into shape, and large silver earrings adding a sparkle to her complexion. She had been hoping to look every inch a modern professional woman, who just happened to be pregnant. She would not let Jess, let anyone, see behind the wall she had built around herself—it was the only way she knew to survive.

Jess gave her some coping strategies, practised deep breathing with her, told her to reach out a bit more to friends and Izzy ran a hand through her gamine-cut blonde hair that had once been long and lush but which she'd cut in a fit of anger. Just when Izzy thought the session was over, Jess spoke again.

'Izzy, nothing can dictate what comes into Emergency, that's the nature of the job.' Jess paused for a moment before continuing. 'No matter what is going on in your life, no matter how difficult your world is right now, you have to be absolutely ready to face whatever comes through the doors. If you feel that you'd rather—'

'Are you going to recommend that I be sent to Outpatients?' Izzy challenged, her grey eyes glittering with tears that so desperately needed to be shed but had, for so long, been held back. 'Or perhaps I can do a couple of months doing staff immunisations—'

'Izzy—' Jess broke in but Izzy would not be silenced.

'I'm a good doctor. I would never compromise my patients' safety. If I didn't feel ready to face A and E, I wouldn't have come back.' She gave an incredulous laugh. 'Everyone seems to be waiting for me to fall apart.' She picked up her bag and headed for the door. 'Well, I'm sorry to disappoint you all, but I refuse to.'

Izzy was a good doctor, of that Jess had no doubt.

As she wrote her notes, she was confident, more than confident, that Izzy would do the right thing by her patients, that she was more than capable to be working in Emergency. But at what cost to herself? Jess thought, resting back in her chair and closing her eyes for a moment.

Jess wanted to send a memo to the universe to insist only gentle, easy patients graced Izzy's path for a little while.

Only life wasn't like.

Jess clicked on her pen and finished writing up her notes, worried for her client and wishing more progress had been made.

Izzy Bailey, while still fighting the most enormous private battle, was stepping straight back into the front line.

CHAPTER TWO

'OBSTETRIC Team to Emergency.'

Izzy heard the chimes as she tossed her coffee and sandwich wrapper in the bin and did a little dance at the sliding door that refused to acknowledge her, no matter how many times she swiped her card. An impatient nurse behind her took over, swiping her own card, and Izzy tailgated her in.

They'd start her in Section B.

Of that she was sure.

Writing up tetanus shots and suturing, examining ankles and wrists… Despite her assured words to Jess earlier, Izzy was actually hoping for a gentle start back and was quietly confident that Ben would have arranged for one.

'Obstetric team to Emergency.'

The chimes sounded again, but Izzy wasn't fazed. It was a fairly familiar call—frenzied fathers-to-be often lost their way and ended up bringing their wives to Emergency rather than Maternity.

Izzy glanced at her watch.

In ten minutes she'd be starting her first shift…

Walking through another set of sliding doors, which

this time opened without the use of her card, Izzy found herself in the inner sanctum of the emergency unit.

She'd timed it well, Izzy thought to herself.

By the time she'd put her bag in her locker, it would be almost time to start, which meant that she could bypass the staffroom, the small talk...

'Izzy!' Beth, an RN she'd worked with over the years, was racing past. 'Cubicle four... Everyone's tied up... She just presented...'

Except Jess *had* been right.

There would be no gentle easing in, Izzy fast realised as Les, the porter, relieved her of her bag. Beth brought her up to speed as best she could in short rapid sentences as they sped across the unit.

'About twenty-three weeks pregnant, though she's vague on dates,' the rapid handover went on. 'She won't make it to Maternity, I've put out a call...'

'Who's seen her?' Izzy asked as she squirted some alcohol rub on her hands.

'You,' came Beth's response

Oh, yes!

She'd forgotten just how unforgiving Emergency could be at times. Just then she saw Ben, wrapping a plastic apron around himself, and Izzy was quite sure he'd take over and usher her off to Section B.

'Have you got this?' Ben said instead, calling over his shoulder as he sped off to Resus.

'Sure!'

'Her name's Nicola,' Beth said as Izzy took one, very quick, deep breath and stepped in.

'Hi, there Nicola. I'm Izzy Bailey, the emergency registrar.' Izzy wasn't sure who looked more petrified, the student nurse who'd been left with the patient while

Beth had dashed for a delivery pack or the mother-to-be who brought Izzy up to date with her rapid progress even before Izzy had time to ask more questions—it was Nicola who pulled back the sheet.

'It's coming.'

'Okay.' Izzy pulled on some gloves as Beth opened the delivery pack, Nicola was in no state to be sped across the floor to Resus. 'Let Resus know to expect the baby,' Izzy said. 'Tell them to get a cot ready.' She took a steadying breath. 'Emergency-page the paediatric team.'

'Vivienne!' Beth instructed the student nurse to carry out Izzy's instructions, and Vivienne sped off.

'There's going to be a lot of overhead chimes,' Izzy explained to Nicola, 'but that's just so we can get the staff we need down here quickly for your baby.'

The membrane was intact, Izzy could see it bulging, and she used those few seconds to question her patient a little more, but there were no straightforward answers.

'I only found out last week. I've got a seven-month-old, I'm breastfeeding…'

'Have you had an ultrasound?' Izzy asked.

'She's just come from there,' Beth said for Nicola, but, as was so often the case in Emergency, a neat list of answers rarely arrived with the patient. They would have to be answered later, because this baby was ready to be born.

He slipped into the world a few seconds later, just as a breathless midwife arrived from Maternity and the overhead speaker chimed its request for the paediatric team to come to Emergency. He was still wrapped in the membrane that should have embraced him for many months more and Izzy parted it, using balloon suction to clear his airway. He was pale and stunned, but stirring into life as Izzy cut the cord. Though outwardly calm, her heart was hammering, because difficult decisions lay ahead for this tiny little man.

'You have a son,' Izzy said, wrapping him up and holding him up briefly for Nicola to see. Though seconds counted in the race for his life, Izzy made one of the many rapid decisions her job entailed and brought the baby up to the mother's head, letting her have a brief glimpse of him. Nicola kissed his little cheek, telling him that she loved him, but those few brief seconds were all there was time for.

Beth had already raced over to Resus, and Izzy left Nicola in the safe hands of the midwife and student nurse as she walked quickly over to Resus holding the infant. A man, dressed in black jeans and a T-shirt, joined her. Walking alongside her, he spoke with a heavy accent.

'What do we know?'

'Mum's dates are hazy,' Izzy said, and though he had no ID on him, there was an air of authority to him that told her this was no nosey relative. 'About twenty-three weeks.'

'*Mierda!*' Izzy more than understood his curse—she was thinking the same—this tiny baby hovered right on the edge of viability. At this stage of pregnancy every day *in utero* mattered, but now he was in their hands and they could only give the tiny baby their best care and attention.

'Diego.' Beth looked up from the warming cot she was rapidly preparing. 'That was quick.' The chimes had only just stopped summoning the staff, but he answered in that rich accent, and Izzy realised he was Spanish.

'I was just passing on my way for a late shift.' He had taken the baby from Izzy and was already getting to work, skilfully suctioning the airway as Izzy placed red dots on the baby's tiny chest. 'I heard the call and I figured you could use me.'

They certainly could!

His large hands were rubbing the baby, trying to stimulate it, and Izzy was incredibly grateful he was there. His dark hair was wet so he must have stepped straight out of the shower before coming to work. He had gone completely overboard on the cologne, the musky scent of him way too heavy for a hospital setting. Still, she was very glad he was there. As an emergency doctor, Izzy was used to dealing with crises, but such a premature baby required very specific skills and was terrifying to handle—Diego was clearly used to it and it showed.

'Diego's the neonatal...' Beth paused. 'What *is* your title, Diego?'

'They are still deciding! Sorry...' Dark brown eyes met Izzy's and amidst controlled chaos he squeezed in a smile. 'I should have introduced myself. I'm Nurse Manager on the neonatal unit.'

'I guessed you weren't a passing relative,' Izzy said, but he wasn't listening, his concentration back on the baby. He was breathing, but his chest was working hard, bubbles at his nose and lips, and his nostrils were flaring as he struggled to drag in oxygen.

'We need his history,' Diego said as he proceeded to bag the baby, helping him to breathe. He was skilled and deft and even though the team was just starting to arrive he already had this particular scene under control. 'You're late.' Diego managed dry humour as the anaesthetist rushed in along with the on-call obstetrician and then Izzy's colleague and friend Megan.

Her fragile looks defied her status. Megan was a paediatric registrar and was the jewel in the paediatric team—fighting for her charges' lives, completely devoted to her profession. Her gentle demeanour defied her steely determination when a life hung in the balance.

Megan would, Izzy knew, give the baby every benefit of every doubt.

'Ring NICU.' This was Diego, giving orders, even though it wasn't his domain. They urgently needed more equipment. Even the tiniest ET tube was proving too big for this babe and feeling just a touch superfluous as Megan and Diego worked on, it was Izzy who made the call to the neonatal intensive care unit, holding the phone to Diego's ear as he rapidly delivered his orders.

Though Megan's long brown hair was tied back, the run from the children's ward had caused a lock to come loose and she gave a soft curse as she tried to concentrate on getting an umbilical line into the baby.

'Here,' Izzy said, and sorted out her friend's hair.

'*About* twenty-three weeks, Megan.' Diego said it as a warning as the baby's heart rate dipped ominously low, but his warning was vital.

'We don't know anything for sure!' Megan words were almost chanted as she shot a warning at Diego. 'I'll do a proper maturation assessment once he's more stable. Izzy, can you start compressions while I get this line in?'

Diego was pulling up the minuscule drug dosages; the anaesthetist taking over in helping the tiny baby to breathe. The baby was so small Izzy compressed the chest rapidly with two fingers, hearing the rapid rhythm on the monitor.

'Nice work.' Megan was always encouraging. The umbilical line in, she took the drugs from Diego and shot them into the little body as Izzy carried on with compressions for another full minute.

'Let's see what we've got.' Megan put a hand up to halt Izzy and the babe's heart rate was up now close to a hundred. There were more staff arriving and a large incubator had arrived from the neonatal unit along with more specialised equipment, but until the baby was more stable it wouldn't be moved up to the first-floor NICU. 'We're going to be here for a while.' Megan gave Izzy a grim smile. 'Sorry to take up all your space.'

'Go right ahead,' Izzy said.

'How are things?' an unfamiliar face came in. 'Ben asked me check in—I'm Josh, A and E consultant.' She'd heard there was a new consultant, that he was Irish and women everywhere were swooning, but no one was swooning here! Izzy couldn't really explain it, but suddenly the mood in the room changed. Izzy wondered if perhaps if Josh's popularity had plummeted, because there was certainly a chill in the air.

'It's all under control.' It was Izzy who broke the strange silence. 'Though the babe might be here for a while.'

'How many weeks?' Josh's voice was gruff, his navy eyes narrowing as he looked down at the tiny infant.

'We're not sure yet,' Megan responded. 'Mum was in Ultrasound when she went into labour.'

'We need to find out.' Josh's was the voice of reason. Before there were any more heroics, some vital facts needed to be established. 'Do you want me to speak with Mum?'

'I'll be the one who speaks with the mother.' Megan's voice was pure ice. 'But right now I'm a bit tied up.'

'There's a full resuscitation taking place in my department on a baby that may not be viable—we need to find out what the mother wants.'

Megan looked up and Izzy was shocked at the blaze of challenge in them. 'It's not like it was eight years ago. We don't wrap them in a blanket now and say we can't do anything for them.'

'I'll tell you what!' A thick Spanish accent waded into the tense debate and abruptly resolved it. 'While you two sort out your own agenda, why don't you…' he looked over at Izzy '…go and speak with the mother? You have already met her, after all. See if you can clarify the dates a bit better—let her know just how ill the baby is and find out if someone can pull up her ultrasound images.'

'Sure!'

She was more than grateful for Diego's presence, and not just for the baby—Izzy hadn't known what was happening in there. She'd never seen Megan like that! Her response had been a blatant snub to Josh's offer to speak with the mother, but Izzy didn't have time to dwell on it—instead she had a most difficult conversation in front of her.

'I don't know…' Nicola sobbed as Izzy gently questioned her. 'My periods are so irregular and it's my fourth baby, I was breast feeding…'

'The doctors will go through your scans and assess your baby and try to get the closest date we can,' Izzy said gently, 'but I have to tell you that things aren't looking very good for your son.' Izzy suddenly felt guilty talking about this to the mother when she was pregnant herself, and was incredibly grateful when Diego came into the cubicle. He gave her a thin smile and, because he would be more than used to this type of conversation, Izzy allowed him to take over.

'Another one of my staff is in with your baby,' he said, having introduced himself to the mother, and did what Megan had insisted Josh didn't. Izzy felt the sting of tears in her eyes as very skilfully, very gently Diego talked Nicola through all that had happened, all that was now taking place and all that could lie ahead if her baby were to survive.

'Right now,' Diego said, 'we are doing everything we can to save your baby, but he is in a very fragile state. Nicola. Do you understand what I said to you about the risks, about the health problems your baby might face if he does survive?'

'Do everything you can.'

'We will,' Diego said. 'Megan, the paediatrician, will come in and speak at more length with you, but right now she needs to be in with your son.' He was very kind, but also very firm. 'We're going to be moving him up to the NICU shortly, but why don't I get you a wheelchair and we can take you in to see him before we head off?'

To Izzy it was too soon, Resus was still a hive of activity, but she also knew that Diego was right, that maybe Nicola needed to see for herself the lengths to which they were going to save the baby and also that, realistically, this might be Nicola's only chance to see her son alive.

She didn't get to hold him, but Diego did ask for a

camera and took some pictures of Nicola next to her son, and some close-up shots of the baby. And then it was time for him to be moved.

'Nice work,' he said to Izzy as his team moved off with its precious cargo, Diego choosing to stay behind. 'Thank you for everything, and sorry to leave so much mess. I'm going to have a quick run-through of your equipment, if that's okay. There are a few things you ought to order.'

'That would be great,' Izzy said. 'And thank you. You've been marvellous!'

'Marvellous!' He repeated the word as if were the first time he'd heard it and grinned, his teeth were so white, so perfect. If the rest of him hadn't been so divine, she'd have sworn they were capped. 'You were *marvellous* too!' Then his eyes narrowed in closer assessment. 'You're new?' Diego checked, because even though he was rarely in Emergency he was quite sure that he'd have noticed her around the hospital.

'No. I've worked here for ages. I've been on...' She didn't really know what to say so she settled for a very simple version. 'Extended leave.' She gave him a wide smile. 'You're the one who's new.'

'How do you know that?' He raised the most perfectly shaped eyebrow, and if eyes could smile, his were. 'I might have been here for years. Perhaps I did my training here...' He was teasing her, with a question she was less prepared to deal with than a premature birth. 'Why do you think I'm new?'

Because I'd have noticed you.

That was the answer and they both knew it.

Now there was no baby, now there was no emergency to deal with, now it was just the two of them,

Izzy, for the first time in, well, the longest time, looked at a man.

Not saw.

Looked.

And as she did so, the strangest thing happened—the four months of endless chatter in her head was silenced. For a delicious moment the fear abated and all she was was a woman.

A woman whose eyes lingered for a fraction too long on a beautiful man.

His hair had dried now and she noticed it was long enough to be sexy and short enough to scrape in as smart. He was a smudge unshaven, but Izzy guessed that even if he met a razor each morning, that shadow would be back in time for lunch. Even in jeans and a T-shirt, even without the olive skin and deep accent, there was a dash of the European about him—his black jeans just a touch tighter, his T-shirt from no high street store that Izzy frequented. He was professional and he was well groomed, but there was a breath of danger about him, a dizzy, musky air that brought Izzy back to a woman she had once known.

'Well,' he said when the silence had gone on too long, 'it's nice to stand here *chatting*, but I have to get back.'

'Of course.'

'A porter took my bag. Do you know where I can find him?'

'Your bag?' Izzy blinked, because it was the sort of thing she would say, but rather than work that one out, she went and called the porter over the Tannoy.

'Come up and see him later,' Diego suggested.

'I will,' Izzy said, consoling herself that he would

have extended that invitation to any doctor, that the invitation wasn't actually for her, that it had nothing to do with him.

Except Diego corrected her racing thoughts.

'I'm on till ten.'

What on earth was that?

She'd never been on a horse, yet she felt as if she'd just been galloping at breakneck speed along the beach. Izzy headed for the staffroom, in need of a cool drink of water before she tackled the next patient, wanting to get her scrambled brain into some sort of order after the adrenaline rush of earlier.

A premature delivery would do that to anyone, Izzy told herself as she grabbed a cup. Except, as a large lazy bubble in the water cooler rose and popped to the surface, she felt as if she were seeing her insides spluttering into life after the longest sleep.

She couldn't have been flirting.

She was in no position to be flirting.

Except, Izzy knew, she had been.

They had been.

The lone figure in the staffroom caught her by surprise and Izzy had begun to back out when she saw who it was. Josh was sitting there, head in hands, his face grey, and Izzy was quite sure she was intruding.

'Don't go on my account,' Josh said. 'I was just heading back. How is she?' he asked.

'Upset,' Izzy admitted. 'I think she was only just getting used to the idea of being pregnant, but...' Her voice trailed off, Josh nodded and stood up and walked out, but before that, even as she spoke, realisation dawned.

Josh hadn't been enquiring how the mother was.

Instead he'd been asking about Megan.

CHAPTER THREE

'ARE you sure you don't want me to stay and help clear the board?' Izzy checked as the clock edged towards ten.

'Go home and get some well-earned rest,' Ben said. 'You haven't had the easiest start back.'

'And I thought you'd break me in gently.'

'Not my style,' Ben said. 'You did great, Izzy. Mind you, you look like you've been dragged through a hedge!'

The power dressing had lasted till about three p.m. when she had changed into more familiar scrubs, her mascara was smudged beneath her eyes and her mouth devoid of lipstick.

It had been Chest Pain Central for the rest of the shift and apart from two minutes on the loo, Izzy had not sat down.

'One day,' Izzy said, 'I'm going to manage to stay in my own clothes for an entire shift. I am!' she insisted as Josh joined them. She'd had a good shift. Josh had been lovely—as sharp as a tack, he had been a pleasure to work with, his strong Irish brogue already familiar to Izzy.

'It will never happen!' Josh said. 'I thought the

same—that maybe when I made consultant... I had some nice suits made, didn't I, Ben?'

They had been friends for years, Izzy had found out, had both worked together in London, and as Izzy grinned and wished them both goodnight she was glad now about her decision to return to work.

It *was* good to be back.

The patients didn't care about the doctor's personal life, didn't know the old Izzy, they just accepted her. Any doubts she might have had about the wisdom of coming back at such a fragile time emotionally had soon faded as she had immersed herself in the busy hub of Emergency, stretching her brain instead of being stuck in that awful loop of wandering around her home, thinking.

It was only now, as she stepped out of her professional role, that the smile faded.

She didn't want to go home.

She stared out past the ambulance bay to the staff car park and she felt a bubble of panic. She could call Security to escort her, of course. Given what had happened, who would blame her for not wanting to walk though the car park alone.

It wasn't even dark. It was one of those lovely summer nights in St Piran when the sky never became fully black.

It wasn't just the car park she was afraid of, though, she decided as she turned and headed up the corridor to the stairwell.

She just wasn't ready to go home.

Her fingers hovered over the NICU intercom, wondering what exactly she was doing. Usually she wouldn't have thought twice about this. The old Izzy had often popped up to the wards to check on cases she had seen in Emergency, but her pregnant status made it seem more personal somehow and it wasn't just the baby she had delivered that had drawn her there tonight. Still, despite more than a passing thought about him now as she neared his territory, it wasn't just Diego pulling her there either—it was after ten, the late staff would long since have gone.

There was a very private answer she was seeking tonight.

It *was* more personal because she was pregnant, Izzy admitted to herself. She wasn't just here to see how the baby was doing, rather to see her reaction to it, to see if the little scrap she had delivered that morning might somehow evoke in her some feeling for the babe she was carrying.

She was being ridiculous, Izzy told herself, as if a trip to the NICU would put her mind at ease.

Turning on her heel, Izzy decided against visiting.

She'd ring the NICU tomorrow and find out how he was doing.

'Hey!' Having made up her mind and turned go, Izzy jumped slightly as the doors opened and she was greeted by the sound of Diego's voice.

Even before she turned and saw him, even though it was just one syllable he'd uttered, she knew that it was him and she felt her cheeks colour up, wondering what reason she could give as to why she was there.

'You're here to see your delivery?' He wasn't really looking at her; instead he was turning on his phone and checking the messages that pinged in.

'If that's okay…' She was incredibly nervous around

him, flustered even, her words coming out too fast as she offered too much of an explanation. 'I often chase up interesting cases. I know it's a bit late, so I decided to ring tomorrow...'

'Day and night are much the same in there,' he said. 'It won't be a problem.'

'I'll just ring tomorrow. I'm sure they're busy'

She'd changed her mind before she'd seen him, yet Diego wouldn't hear it.

'One moment,' he said. 'I'll take you in. Let me just answer this.'

She didn't want him to take her in.

She glanced at the ID badge he now had around his neck.

Diego Ramirez was so not what she needed now.

Still, he was too engrossed in his phone to read her body language, Izzy thought. His *bag* was a large brown leather satchel, which he wore over his shoulder, and on *anyone* else it would have looked, well, stupid, but it just set him aside from the others.

God, what was it about him?

Diego didn't need to look at Izzy to read her. He could *feel* her tense energy, knew she was nervous, and he knew enough to know that a pregnant woman who had delivered a prem baby would, perhaps, have a few questions or need a little reassurance.

Any of his staff could provide that, Diego said to himself as he checked his message from Sally.

The term 'girlfriend' for Sally, would be stretching it, but she *was* gorgeous and she was sitting outside his flat in a car right this minute, texting to see when he'd be home.

He loved women.

He loved curves on women.

He loved confident women

He loved lots of uninhibited, straightforward sex—and it was right there waiting at his door.

Busy at work—txt u tomoz x

Not regretfully enough he hit 'send', but he did wonder what on earth he was doing. Why, instead of heading for home, he was swiping his ID card to gain entry into the area and walking this slinky-malinky long-legs, who was as jumpy as a cat, through his unit?

'Wash your hands,' Diego prompted, following his own instructions and soaping up his hands and rather large forearms for an inordinate amount of time. 'It is a strict rule here,' he explained, 'and one I enforce, no matter the urgency. And,' he chided as Izzy turned off the handle with her elbow, 'I also ask that staff take an extra moment more than is deemed necessary.'

Oh.

Chastised and not liking it a bit, Izzy turned the tap on again and recommenced the rather long ritual.

'I do know how to wash my hands.'

He didn't answer.

'I don't have to be told.'

He turned and looked at her rigid profile.

'Yes, Doctor, you do.' He turned off the tap and pulled out a wad of paper towels. 'Doctors are the worst culprits.'

She rolled her eyes and he just laughed.

'By the way,' Diego said. 'I'm not.'

It was Izzy who didn't answer now, just pursed her lips a touch as she dried her own hands, refusing to give him the satisfaction of asking what the hell he was talking about. Instead she followed him through NICU, past the endless incubators, most with their own staff member working quietly on the occupant.

It was incredibly noisy—Izzy remembered that from her paediatric rotation, but she'd been such a confident young thing then, curious more than nervous. Now it seemed that every bleep, every noise made her jump.

'Here he is. Toby is his name.' Diego looked down into the incubator then spoke with the nurse who was looking after the infant Izzy had, just that afternoon, delivered. Yet when he glanced over at the rather brittle doctor he found himself momentarily distracted, watching Izzy frown down at the tiny infant, then watching as her huge eyes darted around the large ward, then back to the baby.

'He's doing well,' Diego explained, 'though it is minute by minute at the moment—he's extremely premature, but Megan has done a thorough maturation assessment and thinks he's more like twenty-four weeks.'

'That's good news,' Izzy said, only Diego didn't look particularly convinced. 'Well, it's good that she delivered in hospital,' Izzy said, 'even if she was in the wrong department.' She stared at the baby and as she felt her own kicking she willed herself, begged herself to feel something, this surge of connection to her own babe that she knew she should feel.

'Do you get attached?' Izzy asked, and Diego shook his head.

'Too dangerous here. It's the parents who get to me if anything.'

She'd seen enough. The baby was tiny and fragile and she hoped and prayed he would be okay, but the bells weren't ringing for her, the clouds weren't parting. There was no sudden flood of emotion, other than she suddenly felt like crying, but only because of her lack of feeling for her own baby she carried. 'Well, thank you very much.' She gave a tight smile. 'As I said, I just thought I'd pop in on my way home.'

'I'll walk with you,' Diego offered.

'There no need.' Izzy said, but he ignored her and fell into step beside her. She really wished he wouldn't, she just wanted out of the stifling place, away from the machines and equipment, away from babies, away from the endless guilt…

'How far along are you?'

'Sorry?'

'How many weeks pregnant?'

She was momentarily sideswiped by his boldness and also glad for the normality of his question. It was the question everyone *hadn't* asked today—the bump that everyone, bar Jess, seemed to studiously avoid mentioning.

'Twenty-eight weeks,' Izzy said. 'Well, almost,' she continued, but she had lost her audience. Diego had stopped walking and she turned her head to where he stood.

'Here.'

Izzy frowned.

'Over here.' Diego beckoned her over and after a slight hesitation she followed him, coming to a stop at an incubator where a tiny baby lay. Tiny, but comparatively much larger than the little boy she had delivered that afternoon. 'This little one is almost twenty-nine weeks, aren't you, *bebé*?' Diego crooned, then pumped some alcohol rub into his hands. 'You're awake…'

'I thought you said you didn't get attached!' Izzy grinned and so too did the nurse looking after the little girl.

'If that's Diego detached,' joked the nurse, as Diego stroked her little cheek and chatted on in Spanish, 'then we're all dying to see him in love.'

'She's *exceptionally* cute,' Diego said. 'She was a twenty-four-weeker too, though girls are tougher than boys. She's a real fighter...' His voice seemed to fade out then, though Izzy was sort of aware that he was still talking, except she didn't really have room in her head to process anything else other than the baby she was looking at.

This was what was inside her now.

This was what had bought her up to the NICU to-night—a need for some sort of connection to the baby growing inside her. And Diego had led her to it.

Her little eyes were open, her hands stretching, her face scrunching up, her legs kicking, and Izzy watched, transfixed, as the nurse fed her, holding up a syringe of milk and letting gravity work as the syringe emptied through the tube into the infant's stomach as Diego gave her a teat to suck on so she would equate the full feeling with suckling.

'She's perfect,' Izzy said.

'She's doing well,' Diego said. 'We're all really pleased with her.' He glanced at Izzy. 'I imagine it's hard to take in.'

'Very,' Izzy admitted.

'Come on,' he said, when she had stood and looked for a moment or two longer. 'You should be home and resting after they day you've had.' They walked to-gether more easily now, Izzy stopping at the vending machine and trying to choose between chocolate and chocolate.

'You'll spoil your dinner.'

'This is dinner!' Izzy said, and then grimaced, remembering who she was talking to. 'I mean, I'll have something sensible when I get home...'

He just laughed.

'Don't beat yourself up over a bar of chocolate!' Diego said. 'You need lots of calories now, to fatten that baby up.' He could see the effort it took for her just to sustain that smile. 'And you need to relax; they pick up on things.'

'I do relax.'

'Good.'

He fished in his satchel and pulled out a brown bag. 'Here, Brianna forgot to take them.'

'What are they?' For a moment she thought they were sweets. 'Tomatoes?'

'Cherry tomatoes.'

'Miniature cherry tomatoes,' Izzy said peering into the bag. 'Mini-miniature cherry tomatoes.'

'Keep them in the bag and the green ones will redden. I grow them,' Diego said, then corrected himself. 'I grew them.' He frowned. 'Grow or grew? Sometimes I choose the wrong word.'

They were outside now, heading for the car park..

Izzy thought for a moment and it was so nice to think about something so mundane. 'Grow *or* grew. You grow them and you grew these.'

'Thank you, teacher!'

He was rewarded by her first genuine smile and she looked at him again. 'So what's this about your job title?' Izzy remembered a conversation from Resus.

'The powers that be are revising our titles and job descriptions. Two meetings, eight memos and guess what they came up with?' He nudged her as they walked. 'Guess.'

'I can't.'

'Modern Matron!' She could hear someone laughing and realised with a jolt it was her. Not a false laugh but a real laugh, and then he made her laugh some more. 'I said, "Not without a dress!" And I promise I will wear one; if that is the title they give me. Can you imagine when my family rings me at work.' He glanced at her. 'Surgeons, all of them. I'm the *oveja negra*, the black sheep.'

'I like black sheep,' Izzy said, and then wished she hadn't, except it had honestly just slipped out.

They were at her car now and instead of saying goodnight, Izzy lingered. He was sexy and gorgeous but he was also wise and kind and, despite herself, somehow she trusted him, trusted him with more than she had trusted anyone in a very long time.

'You said that babies can pick up on things…' Izzy swallowed. 'Do you believe that?'

'It's proven,' Diego said.

'So if you're stressed or not happy…'

'They know.'

'And if you're not sure…' She wanted him to jump in, but he didn't, he just continued to lean on her car. She should just get in it. Surely she should just drive off rather than admit what she didn't dare to. 'I mean, do you think they could know if you don't…?' She couldn't say it, but Diego did.

'If you don't want them?'

'Shh!' Izzy scolded, appalled at his choice of words.

'Why?' There was a lazy smile on his face that was absolutely out of place with the seriousness of her admission. 'It can't understand your words—they're not *that* clever.'

'Even so!' She was annoyed now, but he just carried on smiling. 'You don't say things like that.'

'Not to an over-protective mum!'

Oh!

She'd never thought of it like that, never thought that her refusal to voice her thoughts, her refusal to even let herself properly *think* them might, in fact, show that she did have feelings for the life inside.

It was her darkest fear.

Of the many things that kept her brain racing through sleepless nights, this was the one that she dreaded exploring most—that her feelings for her baby's father might somehow translate to her baby.

That love might not grow.

'You're not the only woman to be unsure she's ready,' Diego said. 'And lots of mothers-to-be are stressed and unhappy, but I'm sure you're not stressed and unhappy *all* the time.' His smile faded when she didn't agree and they stood for a quiet moment.

'What if I am?'

He was silent for a while, unsure why a woman so beautiful, so vibrant, so competent would be so unhappy, but it wasn't his business and for a dangerous moment Diego wished it was. So instead he smiled. 'You can fake it.'

'Fake it?'

'Fake it!' Diego nodded, that gorgeous smile in full

flood now. 'As I said, they're not *that* clever. Twice a day, fake happiness, say all the things you think you should be saying, dance around the house, go for a walk on the beach, swim. I do each morning, whether I feel like it or not.'

He so didn't get it, but, then, how could he?

'Thanks for the suggestions.' She gave him her best bright smile and pulled out her keys.

'Goodnight, then.'

'Where are you parked?'

'I'm not. I live over there.' He pointed in the direction of the beach. 'I walk to work.'

'You didn't have to escort me.'

'I enjoyed it,' he said. 'Anyway, you shouldn't be walking through car parks on your own at night.'

He really didn't get it, Izzy realised.

He was possibly the only person in the hospital who didn't know her past, or he'd never have said what he just had.

She turned on the engine and as she slid into reverse he knocked on her car window and, irritated now, she wound it down.

'Sing in the shower!' He said. 'Twice a day.'

'Sure' Izzy rolled her eyes. Like *that* was going to help.

'And by the way ,' he said as she was about to close her window, 'I'm not!'

Izzy pulled on her handbrake and let the engine idle and she looked at those lips and those eyes and that smile and she realised exactly why she was annoyed—was she flirting?

Did twenty-eight weeks pregnant, struggling mentally

to just survive, recently widowed women ever even begin to think about flirting?

No.

Because had she thought about it she would never have wound down that window some more.

'Not what?' Izzy asked the question she had refused to ask earlier, her cheeks just a little pink.

'I'm not a frustrated doctor,' Diego said, 'as many of your peers seem to think every male nurse is.'

'Glad to hear it,' Izzy said, and took off the handbrake, the car moving slowly beside him.

'And I'm not the other cliché either!' he called, and her cheeks were on fire, yet for the first time in the longest time she was grinning. Not forcing a smile, no, she was, from ear to ear, grinning.

No, there was absolutely no chance that Diego Ramirez was gay!

'I'd already worked that out!' Izzy called as she pushed up her window. 'Night, Diego!'

'It went well, Mum!' Izzy buttered some toast as she spoke to her mother and added some ginger marmalade. 'Though it was strange being back *after...*' Izzy stopped, because her mother didn't like talking about *before*, so instead she chatted some more, told her mum about Toby, but her mum didn't take the lead and made no mention of Izzy's pregnancy.

'So you had a good day?' her mother checked as Izzy idly opened the brown paper bag and took out a handful of tiny tomatoes. They tasted fantastic, little squirts of summer popping on her tongue, helping Izzy to inject some enthusiasm into her voice.

'Marvellous,' Izzy said, smiling at the choice of word and remembering Diego's smile.

It was actually a relief to hang up.

She was so damn tired of putting others at ease.

So *exhausted* wearing the many different Izzy masks…

Doctor Izzy.

To add to Daughter Izzy.

Domestic Abuse Victim Izzy.

Grieving Izzy.

Mother-to-be Izzy.

Coping Izzy.

She juggled each ball, accepted another as it was tossed in, and sometimes, *sometimes* she'd like to drop the lot, except she knew she wouldn't.

Couldn't.

She could remember her mother's horror when she had for a moment dropped the coping pretence and chopped off her hair. Izzy could still see the pain in her mother's eyes and simply wouldn't put her through it any more.

Oh, but she wanted to, Izzy thought, running her bath and undressing, catching sight of herself in the mirror, her blonde hair way-too-short, her figure too thin for such a pregnant woman.

How she'd love to ring her mum back—ask her to come over, to *take* over.

Except she knew she couldn't.

Wouldn't.

Since that night, there had been a huge wedge between them and Izzy truly didn't know how to fix it. She just hoped that one day it would be fixed, that maybe when the baby came things would improve. Except her mother could hardly bring herself to talk about the impending arrival.

Damn Henry Bailey!

Whoosh!

The anger that Jess had told her was completely normal, was a 'good sign', in fact, came rushing in then and, yes, she should do as Jess said perhaps, and write pages and pages in her journal, or shout, or cry, or read the passage in her self-help book on anger.

Except she was too tired for Henry tonight.

Too fed up to deal with her so-called healthy anger.

Too bone weary to shout or cry.

She wanted a night off!

So she lit six candles instead, the relaxing ones apparently, and lay there and waited for them to work, except they didn't.

She *had* to relax.

It was important for the baby!

Oh, and it would be so easy to cry now, but instead she sat up and pulled the plug out, and then she had another idea, or rather she decided to try out Diego's idea.

She'd fake it.

Cramming the plug back in the hole, she topped up with hot water and feeling stupid, feeling beyond stupid, she lay back as the hot water poured over her toes and she sang the happiest song she could think of.

A stupid happy song.

And then another.

Then she sang a love song, at the top of her voice at midnight, in her smart townhouse.

And she was used to the neighbours banging on the walls during one of her and Henry's fights, so it didn't really faze her when they did just that. Instead she sang louder.

Izzy just lay there in the bath, faking being happy, till her baby was kicking and she was grinning—and even if, for now, she had to fake it, thanks to a male nurse who wasn't a frustrated doctor and certainly wasn't the other cliché, by the time her fingers and toes were all shrivelled up, Izzy wasn't actually sure if she was faking it.

For a second there, if she didn't analyse it too much, if she just said it as it was…

Well, she could have almost passed as happy!

CHAPTER FOUR

DIEGO was not in the best of moods.

Not that anyone would really know.

Though laid back in character, he was always firm in the running of his unit. His babies came first and though friendly and open in communication, he kept a slight distance from his staff that was almost indefinable.

Oh, he chatted. They knew he loved to swim in the Cornish sea, that he came from an affluent long line of doctors in Madrid, they even knew that he was somewhat estranged from his family due to his career choice, for Diego would roll his eyes if any of them rang him at work. His staff knew too about his rather pacy love life—the dark-eyed, good-looking Spaniard was never short of a date but, much to many a St Piran's female staff member's disgust, he never dated anyone from work.

No, the stunning women who occasionally dropped in, waiting for him to finish his shift, or called him on the phone, had nothing to do with hospitals—not public ones anyway. Their hospital stays tended to be in private clinics for little *procedures* to enhance their already polished looks.

There was just this certain aloofness to Diego—an

independent thinker, he never engaged in gossip or mixed his private life with his work.

So no one knew that, despite his zealous attention to detail with his precious charges that day, there was a part of Diego that was unusually distracted.

Cross with himself even.

Okay, his relations with women veered more towards sexual than emotional, and if his moral code appeared loose to some, it actually came with strict guidelines—it was always exclusive. And, a man of honour, he knew it was wrong to suddenly be taking his lunches in the canteen instead of on the ward and looking out for that fragile beauty who was clearly taken.

Wrong, so very wrong to have been thinking of her late, *very late*, into the night.

But why *was* she so stressed and unhappy?

If she were his partner, he'd make damn sure…

Diego blew out a breath, blocked that line of thought and carried on typing up the complicated handover sheet, filling in the updates on his charges, now that Rita the ward clerk had updated the admissions and discharges and changes of cots. It was Monday and there was always a lot to be updated. It was a job he loathed, but he did it quicker and more accurately than anyone else and it was a good way of keeping current with all the patients, even if he couldn't be hands on with them all. So Diego spent a long time on the sheet—speaking with each staff member in turn, checking up on each baby in his care. The NICU handover sheet was a lesson in excellence.

'I'm still trying to chase up some details for Baby Geller,' Rita informed him as Diego typed in the three-days-old latest treatment regime. 'Maternity hasn't sent over forms.'

'He came via Emergency.' Diego didn't look up. 'After you left on Friday.'

'That's right—the emergency obstetric page that went out.' Rita went through his paperwork. 'Do you know the delivering doctor? I need to go to Maternity and get some forms then I can send it all down and he can fill it in.'

'She.' Diego tried to keep his deep voice nonchalant. 'Izzy Bailey, and I think I've got some of the forms in my office. I can take them down.'

'Is she back?' Rita sounded shocked. 'After all that's happened you'd think she'd have stayed off till after the baby. Mind you, the insurance aren't paying up, I've heard. They're dragging their feet, saying it might be suicide—as if! No doubt the poor thing *has* to work.'

Diego hated gossip and Rita was an expert in it. Nearing retirement, she had been there for ever and made everyone's business her own. Rita's latest favourite topic was Megan the paediatrician, who she watched like a hawk, or Brianna Flannigan, the most private of nurses, but today Rita clearly had another interest. Normally Diego would have carried on working or told her to be quiet, but curiosity had the better of him and, not proud of himself, Diego prolonged the unsavoury conversation.

'Suicide?' Diego turned around. 'Are you talking about Izzy's husband?'

'Henry Bailey!' Rita nodded. 'It wasn't suicide, of course; he just drove off in a blind rage. She'd left him, but he turned up at work, waited for her in the car park...' She flushed a little, perhaps aware that she was being terribly indiscreet and that Diego was normally the one to halt her. 'I'm not speaking out of turn; it was all over the newspapers and all over the CCTV, though of course it would have been before you arrived in St Piran's.'

No, it wasn't his proudest morning, because once the handover sheet was complete, Diego headed for his office and closed the door. Feeling as if he was prying but wanting to know all the same, it didn't take long to find out everything Rita had told him and more. Oh, he would never abuse his position and look up personal information, but it was there for everyone, splashed all over the internet, and as he read it he felt his stomach churn in unease for all she had been through.

Pregnant, trying to leave an abusive marriage, real estate agent Henry Bailey had beaten his wife in the darkened hospital car park. Rita was right, the whole, shocking incident had been captured on CCTV and images of footage and the details were spelt out in the press.

He felt sick.

Reading it, he felt physically sick and also strangely proud.

Her first day back.

Mierda! He cursed himself as he remembered his throw-away comment about the car park. He replayed the conversation they had had over and over and wished he could start with her again.

His door knocked and he quickly clicked away from the page he was viewing, before calling whoever it was to come in, but he felt a rare blush on his cheeks as the woman herself stood before him. Diego actually felt as if he'd been caught snooping as Izzy let herself in, a wide smile on her face, and he wondered how on earth she managed it.

She had leggings on again and a bright red dress with bright red lipstick and, Diego noticed, bright red cheeks as he just continued to stare up at her.

'You need me to sign off on the delivery?' It was Izzy who broke the silence; Diego was momentarily lost for words. 'Your ward clerk just rang...'

'We would have sent them down to you.'

'Oh!' Izzy blushed a shade darker as she lied just a little. 'I thought it sounded urgent.'

'I should have some forms...' He was unusually flustered as he rummaged through his desk. 'Or I'll ring Maternity. Here...' Diego found them and was pathetically grateful when the door knocked and one of his team stood there. with a screaming baby with a familiar request.

'Would you mind?'

'Not at all.' He washed his hands, *thoroughly*, then took the screaming baby and plonked it face down on his forearm, its little head at his elbow, and he rocked it easily as he spoke.

'Genevieve!' he introduced. 'Goes home this week, please God! I do not envy her parents.'

Well, Genevieve looked as if she'd happily stay with Diego for ever! The tears had stopped and she was already almost asleep as he bounced away.

'If you want to get started on the forms I'll just go and get the details you'll need.' He paused at the door. 'I was just about to get a drink...'

'Not for me, thanks,' Izzy said, and then changed her mind. 'Actually, water would be great.'

'Would you mind...?' It was his turn to say it and he

gestured to the baby. Izzy went to put out her hands and then laughed.

'Joking!' she said, then went over to his sink and *thoroughly* washed hers. 'Am I clean enough for you?'

Oh, God, there was an answer there!

And they just both stood there, looking a bit stunned.

Izzy flaming red, Diego biting down on his tongue rather than tell her he'd prefer her dirty.

And thank God for Miss Genevieve or he might just have kissed her face off!

Diego got them both water.

Well, he couldn't do much with two polystyrene cups and tap water but he did go to the ice dispenser and then had a little chat with himself in his head as he walked back to his office.

What the hell was wrong with him?

He hardly knew her, she was pregnant, and she obviously had *major* issues.

Why was he acting like a twelve-year-old walking past the underwear department in a department store? Nervous, jumpy, embarrassed, hell, he couldn't actually fancy her, and even if he did, normally that didn't pose a problem—he fancied loads of women.

This, though, felt different.

Maybe he felt sorry for her? Diego wondered as he balanced a file under his arm and two cups in one big hand and opened his office door.

But, no, he'd been thinking about her long before Rita had told him what had happened.

Then she looked up from the form she was filling in and smiled, and Diego was tempted to turn round and walk out.

He more than fancied her.

Not liked, not felt sorry for, no. As he washed his hands and took Genevieve from her and sat down behind his desk it wasn't sympathy that was causing this rather awkward reaction.

Diego was used to women.

Beautiful women.

Ordinary women.

Postnatal women.

Pregnant women were regular visitors to his unit—often he walked a mum-to-be around his unit, telling her what to expect once her baby was born.

He was more than used to women, yet not one, not one single one, had ever had this effect on him.

'How is Toby doing?' Izzy looked up from the forms and Diego made a wobbly gesture with one hand.

'Can I have a peek?' Izzy signed off her name and then reached for her water. 'I'm done.'

'Sure,' Diego said. 'I'll put this one down and take you over—we've moved him.'

Genevieve was sleeping now, and Izzy walked with him to the nursery. It was a far more relaxed atmosphere there.

There were about eight babies, all in clear cribs and dressed in their own clothes, the parents more relaxed and, Izzy noticed, everyone had a smile when Diego walked in and put Genevieve back in her cot.

He was certainly popular, Izzy thought as they head back out to the busy main floor of NICU.

'You need to—'

'Wash my hands,' Izzy interrupted, 'I know.'

'Actually…' Diego gave a small wince. 'Your perfume is very strong. Perhaps you could…'

'I'm not wearing perfume,' Izzy said as she soaped up her hands, 'and you're hardly one to talk, I can smell your cologne from here!'

'I don't wear cologne for work.'

'Oh.' Izzy glanced over. 'Then what...?' She didn't finish, she just turned back to the taps and concentrated really hard on rinsing off the soap.

She could smell him.

If she breathed in now she could taste him—she'd even commented to Megan on his cologne, but Megan had said... Izzy swallowed as she recalled the flip conversation. Megan hadn't even noticed it...

She could smell him and Diego could smell her and they'd just told each other so.

There was no witty comeback from that.

It was the *most* awkward five minutes of her life.

Okay, not *the most* awkward—the last few months had brought many of them. Rather it was the most pleasantly cringe-making, confusingly awkward five minutes of her life.

She peered at Baby Geller and asked after his mother, Nicola. She tried to remember that breathing was a normal bodily function as the nurse who was looking after the babe asked Diego to hold him for a moment while she changed the bedding. The sight of the tiny baby nestled in his strong arms, resting against his broad chest, was just such a contrast between tenderness and masculinity that it had Izzy almost dizzy with the blizzard of emotions it evoked.

'I'd better get back.' Her mouth felt as if was made of rubber—even a simple sentence was difficult.

She managed a smile and then she turned and walked briskly out of the department. Only once she was safely

out did she lean against the wall and close her eyes,
breathing as if she'd run up the emergency exit steps.
Shocked almost because never in her wildest dreams
had she considered this, even ventured the possibility
that she might be attracted to someone.

She was so raw, so scared, so just dealing with func-
tioning, let alone coping, that men weren't even on a
distant horizon yet.

And yet…

She'd never been so strongly attracted to someone.

Never.

Even in the early days with Henry, before he'd shown
his true colours, she hadn't felt like this. Oh, she had
loved him, had been so deeply in love she'd been sure
of it—only it had felt nothing like this attraction.

An attraction that was animal almost.

She *could* smell the delicious fragrance of him.

Right now, on her skin in her hair, she leant against
the wall and dragged in the air, and still his fragrance
lingered in her nostrils.

'Izzy!' Her eyes opened to the concerned voice of
Jess. 'Are you okay?'

'I'm fine!' She smiled. 'I was just in NICU, and it's
so hot in there…' God, she felt like she'd been caught
smoking by the headmistress, as if Jess could see the
little plumes of smoke coming from behind her back.
She tried to carry on as if her world hadn't just upended
itself. Jess would hardly be thrilled to hear what was
going through her patient's mind now.

It was impossible that it was even going through her
mind now.

There wasn't room in her life, in her heart, in her head

for even one single extra emotion, let alone six feet two of made-in-Spain testosterone.

'How are you finding it?' Jess asked as they walked in step back to the emergency department, and then Jess gave a kind smile, 'I'm just making conversation…'

'I know.' Izzy grinned and forced herself back to a safer conversation than the one she was having with herself. 'Actually, it's been really nice. It's good having something else to think about.'

Only she wasn't just talking about work.

CHAPTER FIVE

'THE nurses are all tied up and I've got to dash over to the children's ward,' Megan said into the phone. 'I'll ask Izzy.'

'Ask Izzy what?'

She'd been back a full week now.

It was late.

She was tired.

And the patient she was dealing with wasn't exactly helping Izzy's mood.

'I've got a patient on NICU,' Megan explained. 'A new admission. His mum's bipolar and Diego wants some sedation for her. The baby was an emergency transfer so there's no local GP and her medications are all at home. She's getting really agitated, and really it sounds as if she just needs a good night's sleep and then her husband can bring in her meds in the morning. Diego wants her seen straight away, though. Is there any chance? I'd do it but I've *got* to go up to the ward.'

'You'll have to speak to Josh or one of the nurses,' Izzy was unusually terse. 'I'm about to suture someone and then I'm going home.'

She was aware of the rise of Megan's eyebrow. Normally Izzy was accommodating, but Diego's name seemed to be popping up in her day all too often—and her thoughts were turning to him too, rather more than Izzy was comfortable with.

Still it wasn't just a sexy neonatal nurse that had caused Izzy's terse reaction. Just as Jess had predicted, there would be patients that would touch a very raw nerve with Izzy, and even though she had assured Jess she would have no trouble dealing with them, Evelyn Harris *had* hit a nerve.

In her early forties she had presented having tripped over the cat and cut her head on the edge of the coffee table. Vivienne, the student nurse, had had a quiet word with Izzy before she had examined her, telling her that she had noticed some other bruises on her arms when she had checked her blood pressure and, sure enough when Izzy had *checked* the blood pressure again, she had seen the new fingertip bruises, but had chosen not to comment.

'You're going to need a few stitches!' Izzy had said instead. 'How's the cat?'

The relief in the room at Izzy's small joke had been palpable, Evelyn had laughed and John Harris had said the cat would be in the naughty corner, or some other light-hearted thing, and Izzy had smiled back.

Had let him think, as he no doubt did, that she was stupid.

'Vivienne?' Izzy called out to a student nurse. 'Could you set up the minor theatre?' She smiled at Mrs Harris. 'I'll take you over and I'll be in with you in a moment.'

'I'll stay with you,' Mr Harris reassured his wife, and then explained why to Dumb Doctor Izzy. 'She doesn't like needles.'

'Sorry!' Izzy breezed. 'We can only have the patient.'
She gave a very nice smile. 'We shan't be long, at least
I hope not. You're my last patient for the night…' She
chatted away, not letting the husband get a word in, acted
dizzy and vague and rushed, as if getting home was the
only thing on her mind, telling them both to take a seat
outside minor ops. Then she headed for the annexe,
checked who the on-call social worker was for the night
and was just considering her options when Megan had
asked the favour. With her emotions already bubbling
to the surface, the thought of seeing Diego was the last
thing she needed.

There was something about him that got under her
skin, though in a nice way, and Izzy, right now, just
wasn't comfortable with nice.

Wasn't used to nice.

And was nowhere near ready for it either.

As Izzy came into the minor theatre, Vivienne was
just bringing Evelyn through and Mr Harris's voice came
through the open door as his wife stepped inside.

'I'm right outside, darling,' he said, only Izzy could
hear his clear warning.

'Lie down here, Evelyn,' Izzy said, then headed over
to the small bench in the corner and turned on the radio.
'Let's have some music to distract you.' She washed
her hands and pulled on some gloves and then gently
gave the wound a clean before injecting in some local
anaesthetic. 'I'm fine on my own, Vivienne,' Izzy said.
'It's pretty busy out there.'

'I'm to cut for you,' came the response, but Izzy could
cut her own stitches and wanted to be alone with Evelyn,
except Vivienne wouldn't budge. 'Beth told me to get
into Theatre as much as I could.'

'Could you get me some 3-0 catgut?' Izzy said, knowing they had run out but checking the wound as if that was the thread she needed. 'There's none here, but I think there should be some in the store cupboard.'

'There isn't any,' Vivienne said. 'I did the stock order with Beth this afternoon.'

Vivienne needed a crash course on taking a hint, but Izzy didn't have time right now. Evelyn only needed a couple of stitches and Mr Harris would no doubt start to get impatient soon, so Izzy dragged the stool over with her foot and given the time constraints realised she would have to be more direct than she would normally choose.

'Evelyn,' Izzy said, 'is there anything you want to tell me?'

'Nothing.'

'I know,' Izzy said gently. 'I know that you didn't just trip…' She watched her patient's nervous lick of her dry lips, her eyes anxiously dart to the theatre door. 'He can't hear,' Izzy said. 'That's why I put the radio on. You can talk to me.'

'Can you just do your job and suture me?' Evelyn bristled. 'I tripped! Okay?'

'There's a bruise on the opposite cheek, finger marks on your arms. I can sort out help…'

'Really?' The single word was so loaded with sarcasm, just so scornful and filled with dark energy that Izzy let out a breath before she spoke next.

'I can ring the social worker. There are shelters…'

'I've a seventeen-year-old son.' Evelyn's lip curled in bitter response. 'The shelters won't let me bring him with me. Did you know that?' she challenged, and Izzy shook her head.

'So what do you suggest, Doctor? That I leave him with him?'

'No, of course not, but if I get someone to speak with you, they could go through your options. I can speak to the police. You don't have to go back tonight.'

'You're not helping, Doctor,' Evelyn said. 'In fact, you could very well be making my life a whole lot worse.'

The stitches took no time, and Izzy knew that dragging it out and keeping Evelyn's husband waiting would only make things worse for her patient, but as Vivienne snipped the last thread Izzy had one more go.

'Is there anyone you can talk to? A friend perhaps…'

'You really don't get it, do you?'

Except Izzy did.

'I don't have *friends*! At least, none of my choosing.'

Evelyn struck a dignified pose as she swung her legs down from the gurney and Izzy recognised the glare in her eyes only too well, because she had shot out that look many times before if anyone had dared so much as to assume that her life was less than perfect.

'Do I need to sign anything?' Evelyn asked.

'No.' Izzy shook her head. 'If you…' She looked at Evelyn and her voice trailed off. Evelyn's decision to stay wasn't going to change, not till her son's future was taken care of. Izzy just hoped to God she'd survive that year. 'When was your last tetanus?'

'I had one…' Evelyn swung her bag over her shoulder '…six weeks ago.'

I'll bet she did, Izzy thought as she stood there, clearing the trolley. She could see her hands shaking as she disposed of the sharps and as Evelyn left Theatre, Izzy had to bite on her lip as the young nurse's disbelieving voice filled the still room.

'Straight back to him…' Her voice was incredulous. 'Why doesn't she just lea—' And then Vivienne's voice abruptly halted as perhaps she remembered who she was talking to and what had had happened the night Izzy had tried to *just* leave.

'She has her reasons,' Izzy said. 'And, frankly, if that's your attitude, she's hardly likely to share them with you.'

'I'm sorry, Izzy.'

And she could have left it there, but Izzy chose not to. Vivienne was thinking of a career in Emergency and, well, it was time she faced a few home truths.

'You're a nurse,' Izzy said, and her voice wobbled with long-held-in emotion, 'not the bloody jury. Remember that when you're dealing with patients in Emergency.'

Her shift was nearly over and all she wanted was out, so she left the messy trolley and was tempted to just go to the lockers and get out of there. She was angry and close to tears and there was Evelyn walking out of the department, her husband's arm around her. Then he stopped and fished his phone from his jacket and took a call, and Evelyn patiently waited then she turned and for a second. For just a teeny second their eyes locked and and it was the secret handshake, the password, the club, and Evelyn's expression changed as she realised her doctor was a fully paid up member…

'Mrs Harris…' Izzy scribbled down her mobile number on a head injury information chart and walked briskly over. 'Sorry.' Izzy gave a busy shrug. 'I forgot to give you this. Here's your head injury instructions, have a read through…'

'Thank you.'

'And watch out for that cat!' Izzy added, then gave a vague smile at Evelyn and one to her husband before they walked off into the night. Izzy's heart was thumping, not sure what she had just done and not sure what she would even do if Evelyn did call.

She just wanted to do something.

'Izzy!'

That Spanish voice was too nice for her mood right now.

'Can I ask a favour?' Diego gave her a smile as he poked his head out of a cubicle, but she didn't return it.

'I'm about to go off duty.'

'I was off duty forty minutes ago and I'm back on in the morning.' Diego wasn't quite so nice now. One of his mums was about to tip into trouble, the mother of one his precious babies no less. He had spent two hours dealing with red tape, trying to get hold of her GP to fax a prescription, to no avail, or to get a doctor on NICU to see Maria, but of course she wasn't actually a patient at the hospital.

Yet!

Maria was growing more agitated by the minute and no one seemed to give a damn. 'I have a woman who gave birth four days ago, following twenty-four hours of labour. Her child has multiple anomalies, she has hardly slept since her baby was born and she and her husband have driven one hundred miles today as there was no room for them in the helicopter.' Oh, he told her, even if it was Izzy, he told her, even as she opened her mouth to say that she'd see the patient, still he told her, because Diego knew Izzy was far better than that. 'Now she can't settle and is doing her best not to go into meltdown. Can I get a doctor to prescribe me some sedation?'

'I'm sorry, okay?' Izzy's apology was instant and genuine—she had never been one to dash off at the end of her shift, but Evelyn had unsettled her, not to mention Diego. She was having great trouble keeping her mask from slipping, but it wasn't the patients' fault. 'Of course I'll see her.'

Maria was agitated and pacing and the very last thing she needed was endless questions and an examination, and Izzy could see that. Diego had given her a good brief and on gentle questioning Izzy found out what medications the patient was on.

'If I could just get some sleep,' Maria pleaded, and Izzy nodded.

'I'll be back in just a moment.'

She was and so too was a nurse from the neonatal unit to relieve Diego.

'Take two tablets now,' Izzy said, and gave the hand-over nurse the rest of the bottle. 'She can have two more at two a.m., but don't wake her if she's resting. Will someone be able to check her?'

'Absolutely,' Diego said. 'Maria's staying in the parents' wing, but I'll get my staff to pop in and see her through the night.'

'I'm sure,' Izzy said to her patient, 'that once you've had a decent rest you'll be feeling a lot better. I'm on in the morning,' Izzy added, writing some notes. 'If Maria doesn't settle,' Izzy added to the nurse, 'she'll need to come back down to us.'

It was straightforward and simple and as the nurse took Maria back up to the ward, Diego thanked her.

'I'm sorry if I came on strong.'

'Not at all,' Izzy said. 'She needed to be seen. It's just been a...' She stopped talking; he didn't need to hear about her difficult shift, so she gave him a brief smile and walked on.

Except Diego was going off duty too.

'How's faking it going?' Had he fallen into step beside her that morning, or even an hour ago, Izzy would have managed a laugh and a witty retort, but even a smile seemed like hard work right now, so she just hitched her bag up higher and walked more briskly through the sliding doors and into the ambulance forecourt. But Diego's legs were longer than hers, and he kept up easily.

'Izzy, I was wondering....'

'Do you mind?' She put up her hand to stop him talking, gave an incredulous shake of her head. What was it with people today that they couldn't take a hint if she stood there and semaphored them? 'I just want...' Oh, God, she was going to cry.

Not here.

Not now.

She hadn't yet cried.

Oh, there had been *some* tears, but Izzy had been too scared to really cry, to break down, because if she did, maybe she wouldn't stop.

Scared that if she showed her agony to others they would run when they saw the real her, and scared to do it alone because it was so big, this black, ever-moving shape that had no clear edges, that grew and shrank and transformed.

But she couldn't outrun that black cloud tonight.

She was trying not to cry, trying to breathe and trying to walk away from him to get to her car, as she had tried to that awful night.

No, there was no getting away from it.

Her hands were shaking so much she dropped her keys and it took all her strength not to sink to her knees and break down right there. Instead she got into the car, sat gripping the wheel, holding it in and begging it to pass, but it held her a moment longer, pinning her down. She sat in her car and she was tired, so tired and angry and ashamed and sad…

Sad.

Sad was bigger than angry, bigger than tired, bigger than her.

It was in every cell and it multiplied. It was the membrane of every cell and the nucleus within, it spread and it grew and it consumed and she couldn't escape it any longer. As she doubled over she could feel her baby kick inside and it was so far from the dream, so removed from anything she had envisaged when she had walked down that aisle, that the only word was sad.

She didn't even jump when the passenger door opened and Diego slid into the passenger seat.

'Can't you just leave me alone?'

Diego thought about it for a moment then gave an honest answer. 'It would seem not.'

'You know, don't you?' Izzy said, because everyone else did and so he surely must.

'A little,' Diego admitted. 'I didn't at first, but that morning, when you came to my office, I'd just found out.'

'I thought you were a bit awkward.'

Maybe for a second, Diego thought, but he'd been awkward for another reason that morning, but now wasn't really the time to tell her.

'I've done something stupid…' Izzy said. 'Just then,

when you asked me to see Maria.' He sat patiently, waiting for her to explain. 'I had a woman, I think her husband beats her—actually, I don't think, I know. She wouldn't let me help her. I can see now that I rushed in, but I didn't want her to go home to him. I knew what he'd be like when they got home, you could just tell he was annoyed that she was even at the hospital, even though he'd put her there. Anyway, she wouldn't let me get a social worker or the police….' She turned and saw the flash of worry on his face. 'I didn't confront him or anything, he's none the wiser that I know.'

'You can't help her if she doesn't want it.'

'I gave her my phone number.' Izzy waited for his reaction, waited for him to tell her not to get involved, that she had been foolish, but instead he thought for a long moment before commenting.

'I think,' he said slowly, 'that your phone number would be a very nice thing to have.' She blinked. 'And I'm not flirting,' Diego said, and she actually gave a small smile. 'Other times I flirt, but not then. Did *you* talk to anyone?'

'No,' Izzy admitted. 'Megan, we're friends,' she explained, 'asked me what was wrong once, and I remember then that I nearly told her. God—' regret wrapped her words '—I wish I had. I was on my way to my mum's when it happened—I was going to tell her. Henry and I had had a massive row that morning. I knew I was pregnant, that I had to get out of the marriage. I told him I was leaving, I still wasn't sure how, but I came to work, scraped through the shift and afterwards I was going to land on my parents' doorstep…' she gave a shrug '…or Megan's. All I knew was that I wasn't going home.'

'What if someone had given you a phone number?'

Diego asked. 'If you had known that that person knew what it was like…'

'I'd have rung them,' Izzy said. 'Not straight away perhaps.' Then she nodded, confirmed to herself that she hadn't done a stupid thing. 'What do I say if she rings?'

'What would you have wanted someone to say to you?'

'I don't know,' Izzy admitted. 'Just to listen…'

She'd answered her own question and Izzy leant back on the seat and closed her eyes for a moment, actually glad that he had got into the car, glad that he hadn't left her alone, glad that he was there.

And she didn't want to think about it any more so instead she turned to him.

'I forgive you.'

'*Cómo?*' Diego frowned. 'Forgive me for what?'

'Having a satchel.' She watched as a smile spread across his face and she smiled too. 'I never thought I could,' Izzy said, seriously joking, 'but I do.'

'Leave my satchel alone,' Diego said, and he saw something then, her humour, a glimpse of the real Izzy that would soon be unearthed, because she would come out of this, Diego was sure of that. She would grow and she would rise and she would become more of the woman he was glimpsing now.

He knew.

And he knew if he stayed another minute he'd kiss her.

'I'd better go,' Diego said, because he really thought he'd better.

'I'll drive you.'

'No, because then I would have to ask you in.'

'Would that be so bad?' Izzy asked, because it felt as if he was kissing her, she could see his mouth and almost taste it on hers. Sitting in the car, she didn't want him to get out and she didn't want to drive on. She wanted to stay in this moment, but Diego was moving them along.

'If you come in, I might not want you to leave…' It was big and it was unexpected and the last thing either had planned for, yet, ready or not, it was happening. 'We need to think.'

He climbed out of her car and Izzy sat there. Without him beside her logic seeped in.

It was way too soon.

It was impossibly way too soon.

And yet, had he chosen to, he could have kissed her.

CHAPTER SIX

Qué diablos estás haciendo?

As Diego pushed through the waves, over and over he asked himself what on earth he was doing.

On leaving Izzy, he'd gone home to find Sally in the car outside his flat, with a bottle of wine and a dazzling smile, but instead of asking her in, he'd sent her on her way. The words 'It's been good, but...' had hung in the air, as had the sound of her tears, but it had been the only outcome to their relationship, Diego had realised as he'd let himself into his flat.

It *had* been good.

Sencillo, Diego's favourite word—straightforward, uncomplicated. Sally had been all those things and everything Diego had thought he wanted in a relationship. Only his life had suddenly become a touch more complicated.

He needed to think and he couldn't do that with Sally. Wouldn't do that to Sally and also he needed to be very sure himself.

Walking out of the water towards the beach, he wasn't sure if he was even pleased that Izzy had taken his advice, for there she was, walking along the beach, her face flushing when she saw him.

'I thought you were on an early...'

'I'm on a management day, so I don't have to be in till nine,' Diego explained, then he teased, 'Why? Were you trying to avoid me?'

'Of course not!' Izzy lied.

'It's good to see you out.'

'It's good to be out,' Izzy admitted. 'I used to walk on the beach each morning. I don't know why I stopped.'

'You've had a lot to deal with.'

Which she had, but Izzy hadn't walked since her marriage, another little thing she'd given up in an attempt to please Henry, but she didn't say anything.

'Do you want company?'

And she looked into dark eyes that were squinting against the morning sun, his black hair dripping, unshaven, wet, and his toned body, way smoother than a name like Ramirez suggested, and she didn't know what she wanted because, here was the thing, she'd spent the whole night in turmoil, telling herself she was being ridiculous, that it was impossible, that she should be sorting out herself instead of getting involved with someone.

She didn't actually have to tell herself. The books said the same too, even Jess.

But here, on the beach, when she should be thinking alone, it was his company her heart required. Here in the lovely fresh start of morning it just seemed natural for them to talk.

They walked along the beach, admiring the rugged Cornish coastline. Despite the warmth of summer, the wind was up, making the beach the coolest place as the breeze skimmed off the ocean and stung her cheeks, and it was a relief to talk about him.

'This beach is one of the reasons I choose to settle in St Piran. I love the beach.'

'What about Madrid? Do you miss it?'

'The nearest beach is Valencia. Over a hundred miles away...' Perhaps he realised he was being evasive. 'Sometimes I miss it. I have been away two years now...' She glanced at him when his voice trailed off.

'Go on.'

'My family and I were rowing—we did not part on good terms,' Diego admitted. 'We get on a bit better now. I talk to my mother often on the telephone, but for a while there was no contact.'

He left it there, for now. But there was something about the ocean. It was so vast and endless that it made honesty easier, problems mere specks, which was perhaps why they found themselves there so often over the next few days. They would walk and talk and try to put on hold the chemistry between them and instead work on their history. They sat in the shallows, just enough for the cool water to wash around their ankles and up their calves, and they talked. It was absolutely, for Izzy, the best part of her day and she hoped Diego felt the same.

'I told you it was expected that I would study medicine? It did not go down well when I chose to study nursing instead. Padre said it was women's work...'

'Not any more.'

'He ridiculed it, my brothers too. I also studied *partero*, I'm a midwife too,' Diego explained. 'My mother said she understood, but she would prefer I study medicine to keep my father happy.' He gave a wry smile. 'That was the rule growing up and it is still the rule now— keeping him happy. Getting good grades, melting into the background, anything to keep him happy. I wish she had the guts to leave him.' He looked over at Izzy. 'I admire you for leaving.'

'I didn't have children,' Izzy said. 'And it was still a hard decision. Don't judge her for staying, Diego. What made you want to do nursing?'

'My elder sister had a baby when I was eighteen. He was very premature and my sister was ill afterwards. I used to sit with him and I watched the nurses. They were so skilled, so much more hands on than the doctors, and I knew it was what I wanted to do. Fernando was very sick—I was there night and day for ten days. My sister had a hysterectomy and was very sick too...' There was a long silence. 'She was at another hospital so she didn't get over to see him—she was too ill.' Diego suddenly grimaced. 'I shouldn't be telling you this...'

'I'm not that precious.' Izzy squeezed his hand.

'He died at ten days old. It was tough. In those ten days I really did love him and even now sometimes my sister asks for details about him and I am glad that I can give them to her.'

'What sort of details?'

'He loved to have his feet stroked and he loved to be sing to.' He gave a slight frown and Izzy just sat silent rather than correct his grammar. 'My sister had always sung to him while she was pregnant and I taped her singing and played the songs.'

'It must be hard,' Izzy said. 'Your work must bring it all back...'

'No.' His response surprised her. 'It has certainly made me a better nurse. I know, as much as I can know, how helpless and scared the parents feel. How you constantly watch the monitors and become an armchair expert, but never, not even once, have I come close to the feelings I had for Fernando with a patient. I suppose I detach, of course there are stories and babies that touch you more than others, but you could not do this job and care so deeply at that level.'

And she looked at him and couldn't see how his parents could be anything but proud. She had seen his work at first hand, the way his colleagues and all the parents respected him. There had been an almost audible sigh of relief that Diego had been around when Toby had been born and she told him that.

'There is a managerial position at my father's hospital—I am thinking of applying for it. Of course, it has not gone down well. He says it would be an embarrassment to the Ramirez name if I take it.'

They were only just getting to know each other, but still her breath caught at the impossibility of it all, of anything happening between them, and she tried to keep the needy note from her voice when she asked a question.

'Why would you go back?' Izzy asked, 'After all that, if they don't respect what you do...'

'I respect what I do now,' Diego said. 'That is the difference. I would like to go back and be proud.'

He would go back.

They were sitting in the sand at the water's edge. Izzy's shorts were soaking, the water rushing in then dragging back out, as if taking all the debris of the past away. But the tide returned and bought with it fresh problems and Izzy told herself to slow down, to not even think about it, that his decisions didn't affect her. They were friends, that was all—they hadn't so much as kissed.

Except Diego discounted that theory before it had even properly formed.

She could feel his face near her cheek and knew if she turned her head their lips would meet.

It was six a.m. and the clearest her head would be all day, but she turned to him, to the sweet, confusing relief of his mouth. He tasted like a blast of morning, with the promise of night. It was a kiss that was tender on the outside—a mesh of lips, a slow, measured greeting, but there was raw promise beneath the surface, his tongue sliding in, offering a heady taste of more, and Izzy wanted more. She liked the press of him, the weight of him that pressed her body back to the sand. There was the tranquillity of escape she found as his kiss deepened and his hand moved naturally, sliding around her waist to caress her, and then even before Diego paused, Izzy's lips were still.

She rested her head on his shoulder a moment to steady herself, the weight of her baby between them.

'I think…' Izzy pulled her head up and made herself look at him '…we should pretend that just didn't happen.'

'It did, though,' Diego pointed out.

'Well, it can't again,' Izzy said, and she hoisted herself to standing. 'Let's just keep it as friends,' Izzy insisted, because that was surely all they could be for now, except her lips were tender from the claim of his kiss as she tried to talk about *other* things, and as they walked back her hand bunched in a fist so she didn't reach out and take his.

They were back at her car, his apartment just a short walk away, and how he wanted to take her up there, to peel off her wet clothes and call in sick, spend the day getting to know her in the way he so badly wanted to.

And friends could kiss goodbye on the cheek, except they had passed that now and any contact between them was dangerous.

He faced her, but that only made him want to kiss her again so Diego looked down and saw the swell of her stomach, her belly button just starting to protrude, and his hand ached to capture it, only his mind wasn't so sure.

'We have a lot to think about,' Diego said, 'or maybe it's better not to think about it, just…' He looked up at her and his face was honest and it scared her, but somehow it made her smile as he offered her a very grown-up slant on words said in playgrounds the world over. 'I don't want to be your friend any more.'

CHAPTER SEVEN

'YOU'RE expected to go, Diego!' Rita was adamant. 'You can't not go to the Penhally Ball.'

They'd been having this conversation all morning. Rita had found out that he wasn't going and it seemed every time he passed her work station, she thought of another reason why he must go.

He'd just come from a family meeting with the parents of Toby Geller, which had been difficult at best, and, really, the last thing Diego cared about was if he was *expected* to attend some charity ball that was being held on Saturday.

'You're going, aren't you, Megan?' Rita looked up and Diego rolled his eyes as Megan gave a thin smile.

'It is expected,' Megan agreed, but from her resigned voice it was clear she wasn't looking forward to it.

'All the units send their senior staff,' Rita said, still talking as she answered the phone.

'Spare me,' Diego said. 'Is it awful?'

'No.' Megan shook her head. 'It's actually a great night…'

'So why the long face?' He was friends with Megan. Well, not 'ring each other up every night and why don't we go for coffee type friends', but certainly they were friendly and Diego couldn't help but notice she was unusually low.

'Just one of those days!' Megan said, which given they had just been in with Toby's parents, could have explained it, except Megan hadn't been her usual self lately. Diego suddenly wondered if it had anything to do with the rumours that were flying around the hospital about Izzy and himself.

Diego hadn't realised just how many people he knew. And Izzy too.

It seemed that everywhere they went, be it a walk on the beach or to a café near his flat, they would bump into someone from work. But it wasn't just the rumour mill causing problems. Izzy was almost nine weeks from her due date now, and despite them both trying to be nothing more than just friends, that kiss had unleashed the attraction between them. It was so palpable, so present, it was killing Diego not to whisk her away from the home she was selling and bring her back to his flat, feed her, nurture her and make love to her. Except in a few weeks' time, Izzy would be a mother, which meant there would be a baby, and that was something way down on his list.

So far down, he hadn't actually thought whether one day he might want one of his own—let alone someone else's.

But he wanted her.

'It's a lovely night.' Rita just wouldn't let up; she was off the phone and back to one of her favourite subjects—prying about Megan. 'All the money raised goes to the Penhally Rape Crisis Centre. Will you be taking anyone, Doctor?'

Ah, but Megan was always one step ahead. 'You

heard the man.' Megan flashed Rita a smile that was false. 'He doesn't want to go.'

'Oh!'

Diego couldn't help but grin as a Rita's eyes momentarily widened as she wondered if she'd stumbled on the news of year, but then she remembered the latest information from her sources. She turned back to the computer and resumed typing. Attempting nonchalance, she tested the seemingly gentle waters. 'It's good to support these things.' Rita tap tapped away, 'Look what happened to our own lovely Izzy. I'd have thought you, Diego, more than anyone, would...' And she stopped, just stopped in mid-sentence, because even if she wasn't looking at him, even if Diego hadn't spoken, the atmosphere was so tense, she just knew he wasn't smiling now. 'We should all do our bit,' Rita attempted, typing faster now, hoping she'd rectified it, and hoping Diego hadn't understood what she had implied.

She was wrong on both counts.

'Me? More? Than? Anyone?' Diego's voice was pure ice as he challenged her—each word separate, each word a question, and Diego looked at Megan, who shook her head in disbelief at Rita's insensitivity. 'What do you mean by that, Rita?'

Still she typed on. 'Well, you're a nice young man, I thought you of all people...' Her face was pink and she licked her lips before carrying on. 'Well, that you'd support such a thing.'

'Do you know why I hate gossip, Megan?' Diego looked at his friend.

'Why?' Megan answered.

'Because the fools that spread it get it wrong. Because

the fools that spread it are so miserable in their own lives they have to find that part in others...' Rita stood up.

'I have to get on.' She picked up some papers, *any* papers, and walked off, but Diego's voice chased her.

'Because though they insist their lives are perfect, gossiping about others ensures that for that moment no one is gossiping about them.'

Rita spun on her heel. 'You can't stop people talking.'

'Ah, but you can,' Diego said, and pointedly turned to Megan, ignoring Rita completely. 'Before you go, I've got two in the nursery that need their drug charts re-written and Genevieve is ready to go home. Her mum wants to thank you.'

It was a relief to talk about work.

For Megan to fill in the drug charts and then to head to the nursery where Genevieve was wearing a hot pink all-in-one with a hot pink hat, and a car seat was waiting to finally, against all the odds, take her home. Diego smiled as Megan picked up the little lady and gave her a cuddle, and he could see the tears in her eyes too because, unlike Diego, Megan did get attached. She gave her heart and soul to her patients, took it personally when a battle was lost. Diego wasn't sure it was a healthy thing for her to do, but today was a good day and those, Diego suddenly realised, were the ones Megan struggled with most.

'We can't thank you enough.' Genevieve's mum was effusive in her gratitude. 'It's because of you that we get to take her home.'

Yes, today was a good day.

'Good job,' Diego said before he headed back to his

charges. 'For a while there I didn't think we'd get to this day with Genevieve. You never gave in, though.'

'I never would,' Megan said, and then she paused and her voice was more pensive than jubilant. 'Be careful, Diego.'

He knew exactly what they were talking about.

'We're just friends,' he said, but he could hear the protest in his heart and Megan could hear it in his voice.

'She's fragile…'

'She's getting stronger,' Diego countered, because he would not label Izzy, because he could feel in his soul all she was going to be.

'Just, please,' Megan said, and it was the most she would say to him, 'handle with care.'

'You're looking well.' Gus smiled as he called Izzy into his surgery.

He was a wonderful GP. He read through her charts and checked her blood pressure, even though the midwife had done the same and told Izzy it was fine.

'How is it?'

'Perfect,' Gus said. 'How have you been feeling?'

'Very well,' Izzy said, and it was the truth. For the first time in her pregnancy it wasn't Henry and the nightmare of her past that consumed her, it was something far nicer.

There had been no repeat of that kiss, but there was an energy and promise in her days now and Izzy knew it was just a matter of time.

'You're eating well?' Gus checked, and though his face never flickered, Izzy was a doctor too and could hear the slight probing nature of his question. Often her antenatal visits seemed more like a friendly catch-up, but today Gus was going through her notes, double-checking everything.

'I'm eating really well.' Which was true. In the very dark weeks after Henry's death, even though eating had been the last thing on her mind, Izzy had made herself eat, for the baby's sake. She had even gone as far as to set a reminder on her mobile, forcing down smoothies or even just a piece of toast. But since she'd been back at work, and of course since she'd met Diego, her appetite had returned—for food, for life. She was laughing, she was happy, she was eating—except her weight, Gus said, was down.

It seemed ironic that when she was eating the most, when she was happiest, she hadn't put on any weight. Gus asked her to lie on the examination bed, and though he was always thorough, today his examination took a little longer than usual.

'You're a bit small,' Gus said, and Izzy lay there staring at the ceiling, because if Gus said she was a bit small, then she *was* small. He ran a Doppler over her stomach and listened for a couple of moments to the baby's heartbeat, which was strong and regular. 'How's the baby's movement?'

'There's lots,' Izzy said, trying to keep her voice light and even.

'That's good.' He was very calm, very unruffled and he helped her sit up and then she joined him at his desk.

'Are you worried?' Izzy asked.

'Not unduly,' Gus said. 'Izzy, you've had unbelievable stress throughout this pregnancy—but you're thirty-one weeks now and this is the time that the baby starts to put on weight, so we really do need to keep a slightly closer eye on you. I was going to schedule an ultrasound for a couple of weeks, but let's bring that forward.' He glanced at his watch. It was six on Friday evening. 'Let's get this done early next week and then...' She was due to start coming to fortnightly visits now, but Gus was nothing if not thorough. 'Let's get the scan and I'll see you again next week.'

'You know that I'm working?' Izzy felt incredibly guilty, but Gus moved to reassure her.

'Lots of my mums work right up till their due date, Izzy. You're doing nothing wrong—for now. I just want you to try and reduce your stress and really make sure you're eating well. You need some extra calories. I'd suggest you add a protein shake to your breakfast.'

'I'm supposed to be going to the Penhally Ball tomorrow...'

Out of the blue Diego had suggested they go together— face the gossip and just get it over and done with, and what better way than at the Penhally Ball, when everyone would be there. They had, Diego had pointed out, absolutely nothing to be ashamed of. To the world they were friends and friends went out! Except Izzy still cared what others might think and almost hoped Gus would shake his head and tell her that the weekend might be better spent resting on the couch with her feet up, thus give her a reason not to go, but Gus seemed delighted. 'That's good—I'm glad you're starting to go out.'

'Shouldn't I be resting?'

'Izzy, I'm not prescribing bed rest—I want you to relax and a social life is a part of that. I just want to keep a closer eye on you.'

'The thing is...' She was testing the water, just

dipping in her toe. She respected Gus, and his reaction mattered. 'Things have been awful, but for the last few weeks, for the first time since I've been pregnant, I haven't had any stress or, rather, much less, and I have been eating better...'

'Well, whatever it is you're doing, keep it up,' Gus said, and Izzy gave a small swallow.

'I'm going to the ball with a friend, Diego.'

'Ramirez.' Izzy frowned as Gus said his surname.

'You know him?'

'There aren't too many Diegos around here. The neonatal nurse?'

And she waited for his shock-horror reaction, for him to tell her she should be concentrating on the baby now, not out dancing with male *friends*, but instead Gus smiled.

'He seems a nice man.'

When Izzy just sat there Gus smiled. 'You deserve nice, Izzy.'

She still didn't know it.

CHAPTER EIGHT

SHE'D cancel.

Izzy could hardly hear the hairdresser's comments as she sat with a black cape around her shoulders, pretending to look as a mirror was flashed behind her head.

'It looks fantastic!'

Well, she would say that, Izzy thought to herself. The hairdresser was hardly going to say, 'It looks awful and what on earth were you thinking, taking a pair of scissors to your locks, you stupid tart?' But as the mirror hovered behind her Izzy actually did look, and for once she agreed with the woman who wielded the scissors.

Okay, maybe fantastic was stretching things a touch, but it had been three months and three trips to this chair since that moment of self-loathing and finally, finally, she didn't look like a five-year-old who had taken the kitchen scissors to the bathroom. The last of her home-made crop had been harvested, the once jagged spikes now softened, shades of blonde and caramel moving when her head did, which it did as Izzy craned her neck for a proper look.

'I've hardly taken anything off at the front or sides, just softened it a touch, but I've taken a fair bit off the back...'

Izzy could have kissed her but instead she left a massive tip, booked in for six weeks' time, skipped out to her car and somehow made it home without incident, despite the constant peeks in the rear-view mirror at her very new 'side fringe'.

And then she remembered.

She was cancelling.

So why was she running a bath and getting undressed?

A tepid bath so it didn't fluff up her hair.

She couldn't do it, couldn't go, just couldn't face it.

So instead of climbing in to the water she wrapped herself in a towel and padded out to the living room.

She had every reason to cancel, Izzy told herself as she picked up the telephone, except there was a voicemail message. It wasn't Diego stuck at work, as she had rather hoped, but the real estate agent with a pathetic offer. 'It's a good offer, you should seriously consider it,' played the message. Henry had been a real estate agent and had practically said those words in his sleep so she deleted it and got back to fretting about Diego. The fact that she was pregnant and had worked all morning, the fact that she wasn't ready for the inevitable stares if she walked into the Penhally Ball with a dashing Spaniard on her arm when she should be home...

Doing what? Izzy asked herself.

Grieving, feeling wretched...

Her introspection was halted by the doorbell. No doubt the postman had been while she was out and it was her neighbour with another box of self-help or baby books that she had ordered on the internet during one of her glum times—a book that at the time she had convinced herself would be the one to show her, tell her, inform her how the hell she was supposed to be feeling...

'Diego?'

It was only five p.m. and he shouldn't be there, the ball didn't start till seven.

There was no reason for him to be there now and, worse, she was only wearing a towel.

'I thought I'd come early.' He leant in the doorway and smiled, and either the baby did a big flip or her stomach curled in on itself. He was in evening wear, except he hadn't shaved, and he looked ravishing, so ravishing she wanted to do just that—ravish him, drop the towel she was clinging to, right here at the front door. 'To save you that phone call.'

'What phone call?' Izzy lowered her head a touch as she let him in, wishing there had been a warning sign on the kitchen scissors to inform her that it would be a full twelve to eighteen months before she could again hide her facial expressions with her hair if she chose to lop it all off. A fringe simply wouldn't suffice. Her whole body was on fire, every pulse leaping at the sight of him.

'The one where you tell me your back is aching, or you're tired or that it was lovely of me to ask, but...'

'I was just about to make it,' Izzy admitted.

'Why?'

'Because it's too soon.'

'For what?'

'For me to be out, for me to be...' She blanched at the unsaid word.

'Happy?' Diego offered. 'Living?'

Neither was quite right. Izzy didn't correct him at first, she just clung to her towel, not to keep him from her but to keep her from him, and she stared at a man who had brought nothing but joy into her life. She wanted more of the same.

'For me to be seeing someone,' Izzy corrected. 'Which I think I am.'

'You are,' he confirmed, and crossed the room. It was a relief to be kissed, to kiss him, to be kissed some more, to kiss back. He was less than subtle, he was devouring her, and any vision that their next kiss would be gentle and tender was far removed from delicious reality. Diego had waited long for another kiss and he was claiming it now, pressing her against the wall as she rejoiced in him, her towel falling. He kicked it away and all she wanted was more, more, more.

He tasted as he had that morning but decisiveness made it better. He smelt as he always had, just more concentrated now, and this close to Diego, this into Diego, she forgot to be scared and hold back.

Izzy just forgot.

She could have climbed up the wall and slid onto him he felt so delicious, but just as her senses faded to oblivion, Diego resurrected one of his.

'Is that a bath?'

Now, this bit she didn't get.

Sense *should* have prevailed.

In her mad dash to turn off the taps, okay, yes it was okay that he followed, but then, *then* she should have shown him the door, should have closed it on him and had a few moments' pause, except she let him help her into the bath and then she remembered to be practical. 'Diego, we can't.'

'I know.' He took off his jacket, hung it on the

doorhandle and then sat on the edge and looked at her, and she couldn't believe how normal it felt.

'We can't,' he confirmed, because of the baby she carried. 'How far along are you again?' He grinned and then rolled his eyes as he did the mental arithmetic, because this thing between them had already been going on for a couple of weeks!

'Poor Diego.' Why was she laughing? Lying in the bath and laughing like she was happy. And the fact that she was made her suddenly serious.

'How can this work—ever?' Izzy asked, because surely it was impossible. 'You're going back to Spain.'

'Nope.' He shook his head. 'I didn't apply.'

'There'll be other jobs though. One day you will go back.' And he couldn't argue with that, so instead she watched as he rolled up his sleeves and two tanned olive hands took a lilac bar of soap and worked it. She could see the bubbles between his fingers, see the moist, slippery sheen of his hands, and her body quivered and begged for them to be on her. As his hands met her shoulders her mind stopped looking for reasons to halt this and her brain stopped begging for logic and all she did was feel—feel his strong fingers on her tense shoulders, feel the knots of tight muscles spasm in momentary protest as this large Spaniard had the nerve to tell them to let go. For months, no, maybe a year, or had it been longer, those muscles had been knotted with the serious job of holding her head up high and now they were being told to let go, to give in, that they could relax, regroup and get ready for the next mountain Izzy was certain that she would surely have to climb. But Diego's hands worked on and convinced her shoulders, if not her mind, to do as the master skilfully commanded, and let go.

Her fringe almost met the water with the relief.

Like popping a balloon she just gave in, just groaned as her tension seeped into the water and then steamed out into the room.

She just couldn't let go for long, though.

'I can't get my hair wet!' She flailed at all his hands were offering, she just couldn't relax and enjoy it in long stages. 'How can this work, Diego?' she asked again.

'*Sencillo*,' Diego said, 'It doesn't have to be complicated. Why not just for now? Why not for as long as we make each other happy?'

'Because in nine weeks I'll be diving into postnatal depression and I won't be making anyone happy!'

She wanted guarantees.

Wanted a little piece of paper stamped with *I won't hurt you* to be handed to her now, except she'd had that once, Izzy realised as she lay there, a big piece of paper called a wedding certificate, and it hadn't counted for a thing.

Before Diego had come along living had been like essential surgery without analgesia.

Why would she deny herself the balm of relief?

And there was a wobble of guilt there, but for him. 'What if I'm using you!' God, she had never been so honest, and certainly not with a man. All her relationships had been Izzy pleasing others, Izzy saying the right thing, and now here she was, ten minutes into a new one and saying the wrong thing, saying truthfully what was on her mind. 'What if I'm using you to get through this?'

And he thought about it for a moment, he actually did, and then he came to his decision.

'Use away!'

'What if I'm avoiding my pain by…?'

'Shut up.' He grinned and leaned over and kissed her a nice lazy kiss. Then he kissed her shoulder and along the slippery wet lines of her neck.

Oh, Diego loved women. He loved curves on women and two of Izzy's were floating on the water, just bobbing there, and his hands moved to her shoulders, because it seemed more polite. But then his hands just moved to where they wanted to be and he caressed them, caressed her. His big, dark hands cupped and soaped her very white, rather large, to Izzy rather ugly breasts, but maybe they weren't so ugly, because from the trip in his breathing and the bob of his tongue on his dark lips, she had the feeling that one tug of his tie and he'd be in the water with her, and there would be two empty seats at the Penhally Charity Ball.

'We can't,' she said again and it was the feeblest of protests, because the stubble of his chin was scratching her breast now, his tongue on her nipple and her fingers in his hair.

'You can,' Diego said, as his hand slid beneath the water.

She never fully forgot about the hell of the past months and years. No matter how good, how happy, how busy she was, no matter what conversation she was holding, it never completely left her mind, but as his hand slid beneath the water and Izzy could feel his fingers at the top of her thighs, ever-present thoughts started to fade. She could feel his hot mouth on her cool shoulder and always, always, always she had thought of pleasing *him*, not Diego, but *him*, and the mute button hit and there was nothing to think of but this, nothing to relish but Diego's tender explorations as she wriggled in his palm.

Her cynical voice gave one last call for order. After all, she didn't come with instructions, and he must do this an awful lot, because his fingers read her so well, but she was kissing his neck and above his white collar, coiling her wet fingers in his dark hair as a heavenly regular pressure beat beneath the water. And suddenly she didn't care if he did this a lot, he was doing it to her, right now, and he could go on doing it for ever, it was so divine. He stroked her back to life, cajoled her hibernating clitoris from its dreamless sleep, and it stretched and peeked out and Izzy was sure this feeling must end, that she'd shift or he'd pause and that the magic would stop, and she didn't want it to.

She couldn't lean back because she didn't want to.

She couldn't reach for the sides of the bath because then she couldn't hold him.

She held his shirt-clad back with wet arms and muffled her face in his neck and beneath the cologne that he was wearing tonight was the true scent of him, the one that every cell in her body had flared for on sight and burnt now with direct contact.

Let go, his fingers insisted. *Let go*, the stubble of his chin told her eyelids as she pressed her face into him. She could hear the lap, lap, lap of the water and the patience yet relentlessness of him and she did as his fingers told her, she didn't know what she said and she didn't know what she did—she just let go. She was almost climbing out of the bath and into his arms, but he held her down and it was so much better than being just friends. And as she opened her eyes he closed his; as he struggled to get through the next nine seconds,

Izzy was wondering how they'd get through the next nine weeks. She wanted more of him.

'We're going to be late.' He was trying to sound normal.

Really, really late, because Izzy now had to sort out her hair and do her make-up *and* show him where the ironing board was so he could iron his shirt dry.

But it was more than worth it.

CHAPTER NINE

SHE had known heads would turn and they did, but what Izzy hadn't expected were the smiles that followed the arches of the eyebrows as they walked in together.

Real smiles, because how could they not?

Izzy had been through so very much and her friends and colleagues had been worried about her, had not known how to react in the face of such raw pain and grief, but tonight she was glowing and it wasn't just from the pregnancy.

'Don't you dare say you're just friends, because I won't believe you.' Megan came over as Diego went to the bar. 'Friends,' Megan said, 'are able to go two minutes without eye contact,' she pointed out as she caught Izzy and Diego share a lingering look from across the room. 'Friends don't light up a room with their energy when they walk in. Friends don't cause every head to turn. Friends, my foot...' Megan laughed.

'Okay, 'Izzy said, and though it was all a bit like a runaway train, she felt exhilarated as she rode it, smiled as she said it: 'We're more than friends.'

'Happy?' Megan checked.

'Very.'

'Then I'm happy for you,' Megan said. Izzy was sure

she would have loved to have said more, but sometimes good friends didn't. Sometimes good friends had to let you make your own success or mistakes and be there for you whatever the outcome. Megan confirmed that with her next words.

'I'm always here.'

'I know that.'

'So how did you manage the night off? I thought you were on.'

'No.' Izzy shook her head, 'I told you, I'm only doing days till the baby's born. I thought you were on call?'

'Richard didn't want to come to the ball, so he's covering for me,' Megan said. 'So who's holding the fort in A and E tonight?'

'Mitch,' Izzy said.

'He's only a resident.'

'Oh, Ben is on call, said he might pop in if he can get away....' And her voice trailed off, because Izzy realised then that Megan hadn't actually been enquiring about her roster, she had been fishing to find out the whereabouts of someone else. And as Megan stood and kissed Izzy on the cheek and headed off into the throng of people, Izzy found a corner of an unexpected jigsaw.

She could see Megan, her usually pale cheeks, suddenly flushed and pink, desperately trying to focus on a conversation, but her green eyes kept flicking over to Josh. It was as if there were an invisible thread between them, a thread that tightened. She watched as Josh worked the room, each greeting, each two-minute conversation seemed to be dragging him on a human Mexican wave towards Megan. The pull was so strong,

Izzy could have sworn she could have reached out and grabbed it.

And then it snapped.

Izzy watched as a blonde woman walked over, all smiles, and kissed Josh possessively on the lips. Izzy saw the wedding band glint on her finger and as Megan's face turned away, Izzy knew Megan had just seen it too.

'Excuse me…' All the colour had drained out of Megan's face and she walked quickly to the ladies. Izzy looked over at Josh who was concentrating on something his wife was saying, but then he caught her eye and Izzy couldn't read his expression, but something told her it was a plea to help.

'Here…' Diego was back with the drinks and it was Izzy's turn to excuse herself, but by the time she got to the ladies Megan was on her way out.

'Hey?' Izzy smiled. 'Are you okay?'

'I'm great!' Megan gave a dazzling smile. 'It's always a good night.'

'Megan?' Izzy caught her friend's arm, but Megan shook it off.

'I must get back out there.'

Oh, she wanted to know what was going on, to help, to fix, to share, only it was clear all Megan wanted to do was to get through this night.

'Sit with us,' Izzy suggested. 'I thought we would be with the emergency guys and girls or NICU, but we left the booking too late and we're with the maternity mob. Come and keep us company.' It was the best she could do for Megan right now and when Megan jumped at the suggestion, Izzy knew she had been right.

There was something going on with Megan and Josh.

Or, Izzy pondered, there had been.

It was actually a good night—the food was wonderful, the company great. Diego was clearly a hit with the maternity team as well, but as the table was cleared and the dancing commenced Izzy was uncomfortable all of a sudden in the hard chair. Stretching her spine, she shifted her weight and she was glad to stretch her legs when Diego asked her to dance.

It was such bliss to be in his arms.

To smell him, to be held by him.

She wished the music would last for ever—that somehow she could freeze this moment of time, where there was no past to run from and no future that could change things. She wished she could dance and dance, just hold this moment and forever feel his breath on her neck and his warm hands on her back, to feel the bulge of her pregnant stomach pressed to his and to remember...

She was dizzy almost remembering a couple of hours earlier.

'Glad you came?' Diego asked.

'Very,' Izzy said, and then pulled back and smiled. 'And more than a little surprised that I did.'

Every day he saw another side to her.

Diego was far from stupid. Of course he had questioned the wisdom of getting involved with someone at such a vulnerable time—fatherhood was not on his agenda. After a lifetime of rules and the stuffy confines of his family, he had sworn it would be years before anyone or anything pinned him down. He was devoted to his work and everything else was just a pleasure, but now, holding her in his arms, life was starting to look a little different.

'Hey.' He'd sensed her distraction. 'What are you watching?'

'What's going on,' she asked, 'with Megan and Josh?'

Diego rolled his eyes. 'Not you too? Rita, my ward clerk, is obsessed with them.'

'Megan's been different lately,' Izzy insisted. 'Surely you've noticed?'

'I've had my mind on other things,' he said, pulling her in a little tighter. 'There's nothing going on,' Diego said assuredly, and glanced at the subjects of their conversation. 'They're not even talking to each other.'

Which was such a male thing to say, but Megan was right, Izzy thought, watching Josh's eyes scan the room as he danced with his wife, watched them locate and capture and hold their target, almost in apology, until Megan tore hers away.

Friends don't share looks like that.

But in that moment all thoughts of Josh and Megan faded, all thoughts of Diego and romance too, because the back pain she had felt while sitting returned, spreading out from her spine like two large hands, stretching around to her stomach and squeezing. It wasn't a pain as such, she'd been having Braxton-Hicks' contractions, but this felt different, tighter. This didn't take her breath, neither did it stop her swaying in the darkness with Diego, but she was more than aware of it and then it was gone and she tried to forget that it had happened. only Diego had been aware of it too.

He had felt her stomach, which was pressed into his, tighten.

He didn't want to be one of those paranoid people. She was just dancing on so he did too, but he was almost more aware of her body than his own. He could feel the slight shift and knew that even though she danced on and held him, her mind was no longer there.

'You okay?'

'Great,' she murmured, hoping and praying that she was. The music played on and Diego suggested that they sit this next one out. Izzy was about to agree, only suddenly the walk back to their table seemed rather long. The music tipped into the next ballad and Izzy leant on him as the next small wave hit, only this time it did make her catch her breath and Diego could pretend no more.

'Izzy?' She heard the question in his voice.

'I don't know,' she admitted. 'Can you get me outside?' she said, still leaning on him, waiting for it to pass. 'In a moment.'

Their exit was discreet. He had a hand round her waist and they didn't stop to get her bag, and as the cool night air hit, Izzy wondered if she was overreacting because now she felt completely normal.

'Izzy.' Discreet as their exit had been, Gus must have noticed because he joined them outside, just as another contraction hit.

'They're not strong,' Izzy said as Gus placed a skilled hand on her abdomen.

'How far apart?' Gus asked, and it was Diego who answered.

'Six, maybe seven minutes.'

'Okay.' Gus wasted no time. 'Let's get you over to the hospital and we can pop you on a monitor. I'll bring the Jeep around.'

'Should we call an ambulance?' Diego asked, but Gus shook his head.

'We'll be quicker in my Jeep and if we have to pull over, I've got everything we need.'

'I'm not having it,' Izzy insisted, only neither Diego nor Gus was convinced.

It was a thirty-minute drive from Penhally. Diego felt a wave of unease as Izzy's hand gripped his tighter and she blew out a long breath. He remembered his time on Maternity and often so often it was a false alarm, the midwives could tell. Izzy kept insisting she was fine, that the contractions weren't that bad, but he could feel her fingers digging into his palms at closer intervals, could see Gus glancing in the rear-view mirror when Izzy held her breath every now and then, and the slight acceleration as Gus drove faster.

His mind was racing, awful scenarios playing out, but Izzy could never have guessed. He stayed strong and supportive beside her, held her increasingly tightening fingers as Gus rang through and warned the hospital of their arrival. A staff member was waiting with a wheelchair as they pulled up at the maternity section.

'It's too soon,' Izzy said as he helped her out of the Jeep.

'You're in the right place,' Diego said, only he could feel his heart hammering in his chest, feel the adrenaline coursing through him as she was whisked off and all he could do was give her details as best as he could to a new night receptionist.

'You're the father?' ahe asked, and his lips tightened as he shook his head, and he felt the relegation.

'I'm a friend,' Diego said. 'Her…' But he didn't know what to follow it up with. It had been just a few short weeks, and he wasn't in the least surprised when he was asked to take a seat in a bland waiting room

He waited, unsure what to do, what his role was—if he even had a role here.

Going over and over the night, stunned at how quickly everything had changed. One minute they had been dancing, laughing—now they were at the hospital.

The logical side of his brain told him that thirty-one weeks' gestation was okay. Over and over he tried to console himself, tried to picture his reaction if he knew a woman was labouring and he was preparing a cot to receive the baby. Yet there was nothing logical about the panic that gripped him when he thought of Izzy's baby being born at thirty-one weeks. Every complication, every possibility played over and over. It was way too soon, and even if everything did go well, Izzy would be in for a hellish ride when she surely didn't deserve it.

They could stop the labour, though. Diego swung between hope and despair. She'd only just started to have contractions...

'Diego.' Gus came in and shook his hand.

'How is she?'

'Scared,' Gus said, and gave him a brief rundown of his findings. 'We've given her steroids to mature the baby's lungs and we're trying to stop the labour or at least slow down the process to give the medication time to take effect.'

'Oh, God...' Guilt washed over him, a guilt he knew was senseless, but guilt all the same. However, Gus was one step ahead of him.

'Nothing Izzy or you did contributed to this, Diego. I've spoken with Izzy at length, this was going to happen. In fact...' he gave Diego a grim smile '...an ultrasound and cord study have just been done. Her placenta is small and the cord very thin. This baby really will do better on the outside, though we'd all like to buy another week or two. I knew the baby was small for dates. Izzy was going to have an ultrasound early next week, but from what I've just seen Izzy's baby really will do better by being born.'

'She's been eating well, taking care of herself.'

'She suffered trauma both physically and emotionally early on in the pregnancy,' Gus said. 'Let's just get her through tonight, but guilt isn't going to help anyone.'

Diego knew that. He'd had the same conversation with more parents than he could remember—the endless search for answers, for reasons, when sometimes Mother Nature worked to her own agenda.

'Does she want to see me?'

Gus nodded. 'She doesn't want to call her family just yet.'

When he saw her, Diego remembered the day he had first met her when she had come to the neonatal ward. Wary, guarded, she sat on the bed, looking almost angry, but he knew she was just scared.

'It's going to be okay,' Diego said, and took her hand, but she pulled it away.

'You don't know that.'

She sat there and she had all her make-up on, her hair immaculate, except she was in a hospital gown with a drip and a monitor strapped to her stomach, and Diego wondered if she did actually want him there at all.

She did.

But how could she ask him to be there for her?

She was scared for her baby, yet she resented it almost.

Nine weeks.

They'd had nine weeks left of being just a couple, which was not long by anyone's standards. Nine weeks to get to know each other properly, to enjoy each other, and now even that nine weeks was being denied to them.

How could she admit how much she wanted him to stay—yet how could she land all this on him?

'I think you should go.'

'Izzy.' Diego kept his voice steady. 'Whatever helps you now is fine by me. I can call your family. I can stay with you, or I can wait outside, or if you would prefer that I leave...'

He wanted to leave, Izzy decided, or he wouldn't have said it. The medication they had given her to slow down the labour made her brain work slower, made her thought process muddy.

'I don't know...' Her teeth were chattering, her admission honest. Gus was back, talking to a midwife and Richard Brooke, the paediatric consultant, who had just entered the room. They were all looking at the printout from the monitor and Izzy wanted five minutes alone with Diego, five minutes to try and work out whether or not he wanted to be there, but she wasn't going to get five minutes with her thoughts for a long while.

'Izzy.' She knew that voice and so did Diego, knew that brusque, professional note so well, because they had both used it themselves when they bore bad tidings. 'The baby is struggling; its heartbeat is irregular...'

'It needs time to let the medication take effect.' Izzy's fuzzy logic didn't work on Gus. He just stood over her, next to Diego, both in suits and looking sombre, and she felt as if she were lying in a coffin. 'We want to do a Caesarean, your baby needs to be born.'

Already the room was filling with more staff. She felt the jerk as the brakes were kicked off the bed, the clang as portable oxygen was lifted onto the bed and even in her drugged state she knew this wasn't your standard Caesarean section, this was an emergency Caesarean.

'Is there time…?' She didn't even bother to finish her sentence. Izzy could hear the deceleration in her baby's heartbeat, and knew there wouldn't be time for an epidural, that she would require a general anaesthetic, and it was the scariest, out-of-control feeling. 'Can you be there, Diego?' Her eyes swung from Diego to Gus. 'Can Diego be in there?'

For a general anaesthetic, partners or relatives weren't allowed to come into the theatre, but the NICU team were regularly in Theatre and after just the briefest pause Richard agreed, but with clarification. 'Just for Izzy.'

'Sure,' Diego agreed, and at that moment he'd have agreed to anything, because the thought of being sent to another waiting room, *knowing* all that could go wrong, was unbearable, but as he helped speed the bed the short distance to Theatre, Diego also knew that if there was a problem with the babe, he wanted to be the one dealing with it. This was no time for arrogance neither was it time for feigned modesty—quite simply Diego knew he was the best.

The theatre sister gave Diego a slightly wide-eyed look as she registered he was holding hands with her emergency admission, whom she recognised too.

'Diego's here with Izzy,' the midwife explained. 'Richard has okayed him to go in.'

'Then you'll need to go and get changed,' came the practical response. 'You can say goodbye to her here.'

And that was it.

Diego knew when he saw her again, she would be under anaesthetic.

Izzy knew it too.

'I'm glad you're here...' She was trying not to cry and her face was smothered with the oxygen mask. 'You'll make sure...'

'Everything is going to be fine.' His voice came out gruffer than he was used to hearing it. He was trying to reassure her, but Diego felt it sounded as if he was telling her off. 'Better than fine,' he said again. His voice still didn't soften, but there wasn't time to correct it. 'Thirty-one-weekers do well.'

'Thirty-two's better.'

'I'll be there,' Diego said. 'And it *is* going to be okay.'

He couldn't give her a kiss, because they were already moving her away.

He turned to Gus, who as her GP would also have to wait outside the operating theatre, and exchanged a look with the worried man. 'Go and get changed, Diego,' Gus said, and his words shocked Diego into action. He changed his clothes in a moment, then put on a hat and made his way through to Theatre.

'Diego!' Hugh, the paediatric anaesthetist greeted him from behind a yellow mask. 'Extremely bradycardic, ready for full resus.'

'Diego's here with the mother.' Brianna was there too, ready to receive the baby, and her unusually pointed tone was clearly telling her colleague to shut the hell up.

The surgeon on duty that night had already started

the incision, and Diego knew the man in question was brilliant at getting a baby out urgently when required, but for Diego the world was in slow motion, the theatre clock hand surely sticking as it moved past each second marker.

'Breech.' The surgeon was calling for more traction. Diego could see the two spindly legs the surgeon held in one hand and for the first time in Theatre he felt nausea, understood now why relatives were kept out and almost wished he had been, because suddenly he appreciated how fathers-to-be must feel.

Except he wasn't the father, Diego told himself as the baby's limp body was manoeuvred out and the head delivered.

This baby wasn't his to love, Diego reminded himself as an extremely floppy baby was dashed across to the resuscitation cot.

He *never* wanted to feel like this again.

He never wanted to stand so helpless, just an observer. It would, for Diego, have been easier to work on her himself, yet he was in no state to.

He could feel his fingertips press into her palms with impatience as Hugh called twice for a drug, and though the team was fantastic, their calm professionalism riled him. Richard was fantastic, but Diego would have preferred Megan. Megan pounced on tiny details faster than anyone Diego had seen.

'She's still bradycardic,' Diego said, when surely they should have commenced massage now.

'Out.' Brianna mouthed the word and jerked her head to the theatre doors, but he hesitated.

'Diego!' Brianna said his name, and Diego stiffened in realisation—this wasn't his call, only it felt like it.

Brianna's brown eyes lifted again to his when Diego would have preferred them to stay on the baby, and he knew he was getting in the way, acting more like a father than a professional, so he left before he was formally asked to.

CHAPTER TEN

'THAT'S it, Izzy...' She could hear a male voice she
didn't recognise. 'Stay on your back.'

She was under blankets and wanted to roll onto her
side, except she couldn't seem to move.

'You're doing fine,' came the unfamiliar voice. 'Stay
nice and still.'

'Izzy, it's all okay.'

There was a voice she knew. Strong and deep and
accented, and she knew it was Diego, she just didn't
know why, and then she opened her eyes and saw his
and she remembered.

'You've got a daughter.' His face was inches away.
'She's okay, she's being looked after.'

And then it was fog, followed by pain, followed by
drugs, so many drugs she struggled to focus when Diego
came back in the afternoon with pictures of her baby.

'She looks like you,' Diego said, but all Izzy could
see were tubes.

'Are you working today?'

Diego shook his head. 'No. I just came in to see you.'
And he sat down in the chair by her bed and Izzy went
to sleep. He flicked through the photos and tried very
hard to only see tubes, because this felt uncomfortably

familiar, this felt a little like it had with Fernando and he just couldn't go there again.

He certainly wasn't ready to go there again.

There was a very good reason that a normal pregnancy lasted forty weeks, Diego reflected, putting the photos on her locker and heading for home—and it wasn't just for the baby. The parents needed every week of that time to prepare themselves emotionally for the change to their lives.

He wasn't even a parent.

It was Tuesday night and a vicious UTI later before anything resembling normal thought process occurred and a midwife helped her into a chair and along with her mother wheeled her down to the NICU, where, of course, any new mum would want to be if her baby was.

'We take mums down at night all the time,' the midwife explained, when Izzy said the next day would be fine. 'It's no problem.'

Except, privately, frankly, Izzy would have preferred to sleep.

Izzy knew she was a likely candidate for postnatal depression.

As a doctor she was well versed in the subject and the midwives had also gently warned her and given her leaflets to read. Gus too had talked to her—about her difficult labour, the fact she had been separated from her daughter and her difficult past. He'd told her he was there if she needed to talk and he had been open and upfront and told her not to hesitate to reach out sooner rather than later, as had Jess.

She sat in a wheelchair at the entrance to NICU, at

the very spot where she had first flirted with Diego, where the first thawing of her heart had taken place, and it seemed a lifetime ago, not a few short weeks.

And, just as she had felt that day, Izzy was tempted to ask the midwife to turn the chair around, more nervous at meeting her baby than she could ever let on. Diego was on a stint of night duty and she was nervous of him seeing her in her new role too, because his knowing eyes wouldn't miss anything. What if she couldn't summon whatever feelings and emotions it was that new mums summoned?

'I bet you can't wait!' Izzy's mum said as the midwife pressed the intercom and informed the voice on the end of their arrival. Then the doors buzzed and she was let in. Diego came straight over and gave her a very nice smile and they made some introductions. 'Perhaps you could show Izzy's mother the coffee room.' Diego was firm on this as he would be with any of his mothers. If Izzy had stepped in and said she'd prefer her mum to come, then of course it would have happened, but Izzy stayed quiet, very glad of a chance to meet her daughter alone.

'I already know where the coffee room is,' Gwen said, 'and I've already seen the baby.'

'Izzy hasn't.' Diego was straight down the line. 'We can't re-create the delivery room but we try—she needs time alone to greet her baby.'

Which told her.

'You know the rules.' He treated Izzy professionally and she was very glad of it. They went through the hand-washing ritual and he spoke to her as they did so.

'Brianna is looking after her tonight,' Diego said. 'Do you know her?'

'I don't think so.'

'She's great—she was there at the delivery. I'll take you over.'

Nicola, Toby's mother, was there and gave Izzy a sympathetic smile as she was wheeled past, which Izzy returned too late, because she was already there at her baby's cot.

Brianna greeted her, but Izzy was hardly listening. Instead she stared into the cot and there she was—her baby. And months of fear and wondering all hushed for a moment as she saw her, her little red scrunched-up face and huge dark blue eyes that stared right into Izzy's.

Over the last three days Diego had bought her plenty of photos, told her how well she was doing and how beautiful she was, but seeing her in the flesh she was better than beautiful, she was hers.

'We're just giving her a little oxygen,' Brianna explained as Diego was called away. 'Which we will be for a couple more weeks, I'd expect...' She opened the porthole and Izzy needed no invitation. She held her daughter's hand, marvelling that such a tiny hand instinctively curled around her index finger, and Izzy knew there and then that she was in love.

'She looks better than I thought...' Izzy couldn't actually believe just how well she looked. Her mum had been crying when she'd returned the first day from visiting her granddaughter and Richard, the consultant paediatrician, had told her that her baby had got off to a rocky start.

'She struggled for the first forty-eight hours, which we were expecting,' Brianna said calmly, 'but she picked up well.'

Diego had said the same, but she'd been worried he'd

just been reassuring her, but now she was here, now she could see her, all Izzy could feel was relief and this overwhelming surge charging through her veins that she figured felt a lot like love.

'Now, would you like to hold her?' Brianna said to Izzy's surprise. 'She's due for a feed, but she needs it soon, so would you like to give her a cuddle first?'

She very much would.

Brianna brought over a large chair and Izzy sat, exhausted, then got a new surge of energy.

'Open up your pyjama top,' Brianna said

'It's popping open all the time...' Izzy said, staring down at her newly massive breasts that strained the buttons.

'Your skin will keep her warm and it's good for both of you.'

She hadn't expected so much so soon. Her dreams had been filled with tiny floppy babies like ugly skinned rabbits, yet her baby was prettier and healthier than her photos had shown. Brianna was calm and confident and then there she was, wearing just a nappy and hat and resting on her chest, a blanket being wrapped around them both, skin on skin, and Izzy at that moment knew...

She knew, as far as anyone could possibly know, that the doom and gloom and the shadow of PND was not going to darken her door.

She could feel her baby on her skin and it was almost, Izzy was sure, as if all the darkness just fell away from her now, as pure love flooded in.

A white, pure love that was tangible, that was real. All the fears, the doubts, the dark, dark dread faded, because she had never been sure, really, truly sure that love *could* win, that love would come, that it would happen.

But it just did.

Diego witnessed it too.

He had seen many moments like this one, both in NICU and in the delivery room, and it was more something he ticked off his list than felt moved by—especially in NICU, where bonding was more difficult to achieve. Only it wasn't a list with Izzy, because it did move him, so much so that he came over and smiled down as he watched.

It crossed so many lines, because he didn't want to feel it, and also, as Gwen came over, Diego realised he had sent her own mother away.

Yet he was here.

'She's a Ross all over, isn't she?' Gwen said, and Diego saw Izzy's jaw clench as her mother stamped her territory on her granddaughter and told her how it would be. 'There's nothing of him in her.'

Of course, Henry's parents begged to differ when they came two days later to visit.

They had been in France, trying to have a break, after the most traumatic of months, and had cut their holiday short to come in and visit what was left of their son.

It was an agonising visit. Emotions frayed, Henry's mother teary, his father trying to control things, telling Izzy their rights, blaming her at every turn till she could see clearly where Henry had got it from! And, that evening, as soon as they left, Izzy sat on the bed with her fingers pressed into her eyes, trying to hold it together, wondering if now tears would come.

'Bad timing?' Izzy jumped as heard footsteps and

saw Josh, the new consultant, at her door. 'I'll come by another time.'

'I'm fine.' Izzy forced a smile. 'Come in.'

'You're sure?' he checked, and Izzy nodded.

'I'm sorry to mess up the roster.'

'That's the last thing you should be worrying about,' Josh replied, just as any boss would in the circumstances, and it was going to be an awkward visit, Izzy knew that. A guy like Josh didn't really belong in the maternity ward with teary women. 'Ben's on leave, but he rang and told me you'd be stressing about details like that, and could I come up and tell you that you're not to worry about a thing and that if there's anything we can do for you, you're to ask.'

'Is there anything,' Josh pushed, 'that we can do for you now?'

'I'm being very well looked after. I'm fine, really, it's just been a difficult evening.' She waited for a thin line from Josh about the baby blues, or something like that, but he just looked at her for a long time before he spoke.

'I'm quite sure this is all very difficult for you,' Josh said.

And he was just so disarmingly nice that Izzy found herself admitting a little more. 'Henry's parents just stopped by. They've gone to see the baby.'

'Henry's your late husband?' Josh checked, and Izzy nodded.

'I'm sure you've heard all the gossip.'

'I don't listen to gossip,' Josh said, 'though Ben did bring me up to date on what happened before you came back to work, just so that I would know to look out for you. You know Ben's not into gossip either, but he felt

I should know—not all of it, I'm sure, but he told me enough that I can see you'd be having a tough time of it.'

His directness surprised her. Instead of sitting stiffly in the chair and making painful small talk, he came over and sat on the bed, took her hand and gave it a squeeze and a bit of that Irish charm, and Izzy could see why he was such a wonderful doctor.

'Henry's parents blame me,' Izzy admitted. 'They thought our marriage was perfect, they think I'm making it all up.'

'They probably want to believe that you're making it all up,' Josh said wisely.

'They were in tears just before, saying what a wonderful father Henry would have been, how a baby would have changed things, would have saved our marriage, if only I hadn't asked him to leave. They don't know what went on behind closed doors.'

'They need to believe that you're lying,' Josh said. 'But you know the truth.'

'A baby wouldn't have changed things.' With his gentle guidance Izzy's voice was finally adamant. 'Babies don't fix a damaged marriage. That was why I had to leave. I can't even begin to imagine us together as parents. A baby should come from love...'

'Do you want me to call Diego for you?' Josh said, but Izzy shook her head.

'He's already been to visit,' Izzy said. 'He's on a night shift tonight. I can't ring him for every little thing.'

'Yes,' a voice said from the doorway, 'you can.' There stood Diego, but only for a moment, and she dropped Josh's hand as he walked over.

'I'll leave you to it.' Josh smiled and stood up. 'Now,

remember, if there's anything we can do, you just pick up that phone. Even if it's just a decent coffee, you've got a whole team behind you twenty-four seven. Just let us know.'

Izzy thanked him, but she sat there blushing as he left and waited till the door was closed.

'Nothing was happening.' Izzy was awash with guilt. 'I was just upset, so he held my hand—'

'Izzy!' Diego interrupted. 'I'm glad Josh was here, I'm glad you had someone to hold your hand.'

Yet she still felt more explanation was needed. 'Henry would have had a fit if he'd—'

'Izzy! I'm not Henry—I don't care how many times I have to say it—I'm nothing like him.'

And he wasn't.

She leant on his broad chest and heard the regular beat of his heart, felt the safe wall of his chest and the wrap of his arms, and if she didn't love her so, it would be so easy to resent her baby—because nine weeks of just them would have been so very nice.

'I'd better go.' Reluctantly he stood up. 'I'll drop by in the morning and let you know what sort of night she had.'

'Tilia,' Izzy said.

'Tilia,' Diego repeated, and a smile spread over his face. 'I like it. What does it mean?'

'It's actually a tree…' Izzy's eyes never left his face, because somehow his reaction was important. 'I'm only telling you this—my mum would freak and I can't have a proper conversation with Henry's parents. It's a lime tree. Henry proposed under this gorgeous old lime tree…' Still he just looked. 'We were happy then.'

'I think it's wonderful,' Diego said. 'And one day,

Izzy, you'll be able to talk about him to Tilia, and tell her about those good times.' He gave her a kiss and headed for work, and Izzy lay back on the pillow and even though he'd said everything right, she still couldn't settle.

She looked at new photos of herself holding Tilia and she didn't see the drips or tubes, she just saw her baby.

And there in one photo was a side view of Diego.

The three of them together, except he wasn't kneeling down with his arms around her.

She couldn't imagine these past weeks without him.

Yet she was too scared to indulge in a glimpse of a future with him.

She kept waiting for the axe to fall—sure, quite sure that something this good could never last.

A midwife took her drip down and turned off the lights but the room was still bright thanks to the full moon bathing St Piran's, and while Izzy couldn't get to sleep, Diego on the other hand would have loved to be-cause between visiting Izzy and working he still hadn't caught up from Tilia's rapid arrival.

It was a busy night that kept him at the nurses' sta-tion rather than the shop floor, where Diego preferred to be.

And, worse, from the computer he could hear her crying.

He glanced up and Brianna was checking a drug with another nurse working at the next cot, and Diego could hear Tilia crying. Brianna must have asked the other nurse for an opinion on something, because they were reading through the obs sheet. It was *normal* for babies to cry—he barely even heard it, so why did he stand up and head over?

'Brianna.' He jerked his head to Tilia's cot and he wished he hadn't, knew he was doing something he never would have done previously. If a baby was crying it was breathing was the mantra when matters where pressing. But Brianna didn't seem worried at his snap. Actually, she was more discreet than anyone he had ever met, but he could have sworn he saw her lips suppress a smile.

And as for Josh, well, as tired as he might be, bed was the last thing he wanted.

He'd visited Izzy when really he hadn't had to. Ben had actually asked for him to drop in over the next couple of days, but Josh had convinced himself that it was his duty to go after his shift.

Then, having visited her, he had hung around till someone had made some joke about him not having a home to go to, so eventually he'd headed there, but had stopped at the garage first.

As he pulled up at the smart gated community and the gates opened, Josh checked his pager and knew in his heart of hearts he was hoping against hope for something urgent to call him in.

God, had it really come to this, sitting in his driveway, steeling himself to go inside?

Izzy's words rang in his ears.

'*A baby wouldn't have changed things… Babies don't fix a damaged marriage… I can't even begin to imagine us together as parents… A baby should come from love…*'

There *had* been love between him and Rebecca.

A different sort of love, though, not the intense,

dangerous love he had once briefly known. That had been a love so consuming that it had bulldozed everything in its path. He closed his eyes and leant back on the headrest and for the first time in years he fully let himself visit that time.

Felt the grief and the agony, but it was too painful to recall so instead he dwelt on the consequences of raw love—a love that ruined lives and could destroy plans, a love that had threatened his rapid ascent in his career.

His and Rebecca's love had been different—safer certainly.

She wanted a successful doctor—*that* he could provide.

They had been good for each other, had wanted the same, at least for a while.

Josh could see her shadow behind the blinds, see her earrings, her jewellery, the skimpy outlines of her nightdress that left nothing to the imagination, and knew what Rebecca wanted from him tonight.

And he also knew that it wasn't about him.

'At least I'll have something to show for four years of marriage...' He recalled the harsh words of their latest row and then watched as she poured herself a drink from the decanter. He felt a stab of sympathy as he realised that Rebecca needed a bit of Dutch courage to go through with tonight.

Maybe he should get a vasectomy without her knowing, but what sort of coward, or husband, did that? Josh reeled at his own thought.

So he checked his pocket for his purchase from the garage, because he couldn't face her tears from another rejection. They hadn't slept together in weeks, not since...

Josh slammed that door in his mind closed, simply refused to go there, and tried very hard not to cloud the issue. In truth his and Rebecca's marriage had been well into injury time long before they had come to St Piran.

He went to pocket the condoms, to have them conveniently to hand, because no doubt Rebecca would ensure they never made it up the stairs and he knew for a fact she'd stopped taking the Pill.

'What the hell am I doing?' he groaned.

Yes, it would be so much easier to go in and make love.

Easier in the short term perhaps to give her the baby Rebecca said she wanted.

But since when had Josh chosen the easy path?

He tossed the condoms back into the glove box, a guarantee of sorts that he wouldn't give in and take the easy way out.

There was a conversation that needed to take place and, no matter how painful, it really was time.

They owed each other that at least.

Taking a breath, he walked up the neat path of his low-maintenance garden, waved to his neighbours, who were sipping wine on their little balcony and watching the world go by.

'Beautiful night, Josh.'

'It's grand, isn't it?' Josh agreed, and turned the key and stepped inside.

To the world, to his neighbours, the dashing doctor was coming home after a hellishly long day to his wonderful smart home and into the loving arms of his beautiful trophy wife.

* * *

It *was* a beautiful night.

The moon was big and round and it just accentuated the chaos as Evelyn Harris surveyed the ruin of her kitchen, plates smashed and broken, her ribs bruised and tender, the taste of blood in her mouth. She heard her husband snoring upstairs in bed.

She picked up the phone and not for the first time wondered about calling Izzy—but would the doctor even remember her? Surely it was too late to ring at this hour, and her son had an exam in the morning and she had lunch with John's boss's wife to get through, so she put down the phone and chose to sleep on the plush leather sofa.

Izzy was right.

Nobody *did* know what went on behind closed doors.

CHAPTER ELEVEN

'SHE'S a tough little one.'

Like her mother, Diego thought.

Tilia, though small for dates and premature, was also incredibly active and strong. She had only required a short time on CPAP and was doing well on oxygen.

It really was a case of better out than in—now she could gain weight and as was often the case with babies who had been deprived nutrition *in utero*, Tilia's forehead often creased in concern as if she was constantly worried as to where her next meal was coming from.

'She wants her mum.' Brianna could not get Tilia to settle. 'I might ring Maternity and see if Izzy's still awake, she might get a nice cuddle. Then I'm going to have my coffee break. Could you watch mine for a moment while I call?'

They often rang Maternity, especially when babies were active and if there was a nurse who could bring the mother over—well, the middle of the night was a nice time to sit in rocking chair and bond a little. But when Diego had left Izzy she had been drained and exhausted and she could really use a full night's sleep—not that he was going to say that to Brianna. The gossip was already flying around the hospital since their appearance at the ball—had a certain little lady not put in such an early appearance, they might have been old news now, but given the turn of events and that Diego had been in the labour ward and was up twice day visiting on Maternity, he felt as if all eyes were on them. The scrutiny was just too fierce and strong at such a fragile time.

He was actually more than glad to be on nights, away from Rita's probing, and he had deliberately allocated Brianna to care for Tilia.

Brianna was one of the most private people Diego had met. She said nothing about her private life. She was there to work and work she did, loving and caring for her charges—gossip the last thing she was interested in.

'They've given Izzy a sleeping tablet,' Brianna said when she came back. 'Never mind, little lady, I'll give you a cuddle.'

'You go and have your break,' Diego said. 'I'll sort her.'

He didn't want to be doing this.

Or had he engineered it?

Diego didn't want to examine his feelings. Brianna was long overdue her coffee break, it was as simple as that. So he washed his hands in his usual thorough manner, put on a gown and then unclipped the sides of the incubator.

Often, so very often he did this—soothed a restless baby, or took over care while one of his team took their break.

And tonight it would be far safer to remember that.

He would sit and get this baby settled and perhaps chat with another nurse as he did so, or watch the ward from a chair.

He sat and expertly held Tilia, spoke as he always did to his charges—joking that he would teach her a little Spanish.

Which he did.

Then Chris, another of the nurses on duty that night, came over and asked him to run his eyes over a drug.

Which he did.

And then he felt something he hadn't in more than a decade.

Something he had tried never to feel since Fernando.

He adored his babies, but they weren't *his* to love.

He had loved Fernando, had held him three times in his little life, and it had never come close since.

But holding Tilia, it came close.

Dangerously close.

She wasn't a patient and she wasn't his new girl-friend's baby.

She was Tilia.

Izzy's baby.

But more than that.

He smelt that unmistakable baby smell that sur-rounded him each day but which he never noticed, he looked into huge eyes that were the same shape as her mother's and she had the same shape mouth. Even her nostrils were the same.

And there, sitting with all the hissing and bleeping and noise that was a busy neonatal unit, Diego, felt a stab of dread.

That he might lose her too.

He looked over to where Toby's mother had come in, restless and unable to sleep, for just one more check on her son, and he knew how she felt—how many times in the night at eighteen he had woken with a sudden shock of fright and rushed to check on Fernando, asking the nurses to check and check again, petrified that they had missed something, but it wasn't that fear that gripped him as he held Tilia.

'You're going to be fine,' Diego said to Tilia in Spanish. 'You're going to be clever and grow healthy and strong...'

Only would he be around to see it?

'And your mother's getting stronger each day too,' Diego went on. 'Just watch her grow too.'

He wanted that for Izzy. He vowed as he sat there, holding her baby while she could not, that he would help Izzy grow, would do everything to encourage her, even if that meant that she grew away from him.

How could he let himself fall in love with this little babe when who knew what her mother might want days, weeks or months from now? When who knew what he might want?

Diego ran a finger down her little cheek.

But how could he not?

Staying in the parents' wing had been the right choice.

It was a precious time, one where she caught up on all she had missed out on, one where there was nothing to focus on other than her baby.

Always Diego was friendly, professional, calm, except for the visits before or after her shift, when he was friendly and calm but he dropped the professional for tender, but there was never any pressure, no demands for her time. Now, as Tilia hit four weeks, the world outside was starting to creep back in and for the first time since her daughter's birth, Izzy truly assessed the situation, wondering, fearing that it was as she had suspected—that her daughter's birth had changed everything for them, that his lack of demands meant a lack of passion.

A soft rap at her door at six-thirty a.m. didn't wake her. She'd been up and fed Tilia and had had her shower, and often Diego popped in at this time if he was on an early shift, bearing two cups of decent coffee and, this morning, two croissants.

'She went the whole night without oxygen.' Izzy beamed.

'We'll be asking her to leave if she carries on like this!' Diego joked, and though Izzy smiled and they chatted easily, when he left a familiar flutter took place in her stomach. Tilia was doing well, really well, and though at first the doctors had warned it could be several weeks before her discharge, just four short weeks on Tilia was defying everyone—putting on weight, managing the occasional bottle, and now a whole night without oxygen and no de-sats. Discharge day would be coming soon, Izzy knew, but if Tilia was ready, Izzy wasn't so sure she was.

Diego was working the floor today. Once a week he left his office and insisted on doing the job he adored. From nine a.m. he was working in Theatre with a multiple birth and a baby with a cardiac defect scheduled for delivery. The unit was expecting a lot of new arrivals, and it fell to him to tell the mother of a thriving thirty-five-weeker that her room would be needed in a couple of days.

He'd stretched it to the limit, of course.

Not just because it was Izzy, not just that she was a doctor at this hospital, but with all she had been through, he would have done his best for any woman in that situation—though he waited till he was working to tell her.

'She won't take it.' Izzy was in the nursery, feeding her daughter, jiggling the teat in Tilia's slack mouth. 'She took the last one really well...'

He tickled her little feet and held his hand over Izzy's and pushed the teat in a bit more firmly, tried to stimulate the baby to suck, but Tilia was having none of it, her little eyelids flickering as she drifted deeper into sleep. Izzy actually laughed as she gave in.

'She's not going to take it.' There was no panic in her voice, Diego noted. Izzy was a pretty amazing mum. Often with doctors or nurses they were more anxious than most new parents and even though he'd expected that from Izzy, she'd surprised him. She revelled in her new motherhood role and was far more relaxed than most.

'They're like teenagers,' Diego said, 'party all night, and sleep all day. That last feed would have exhausted her.'

Chris, one of the nurses, came over and saw the full bottle, and because Tilia was so small and needed her calories, she suggested they tube-feed her, and Izzy went to stand to help.

'Actually, Chris, I need a word with Izzy.'

'Sure.' Chris took Tilia and Izzy sat, frowning just a little, worried what was to come because Diego, when at work, never brought his problems to the shop floor.

'Is she okay?' Her first thought was something had been said on the ward round that morning and he was about to give her bad news.

'She's wonderful,' Diego assured her. 'So wonderful,

in fact, that I need your room for some parents we are getting whose baby will not be doing so well.'

'Oh.'

'I know it seems pretty empty over in the parents' wing at the moment, but I'm getting some transfers from other hospitals today, and I have some mothers in Maternity now needing accommodation too. You don't need to leave today...'

'But it would help?'

'It would,' Diego admitted. Normally they gave more notice, but Izzy had been told last week that if the room was needed, given her close proximity to the hospital and Tilia's improving status, she was top of the list to leave if required. Izzy had been happy with that. Well, till the inevitable happened.

How could she tell Diego that she didn't want to go home?

More than that, she had never wanted to bring her baby back to the home she had shared with Henry.

'Izzy!' Rita was at the nursery door. 'You've got visitors. Mr and Mrs Bailey, Tilia's grandparents...'

He saw her lips tense and then stretch out into a smile and he'd have given anything not to be on duty now, to just be here with her as she faced all this, but Diego knew it would surly only make things worse. So instead he stood, smiled as he would at any other relatives and said to Izzy, 'I'll leave you to it.' Just as he would to any of the mums—except he knew so much more.

'Could I have a word, Doctor?' Mr. Bailey followed him out.

'I'm not a doctor; I'm the nurse unit manager. Is there anything I can help you with?'

Up shot the eyebrows, just as Diego expected. 'I'd

prefer to speak to a doctor,' Mr Bailey said. 'You see, we're not getting enough information from Izzy. She just says that Tilia is doing well and as her grandparents we have a right to know more.'

'Tilia *is* doing well,' Diego said. 'We're very pleased with her progress.'

'I'm not sure if you're aware of the circumstances. Our beloved son passed away and Izzy is doing her level best to keep us out of the picture. Tilia's extremely precious to us and we will not be shut out.'

And at that moment all Diego felt was tired for Izzy.

'I'd really prefer to speak with a doctor.'

Which suited Diego fine. 'I'll just check with Izzy and then I can page—'

'Why would you check with her? I've already told you that she's doing her level best to keep us misinformed. I know she seems quite pleasant, but she's a manipulative—'

'Mr Bailey.' Diego halted him—oh, there were many things, so many things he would have loved to have said, but he was far better than that. 'I will first speak to Tilia's mother. Let's see what she says and then we can take it from there.'

Of course she said yes.

Diego looked over when Richard agreed to speak to them and could see Izzy sitting by Tilia, looking bemused and bewildered, and if he'd done his level best to keep work and his private life separate, right now he didn't care.

'They don't trust me to tell them everything!' Izzy blew her fringe upwards. 'They're annoyed I waited two days to ring them after she was born...'

'They're just scared you'll keep them from see-ing her.'

'Well, they're going the right way about it!' Izzy shot back, but Diego shook his head.

'Don't go there, Izzy.'

'I won't!' Izzy said, but she was exasperated. 'They've been in every day, I've dressed her in the outfits they've bought, I text them a photo of her each night. What more do they want?'

'Time,' Diego said. 'And so do we.' He glanced over to make sure no one was in earshot 'Do you want to come to my place tonight?' He saw her swallow. 'I'm closer to the hospital. If it makes the transition easier…'

'Just for tonight,' Izzy said, because she didn't want to foist herself on him, but she couldn't stand to be alone at the house on her first night away from Tilia.

'Sure.'

He got called away then, and Izzy sat there awash with relief, grateful for the reprieve, until it dawned on her.

She was staying the night with Diego.

How the hell could she have overlooked that?

CHAPTER TWELVE

SHE felt incredibly gauche, knocking at his door that evening. 'Where did you disappear to?' he asked as he let her in. 'I wasn't sure if you were coming.'

'I got a taxi and took my stuff home,' Izzy said airily, because she certainly wasn't going to admit she'd spent the afternoon in the bathroom—trying and failing to whip her postnatal body into suitable shape for Diego's eyes. 'By the time I got back for her evening feed, your shift had ended.'

'You've got hospital colour!' Diego smiled as she stood in the lounge. 'I never noticed it on the ward but now you are here in the real world, I can see it.'

There was a distinct lack of mirrors in Diego's flat, so Izzy would just have to take his word for it, but she was quite sure he was right. Apart from an occasional walk around the hospital grounds, a few very brief trips home and one trip out with Megan, she'd been living under fluorescent lighting and breathing hospital air, and no doubt her skin had that sallow tinge that patients often had when they were discharged after a long stay.

'Have a seat out on the balcony,' Diego suggested. 'Get some sun. I'll join you in a minute.'

It *was* good to sit in the evening sun. Izzy could feel

it warming her cheeks and she drank in the delicious view—the moored boats and a few making their way back in. There was no place nicer than St Piran on a rosy summer evening, made nicer when Diego pressed a nice cold glass of champagne in her hand.

'One of the joys of bottle-feeding!' Diego said, because Izzy's milk supply had died out two weeks in.

And then he was back to his kitchen and Izzy could only sit and smile.

He was such a delicious mix.

So male, so sexy, yet there was this side to him that could address, without a hint of a blush or a bat of an eyelid, things that most men knew little about.

'How does it feel to be free?' Diego called from the kitchen as she picked a couple of tomatoes out of the pots that lined his balcony.

'Strange,' Izzy called, but he was already back. 'I keep waiting for my little pager to go off to let me know she needs feeding. I feel guilty, actually.'

'It's good to have a break before you bring her home.'

'Most new mums don't get it.'

'Most new mums have those extra weeks to prepare,' Diego said, arranging some roasted Camembert cheese and breadsticks on the table, which Izzy fell on, scooping up the sticky warm goo with a large piece of bread.

'I've been craving this,' Izzy said. 'How did you know?'

'Tonight, you get everything that has been forbidden to you in pregnancy, well, almost everything. Some things can wait!' Diego said, as Izzy's toes curled in her sandals. His grin was lazy and slow and she hated how he never blushed, hated that her cheeks were surely scarlet. God, she'd forgotten how they sizzled, Izzy thought as he headed back to prepare dinner.

There *were* so many sides to Diego and recently she'd been grateful for the professional side to him and for the care he had shown off duty too, but she was in his territory now, not pregnant, not a patient, not a parent on the unit. Tonight she was just Izzy, whoever Izzy was.

And that night she started to remember.

'You can cook!' Izzy exclaimed as he brought a feast out to her—shellfish, mussels, oysters, prawns and cream cheese wrapped in roast peppers, and all the stuff she'd craved in the last few weeks of her pregnancy.

'Not really. You could train a monkey to cook seafood.' Diego shrugged. 'And the antipasto is from our favourite café...'

She didn't know if it was the champagne or the company, but talking to Diego was always easy so she figured it was the latter. They talked, and as the sky turned to navy they laughed and they talked, and more and more she came back.

Not even Izzy Bailey, but a younger Izzy, an Izzy Ross, who she had stifled and buried and forgotten.

Izzy Ross, who teased and joked and did things like lean back in her seat and put her feet up on his thighs, Izzy Ross, who expected a foot rub and Diego obliged.

But it was Izzy Bailey who was convinced things were all about to change.

'So, what did the real estate agent say?'

'That it's a good offer!' Izzy poked out her tongue. 'It's not, of course, but it's better than the last one, though they want a quick settlement.'

'Which is what you wanted?'

'When I was pregnant and hoping to find somewhere before she was born.' She looked at him. 'In a few days she'll be home,' Izzy said, 'and as well as having a baby home, I'm going to have to pack up a house and find a new one, and I'm going to have to find a babysitter just so we can *date*.' Her voice wobbled. 'We haven't even slept together and we're talking nappies and babysitters...'

He had the audacity to laugh.

'It's not funny, Diego.'

'You're making problems where there are none. Sex is hardly going to be a problem.'

God, he was so relaxed and assured about it, like it was a given it was going to be marvellous.

The icing on the cake.

'Come on.' He stood up.

'Where are we going?'

'The movies and then there's a nice wine bar, they do music till late...'

'I don't want to go to the movies!' Izzy couldn't believe Mr Sensitive could get it so wrong. 'And if you think I've got the energy to be sitting in a wine bar...'

'I thought you wanted us to date!'

'Ha, ha.'

'Izzy, you need time with your baby and that's the priority. I'll slot in, and if it's an issue that we haven't slept together yet, well, we both know it's going to be great.'

'You don't know that.'

'Oh, I do.' Diego grinned. 'I'm looking forward to getting rid of your hang-ups.'

'Can you get rid of them tonight?'

And suddenly he didn't look so assured.

'It's too soon…'

'No,' Izzy said slowly. 'No heavy lifting, no strenuous exercise…'

'Do you want me, Izzy?' He was always direct and now never more so. 'Or do you just want it over?'

'I don't know,' Izzy admitted, and there should have been a big horn to denote she was giving the wrong answer, but she was incapable of dishonesty with him—or rather she didn't want to go down that route, saying the right thing just to keep *him* happy. She wanted the truth with Diego even if it wasn't what he wanted to hear.

'What are you scared of?'

'That I'll disappoint you,' she admitted. 'Because on so many levels I disappointed him.' She snapped her mouth closed. Diego had made it very clear that he didn't compare to Henry, which he didn't, but… She looked over to where he stood, tried to choose words that could explain her insecurities, but there were none that could do them justice. 'Things weren't great in that department,' she settled for, but Diego's frown just deepened. 'I know I was pregnant and so there must have been a relationship…' She swallowed. 'His parents take it as proof that our marriage was healthy, that…' She couldn't explain further and thankfully she didn't have to because Diego spoke.

'It would be nice,' Diego said slowly, 'if babies were only conceived in love…' There was silence that she didn't break as he thought for a moment. 'If there was some sort of…' Again he paused, trying to find the English for a word he hadn't used in his time in the country '*Cósmico*, contraception.' It was Izzy who then frowned and she gave a small smile.

'Cosmic.'

'Cosmic contraception,' Diego continued, 'where no experimenting teenagers, no rape victims, no women in a terrible relationship who just go along with it to keep the peace...' His strange logic soothed some of the jagged parts of her mind. She liked his vision and it made her smile. 'Here's a happy couple,' Diego continued, 'said the sperm to the egg. You know it doesn't work like that.'

'People think...'

'People are stupid, then.' Diego would not let her go there, would not let her care what others thought. 'People choose to be ignorant rather than face unpleasant truths. You know what your marriage was like and you don't have to live it again, explaining details to me, to justify why you're pregnant. But I will say this.' For the first time his voice bordered on angry. 'If he expected a great sex life, if he was disappointed by your lack of enthusiasm in that department after the way he treated you, then he was the most stupid them all.'

And he was so convincing that she was almost... convinced.

Almost.

But still the cloud of doubt hung over her and Diego could see it.

It had never been his intention to sleep with her tonight.

For her to stay was a hope, but sex—hell, wasn't that supposed to be the last thing on her mind?

Wasn't it too soon?

And he liked straightforward, only this was anything but.

But he looked over to where she sat, not in the least

offended that she wanted it over with, another thing to tick off her list as she moved on with her life. And again it wasn't a time for arrogance or feigned modesty. He knew he was good, knew he could make her happy—and wasn't happy part of their deal?

'I'll sleep with you on one condition.'

Why did he always make her smile?

'That you never fake it for me.'

'Or you.'

'Er, Izzy,' he said, and that made her blush and give an embarrassed laugh.

'I mean, don't pretend afterwards that it's okay, just so you don't upset me.'

Diego rolled his eyes, but he was smiling now too. 'The talking doesn't stop when we get to the bedroom. I can do both!'

And he knew then that they could talk about it for ever, but words could only reassure so far. This was so not what he had imagined for tonight. There was something almost clinical about it and yet Diego had so much confidence in her, in them, in all they were going to be, that if this was a hurdle for her, perhaps it was better to jump it.

He pulled her onto his lap, but his kisses weren't working. He could feel her trying, feel her doing her very best to relax, but he wouldn't put her through it. He pulled back his lips, looked into her eyes and feigned a martyred sigh 'Shall we just get this over with?'

She almost wept with relief.

'Please.'

'Ring the hospital.'

Which took away her little excuse to suddenly stop later. Diego was onto her, she realised.

So she rang and, no, Tilia didn't need her to come in.

Oh, God, what was she doing?

She felt as if she was walking into Theatre for surgery as he took her hand and they headed for the bedroom. Izzy half expected him to tell her to get undressed and pop on a gown and that he'd be back in five minutes.

Couldn't it happen more seamlessly?

Couldn't they just have had a kiss on the balcony and somehow ended up naked on his massive bed without the awkward bit in the middle? But that hadn't worked and Izzy realised she would have been faking it because she would know where it would lead, to this, the bit she was dreading, the part that was holding her back from moving on.

God, it was a room built for nothing but a bed. Izzy gulped.

Massive windows, floorboards and one very large, very low bed and not much else, bar a table that doubled as a washing basket.

'Where are your things?' Izzy would rather deal with basics than the bed.

'What things?'

'Alarm clock, books...' Her hands flailed. 'A mirror, a wardrobe...'

'Here's the wardrobe.'

Okay, there it was, hidden in the wall, but apart from that...

'Curtains?' Izzy begged.

'It looks out to the ocean,' Diego said, and to her horror he was stripping off. 'And I don't need an alarm clock—I wake at five.' He was unbuckling his belt, his top already off, stripping off like a professional and chatting about nothing as Izzy stood, champagne in hand, wishing she'd never started this.

'Five?'

'It's hell.' He pushed his denim jeans down past thick thighs as he explained his plight to a distracted audience. 'Even when the clocks change my brain knows and I wake up.'

Oh, God.

He wasn't *erect* erect, but he was erect enough that it was pointing at her—this conversation going on as this thing waggled and danced and she did her best not to look at it, tried to worry about windows and passing ships, but he was completely naked now.

'Are you always this uninhibited?'

'I've been undressing for bed for many years now,' Diego said, and then his voice was serious. 'Let's just start as we mean to go on.'

But would he want to go on afterwards?

'I've changed my mind,' Izzy said, in the hope of delaying the inevitable, so sure was she that when he found out just how hopeless she was, he wouldn't want her or, worse, would feel stuck with her.

'Why don't we just sleep together?' Diego suggested. 'Given it will probably be our one interrupted night for the foreseeable future.'

And though she wanted to turn and flee, he was right, Izzy realised, because as hellish as this was for her, next time there might be more than passing ships to worry about. There might be a baby in the room too!

'I forgot my phone…'

'Your phone?' Izzy said to his departing back, and as he spoke about staff ringing some nights if there was a problem, and he'd rather that… Izzy took the moment to get out of her clothes and under the sheet before he returned.

Just as Diego had expected her to do.

He didn't need his phone, of course.

And he was, in fact, nervous.

Just not for the same reasons as Izzy.

Diego liked sex.

Correction.

Diego *loved* sex.

And he liked relationships too, but short-term ones.

There was nothing short term about Izzy.

As he climbed into bed and turned and faced her, it was the sense of responsibility that unnerved him a touch.

Not just the obvious, not just Izzy and her baby, but a self-imposed responsibility towards Izzy, because in every area of her life she was getting it together, managing it herself, but for this part to be right she needed another, and she had trusted herself to him.

'Better?' Diego asked, and, yes, it was.

Much, much better, not because she was in the dark and under a sheet, just better because she was, for the first time, lying next to him and he was so solid and bulky and just him.

'In a few short weeks,' Diego said into the darkness, 'you'll be ripping your clothes off in the middle of the day and we'll be on the kitchen floor!'

'Your confidence is inspiring.'

'Oh, you will!' Diego said. 'Remember the bath?'

How could she forget?

'That just sort of happened.'

Izzy lived on her nerves.

Diego lived on instinct.

Instinct that told him his parents were wrong, that he'd do better by not following their chosen course for him.

Instinct that had told him over and over again that, despite neat numbers on a chart, a baby was struggling.

And instinct was all very well, but it got in the way sometimes.

Like now, when he knew he should be closing his eyes and trying to sleep, to let her come to him, a little problem arose.

Or rather quite a big problem that crept along the side of her thigh, nudging her like a puppy that wanted to be stroked.

'*Perdón!*' Diego said, and he would have moved away but he heard her sort of laugh and he wasn't a saint. She was right there next to him and naked and warm and he'd had to go and remind them both of that bath.

Yes, it was instinct that drove his lips to her neck, the hand that wasn't under her roaming her body a little and then, for Izzy, instinct overrode nerves.

His lips were soft but firm at the same time, kissing her, breathing onto her skin. Diego, a man who had only ever given, now wanting badly, and from his deep murmurs of approval as his hands slid to her breasts it was her that he wanted.

And she wanted a little more of him too.

She turned and faced him, so she could kiss him properly, not the nervous kiss about where this might lead she had endured on the balcony, but a bolder kiss, knowing where this might lead, in the bedroom.

He tasted of him, his tongue cool and lazy and then suddenly insistent and then back to lazy. He drove her wild with his mouth, because her body was at its own bidding now. Her thighs parted a little and captured him as they kissed, he could feel himself hard but smooth between the tender skin of her thighs, and she wanted him higher, her legs parting, only Diego wasn't rushing.

'I know where you were this afternoon...' His hand was there, exploring where she had shaved. 'Next time I'll do it.' And she felt this bubble of moisture at the very thought as his fingers slipped in and it felt divine.

'Condoms!' Izzy said, common sense prevailing, even if the last thing she wanted was him getting up and heading for the bathroom.

But this was Diego.

He sort of stretched over her and she felt his arm rummage in the dark beneath the bed and come up with the goods.

Oh, God, he was so male, so... She flailed for a word...basic.

It was the only one she could think of and it didn't really suit, but it was the best she could do.

And then he rolled off her and lay on his back and Izzy came up with another word.

Raw.

He didn't slip it on discreetly as he kissed her. No, he lay back and she watched, she actually propped up on her elbow and watched, this shiver inside as he gave himself two slow strokes, two long, slow strokes that had Izzy licking her lips and feeling suddenly contrary. This was something she had wanted over and done with, something she still wanted over and done with, except she was balling her fist not to reach out and touch him.

So she did.

Like warm silk he slid down her palm, the pulse of

him beneath her fingers, and she did it again and it felt so nice that she did it again, till his hand closed around hers and halted her.

'Aren't I doing it right?' said her old fears, and for a moment there was no reply.

'Izzy.' He paused again. 'Any more right and we won't need the condom.'

And then she got her seamless kiss, because that was what he did, he rolled over and kissed her, his tongue, his breath filling her mouth and his body over her and then the nudge of him between her legs.

And she was scared, but she wanted him.

Like hating flying and preparing for take-off, wanting just to get there, except there's a slight delay in departure and cabin crew are bringing round drinks and you taste your first Singapore sling.

Oh, my!

He was slow and tender and, yes, she was ready, and it had little to do with nerves that he had to squeeze inside. Izzy screwed her eyes closed, told herself to breathe as her body stretched to greet him, the slow fill of him more than she could accommodate, except slowly she did.

And then she breathed out as he slid out, right to the tip and she braced herself for him to fill her again, which he did.

And then again and each time she had to remember to breathe.

His elbows held most of his weight, his rough chin was on her cheek and his breath tickled at her ear, and suddenly Izzy remembered where she was and it wasn't happening so easily. She knew she should be a touch more enthusiastic, but she was a mother now and surely sensible, so she made the right noises and lifted her hips and would have settled for his pleasure, except Diego had other ideas.

He smothered her feigned gasps with his mouth and offered her more weight, wrapping his arms around her, kissing her, not harder but deeper, and she remembered his demand that she not fake it. So she lay there and let herself just feel him—lay there as he kissed her eyes and then her cheeks and then she felt the shift in him, the kissing stopping, his heavier weight and the ragged breathing in her ear, and she forgot where she was again, forgot about rather a lot of things, just the delicious feel of him, and the scratch of his jaw and the stirrings of the orgasm he had given her before. Then she found that she *was* making noises now, but of her body's own accord, and as he bucked deep inside her, she did something she would never have envisaged from this night.

'Not yet.'

She was too deep into herself to wonder at the transition to voicing her wants, her real wants, but Diego recognised it and it gave a surge of pleasure that almost tipped him over. He would have waited for this for ever, yet now was struggling to wait another minute, but for Izzy he did.

He could feel her pleasure and it was his.

Both locked in a dance that moved faster than them.

'Not yet!' She was in another place and he could hear her calling and he chased her, he was holding back and driving harder, he could hear her moans, feel the surge in her that was akin to panic, but he knew her body too, could feel her body tight around him, feel her trip and he just knew.

Knew she needed all of him before she could give that bit more.

Her words were futile, Izzy realised, because Diego was moving at a different speed now, reaching for the finish line with a surge of energy that had her breathless.

She could hear her name, feel the unbridled passion and just the sheer strength of him as he thrust inside her. And she stopped trying then, stopped trying to chase or catch him, she just felt the moment.

Felt him over her, in her and his arms behind her, she could hear her name, taste his skin, and then it was his name she heard her voice calling, his name said in a tone she didn't recognise, then a shout of surprise as she let go.

Her thighs were shaking and her hips pushing up against his, her hands digging into his back, and deep inside she trembled as Diego pulsed into her.

And most delicious of all, it didn't matter that she was a teeny bit late for the party, she was there, she had made it, her late entrance dazzling, because he got to feel every beat of it as he delivered those last emptying strokes and instinct had served him well.

As he felt her crash and burn beneath him, as he tried to get his head out of white light and back to the dark, he knew he had just met the real Izzy.

'Tell me again,' Diego said, when he could get the words out, 'what exactly your hang-ups are.'

CHAPTER THIRTEEN

'SHE'S fine!' a night nurse greeted her as Izzy dashed in at seven a.m.

She'd given Diego a fifteen-minute head start so they didn't arrive together and it seemed to take ages for the intercom to answer when she buzzed, because the staff were all in handover.

Izzy felt guilty with pleasure and was sure there must be a penance to pay for having such a wonderful night, except Tilia was fine—completely adorable and wide awake. Chris, her nurse for the day, informed Izzy when she came out of handover that Tilia might even be ready for her first bath.

Izzy was glad to have Chris beside her, encouraging her.

Tilia seemed so small and slippery and she wouldn't stop crying.

'I thought they liked their bath,' Izzy said.

'Just rock her a little.'

Which Izzy did, and Tilia's cries softened.

Her tufts of hair were shampooed and by the time Izzy had dried and dressed her, it was all sticking up and Izzy thought her heart would burst as she sat in the rocking chair and held her.

'How soon do you think?' Izzy asked the perpetual question.

'When she's taking all her feeds and just a bit bigger,' Chris said. 'She's doing so well. I know you're impatient to get her home, but she still needs top-ups and a little one like this...' She took an exhausted Tilia from Izzy and popped her in her cot then put the saturation probe on her, checked her obs and popped a little hat on. 'Even a bath wears them out. Why don't you go down to the canteen and get some breakfast?' Chris suggested, rightly guessing that Izzy hadn't eaten.

'Good idea,' Izzy agreed. 'I'll go and see if Nicola wants to come down with me.'

'Actually,' Chris said gently, 'maybe it's best if you leave Nicola for now.'

'Oh!' Izzy waited for more information, only she wasn't a doctor on duty here and there was no information forthcoming. 'I'll be at the canteen, then,' Izzy said. 'I've got my pager.'

She walked through the unit, her eyes drawn to Toby's cot. There was Nicola and her husband, and Diego was sitting with them. His face was more serious than she had ever seen it and Izzy felt sick as Megan came into the unit and instead of waving to Izzy just gave a very brief nod and headed over to them.

It was the longest morning.

Tilia awoke at eleven but wouldn't take her bottle and Izzy came close to crying, except she shook her head when Chris passed her a box of tissues.

'You are allowed to cry.'

But it seemed so petty. Tilia was thriving, okay, a little slower than Izzy would like, but she was getting bigger and stronger every day and, anyway, Izzy knew, there was a lot more to cry over than that—and now just wasn't the time to.

'Hey, where's Chris?' Diego gave her a tired smile as he came in later to get an update.

'Two minutes,' Chris called from the sinks, where she was helping another mum with a bath.

'How are you?' Diego asked.

'Good.'

'Tilia?'

'Misbehaving—she won't take her feeds.'

'She had a bath, though,' Diego said, but she could tell he was distracted and who could blame him?

'How's Toby?'

'He's not good,' Diego said. 'I know you helped deliver him.' He was walking a fine line. 'We can talk another time.'

'Sure.'

'Two more minutes!' Chris called again.

'I'm going to be working late tonight.' His voice was low. 'I can give you a key if you want…'

'I might go home tonight,' Izzy said, hoping he wouldn't take up her offer of an out. 'I'm really tired and you're working…'

Except he took it. 'Sure.'

And then Chris was walking over, ready to bring Diego up to date with her charges, and Izzy didn't see him again apart from the back of his shoulders for the rest of the day.

And that night, when she sat at home, she told herself she was being ridiculous—he was working late, he had every reason to be sombre, and she had been the one to say she'd prefer to go home, but, just as a mother could often pin-point the moment their child became sick long before the doctors were concerned even when the child itself said it was well, Izzy could sense change.

Even as she tried to leave the past where it belonged, she could sense a shift, could sense a black cloud forming, and it had hovered over Diego today.

'Neonatal Unit—Diego speaking.'

'It's me.' Izzy hadn't really expected him to answer the phone. It was edging towards ten p.m., which meant he had done a double shift. 'I was just ringing to check up on Tilia.'

'She's had a good night so far, I think,' Diego said. 'I'll just have a word with the nurse who's looking after her.' And she sat there and held her breath as he did what all the nursing staff did when a mother rang at night to check on their baby. She could even hear his voice in the background and Izzy held her breath as he came to the phone. 'She's settled and she's taken her bottle. You can relax, she's having a good night.'

'Thank you.'

He said goodnight, he was lovely and kind, but he was Nurse Unit Manager and that was all.

Something had changed.

Izzy just knew it.

The phone rang again and Izzy pounced on it, sure it was Diego, only it wasn't, and she frowned at the vaguely familiar voice. 'I'm sorry to trouble you. It's just that you gave me your number. You're the only one who seemed to understand it's not as simple as just leaving...'

'Evelyn?'

'I can't go on like this.'

'Evelyn.' Izzy kept her voice calmer than she felt. 'Where are you now?'

'I'm at home. He's at the pub...' Even if she wanted

to dwell on Diego or Tilia, or to just go to bed, Izzy pushed it aside and listened. So badly she wanted to tell Evelyn to get out, to just pack her bags and go, but Izzy remembered how she had rushed it last time, knew that it was good Evelyn was taking this small step, so, instead of jumping in and fixing, Izzy bit her tongue and just listened, learning fast that sometimes it was the best you could do.

'Are you okay?' Izzy was quite sure Megan wasn't. She had come and sat with her in the canteen and Izzy could tell she'd been crying, but, then, so had a lot of people.

Toby had passed away last night and both Diego and Megan, Izzy had heard from another mother, had stayed till the end.

'I've been better,' Megan admitted. 'All I put that baby through and the parents too—and for what?'

'Don't,' Izzy said, because they'd had these conversations before. Megan set impossible standards for herself, wanted to save each and every baby, and took it right to her heart when nature chose otherwise. 'Look at Genevieve!' Izzy said.

'I know.' Megan blew out a breath. 'This really got to me, though, and Diego—he doesn't normally get upset, but I guess finding out his dad's so sick...' Her voice trailed off, realising she was being indiscreet. 'I shouldn't have said that.'

'I'm not going to tell him.' Izzy felt her throat tighten. It was such a tightrope—they were all friends, all colleagues, all different things to each other. 'What's wrong with him?'

Megan screwed her eyes closed. 'Izzy, please don't.'

'Just because I've had a baby it doesn't mean my

brain's softened. Nobody would tell me anything about Toby, forgetting the fact I delivered him, and now I'm not supposed to be told Diego's father's sick. I knew there was something wrong last night.'

'He probably doesn't want to worry you.'

'Well, I am worried,' Izzy said. 'Is it bad?'

Reluctantly Megan nodded but no more information was forthcoming and Izzy sat quietly for a moment with her thoughts. 'I've had an offer on the house,' Izzy said, 'but they want a quick settlement. Thirty days.'

'Ouch!' Megan said. 'Will you be able to find somewhere?'

'Probably.'

'What about your mum's?' Megan managed a smile at Izzy's reaction. 'Okay, bad idea.'

'I think I should be concentrating on Tilia, not trying to find somewhere to live.'

'There's always Diego's,' Megan teased, adding when she saw Izzy close her eyes, 'I was joking—I know it's way too soon to even be thinking—'

'But I do,' Izzy admitted, and Megan's eyes widened.

'You hardly know each other.'

'I know that.' Izzy nodded. 'I can't stand being in the house, but I think it's best for now...' She was trying to be practical, logical, sensible. 'I don't want to force any decisions on us.' She looked at her friend. 'I'm trying to hold onto my heart here. I'm trying to just be in the now with him, but practically the day I met him I was knocked sideways. I felt it, this connection, this chemistry.' She looked at Megan, who was frowning. 'Sounds crazy, doesn't it?'

'No.' Megan swallowed and then her voice was urgent. 'Don't sell your house.' Megan, who normally was happy to sit and just listen, was practically hopping in her seat to give advice. 'Izzy, Diego's lovely and everything…' She was struggling to give the right advice, tempted to tell Izzy to turn tail and run because she'd felt that way once too and look where it had left her. Love had swept in for Megan and left a trail of devastation that all these years on she was still struggling to come to terms with—pain so real that she still woke some nights in tears, still lived with the consequences and would till the day she left the earth. 'Be careful, Izzy,' Megan said, even if wasn't the advice Izzy wanted. 'Maybe you should have some time on your own. At least, don't rush into anything with Diego—you've got Tilia to think of. Diego's father's sick, he could just up and go to Spain…' And then Megan stopped herself, saw Izzy's stunned expression and realised she had been too harsh, realised perhaps she was talking more about herself than her friend.

'Izzy, don't listen to me,' Megan begged. 'Who am I to give advice? I haven't been in a relationship in ages, I'm married to my career.' Megan swallowed. 'And I don't have a child. I'm the last person to tell you what you should be doing. Maybe speak to Jess…' She was close to tears and feeling wretched. The last thing Megan had wanted to do was project her own bitterness onto Izzy, especially at such a vulnerable time, but the last few weeks had been hell for Megan—sheer hell. Since Josh had come to work at St Piran's she was struggling to even think straight. 'Maybe you should talk to Jess,' Megan said again as her pager went off, summoning her to the children's ward. She gave her friend's hand a squeeze. 'You'll make the right choice.' She turned to leave, but there he was, right there in front of her.

'Megan…' Josh said. 'Did you get my message?'

She went to walk on, but Josh was insistent.

'Megan, we need to talk—there are things we need to discuss.' He caught her wrist and Megan looked at his hand around hers, their first physical contact in years, and she couldn't stand it because it was there, the chemistry, the reaction, her skin leaping at the memory of him, and it terrified her—it truly terrified her. She shook him off.

'There's nothing to discuss,' Megan said.

'There's plenty,' Josh insisted, and she felt herself waver, because there *was* so much to discuss but, worse, she knew that he felt her waver, knew they were still in sync. 'Not here,' Josh said, because heads in the corridor were turning.

Megan grappled for control of her mind, held onto the pain he had caused as if it were a liferaft, because if she forgot for a moment she would sink back into his charm.

And she remembered more, enough for a sneer to curl her lips.

Then she let herself remember just a little bit more, enough to force harsh words from her lips.

'Where, then, Josh?' Megan spat. 'Where should we meet?' She watched as he ran a tongue over his lips, knew then he hadn't thought this out, perhaps hadn't expected her to agree. 'There's a nice restaurant on the foreshore,' she sneered. 'Oh, but we might be seen!' she jeered. 'How about Penhally, or is that too close? Maybe you could pop over to mine...' She was blind with rage now, shaking just to stop herself from shouting. 'You're married, Josh, so, no, we can't meet. You're a married man.' If she said it again, maybe if she said it enough times, she would come to accept it. 'Which means there is absolutely nothing to discuss.'

And she remembered some more then, not all of it, because that would be too cruel to herself, but Megan remembered just enough of what she had been through to make the only sensible choice—to turn on her heel and walk quickly away.

She wasn't upset that he hadn't told her about his father.

In truth, Izzy knew he hadn't had a chance. Her dad had been over the last two nights trying to get the spare room ready for Tilia, who had, after twelve hours of not taking a drop from the bottle, awoken from her slumber and had taken her feeds like a dream. Now on the eve of her discharge, they were scrambling to find two minutes alone.

She was sitting in the nursery, feeding Tilia her bottle, Brianna was on her break and Diego was doing Tilia's obs.

'Do you want me to come over tonight?' Diego offered. 'Help you get everything ready for tomorrow?'

'My mum's coming,' Izzy said, but right now she didn't care about her mother's reaction. 'I could cancel, tell her why perhaps…about us.'

'I think…' she sensed his reluctance '…you should wait till Tilia is no longer a patient.'

He was right, of course he was right, but though there were a million and one reasons they hadn't had any time together, Megan's words had hit home. Izzy was sure, quite sure, that Diego was pulling back—he looked terrible. Well, still absolutely gorgeous, except there were black rings under his eyes and he was more unshaven than usual and there was just this air to him that his world was heavy. And Izzy was quite sure she was a part of his problem. 'Her obs are good.' He checked Tilia's chart. 'She's put on more weight.' And then he suggested that while Tilia was sleeping she watch a video in the parents' room, but apnoea was the last thing Izzy wanted to deal with right now, she was having enough trouble remembering to breathe herself.

'I'm going to go home now.' She looked down at her sleeping daughter, because it was easier than looking at him with tears in her eyes. She didn't want to push or question, because she didn't want to sound needy—but, hell, she felt needy.

They had made love and suddenly everything had changed.

'I'd better make sure everything's ready for the big day. I'll see you in the morning,' Izzy said, and watched him swallow. 'You can wave her off...'

'I've got a meeting tomorrow morning,' Diego said, and she couldn't mask her disappointment. She wasn't asking him to take her baby home with him, or to out them to her family, just for him to be there, even if all he could manage was professional on the day she took her daughter home, she wanted that at least.

'Can you reschedule?' She hated to nag but hated it more that he shook his head.

'I really can't.'

'There's a call for you, Diego.' Rita came over.

'Thanks.'

'The travel agent,' Rita added, and Diego wasn't sure if she'd done it deliberately, but Rita must have felt her back burning as she walked off, with the blistering look Diego gave her.

'My father,' Diego said eventually, but he could barely look her in the eyes. 'He's sick. Very sick,' he added. 'I wanted to speak to you properly—I need to go back.'

Izzy nodded and held Tilia just a little bit tighter, felt her warm weight, and it was actually Tilia who gave her strength. 'Of course you do.'

'Diego!' She could hear shouts for his attention, hear

the summons of the emergency bell, and for now the travel agent would be forgotten, but only for now. His real future was just being placed temporarily on hold.

Izzy sat there and held her baby, her world, her family, and she was sure, quite sure, that she was about to lose Diego to his.

'Thank you.' Izzy said it a hundred times or more.

To Richard, to Chris, to Rita, to all the staff that popped in to say goodbye and wish her and Tilia well, but the people that mattered most weren't there. Megan, Brianna and Diego had a 'meeting'. And though the NICU was used to babies going home, Izzy wasn't used to taking one home and wished they could have been there for this moment.

'She looks such a big girl.' Gwen was the doting grandmother now and her father carried the car seat with Tilia inside. Finally she was out of the neonatal unit and taking her baby home.

'You know I'm happy to stay over. Between your mother and I, you don't have to be on your own for a few weeks....'

Except she wanted to be alone.

Or not quite alone.

There was the one she wanted to share this moment walking towards her now, with Brianna and Megan at his side, and with a stab of realisation at her own selfishness Izzy realised just how important their 'meeting' had been.

Diego was in a suit and he'd discarded the tie, but Izzy knew it had been a black one. Megan was in dark grey and Brianna too.

'Hey! Looks who's going home.' Brianna snapped to happy, fussed and cooed over Tilia, and Megan gave her friend a hug, but it was more than a little awkward, almost a relief when Megan had to dash off.

Had to dash off.

Megan actually thought she might vomit.

She felt like this each and every time she had to attend one of her precious patients' funerals, but today had been worse. With Josh back in her life Megan was having enough trouble holding things together, but when even Diego had struggled through a hymn, when the one who never got too involved held the song sheet and she could see his hand shaking, this morning had been the worst of them all.

Bar one.

'Megan!' Josh caught her arm as she tried to dash past him, his face the last she needed to see now. He took in her clothes and pale cheeks, her lips so white she looked as if she might faint at any moment. 'I'm sorry...'

'Sorry?' She was close to ballistic as she shot the word out and Josh blinked.

'You've clearly just been to a funeral...'

'Perk of the job,' Megan spat. 'I get to go to lots. I get to stand there and relive it over and over.'

'Is Megan okay?' Izzy watched from a distance as her friend ran up the corridor.

'It's been a tough morning,' Diego said. 'I'll talk to her later. You concentrate on you for now—enjoy taking Tilia home.'

'Thanks for everything,' Gwen said. 'Everyone's been marvellous.' And Izzy caught Diego's eyes and they shared a teeny private smile at her mother's choice of words.

'Thank you,' she said, and because she had hugged Brianna and Megan, she got to hug him, and then he had to go and so did Izzy, but she wished, how she wished, it was him taking them home.

CHAPTER FOURTEEN

HER parents adored Tilia.

It was, of course, a relief, but it came with a down side.

Instead of Gwen bossing and taking over and whizzing round the house doing the little jobs that were rapidly turning into big jobs, the doting grandparents sat on the sofa, cooing over their granddaughter, occasionally rising to make a drink or lunch, then it was back to admiring their granddaughter. Then when Tilia fell asleep Gwen shooed Izzy off for a sleep of her own as she headed for the door, keen to get out of the way before Henry's parents arrived, because Tilia's two sets of grandparents in the same room wasn't going to happen for a while yet.

'You're supposed to sleep when the baby does,' was Gwen's less than helpful advice.

Except Izzy couldn't.

She lay in her bed and stared at her daughter—wished her homecoming could somehow have been different, wished for so many things for her, and for herself too. Unable to settle, Izzy headed downstairs, made herself a coffee and rather listlessly flicked through her neglected post as she waited for the kettle to boil.

And it came with no ceremony no warning.

What she'd expected Izzy didn't really know. The envelope looked like any of the others from the insurance company and she just assumed there was something else they were requesting that she send. She briefly skimmed the letter, intending to read it properly later, but it wasn't a request for more information.

Instead, it was closure.

No relief washed over her. She read the letter again and stared at the cheque, and she didn't know how she felt, except it was starting to look a lot like angry. Angry at Henry for what he had done to her life, for the money that couldn't fix this, for her daughter who was without a father and for all that Izzy would have to tell her one day.

Izzy had never felt so alone.

The only person she wanted now was Diego.

Except how could she foist more of her drama on him? And, anyway, he would soon be back in Spain.

Lonely was a place she had better start to get used to.

Though she was beyond tired, when Henry's parents arrived she made them coffee and put out cake and tried small talk as Tilia slept on. In the end, Izzy gave in and brought her daughter down. She watched her mother-in-law's lips disappear when Izzy said, no, Tilia wasn't due for a feed yet and, no, she didn't need a bath.

'I'll do it,' Mrs Bailey fussed. 'You won't have to do a thing.'

'She's asleep,' Izzy pointed out, 'and a bath exhausts her.' And exhausted was all she felt when, clearly disappointed with the social skills of a tiny baby, Henry's parents left.

The house that had been so tidy looked like a bomb

site; there were coffee cups and plates all over the kitchen and Izzy went to load the dishwasher but realised that she had to empty if first and right now that task seemed too big.

There were bottles to be made up, once she had sterilised them, washing to be put on—eight hours home and Izzy, who had felt so confident, who had wished for this moment, when finally she was home alone with her daughter, wanted to go back to the safety of the nursery.

She could hear Tilia waking up at completely the wrong moment, because long held-back tears were coming to the fore.

She didn't want an insurance payout, she didn't want to raise her baby alone. She wanted to have met Diego when she was who she had once been, except this was who she was now.

A mother.

Which meant even when her own heart was bleeding, she had to somehow put her grief on hold and pick up her screaming baby at the same time the phone rang and the doorbell went and she remembered that it was bin night tonight.

'She's fine,' Izzy said down the phone through gritted teeth to her mother and, holding a phone and her baby, somehow answered the front door, and there, out of his suit and in his white nursing uniform, was Diego, carrying a tray with two coffees, which he quickly put down and took from Izzy a screaming, red-faced Tilia. 'She's due for a feed,' Izzy said to Gwen. 'Babies are supposed to cry.' As she reassured her mother, Izzy glanced at Diego. She so hadn't wanted him to catch her like this. He was gorgeous amidst the chaos and started to make up bottles with his free hand far more skilfully than she could with two. The last time he had been here, her house had been spotless, ready at any given second for the real estate agent to warn her he was bringing someone round. Her intention, if Diego ever came over, had been to have Tilia asleep and the house looking fantastic. Oh, and for her to be looking pretty good too—just to show him that a baby didn't have to change things!

By the time she had hung up the phone to her mother, Diego was cooling a bottle under the tap and though pleased to see him, Izzy could hardly stand what was about to come next. She tried to make a little joke, tried to lighten the tense mood, tried to tell him in one line how she knew and understood that everything must now change.

'If you've come for torrid sex…' Izzy smiled as he came in '…you've come to the wrong house!'

'I couldn't even manage a slow one!' For the first time in days Diego grinned. 'All I want to do is sleep.'

'The perfect guy.'

She wasn't joking.

She so wasn't joking.

'I wore my uniform in case you had visitors.' He was changing Tilia's nappy. 'I was going to say it was a house call!' He smiled down at Tilia. 'Do you think they'd have believed me?'

'I have no idea,' Izzy admitted.

'It's a good idea…' Diego seemed to ponder it for a moment. 'It's always hard when you leave NICU.'

'I would have been fine…' Izzy said, and then she paused and then she told them what she couldn't face telling her own parents yet, what she dreaded telling

Henry's. 'The insurance paid.' She was so glad he didn't comment. 'The mortgage and everything,' Izzy elaborated, and Diego knew this was the very last thing she needed to deal with today. 'I just wanted to bring her home,' Izzy said. 'I just wanted one day where I can pretend it's normal for her.'

'Here.' He took the letter and folded it, threw it in the kitchen drawer as if it was a shopping list. 'Think about it later.'

But it was already there and she told Diego that and he just stood there, let her rant and rave for a while and then told her an impossible truth.

'You need to forgive him, Izzy.'

'Forgive him?' Diego was supposed to be on her side, Diego was supposed to be as angry with Henry as she was, yet he steadfastly refused to go there.

'For your daughter's sake.' Diego stood firm. 'Don't you think he'd rather be here?' Diego demanded. 'Don't you think he'd rather be here today, bringing his daughter home from the hospital, enjoying this moment? Without forgiveness you won't get peace.'

'And you know all about it, do you?'

Diego didn't answer. Instead he sat on the sofa, put his feet up on the coffee table and fed Tilia as Izzy sat there, refusing to believe it was that simple to move on.

'He's looking after her.' Diego fed Tilia her bottle. 'Maybe this is the only way he could look after you both.' He looked down at Tilia. 'You need to forgive him for this little girl's sake.' He handed her baby to her. 'You need to be able to speak to her about her father without bitterness in your voice, because you don't want her to grow up feeling it.'

'It's so hard, though.' She knew he was right, but it was *so* hard.

'Then keep working on it.' Diego was resolute. 'Fake it,' he said, 'like I told you that first day, and eventually it might even be real.'

He made it sound doable. He knelt beside her as she cradled Tilia and she couldn't imagine these past weeks without him, or rather she could and how very different they would have been!

He turned things around. His calm reason, his humour, he himself allowed rapid healing. He made her stronger, made her get there sooner, so much sooner and so much stronger that as she sat in the silence and nursed her baby, Izzy knew she could face it, could do it alone if she had to.

Thanks to Diego.

She changed Tilia, put her back into her cot and stood as she watched her daughter sleeping, and the strength of his arms around her made her able to say it.

'Your father loves you, Tilia. He's looking after you.'

And then she did what she had never done and certainly didn't want to on the day she bought her baby home. She sobbed and she cried and Tilia slept right through it, and Diego lay on the bed with her and with his help she got through another bit she had dreaded.

'You should sleep when the baby does,' Diego said, only he didn't leave her to it. Instead he took off his uniform and climbed into bed beside her. Maybe he didn't have the heart to dump her on the day her baby came home, and maybe she should just be grateful for the reprieve, but Izzy was fast realising it was better to face things and so, in the semi-dark room with his arms around her she did the next bit she was dreading and asked him about his father.

'He had a seizure. They did an MRI and he has a brain tumour—they're operating next Thursday. Izzy, I don't want to leave now, but I really feel I should go home and see him before the operation. It's just for a few days.'

'Of course you have to see him. He's your father.' And then she took a breath and made herself say it. 'Have they asked you to move home?'

There was a long silence.

'My mother asked if I could take some time and come home for a while. If he survives the surgery it will be a long rehabilitation. He won't be operating again—they expect some paralysis.' She felt the tension build in him. 'I've said I can't. The truth is, I won't. The way my father treated me, the names he called me, the taunts even now. He still goads me because I choose to nurse.' He shook his head. 'I want time with you…'

And it was the answer she wanted. It just wasn't the right one.

'You need to resolve things, Diego.'

'Flights are cheap, I can come and go. Don't worry about it, Izzy. I've been trying not to burden you with it.'

'Talk to me,' Izzy said, because she wanted more of him than he was giving.

'Okay.' He told her the truth. 'How are we supposed to get to know each other if I am in Spain? How are we supposed to make each other happy, if you are here and I am there? There's taking it slowly and then there's a place where you take it so slowly you stop.' And so then did Diego. 'We can't do this tonight. Let's not worry about it now and just try and enjoy the rest of tonight—having Tilia home...'

There was no hope of pretending a baby didn't change things because there wasn't even a crackle of sexual tension in the air. She slept like a log and actually so did Diego. And how nice it was to have her own modern matron to get up at midnight and again at four and bring her Tilia's bottle and then to put her back in her crib and to sleep again.

Diego was asleep and he rolled into Izzy, his large, warm body cradling, spooning into hers, and it was the nicest place she had ever known in her life—Tilia sleeping safely, Diego beside her, peace in her heart about Henry, summer rain rattling the windows. She had everything here in this room, only she wanted still more.

She just didn't quite know what.

Izzy found out what woke Diego at five as the most basic alarm clock stirred and she lay with him in this lovely silent place, just before waking, and Izzy closed her eyes and felt the lazy roam of his body, the natural wander of his hands before he awakened, and it wasn't sleep she wanted but him, so she pushed herself a little into him, loving the feel of a half-asleep Diego, a man following his instinctive want and her want calling him. Sex, Izzy learnt, could be peaceful and healing. She was warm and he slipped in and filled her, he was wrapped around her and deep within her, with no words needed because the air tasted of them.

She could never have imagined such peace, even as he drove in deeper, even as she throbbed in orgasm. All she wanted was peace and this every morning and the only person who could give her that was him.

'*Mierda*!' His curse woke her up an hour later, and was completely merited as it was the first time in his life he'd overslept. She drifted back to sleep as Diego dived under the shower and Izzy suddenly let out a curse of her own a few minutes later as she heard the garbage truck thumping down the street. She had to quickly find a dressing gown and race to get the bins out, then she took two coffees back to bed.

'Your razor's blunt.' He grinned as he came out of the shower and then he looked at her. 'Why is your hair wet?'

'I forgot to put the bins out last night.'

'Did you catch them?' Diego asked, and the conversation was normal and Diego looked so much better than he had last night. More than that, Izzy felt better too. 'I'll get it from everyone this morning—at least I'm only on till one,' Diego said as he hauled on his clothes.

'You'll only be a few minutes late.' Izzy grimaced as she looked at the clock, only Diego wasn't worried about the time. He drank the coffee she had made, glanced in at Tilia who was starting to stir and then went downstairs and came back with a bottle in a jug and his satchel, which looked curiously sexy over his shoulder. He mimicked nosy Rita. '*You look tired, Diego. Did you not get much sleep, Diego?* And then...' he rolled his eyes '...she'll subtly talk about the Dark Ages, when she brought her baby home from the hospital! You wait,' Diego said, and drained his coffee. 'I guarantee it.'

He didn't need to.

As he kissed her and left, Izzy lay there and tried to wrap her head around what had happened. Somehow, despite everything, last night, Tilia's first night home, *had* been wonderful, but more than that, Izzy realised, she didn't need Diego's guarantees—she was starting to find her own.

CHAPTER FIFTEEN

'THANKS for seeing me.'

She was back again, only this time she wanted to be there.

And Izzy didn't insist on the office, it was nice to just walk around the hospital grounds and not try to convince Jess everything was perfect. In fact, she rather hoped Jess would convince her that she was going out of her mind.

That she was mad, that it was absolutely ridiculous to be even considering going to Spain.

Izzy wanted logic and reason to preside, for Jess to tell her to wait twelve months, for her to tell her she was rushing in, for her to warn her to be careful.

Only when she spilled it all out, Jess didn't do that.

'I let Henry consume me,' Izzy said. 'In the end, I hardly saw my family and friends.'

'Is Diego anything like Henry?'

'No,' Izzy said. 'But as you said, people suggest you wait twelve months before making any major life decisions…'

'I offered you a theory,' Jess said, 'but as you pointed out yourself, we don't all have the requisite twelve months to lick our wounds and heal. Life keeps coming at us, bad things, good things, wonderful things…'

'So you don't think I'm crazy to be considering going to Spain.'

'I'd think you were crazy if you were going with no consideration.' Izzy's face tightened in frustration at Jess's refusal to commit.

'Even my friends are warning me to be careful!' Izzy said, still reeling from Megan's warning. 'Megan was so...' She tried to find the right words. 'I've never seen her so upset.'

'And then she apologised,' Jess pointed out. 'Izzy, in medicine we are used to coming up with solutions.' Izzy frowned and then Jess corrected herself. 'As a doctor you are used to coming up with an answer, finding the best course of treatment, perhaps telling the patient what needs to be done. My job is different,' Jess explained. 'Of course I would love to rush in at times, but I have to ask myself, would that really help? The best I can do is allow you to explore your options—which,' she added, 'you're doing.'

'This morning,' Izzy explained, 'it was normal.' She looked at Jess. 'We could have been anywhere in the world and it wouldn't have mattered. Diego says that he doesn't want to burden me with his stuff...'

'Is it a burden?' Jess asked.

'No,' Izzy admitted. 'It's harder not knowing how he's feeling.' And Jess *was* so easy to talk to that Izzy admitted something else on her mind. 'Shouldn't I just know?' Izzy asked. 'If it's so right, what I am doing here?'

'You're looking out for you,' Jess said. 'Which shows how far you've come.' Jess gave her a smile. 'For many years, Izzy, you've had your inner voice turned off. You told yourself and others that everything was okay, when, in fact, it was far from it. Can I suggest your inner voice is coming back?'

Izzy nodded.

'You might need a little help recognising it at times, but it's there, if only you listen.'

Jess was right.

So right that there was somewhere else Izzy needed to be.

'I need to talk to Diego. I need to tell him just how much he means to me.' She stalled for a second, wondered how she could be so absolutely honest with someone if it was going to freak him out, that his girlfriend of a few weeks would drop everything and follow him to Spain with a baby in tow. 'How?'

'Maybe ring him, ask him to come over tonight.'

But she didn't mean that. 'He's at my house now,' Izzy said. 'Watching Tilia.'

'Can I ask where he thinks you are?'

'Oh, I told him I was seeing you.' Jess watched Izzy's slow reaction as her own words registered with herself. Her casual words sinking in. She had, on ringing Jess, asked Diego if he'd mind watching Tilia for an hour or so. He hadn't probed, hadn't asked why. Diego had come straight over from his half-day shift, had just accepted that this was where she wanted to be, that this was what she needed now.

'Not many people who come into my office can say that,' Jess said. 'Izzy, I think it's wonderful that you're going to talk with Diego and be honest, but can I suggest when you are telling him how you feel that you also listen? He might surprise you with what he has to say.'

* * *

'Shh!' Diego put a finger up to his lips as Izzy burst in the house. She'd practised her speech, gathering strength all the way home, and had swept into her house, ready to blurt it all out, but as she'd entered the living room Diego, lying on the sofa with Tilia on his shoulder, had halted her. 'She's nearly asleep.'

Izzy could tell from her little red face that it had been a noisy hour. There were bottles and soothers and half the contents of the nappy bag all strewn around the sofa and they sat quietly, Diego chatting low and soft in Spanish, till finally, *finally* Tilia gave in and Diego gingerly stood, taking her to her cot. Izzy had to sit, tapping her toes in nervousness, as she waited for Diego. She listened to the intercom and heard Tilia, on being laid in the cot, protest for a few minutes at being out of his arms.

Who could blame her?

'Diego.' Izzy's voice was firm when he came into the room, because if she didn't tell him now, she might never do so.

'One moment…' He flashed that lovely smile. 'I *must* eat, and make a phone call.' He picked up his phone and headed to the kitchen. 'My mother rang. I told her I would call her back as soon as I got Tilia to sleep.' He rolled his eyes, clearly not relishing the prospect.

'How is she?'

'The same,' Diego said, and he was chatting easily, slicing up bread and tomatoes as Izzy talked on.

'She wants you to come to Spain, doesn't she?'

'And as I told her, I am coming.'

She could hear him keeping his voice light, but she could see the dark smudges under his eyes, almost feel the burden he was carrying alone, and her speech went out of the window because Izzy realised it wasn't about whether she'd follow him or not—it wasn't about her, this was about Diego.

'I can understand her being upset. She knows that you need to spend some time with your father,' Izzy said. 'Not just a quick visit.'

'I have a job, I have a life here.'

'And your family is there,' Izzy said, and she watched his tongue roll in his cheek.

'Do you want pepper?' was his response, and then he changed the subject. 'I was right about Rita. All morning she spoke about bringing her daughter home from the hospital, her daughter bringing her daughter home from the hospital…' Izzy would be sneezing till next year with the amount of pepper he was shaking! 'Then she started about how the place was quiet without Tilia, how she'd love to know how she was getting on.' He looked at Izzy, a guilty smile on his face. 'Do you know what I did?'

Izzy shook her head. She didn't want to hear about Rita, she wanted to sort out their own situation, but he did make her smile and he did make her laugh, he did make her happy, then she frowned as he continued, because in all of this he made her happy.

'She was at lunch when I left and I got a piece of A4 paper and wrote *Gone Fishing* and stuck it on her computer.'

And she could have laughed, could have just stayed happy, but Izzy was realising that wasn't quite what she wanted.

'You told me I needed to forgive Henry,' Izzy said. 'And it's the best thing I've done. You need to make peace with your father and if it means going to Spain, then that's what it means. This is something you need to sort out and I'll be okay with whatever you decide.' She took a deep breath and made herself say it. 'Whatever *we* decide.' And she was so, so wary of making demands on him, of foisting herself and her baby and all her problems onto a man who she had so recently met, so she offered a word, *we* instead of *you*, and she held that deep breath and wondered if he'd even notice.

He did.

'There's nothing to decide. We don't have to discuss it. I'm so angry with him, Izzy. Part of me doesn't even want to go for a few days, and still he goads—women's work...' He shook his head. 'You don't need this now.'

'But I do,' Izzy said. 'Because I'm a lot stronger than you think. I'm certainly stronger than I was even a few weeks ago, even since yesterday. You can tell me about things like Toby and that you've just got a call that your father is sick and how difficult that must be for you, how hard it was to get through Toby's funeral with your father so ill... We chose the wrong words, Diego—that we will last for as long as we make each other happy. Well, that's not real life. How about we will last as long as we make the world better for each other than it would be without?'

'Better?'

'Better.' Izzy nodded. 'Because I'd have got through all this and I'd have been fine, but it's been better with you. The same way you'll get through your father's illness and whatever lies ahead...'

It was a new contract, a different agreement, and Diego checked the small print.

'What do *you* want, Izzy?' Diego asked.

And she screwed her eyes closed and made herself say it.

'You,' Izzy admitted. 'And I'm sorry if it's too soon and too much and too everything, but that's how I feel.'

'Where do *you* want to be?' She peeled her eyes open just a little bit and he wasn't running out of the door and collapsing under the pressure of her honest admission—he was just standing there, smiling.

'With you,' Izzy said, and then made herself elaborate. 'And if that means going to Spain, I will. As soon as she's big enough…'

'Tilia comes first.' Diego stood firm. 'Always in this, she must come first.' And he sounded like a father and then she found out, he felt like a father. 'Always people tell me that my job will get tougher when I am a father—it annoys me, because I was there for Fernando. Always I tell them they don't know what they are talking about.' He looked right at her. 'They were right. Toby's funeral was awful, for all the reasons they are all awful, only it wasn't that my father was sick that upset me, it was how I felt about Tilia. She was a patient on my ward and I had to work, to look after her instead of be there for her…' He closed his eyes in frustration. 'Do you know what I want, Izzy?' She shook her head. 'Today, when Rita was going on, I wanted to take out my phone and show her a photo of Tilia, and I want to tell my mother when she calls and she thinks it is a baby crying at work that I am not at work—I am with my family.' She caught her breath. 'I want you and Tilia as my family.'

And good families tried to sort things out, even when the phone rang during important conversations. Diego let it continue to ring.

'Then tell her,' Izzy said.

'Tell her?' Diego checked, and Izzy nodded. 'You're sure?'

'Very,' Izzy said. 'We don't have to hide anything, we can tell people and it's up to them what they think.'

'We know,' Diego said, because they did.

It was time for the world to know the truth they had just confirmed. He pressed redial and put it on speaker and then took a deep breath as his mother answered. *'Qué pasa?'* He tipped into Spanish, chatting away to his mother, and she heard the words *bebé* and Tilia and *novia,* which Izzy knew meant girlfriend, and he occasionally rolled his eyes as his mother's voice got louder, but Diego never matched it, talking in his deep, even voice as *madre* got a little more demanding. And Izzy guessed when he used the word *prematuro* and his mother became more insistent that he was telling her it wasn't so easy—that his *familia* couldn't just pack up and come, and she stood there in wonder because he was talking to them about her, that she too was his family.

'Te quiero.'

He ended the most difficult call with *I love you* and when Señora Ramirez huffed, Diego grinned and said it again. *'Te quiero.'*

'Te quiero, Diego,' his mother admitted finally.

'Better?' Izzy asked, and after a moment he nodded. 'I said that I will be there for the operation and I have said I will come out again just as soon as I can...'

'What did she say about us?'

'That it's too fast, too soon—even though I lied.' Diego gave a bit of a sheepish grin. 'I hope you don't mind but we've been together a few months, not a few weeks.'

And then he kissed her and that made it better too.

His kiss made things better—they didn't fix, they didn't solve anything, they just made it all so much nicer.

'*Te amo*,' Diego said. 'It means I love you.'

'I thought it was *Te quiero*,' Izzy said, and she smiled because there was a lot to suddenly get used to and, oh, yes, a new language to learn too!

'*Te quiero*, what I said to my mother, does mean I love you,' Diego explained, 'but it's a different I love you. *Te amo* I save for you.' Then he kissed her again, made the world just that bit better till it was Izzy's turn to admit it.

'*Te amo*.' She spoke her first two words in Spanish to the only person who would ever hear them, to the man she had loved from the moment she had met him, to the man who, it turned out, felt the same.

And now they were a family.

EPILOGUE

You can't do it for her.

You can't change the world.

She might go back...

Diego didn't say any of those words and Izzy would love him for ever for it.

There was a trust fund for Tilia and when she was old enough and deciding her options, Izzy could tell her that her father was still supporting her.

And there was the house to fall back on as well.

A house Izzy had wanted to get rid of, a house she had hated, but now she could remember the good times there too.

And perhaps she could just sell. There were some gorgeous cottages along the coast she had considered but, as Diego had pointed out, his apartment had brilliant views and they could babyproof the balcony.

Diego was Daddy, or Papà.

They didn't ram it down anyone's throats, and certainly not to Henry's parents, but behind closed doors, when it was just they three, no one really knew that this very new couple were an established family.

And, no, Izzy couldn't change the world.

But she could help when someone wanted to change theirs.

'The washing machine jumps,' Izzy explained. 'If you put in too many towels, you'll find it halfway across the kitchen.'

'Thank you.' Evelyn stood in the hall, her face bruised and swollen, leaning on her son for support. 'We won't stay for long…'

'Stay for as long as you need,' Izzy said, and she meant it. 'Get your son through his exams, take your time…'

Many phone conversations, and a couple of sessions Izzy had arranged for Evelyn with a counsellor who specialised in these things had all helped Evelyn in her decision to take those first steps to empowerment. And on the eve of Izzy heading back to Spain, she realised why she'd chosen to keep the house.

'How long are you away for?' Evelyn asked.

'A couple of months this time around,' Izzy said. 'We're back and forth a bit. Diego's father hasn't been too well, but he's improving.' She glanced at her watch. 'I really have to go.'

And she knew, she just knew as she handed Evelyn the keys, that in six months or a year those keys would go to someone else who needed them—and Izzy wished she had a thousand keys, or a hundred thousand keys, except she didn't. She had one set and she would do her level best to use them wisely.

'How is she?' Diego asked, as Izzy climbed into the car, and looked over at four-month-old Tilia, who was sleeping in the back.

'She's going to be fine,' Izzy said. 'She just doesn't know it yet.' She looked at Diego, his face surly as it always was as they were about to head for his home. He loved St Piran but, despite it all, he loved his family too and so, after a lot of toing and froing, they were heading for a few months in Madrid. Diego had a temporary position at his father's old hospital and Izzy, well, she wanted to practise her Spanish.

'It'll be fine.' Izzy grinned. 'Your dad's being lovely now.'

'Yes, there's nothing like a brain tumour to help you get your priorities straight in life. At least he's stopped saying I'm gay.'

That still made her laugh.

She looked at the love of her life, at a man who hadn't stuck by her—no, instead he had pushed her.

Pushed her to be the best, the happiest she could be.

To go out, to make friends, to work, to laugh, to love, to heal, and she was ticking every box.

He put a smile on her face every day and watching him scowl as Heathrow approached, and later, watching him haul the luggage off the conveyor belt when they landed in Madrid and Diego braced himself for another round of facing his demons, Izzy was more than happy to put a smile on his.

'I'd help, but I shouldn't be lifting.'

'I can manage.'

There was the stroller and another of their suitcases whizzing past but Diego missed them and turned round, that frown on his face he got when he didn't quite get what she was saying.

'Tell him he's going to be a grandfather,' Izzy said. 'That should keep him happy.'

'A grandfather *again*,' Diego said, because at every turn, with everyone, Tilia was his, and Izzy knew a new baby wouldn't change that fact.

She knew.

'What took us so long?' Diego pulled her and Tilia into his arms, and kissed Izzy thoroughly right there in the airport, but this was Spain so no one batted an eyelid.

Six months from meeting and now two babies between them—and Izzy defied anyone to say it was way too soon.

They'd been waiting for each other all their lives.

ST. PIRAN'S: ITALIAN SURGEON, FORBIDDEN BRIDE

MARGARET McDONAGH

With special thanks to:

The Medical Romance team for inviting me to
be a part of this wonderful project and my fellow
authors for their support, especially…

Jo, Lucy, Mimi, Sheila, Carol, Caroline,
Kate and Maggie
Charlie & Will—for *'Charlie'*…
and for making the best bears in the world!

Namlife for the information on living with HIV:
www.namlife.org

CHAPTER ONE

'YOU need Jessica Carmichael.'

He didn't *need* anyone…not any more.

Giovanni Corezzi bit back his instant denial of the suggestion made by paediatric registrar Dr Megan Phillips. It was his first day as consultant neurosurgeon at St Piran's Hospital in Cornwall and although his primary focus was always on doing his best for his patients, he also hoped to make a good impression and to form a friendly working relationship with his new colleagues.

'Jessica Carmichael?'

He frowned, disturbed at the way the unknown woman's name flowed from his tongue. As if it were a caress. And somehow important. What nonsense was he thinking? With an impatient shake of his head, he refocused on Megan.

'Jess is a hospital counsellor. She's very knowledge-able and good with patients and their relatives,' the paediatric registrar explained with obvious admiration. 'Unfortunately we don't have extra time for everyone. Jess fills that gap.'

'I'll bear it in mind,' Gio replied, knowing the involvement of a counsellor was often helpful to his patients but reluctant to bring one in now.

'It's your decision.' Megan's disappointment and disagreement were apparent. 'I think you'd find Jess useful in Cody Rowland's case.'

Gio bit back irritation as the young registrar questioned his judgement. Instead of an instant retort, however, he considered whether he had missed anything regarding the young boy admitted to his care. Three-year-old Cody had fallen from a climbing frame two weeks previously, but had not shown any symptoms at the time. Recently he had become increasingly listless, complaining of a headache, going off his food and feeling nauseous. His frightened parents had brought him to the hospital that morning.

A and E consultant Josh O'Hara had examined Cody and called the neurology team. Busy in Theatre, Gio had sent his registrar to do an assessment. The subsequent tests, including a CT scan, had revealed the presence of a chronic subdural haematoma. As the bleed had continued and the clot had increased in size, it had caused a rise in pressure and the swelling brain to press on the skull, causing bruising and a restriction in blood flow.

Cody was now on the children's ward and awaiting surgery. Unless he carried out the operation soon, Gio feared the boy's condition would deteriorate and, if the clot and pressure continued to grow, there was a possibility of irreversible brain damage.

It was after noon and his first day was proving to be a hectic one. That morning he had undertaken three minor and routine operations—as minor and routine as any brain surgery procedures could be—and his first neurological clinic was scheduled later that afternoon.

Before that, he needed to return to the operating theatre with Cody.

'I'm sure this woman is good at her job,' he commented, 'but Cody—'

'Cody might need Jess at some point. Right now I'm thinking of his parents.'

Gio hated to admit it, but she was right. He *did* have concerns about the Rowlands and that Megan had picked up on the same signs was something he should find pleasing, not irritating.

'They aren't coping well,' he conceded with frustration. 'And their anxiety is distressing Cody. I need him to be settled for surgery—and for his parents to be calm and understand why we need to operate. I wish to press on them the urgency without further panicking them. They are listening but not hearing, you know?'

'I know,' Megan agreed. 'They're in denial…Mrs Rowland particularly.'

'Exactly so. Which is understandable. I'm not unsympathetic but I don't know how much time we have to play with.'

Megan hesitated, as if unsure of her ground. 'That's why I suggested Jess. I'm sorry to keep on about her, and I'm not questioning your skills,' she added hastily as his eyebrows snapped together. 'But I know how helpful she is in these situations. Everyone in the hospital likes Jess. She's a wonderful listener…and it isn't just the patients and their relatives who benefit. The staff frequently offload their problems on her, too. She's definitely your woman.'

Gio's frown returned in earnest, both at Megan's phraseology and the implication of her words. 'I don't know…'

Was he being too hasty? It was uncharacteristic of him not to listen to the suggestions of others, even if they were his juniors. He considered his reluctance to follow Megan's advice. Was it because he didn't want his new colleagues to think he couldn't do his job? Here he was, halfway through his first day and already needing to call in someone else to help with a case! He shook his head. What mattered was the well-being of his patients, not his own status.

Checking his watch, aware that *he* was now the one wasting precious time, he wondered how long it would take for Ms Carmichael to arrive. Once she was there, he would need to bring her up to date on the case and, as yet, he had no idea how much she understood of medical issues.

'Won't she be tied up with existing appointments?' he asked Megan. 'Cody can't afford to wait much longer.'

'Jess doesn't work like that, Mr Corezzi. She's on call and responds to whichever department or ward has need of her. It's just a matter of paging her—she usually comes right away,' the paediatric registrar explained, jotting a note on the front of Cody's file.

'Call me Gio.' He made the invitation with a distracted smile as he considered his options. He needed Cody in Theatre without further delay. If this counsellor could help facilitate that, then so be it. 'All right, Megan, please call her,' he invited, decision made, adding a word of caution. 'However, if she's not here soon, we may have to move without her.'

Megan's smile was swift. 'You won't be sorry, Gio,' she assured him, and he could only hope she was right.

'I'll ensure the operating theatre and my team are

ready. And I'll arrange for the anaesthetist to assess Cody,' he informed her. 'Everything will be in place and we can move quickly—*when* we have the Rowlands' consent.'

As Megan went to the ward office to organise the page, an inexplicable shiver of apprehension and anticipation rippled down Gio's spine. He had done the right thing for Cody. So why did he feel unsettled? And why did he have the disturbing notion that in bringing Jessica Carmichael on board he would be taking on much more than he had bargained for?

'Consultants don't spend time taking histories or chatting to patients and their relatives. That's why they have registrars and juniors,' Jess protested with a mix of wry cynicism and surprise.

Megan chuckled. 'This consultant does. He's pretty amazing, Jess, and very hands on.'

The news that Mr Corezzi remained on the ward was disturbing enough, but knowing Megan was so taken with their new consultant neurosurgeon left Jess feeling more unsettled. A sense of premonition refused to be banished. On edge, she opened her notebook and balanced it on top of the other items she carried, jotting down a few pointers as her friend gave a brief summation of Cody's case.

'Mr Corezzi…Gio…will give you more detail,' Megan added, the prospect making Jess feel more nervous.

'And Cody is three,' she mused, considering how best to help. 'I'll get Charlie.'

'Who is Charlie?'

The question came from behind her and the deep, throaty voice with its distinctive Italian accent not only

identified its owner but set every nerve-ending tingling.
Jess knew it was his first day there, and within moments
of his arrival the overactive grapevine had been buzzing
about the gorgeous new consultant. Female staff the
length and breadth of the hospital had been preening
themselves, eager to meet him and make an impression
on him.

She had not been one of them.

Jess tensed, her knuckles whitening as her fingers
tightened their grip on her files. Clutching them like
a protective shield, and feeling suddenly scared in a
way she didn't understand, she turned around and saw
Giovanni Corezzi for the first time.

Oh, my!

For once the rumourmill had been right. The new
Italian surgeon *was* something special to look at and
even she, who had sworn off men a long time ago, could
appreciate the view. A bit like window-shopping, she
thought, smothering an inappropriate smile. You could
admire the goods even though you had no intention of
buying. But her inner humour vanished in the face of
her body's impossible-to-ignore reaction.

She hated the breathless feeling that made it difficult
to fill her lungs, the ache that knotted her stomach, the
too-fast beat of her heart, and jelly-like knees that felt
unable to support her. The instinctive responses were
unnerving and unwanted. She had not been attracted to
any man for a long time—had not expected or wished
to be. Not since her life had taken an abrupt change of
direction four years ago, turning her world upside down
and having an irrevocable impact on her future, forcing
her not only to abandon her hopes and dreams but to
reinvent herself to survive. The Jess Carmichael of today

was a very different person from the one then…one who could no longer indulge in many things, including uncharacteristic flights of fancy over a good-looking man, even if he did stir her blood in ways it had never been stirred before.

Trying to shrug off the disturbing feelings, she allowed herself a quick inspection of the imposing man who stood before her looking relaxed and at ease. His dark hair was short, thick and well groomed. In his early thirties, and topping six feet, he had an olive-toned complexion and the kind of chiselled jawline that would make him sought after in Hollywood or gracing the pages of fashion magazines. Not that he was fashionable at the moment, dressed as he was in hospital scrubs, suggesting he had come to the ward from the operating theatre.

The shapeless trousers and short-sleeved tunic should have been unflattering but they failed to mask the strength and lean athleticism of his body, while their colour emphasised the intense blueness of his eyes. Under straight, dark brows and fringed by long, dusky lashes, they were the shade of the rarest tanzanite. They regarded her with a wariness she shared, a suspicion that had her shifting uncomfortably, and the kind of masculine interest and sensual awareness that frightened her witless.

Aware that Megan was making the introductions, Jess struggled to pull herself together.

'Ms Carmichael.'

The throaty rumble of his voice made her pulse race and ruined her attempt at sang-froid. 'Hello, Mr Corezzi.'

Jess dragged her gaze free and focused on the leanly

muscled forearms crossed over his broad chest. As he
moved, she juggled the files and assorted items she carried around the hospital, anxious to avoid shaking hands.
Instead, she fished out one of her cards, careful to ensure
she didn't touch him. His fingers closed around the card
and she couldn't help but notice that he had nice hands.
Surgeon's hands…capable, cared for and with short,
well-manicured nails. There was no wedding ring and
no tell-tale sign to suggest he had recently worn one.
His only accessory was the watch on his left wrist with
its mesh strap and midnight-blue dial.

The sound of Megan's pager made Jess jump but the
distraction helped cut the growing tension.

'I'm needed in A and E,' Megan told them with
evident reluctance, her cheeks pale and lines of strain
around her mouth.

'Are you OK?' Jess asked, knowing her friend's reluctance stemmed from some unexplained issues she
had with Josh O'Hara, the charismatic consultant who
had joined St Piran's trauma team in the spring.

'I'll be fine.'

The words lacked conviction and Jess was concerned.
Tall and slender, Megan appeared delicate, but although
she possessed an inner strength, she had seemed more
fragile than usual these last few weeks. Instinct made
Jess want to give her friend a hug, but she hung back,
keeping the physical distance she had maintained between herself and everyone else these last four years.

'I'm here if you need me,' she offered instead, conscious of the disturbing nearness of Giovanni Corezzi,
whose presence prevented her saying more.

'Thanks.' Megan squared her shoulders, determination mixing with anxiety and inner hurt that shadowed

her green eyes. 'I'll see you later. Good luck with the Rowlands. And Cody's surgery.'

Alone with Giovanni Corezzi, Jess felt a return of the tension and awareness that surged between them. Determined to focus on work, and needing to put distance between herself and the disturbing new surgeon, Jess murmured an apology and escaped to the ward office to track down Charlie.

Gio released a shaky breath as the surprising Jessica Carmichael walked away. He had no idea who Charlie was, or how he was relevant to the current problem, but he had greater things to worry about. Namely Jessica and his unaccountably disturbing reaction to her.

As the staff went about their work on the busy ward, he leaned against the wall and pressed one hand to his stomach. The moment he'd seen Jessica, it had felt as if he'd been sat on by an elephant. She was younger than he'd expected, perhaps in her late twenties. Below average height, she looked smart but casual, dressed for the August heat in a multi-coloured crinkle-cotton skirt that fell to her knees and a short-sleeved green shirt, her hospital ID clipped, like his own, to the top pocket.

Her eyes were a captivating and unusual olive green, while her hair—a gift from mother nature—was a vibrant auburn, with shades from burnished chestnut, like a conker fresh from its casing, to rich copper red. The luxuriant waves were confined in a thick plait which bobbed between her shoulder blades. He longed to see it unrestrained and to run his fingers through its glory.

When Jessica emerged from the ward office, the disturbing heaviness pressed on him once more. He straightened, shocked by the slam of attraction that shot through him. The cut of her shirt highlighted firm, full breasts, while the sway of her skirt hinted at curvy hips and thighs. He found her rounded, feminine figure so much more appealing than the reed-thin bodies many women aspired to.

Gio took an involuntary step back, disturbed by the surge of desire that threatened to overwhelm him with its unexpected intensity. This was the first time he had even *noticed* a woman for a long time. He couldn't believe it had been five years— No! He slammed his brain shut on *those* thoughts. This was neither the time nor the place. But he'd allowed a crack in the internal armour encasing the memories, the pain and his heart, and panic swelled within him. He didn't want to be attracted to anyone, yet he could not deny the strength of his reaction to Jessica or the way his body was reawakening and making new desires and needs known.

Disconcerted, he met her gaze and saw her eyes widen in shock at the unmasked emotions she read in his. She kept a safe gap between them, but she was close enough for him to see her shock turn to confusion, followed by answering knowledge and then alarm. Silence stretched and the air crackled with electricity. It was clear Jessica didn't want the attraction any more than he did, but that didn't make it go away. And, perversely, her reluctance intrigued him and made him want to learn more about her.

She stepped aside to allow a nurse pushing a wheel-chair to pass, her smile transforming her pretty face and trapping the air in his lungs. Cross with himself, he was about to return to the business of Cody Rowland when she shifted the things she was carrying and he noticed the teddy-bear puppet she wore on one hand.

'Meet Charlie,' she invited, holding up the plush toy, which had marbled brown fur and a friendly, mischievous face, its mouth open as if laughing. 'He helps break the ice and explain things to young children, calming their fears.'

The husky but melodic burr of her soft Scottish accent was sensual and set his heart thudding. Feeling as flustered as a teenager with his first crush, he struggled to ignore his unwanted reaction and focus on the matter at hand.

'Very clever.' Her innovative method impressed him. He reached out and gently shook the teddy bear by the paw. 'It's nice to meet you, Charlie.'

Jessica's flustered reaction confirmed his suspicion that giving him her card had been a ruse to avoid shaking hands. Was it him, or did she dislike touching other people, too? That he was immediately attuned to her unsettled him further.

'What are the priorities with Cody?' Jessica asked, moving them onto ground which, he felt sure, made her feel more comfortable. 'Have his parents signed the consent form?'

'Not yet.' Gio ran the fingers of one hand through his hair in frustration. 'The injury occurred over two weeks ago,' he explained, unsure how much Megan had told her. 'The parents are too upset to understand that while Cody may have appeared fine at first, the situation has changed.'

'And you don't want to waste more time.'

Grateful that Jessica was on his wavelength, Gio smiled. 'Exactly so.'

'He's deteriorating more quickly?' she asked, glancing at the notes.

'What was a slow bleed building a chronic subdural haematoma could be worsening,' he outlined, sharing his concerns. 'Or something more serious could be underlying it.'

Jessica nodded, making her beautiful hair gleam. 'And the longer you wait, the more chance there is of permanent brain damage.'

'I'm afraid so.'

'His parents must be very confused.' Her expression softened with understanding. 'They may feel guilty for not realising that what seemed an innocuous incident has become something so serious.'

'There is no question of blame, although such feelings are common,' he agreed, impressed by Jessica.

Her smile was rueful. 'I come across this in a wide variety of circumstances. We need to explain things to the Rowlands without frightening them further.'

'Yes…and Megan says you're the best person to help.'

A wash of colour warmed her flawless alabaster cheeks. 'I'll do what I can, of course.'

'Thank you, Jessica.'

Again her name felt right, unsettling him and curbing his amusement at her flustered reaction. Ignoring the hum of attraction between them by concentrating on work might not be effective long term, but hopefully it would get them through this encounter.

'Do you have suggestions about the Rowlands?'

Her relief was evident and she nodded again, loosening some strands of fiery hair, which tumbled around her face. As she raised her free hand, he saw that her fingers were ring free, and that she wore a narrow silver-toned watch around her wrist. She tucked the errant curls behind her ear, drawing his attention to the attractive stud earrings she wore. Set in white metal, the olive green stones matched her eyes and he made a mental note to discover the identity of the gem that so suited her.

'We need their consent so Cody can go to Theatre without delay. Then I can spend time with them and run through everything in more detail.' Even, white teeth nibbled the sensual swell of her rosy lower lip, nearly giving him heart failure. 'Do you have a rough guestimate on how long the operation might take?' she queried, snapping his attention back to business. 'The Rowlands will ask—and I need to reorganise my schedule to support them.'

Gio was encouraged by Jessica's common-sense approach, knowledge and apparent dedication to her patients. With real hope of a resolution, he gave her all the information he could.

'Can you talk with the father while I try the mother?' she asked next, walking briskly towards Cody's room.

He would happily do anything to speed things along. 'No problem.'

Following her, he admired her gently rounded, mouth-watering curves. As she stepped into Cody's room, sunlight spilling through the window made the natural red, copper and chestnut tones of her hair glow like living flames, captivating him. And, for the briefest instant, as he stood close behind her before she shifted to give him more room, he could have sworn he caught a faint, tantalising aroma of chocolate.

Fanciful notions vanished as he observed that Cody appeared more listless than when he had checked him several minutes ago. His frightened young mother sat close to him, clinging to his hand, tears spilling down her cheeks. The father, scarcely more than a boy himself, stood to one side, pale and withdrawn, at a loss to know what to do.

Jessica glanced over her shoulder and he met her gaze. The connection between them felt electric and intense, and it took a huge effort to look away. Clearing his throat, he introduced her to the Rowlands.

As Jessica began the delicate process of winning the trust of the troubled young family, Gio released another shaky breath. He was in big trouble. He had sensed Jessica would be more than he'd bargained for. Professionally. What he could never have foreseen was the impact she would have on him personally. It was unexpected, unwanted and scary. But bubbling within, as yet unacknowledged and unexplored, was growing excitement.

Even as they worked together to see Cody and his parents through the trauma that had befallen them, Gio was aware of the simmering connection between himself and Jessica. However hard they fought it, it was not going away.

All he knew for sure was that Jessica threatened to blow the ordered and lonely world he had lived in these last five years wide apart, and that her impact on his life would not leave him unscathed.

CHAPTER TWO

SHE didn't *look* any different.

Jess peered at her reflection in the mirror above the basin in the tiny bathroom next to her office. She wasn't sure what she'd expected to see, but she *felt* different. Changed somehow. And scared. Because of Giovanni Corezzi. Thinking about him made her pulse race and raised her temperature to an uncomfortable level—one she couldn't blame on the scorching August weather.

After splashing cool water on her overheated cheeks, she buried her face in the softness of her towel. Even with her eyes closed, images of St Piran's new Italian surgeon filled her mind. Unsettled by her reaction to him, she had endeavoured to keep things on a professional footing, determined to banish the disturbing feelings he roused within her.

She hadn't wanted to like him, but it had proved impossible not to. Ignoring the inexplicable and overwhelming blaze of attraction would have been easier had he been arrogant and horrible to work with, but nothing was further from the truth. He'd been compassionate and patient. As his initial suspicion had evaporated once he had witnessed her with the Rowlands, the likelihood was that she would be called to work with him again.

What was she going to do?

Jess sighed, discarding the towel and glancing at her reflection again. Less than an hour in his company had left her shaken and anxious. Megan had been right to describe him as hands on and caring. It was something Jess admired, yet it made him even more dangerous to her.

She had to find a way to limit his impact on her. He had reawakened things long forgotten, things she would sooner remained buried. She had to fight the desire he roused in her...because nothing could come of it. *Ever.* And she was leaving herself open to heartache if, even for a moment, she allowed herself to imagine anything else.

For the last four years, since the bombshell had hit her, changing her life for ever, she had turned in on herself, keeping focused on her new career and keeping people at bay. She hadn't worked so hard to reinvent herself to allow the first man to stir her long-dormant hormones into action to undo everything she had achieved. In the unlikely event she could ever trust a man again, there was no way she could allow any kind of relationship to develop. Not beyond friendship. To do so would be too great a risk. Besides, once Giovanni learned the truth she had kept secret for so long, he wouldn't want her anyway.

Quashing disobedient feelings of disappointment and regret—and, worse, a flash of self-pity—Jess hardened her battered heart. She had to keep Giovanni Corezzi at a distance and ensure any meetings with him were kept as professional and brief as possible.

Shocked how late it was, she returned to her office. She'd had to rearrange her schedule for the Rowlands, which meant she had much to catch up on and now she would have to rush if she was not to be late for an important appointment.

Five days ago, and less than three weeks after moving into the run-down cottage she had bought near Penhally village, an unseasonal storm had caused serious damage. Today the insurance company's assessor was carrying out an inspection, after which Jess hoped permission would be given for the repairs. The sooner the better... before anyone discovered the unconventional lengths she was going to to keep a roof over her head.

Smothering her guilt, she took care of a few urgent tasks before shutting down her computer. She just had time to dash across the grounds to see hospital handy-man Sid Evans and collect the precious cargo he was watching for her.

'Hello, Jess, love,' the kindly man greeted her as she hurried through his open workshop door. 'Everything is ready for you.'

'Thanks, Sid.'

'Here we are, all present and correct,' he told her in his lilting Welsh accent as he handed her a basket.

'I'm sorry to rush, Sid. Thanks for your help.'

'No worries.' He smiled, but Jess could see the sadness that lurked in his eyes. Following the recent death of Winnie, Sid's beloved wife of forty years, Jess had taken time to visit with him. 'And I'm the one who's grateful. You've been wonderful, love, letting me talk about my Winnie. I'll not forget it.'

'It's been my privilege,' she replied, a lump in her throat.

Jess hurried back to the psychology unit, glad every-one had left for the day, allowing her to sneak the basket into her odd little annexe at the back of the building. Dubbed the 'cubby hole', it had been assigned to her as the only spare room available, but she couldn't have been more pleased. Apart from the office and next-door bathroom, it had an adjoining anteroom and a basic kitchen. Away from the main offices, it gave her privacy, which suited her just fine. Especially with circumstances as they were…circumstances no one else knew about and which brought another surge of guilt.

Setting down the basket, Jess checked the contents then picked up her bag and keys. The sooner she went home, the sooner she could return to St Piran's. Hopefully she would be too busy in the coming hours to think about Giovanni Corezzi.

Opening her office door, she hurried out, only to collide with something solid and warm and smelling divinely of clean male with a hint of citrus and musk. Her 'Oh' of surprise was muffled against a broad chest as she lost her balance.

'Easy there,' Giovanni's voice soothed.

His hands steadied her, closing on her bare arms above the elbows. She felt the impact of his touch in every particle of her being, the brush of his fingers on sensitive skin making her tingle. She felt as if she'd been branded. A bolt of awareness and long-suppressed need blazed through her, scaring her.

The urge to lean into him and savour the moment was very strong. It seemed for ever since she had been touched and held, even in a platonic way. Not that there was anything *platonic* about the way Giovanni made her feel! But that knowledge acted like a bucket of icy water. Panic gripped her, both at the physical contact and her overwhelming reaction to this man. The need to break the spell overrode everything else and she struggled free, her desperation causing her to push away from him with more force than she had intended.

'What are you doing here?' she challenged brusquely.

Intense blue eyes regarded her with curiosity. 'Forgive me, I didn't know this part of the hospital was out of bounds.' His tone was gently teasing, but a blush stained her cheeks in acknowledgement of her uncharacteristic rudeness.

'It's not, of course, Mr Corezzi, but—' Jess broke off. Everything about him threw her into confusion.

'Please, call me Gio. I came to update you on Cody,' he explained, his throaty voice and sexy accent sending a shiver down her spine. 'And to thank you for your help.'

Her breath locked in her lungs as he rewarded her with a full-wattage smile. 'I was just doing my job.'

'I also wish to discuss another patient soon to be admitted whom I feel will benefit from your involvement,' he continued.

'That's fine. But is it urgent? I'm in a hurry.'

Although she had softened her tone, his dark eyebrows drew together in a frown. 'It's not urgent, but I hoped you'd have a minute…'

'I'm afraid I don't.' Jess cursed her stiltedness. She seemed unable to behave normally around him. 'I'm sorry, I have to rush home. I'll talk with you later.'

Eager to make her escape without him seeing inside her office and discovering the secret she had kept hidden so far, Jess fumbled behind her for the handle and pulled the door closed with a determined snap. She turned round, removing herself from his inspection, locked her office and pocketed the key. Then, carefully skirting him, she walked briskly to the main entrance, conscious of him following her.

'Jessica…'

The way he said her name tied her insides into knots. It wasn't just his voice or pronunciation but that he alone used her full name and made it sound like a caress. Thankful she had a genuine excuse to escape, she opened the front door and stepped aside for him to exit ahead of her.

'I have to run,' she said, concerned at his reluctance to leave.

A muscle pulsed along the masculine line of his jaw, indicating his dissatisfaction. When he stepped outside, allowing her to do the same, the door swinging closed and the lock clicking into place, Jess released the breath she hadn't realised she'd been holding.

He looked down at her, a brooding expression on his far-too-handsome face. 'Later.'

It was more demand than question and it filled Jess with alarm…and a dangerous sense of excited anticipation that was the most scary of all.

'Later,' she allowed reluctantly.

As she hurried towards her car, she sensed him watching her. So much for her earlier resolution. He was going to be more difficult to avoid than she'd anticipated. And this second encounter had confirmed what a risk he posed to the carefully constructed world she had manufactured for herself. Now a sexy Italian neurosurgeon had bulldozed his way into her life and was in danger of unravelling everything she had worked so hard for.

* * *

Heavy-hearted at the way his first day at St Piran's was ending, Gio washed, disposed of his scrubs and dressed in the jeans and short-sleeved shirt he had pulled on after arriving home. He'd not long left the hospital after making a final check of his patients when the emergency call had come for him to return.

A multidisciplinary team had assembled in Theatre, but despite their best efforts their nineteen-year-old casualty had succumbed to severe chest trauma and brain damage after an alcohol-induced accident.

Gio sighed at the waste of a life. Pain stabbed inside him as his thoughts strayed to another young life that had been cut cruelly short and he closed his eyes, determined to control his emotions and push the destructive memories away. Instead, he found himself thinking of Jessica Carmichael.

His impulsive visit to her office in the psychology unit—situated in one of the buildings adjacent to the main hospital and abutting the consultants' car park—had not gone to plan. He usually got on well with people. *'You could sell sand in the desert, Cori!'* Remembering the teasing words brought both amusement and an ache to his heart. Friendliness, politeness and a touch of flattery soothed troubled waters, but it wasn't working with Jessica, who remained tense and reserved.

Their unsatisfactory encounter had disappointed and confused him. He lived for his job, trying each day to make up for the failings that had haunted him for the last five years. Which was why his immediate and intense response to Jessica had shocked him. She had affected him on a deeply personal level. And he didn't *do* personal. Not any more. His reaction—and the attraction he wished he could deny—left him disconcerted and off balance.

When she had rushed out of her office and cannoned into him, instinct had taken over and he'd caught her as she'd stumbled. He'd felt the incredible softness of her skin under his fingers, the press of her femininely curved body against him, and he'd breathed in the teasing aroma of chocolate that lingered on her hair and skin. His attraction and body's response to her had been instant and undeniable.

But it was Jessica's reactions that had left him puzzled and unsettled. Her alarm had been real, and he had not imagined the panic in her beautiful green eyes as she'd wrenched herself free. For some reason Jessica didn't like to touch or be touched and he was determined to find out what lay behind it. There were several possibilities and each one caused him concern.

Gio stepped out of the surgeons' wash room, unsure what to do next. Why had Jessica been so dismissive of him and in such a rush to leave? He was positive she had felt the same bolt of awareness that had slammed into him when they'd first met. And that it had scared her. So could it be, he wondered, heading to the paediatric intensive care unit to check on Cody, that Jessica's cool professionalism and anxiety were flight responses? Was she trying to ignore the feelings and make them go away? If so, he could tell her it didn't work.

Using his swipe card, he let himself into PICU. Aside from the noise of the various monitoring machines and ventilators, the unit was quiet and dimly lit. He nodded to the charge nurse on duty and made his way to the bay that held Cody's bed. As he approached, he heard voices, one of which was Jessica's. He halted, surprised. What was she doing back here at this time of night? Curious, he listened before making his presence known.

'And when I think what could have happened,' Elsa Rowland commented, fear and guilt lacing her voice.

'You mustn't blame yourself, Elsa,' he heard Jessica respond softly, the gentle burr of her Scottish accent so attractive to him. 'A chronic subdural haematoma builds gradually. It can be weeks, even months, before the symptoms show. You did the right thing bringing Cody to A and E as soon as you realised something was wrong.'

'Thank you.' The woman's relief was tangible. 'I know Mr Corezzi explained it all to us but I didn't take anything in. And someone told me he's new. The thought of Cody's head being cut open is frightening.'

'Of course it is. But you can trust Mr Corezzi. He might be new to St Piran's but he's a very skilled and highly respected consultant neurosurgeon and he's come to us from London with a tremendous reputation,' Jessica explained to the anxious woman, her glowing endorsement of him taking Gio by surprise.

'Cody looks so still and small. Are you sure everything is all right?' the tearful mother asked, and although Gio wanted to reassure her, he was keen to hear what Jessica would say.

'He's doing very well,' she replied, her tone conveying sympathy and authority. 'It's standard procedure for him to be in Intensive Care following the operation.'

Gio was impressed. He was also intrigued by the depth of Jessica's knowledge. She seemed too assured and informed for someone with no medical training.

'Ally's gone to get something to eat. The nurses want

us to go home, but I can't bear to be away from Cody,' Elsa fretted.

'There's a cot in a room nearby for parents to use, and I'd advise you both to get what sleep you can there. But after tonight it would be best to get back into a normal routine. You and Ally need to keep strong so you are fit and ready to take Cody home,' Jessica urged, her common-sense approach pleasing him. 'I'll see you again tomorrow, but you can ring me if you need anything.'

There was a pause in the conversation and Gio waited a moment before making a sound and entering the bay. Elsa Rowland gave him a weary smile as he greeted her, but his attention immediately strayed to Jessica. She tensed, her gaze skittering to his and away again, a delicate flush of colour staining her cheeks.

As he checked Cody, who was sleeping peacefully, and looked over his chart, Gio was attuned to Jessica. What was she doing back at the hospital? Had she misled him when she'd said she was leaving for the day? He hoped to find answers as soon as Cody's father returned and, after a few pleasantries, Gio was able to escort Jessica out.

'I was surprised to see you,' he told her once they had left the unit and were in no danger of being overheard. 'I thought you had left for the day.'

Once more a tinge of colour warmed her smooth cheeks. 'I had to rush home to meet the insurance company's assessor. I said I'd be back,' she added defensively, refusing to meet his gaze.

She *had* said that but he'd assumed she had meant the next day. Apparently unsure what to do with her hands now that she was no longer carrying the assorted paraphernalia he'd seen her with before, she pushed them into her skirt pockets.

'What about you? Why are you still here?'

Her questions cut across the electrically charged atmosphere that hummed between them.

'I was called in after a young woman was knocked down by a coach.' He gave her a brief summary of the events and the unsuccessful struggle in the operating theatre. 'Her injuries were too severe…there was nothing we could do.'

Jessica's expression softened, understanding and sympathy visible in her olive-green eyes, and in her voice when she spoke. 'What a rotten end to your first day.'

'It could have finished on a better note,' Gio admitted with a rueful shrug, running the fingers of one hand through his hair.

Leaning back against the wall, Jessica met his gaze, and he witnessed her first real smile for him. *Dio*, but she was beautiful! The heavy weight settled back on his chest, making it difficult to breathe, and he felt each rapid thud of his heart.

'If it's not too late and you still want to talk about your patient…' Jessica's words trailed off and she bit her lip, looking hesitant and unsure.

'That would be good, thank you.' He'd take any opportunity to spend time with this elusive and most puzzling woman. 'Shall we go to the canteen? I've not eaten and the now congealed ready meal waiting in my microwave holds no appeal.'

Gio thought she was going to refuse and he found himself holding his breath as he waited for her answer. That it meant so much to him and he wanted so badly to be in her company should have worried him—*would*

have worried him even one day ago. But in the short
hours since he had met Jessica he felt changed somehow.
Where this inexplicable but intense attraction was heading he had no idea, but he was keen to find out.

'All right.'

However reluctantly given, her agreement cheered
him, and as he walked by her side down the deserted
hospital corridor he felt as if he was setting out on one of
the most important journeys of his life…with no map to
help guide him and no clue as to the final destination.

CHAPTER THREE

'THAT wretched woman!'

Jess looked up in surprise as Brianna Flannigan, a nursing sister from the neonatal intensive care and special care baby units, banged a plate down on the canteen table and sat down, joining Megan and herself.

'What woman?' Jess and Megan asked in unison, concerned that the gentle, dedicated and softly spoken Brianna was so upset.

'Rita.'

Rita was the ward clerk in NICU/SCBU and renowned for nosing into other people's business, making her opinions, and often her disapproval, known. Few people took notice of her, but none wanted to fall under her spotlight. Both Brianna and Megan had suffered when Rita had picked on them in the past, and news she was hassling Brianna again brought out Jess's protective instincts.

'I'm sorry.' She sent her friend a sympathetic smile. 'What brought this on?'

Brianna idly pushed her salad around the plate. 'Now Diego and Izzy are no longer occupying Rita, she's refocused on me,' Brianna explained, frustration and displeasure in her lilting Irish voice.

'Tell her to mind her own business…that's what I do,' Megan riposted, stirring a sugar into her mug of tea. 'Not that it stops her. She's started making comments about me again, too.'

Jess knew Rita wasn't easily diverted once she set her mind on something. She suppressed a shiver. The idea of anyone probing into her past and her secrets was too awful to contemplate.

'She's always been nosy and judgemental. I thought she'd given up on me, but now she's asking where I came from and what I did before I joined St Piran's,' Brianna continued.

Jess recognised the dark shadows in her friend's brown eyes and couldn't help but wonder what had put them there.

'She'll never change,' Megan predicted. 'If she's not prying into someone's business, she's having a go about single mothers…or teenage ones. And don't get her started on her daughter.'

'What's wrong with her daughter?' Jess queried with a frown.

Megan dunked a biscuit in her tea. 'Nothing. That's the point. Marina's been happily married for twenty years and has several children—I've treated some of them for the usual childhood accidents and illnesses. They're a great family. Noisy and loving. Maybe that's what bugs Rita. She claims Marina married beneath her and shouldn't have had such a big family,' Megan finished, brushing crumbs from her lip.

'It's true she picks on Marina,' Brianna agreed. 'She finds fault with her grandchildren, too.'

The talk made Jess even more grateful that she had managed to avoid Rita's attention and speculation.

Megan and Brianna were the closest she had to friends, yet they knew no more about her than she did about them, even after the years they had known each other. Which was probably why they got along so well. The mutual trust was there and they guarded each other's privacy, sharing an unspoken agreement not to ask personal questions, yet they could turn to one another should they need to, knowing their confidence would be respected.

'Rita's also asking questions about Gio Corezzi,' Brianna added, snapping Jess from her thoughts.

'Why would she start on him?' she asked, fighting a blush at the mention of Gio's name. 'She hasn't even met him, has she?'

Brianna nodded. 'She met him this morning. We all did. We have a baby with hydrocephalus—along with several other problems, the poor mite—and Richard Brooke called Gio up to the unit for advice,' the caring Irish woman explained, referring to the consultant who headed NICU.

'What sort of questions is Rita asking?' Jess queried, striving for casual indifference.

'She wants to know why someone who was such a wow in London would chose to "*bury himself*" in Cornwall,' Brianna told them, spearing some food with her fork. 'She saw Gio in the consultants' car park with James Alexander, chatting about cars—apparently they own the same model Aston Martin, but in different colours, so Rita's sure Gio's loaded.'

'For goodness' sake,' Megan responded, with the same disgust Jess was feeling.

'Rita asked Gio if his wife would be joining him here.' Brianna paused, and Jess steeled herself for what her friend would reveal next. 'Gio said, "Unfortunately not," and you could see the speculation in Rita's eyes until Gio added, after a deliberate pause, "She's *dead*." It was just awful. I felt terrible for him. He looked so sad. Even Rita was embarrassed, and that's saying something.'

As Brianna and Megan discussed Rita-avoidance tactics, Jess sat back and battled her emotions. Her heart squeezed with pain at the news of Gio's loss. Concerned for him, she also felt guilty for the unstoppable flicker of relief that he wasn't already taken. Not that *she* had any future with him. Or with anyone. But she couldn't help wondering what had happened…or question why he hadn't told her himself. Not that it was her business. She respected his privacy. And she hadn't told him *her* secrets.

Discovering how protective and possessive she felt of Gio was disconcerting. She knew the answer to some of Rita's questions, but she would never divulge them. Not even to Brianna and Megan. Not because they might gossip, they wouldn't, but for much more complicated reasons. She didn't want to admit to her friends, or to herself, how much she enjoyed and looked forward to Gio's company.

After Gio had returned to the hospital on the evening of his first day and had found her in PICU with the Rowlands, they had spent well over an hour in the canteen together. She'd had little time to wonder if he'd overheard any of her conversation with Cody's mother because she'd been pole-axed by the charge of electricity and blaze of sensual awareness that hit her every time she saw him. He'd looked gorgeous in jeans and a blue shirt, the shadow of stubble darkening his masculine jaw making him seem rakish and dangerous.

The canteen had been far less crowded than it was now, Jess acknowledged, shifting her chair in to allow a group of nurses to pass and access a nearby table. Gio had chosen a full meal, while she'd opted for a small bottle of mineral water and a packet of sandwiches... out of habit selecting things in disposable packaging. She hadn't budgeted for an extra snack, but as she'd not eaten anything but a banana and an apple since break-fast, she'd been hungry.

Having sunk everything she'd had into buying her cottage, she was counting every penny. The storm damage had been an unforeseen disaster but the insur-ance company was going to cover repairs for her roof despite the policy only being a month old. Having over-stretched herself on the property, she was having to be frugal with everything else, not that she had hinted at the sorry state of her finances to Gio—or anyone else.

'Have you always worked here?' Gio had asked, turn-ing their conversation that first night away from his patients and to work in general as he'd tucked into his dessert.

'No. I joined St Piran's when I was in the final year of my training,' she'd explained to him, amazed he'd found room for apple pie and cream after the large portion of lasagne that had preceded it. 'They asked me to stay on once I'd qualified.'

What she hadn't told him had been the extent of her relief that she'd not needed to move on again, some-thing she had done several times since the life-changing bombshell had brought things crashing down around her. She'd carved out a niche for herself in St Piran, fulfilling a role that patients, relatives and staff all appreciated and which allowed her some welcome autonomy.

'You don't see patients in your office?' Gio had queried.

'Very rarely—although I have done so if circumstances required it,' she replied, thinking of Izzy, the young A and E doctor who, then six months pregnant, had wanted to return to work after taking leave following the traumatic time she had experienced.

It hadn't been easy, for Izzy or herself, but things had worked out well. Now Izzy had a beautiful baby girl and an amazing new man in her life in the shape of attractive Spaniard Diego, who had been a charge nurse in NICU/SCBU, and Jess wished them all the happiness in the world.

'My role is more immediate,' she had gone on to tell Gio. 'I give emergency help to those who need it, be that on the wards, in A and E, or elsewhere in the hospital.'

'Like the Rowlands.' Gio's smile had nearly stopped her heart.

'Y-yes.' Flustered, she'd tried to get a grip. 'There can be a wide variety of situations…parents making difficult decisions about treatment for their child, or a young man who has crashed his motorbike and, overnight, has gone from being fit and active to waking up in hospital to the news he'll never walk again. Or it could be an older person who's had a stroke and is unable to return to their home. Or a relative in A and E trying to come to terms with a sudden bereavement.'

Something dark and painful had flashed in Gio's intense blue eyes, alerting Jess to the possibility there had been some traumatic event in his past. She hadn't pried, and Gio had declined to refer to it, but she had wondered about his background.

'So you see people through those first stages?' he'd asked next, pushing his empty dish aside and reclaiming her attention.

'That's right. Sometimes people need a shoulder to cry on and a friend in their corner. Others need greater help and back-up. I can liaise with other departments and with agencies outside the hospital that can offer care, advice and support, like social services, or relatives who have expectations that the patient may not want,' she'd explained, finding him easy to talk to. 'My job is to support them and their rights, and to help them achieve the best solution to whatever problem they're facing. If they need ongoing counselling once they leave hospital, they are assigned to one of my colleagues through Outpatients, or to an outside support organisation.'

Gio had shaken his head. 'I hadn't realised the full extent of what you do for people. It's very impressive... *you're* very impressive. I can see why everyone here respects you so much.'

The admiration in his eyes and praise in his sexy voice had warmed her right through and brought an uncharacteristic sting of tears to her eyes. 'It's hardly brain surgery,' she'd quipped to mask her embarrassment.

Gio's husky chuckle of appreciation had tightened the knot of awareness low in her tummy, and a sudden wave of longing had stolen her breath and made her realise how alone she had been these last four years. She enjoyed a friendship with Megan and Brianna, but it didn't extended beyond work and could never fill the cold and lonely void that had grown inside her since her life had turned upside down.

'Your first day's been hectic and hasn't ended in the best of ways, but how have you found St Piran's?' Jess had asked, anxious to move the conversation away from herself.

'I would rather not have returned to Theatre for that poor girl tonight,' he'd admitted, and she had seen the lines of tiredness around his eyes. 'But I've enjoyed today and it's good to be in near the beginning of a new unit for the hospital. It was one of the reasons I took the job. I was impressed with Gordon Ainsworth, the senior neurological consultant, the state-of-the-art equipment and the plans to increase the neurosurgical services here. Being able to help shape those services and build my own team appealed to me. Of course, many people cannot understand why I would leave London to come here.'

'It's none of their business, is it? If it's what you want, that's all that matters,' she'd told him, his surprised expression suggesting her matter-of-fact support had been in short supply.

'Thank you.' His slow, intimate smile had threatened to unravel her completely. 'St Piran's offered me new challenges and fresh opportunities, as well as the chance of more rapid career progression.'

It had made sense to her. 'Better to be a big fish in a small pond?'

Again the smile with its devastating effect on her. 'But it's much more than that…more than what I might gain for myself.' He'd leaned forward and folded his arms on the table, a pout of consideration shaping his sexy mouth. 'I commit a fair bit of time and money to a charitable trust that not only funds research, equipment for hospitals in various countries and support for patients

and their families with brain tumours and other neurological conditions. We also bring children in desperate
need of specialist treatment to the UK.'

She hadn't been surprised to learn of this side to him.
She'd seen the kind of doctor he was. Instinct had told
her how important the charity work was to him, and
she'd suspected there was far more to it than he had told
her…reasons why the trust was so close to his heart.

'That's fantastic. And it must be so rewarding.'

'It is. That St Piran's is interested and has given permission for me to continue to bring over a number of
children each year, donating the hospital facilities free
of charge, was a huge factor in my decision to come
here.'

Jess had been fascinated as he'd talked more about
the work he'd done with the trust. Her heart had swelled
with pride as she'd thought about his selflessness and
determination to use his skills to help others.

'He is *very* handsome, isn't he?'

Brianna's comment impinged on Jess's consciousness
and she blinked, looking up and following her friend's
gaze in time to see Gio carrying a tray across the canteen and sitting at a table with Ben Carter and James
Alexander. Her pulse raced at the sight of him and she
had to beat back a dart of jealousy at Brianna's evident
appreciation of Gio's looks.

The man in question turned his head and met her
gaze. For several moments it was as if there was no one
else in the canteen—the myriad conversations going on
all around her faded to a background hum and everything was a blur but Gio himself. A shiver ran down
her spine and a very real sense of fear clutched at her.

Less than a week and already this man had breached her defences and become all too important to her.

What was she going to do? If she allowed the friendship to develop, she knew things would end in heartbreak. Despite knowing that, and despite a desperate need to preserve all she had achieved these last four years, she wasn't sure she could give Gio up.

A sudden clatter and burst of laughter from across the room caught the attention of everyone in the canteen and snapped Gio's gaze away from Jessica. He glanced round in time to see three junior doctors trying to contain the mess from a can of fizzy drink as the liquid spewed from the top in a bubbly fountain, soaking everything and everyone within range.

'The Three Stooges,' Ben commented wryly.

James chuckled. 'Were we ever that young and foolish and confident?'

'Probably!' Ben allowed.

Gio tried not to dwell on the past. His memories were mixed, all the happy ones overshadowed by the bad ones and the blackest time of his life. Ben and James, fellow consultants with whom he had struck up an immediate rapport, began detailing the merits of the three rowdy young doctors, but Gio's attention was inexorably drawn back to Jessica. The now familiar awareness surged through him, tightening his gut and making it difficult to breathe.

Jessica was sitting with two other women. Megan Phillips, the paediatric registrar with whom he worked frequently. And Brianna Flannigan, a kind and dedicated nursing sister in NICU/PICU, whom he'd met for the first time that morning. On the surface, the three women shared many similarities and yet they were distinctly different. And it was only Jessica who made his pulse race and caused his heart, which he had believed to be in permanent cold storage, to flutter with long-forgotten excitement.

They had sat in this very canteen and talked for a long time that first night, yet he'd discovered precious little about her. He, on the other hand, had revealed far more than he'd intended.

Her understanding and support about his move to Cornwall had warmed him. Many people had appreciated his need to leave Italy for New York five years ago. Some had comprehended his decision to leave New York, and the team of the neurosurgeon who had taught him so much, to move to London. But very few had grasped why he had chosen St Piran's over the other options that had been open to him—options that would have meant more money and working at bigger hospitals.

Those things hadn't interested him, which had not surprised Jessica. St Piran's offered the opportunity of advancing to head of department within a decade, Gordon Ainsworth grooming him to take over when he retired, but it had been the administration's support of his charity work that had swayed his decision.

He'd told Jessica about the trust but *not* why it was so important to him. Not yet. That he was thinking of doing so showed how far she had burrowed under his skin. Even as warning bells rang in his head, suggesting he was getting too close too quickly, he couldn't stop himself craving her company and wanting to know more about her.

They'd seen each other often during the week, working together with a couple of new patients and a rapidly improving Cody Rowland. Their friendship grew tighter all the time but Jessica remained nervous. She'd relax for a time then something would cause her to raise her defensive wall again. Her working hours puzzled him, and the extent of her medical knowledge continued to intrigue him.

The little she had revealed about herself centred around her work at St Piran's. Listening to her describe her role, and witnessing her way with people—including the use of Charlie, the teddy-bear hand puppet, to interact with frightened children—had left him full of admiration for her devotion and skill.

'Much of my work involves supporting people who face life changes and difficult decisions caused by illness or accident. It's a huge shock to the system,' she'd told him and, for a moment her eyes had revealed such intense pain that it had taken his breath away.

He'd wanted to comfort and hug her, but he'd resisted the instinctive urge, aware of Jessica's aversion to touching and being touched…one of her mysteries he hoped to unravel. But the incident had left him in little doubt that she'd experienced some similar trauma. As had he, he allowed, with his own dart of inner pain.

'Patients and relatives often try to be strong for each other,' Jessica had continued with perceptive insight, 'when often they need to admit that they're scared and have a bloody good cry.' She'd sent him a sweet, sad smile that had ripped at his already shredded heart. 'I'm merely a vehicle, a sounding board, someone outside their normal lives on whom they can offload all the emotion.'

What toll did that take on her? Gio wondered

with concern. And who was there for her? They were questions to which he still had no answers.

Without conscious decision or prior arrangement, they'd met each evening in the canteen, lingering over something to eat, discussing work, finding all manner of common interests in books, music and politics, both of them steering clear of anything too personal.

He'd learned very quickly to tread carefully, watching for the triggers that caused her withdrawal. He liked her, enjoyed her company and was comfortable with her but also alive, aroused and challenged, feeling things he'd not experienced in the five long years since his world had come crashing down around him.

Taking things slowly was a necessity. For both of them. But every day he became more deeply involved. So much so that having to say goodnight to her and return alone to his rented house was becoming increasingly difficult.

'Oh, to be that young and free from responsibility.'

Edged with bitterness, the words were voiced by Josh O'Hara and pulled Gio from his reverie. The Irishman took the final empty chair and set his plate down on the table. Gio regarded the other man, wondering what had sparked his reaction.

'Something wrong, Josh?' Ben asked, a frown on his face.

'Bad day.' He pushed his food aside untouched. 'I've just had to DOA an eighteen-year-old…I was going to say *man*, but he was scarcely more than a boy with his whole life ahead of him.'

Gio sympathised, recalling how he'd felt a few days ago when the young woman had died in Theatre from multiple injuries. 'What happened?'

'He was an apprentice mechanic at a local garage, driving the work van and following another mechanic who was returning a customer's car after service,' Josh explained, emotion in his accented voice as he told the story. 'Some bozo going home from a liquid lunch at the golf club and driving far too fast ploughed into the van. The boy wasn't wearing his seat belt, the van had no air-bags, and he went through the windscreen. He had horrible head and facial injuries—apparently he'd been a good-looking boy, not that I could tell—and a broken neck.'

Gio exchanged glances with Ben and James, both of whom were listening with equal solemnity and empathy. 'And the drunk driver?' Ben queried, voicing the question in all their minds.

'Yeah, well, there's the rub. There's no justice in this world.' Josh gave a humourless laugh. 'The boy's colleague, who witnessed the crash, is in shock. The drunk driver hasn't got a scratch on him. The police have arrested him and I hope they throw the book at him, but whatever sentence he gets won't be enough to make up for that young life, will it?'

'No,' Gio murmured with feeling.

As his three companions discussed the case, Gio struggled to contain memories of another injustice and senseless loss of life, one he had been unable to prevent and which had plunged him into the darkest despair he had ever known. A darkness he had believed he would never escape. His gaze returned to Jessica, who, in just a few days, had brought flickerings of light and hope back into his life.

A shaft of sunshine from the window beside her made the vibrancy of her rich auburn hair gleam like pure flame. Brianna also had auburn hair but hers was a much lighter shade, lacking the coppery chestnut richness of Jessica's. Megan, whose hair was darker, was the tallest of the three, slender and fragile-looking. Brianna, an inch or two shorter, was lithe and athletic, while Jessica was shorter still and more rounded, her shapely feminine curves so appealing to him. She looked up and, as their gazes clashed once more, she sent him a tiny smile.

'From the Three Stooges to the Three Enigmas,' Ben remarked, his gaze following Gio's to Jessica's table, just as the rowdy young doctors left the canteen.

Fearing his new friend would detect his interest in Jessica, Gio dragged his gaze away and pretended not to know what Ben meant. 'Sorry?'

'Brianna, Jess and Megan,' Ben enlightened him. 'St Piran's Three Enigmas.'

'It's interesting that the three of them gravitated to each other,' James said, as he looked across at them.

Ben shrugged. 'I'm not surprised. They have so much in common. All three are intensely private and have somehow managed to elude the gossip-mongers. And all three have also ignored the attention showered on them by the majority of the single—and some not-so-single—men in the hospital. I don't think anyone knows anything more about them, or their lives outside work, than they did the day each of them began working here,' Ben finished.

'How long *has* Megan been here?' Josh asked, his apparent nonchalance only surface deep, Gio was sure.

'It must be, what…seven years? Maybe eight,' Ben pondered, and Gio noticed the set of Josh's jaw and the way he flinched, as if the time was somehow important.

Gio glanced over to Jessica's table again, his gaze resting a moment on Megan. He was just about to smile at her when he realised that she wasn't looking at him but at Josh. Pale faced and seemingly upset, Megan turned away.

Across from him Josh looked strained and affected by the silent exchange. There was a story there, Gio realised, but it was none of his business. He had enough to concern him settling into a new job, a new town, and dealing with the sudden and unexpected resurgence of his libido.

As the four of them prepared to return to their respective departments, their break over, Gio noticed activity at Jessica's table, too. She was standing up and reaching for her pager, a frown on her face as she read the message.

He wondered what had happened and who needed her now. Like a schoolboy with his first crush, he hoped he would meet up with Jessica later, craving the moments at the end of the day when he had her to himself, at least for a while.

She was becoming ever more important to him and he was both scared and excited to discover what was going to happen.

CHAPTER FOUR

As HER pager sounded, Jess rose to her feet, frowning as she read the call for her to attend A and E urgently.

'I have to go,' she explained as her friends said goodbye. 'I'll see you later.'

Jess squeezed her way between the tables, wishing she was as slender as Megan and Brianna. Before she left the canteen, she couldn't resist looking back at Gio. Her gaze clashed with his, delaying her, her footsteps slowing as if ruled by an inbuilt reluctance to leave him.

Gio waved, drawing Ben's attention as the men stood up from their table. Ben smiled at her, and she blushed, hoping he would think she was including all of them, and not that she had any special interest in Gio, as she sketched a wave in return and hurried out of the canteen.

As she made her way to A and E, her thoughts remained with Gio. Beyond the dangerous attraction, she enjoyed his company, admired him, professionally and personally, and felt good with him. If she had any sense, she'd guard her heart and keep her distance, but she feared it was already too late. She'd begun to slide down the slippery slope by foolishly convincing herself it was

OK to be friends with him…provided they both knew friendship was all it could be.

She knew Gio was curious and wanted to know more about her, but he'd been circumspect so far and she was grateful. Meeting in the canteen each evening challenged her resolve but his comments on how he hated returning to the empty house he was renting had touched a chord within her. She knew all about the loneliness found between the walls of somewhere that didn't feel like home. One more of the many things they had in common.

Arriving in A and E, Jess set thoughts of Gio aside. Ellen, a senior staff nurse in the department, greeted her and outlined the reason for the call.

'The girl came in very distressed, asking after a young man killed in a road accident,' the middle-aged woman explained, shaking her head. 'She's terribly young, Jess, but she insists she's the girlfriend. Unfortunately we're rushed off our feet and as she's not physically injured or ill, we don't have time to spend with her, but we didn't want her to leave in such a state.'

'I understand. Has she been told anything?' Jess asked, her heart going out to the unknown girl.

Ellen sighed again. 'I'm afraid one of the inexperienced clerks told her the boyfriend, a lad named Colin Maddern, had died.'

'Oh, hell.'

'Exactly.' The nurse's displeasure matched her own. 'The girl wants Colin's things. He had no one but her. And there are photographs of her in his jacket, so she's genuine. I've checked with the police and they don't need anything, so I'll arrange to have the jacket and the possessions we salvaged brought to her.' Ellen nodded in the direction of the closed door to one of the quiet rooms used for relatives. 'She's in there. She wants to see him, but…'

'You don't think it's a good idea,' Jess finished for her.

'No, I don't. The poor boy wasn't wearing a seat belt and there was no air-bag fitted. He was hit at speed, went through the windscreen and was killed. A broken neck. And his face is a mess.'

Jess struggled to keep her emotions from showing. 'And the other driver?'

'Returning home drunk after lunch at the golf club. The police have arrested him. Needless to say he's not even bruised. Josh had to deal with both of them and he's furious. It's so unfair,' Ellen finished, mirroring Jess's own sentiments and explaining the grim expression on Josh's face when he'd arrived in the canteen.

'Do we know the girl's name?' Jess queried, jotting a few notes on her pad.

'No. Other than asking for Colin—and his things—she's not said anything. She broke down after she learnt of his death.'

'Thanks, Ellen.' She would not have relished the task of delivering the news, but Jess wished the girl had learned the truth in a more gentle and caring way. 'I'll see what I can do.'

The woman smiled. 'If anyone can help her, love, it's you.'

Jess hoped so. After Ellen had gone, she drew in a breath, hoping to find the right things to say in an impossible situation. Tapping on the door, she opened it and stepped inside. A junior nurse sat awkwardly near the sobbing girl, and jumped to her feet, clearly glad to leave.

Once they were alone, Jess pulled a chair closer and sat opposite the plump form huddled on the two-seater sofa. With her face buried in her hands, a curtain of straight, corn-coloured blonde hair swung forward, hiding her face from view. A cooling cup of tea remained untouched on the table beside her.

'Hello. I'm Jess Carmichael. I've come to see if there's anything I can help you with.' Jess waited for some kind of response or acknowledgement of her presence. 'I'm very sorry to hear about the accident.'

Slowly the girl looked up, her hands dropping away from her face and falling to her lap. Jess barely managed to smother a shocked gasp as she discovered how terribly young she was...no more than sixteen. Grey eyes were awash with tears, leaving no doubt at the depth of her devastation.

'They won't let me see him,' she murmured. 'Is it because I'm not officially family?'

Jess hesitated, unsure how to explain without causing further upset. 'It's a difficult decision. I'd urge you to think carefully, because once it's done, it can't be undone. They advised you against seeing Colin because of the nature of his injuries,' she continued, deciding it was important to tell the truth, even as the words caused the girl to flinch. 'Wouldn't you rather your last memory of him was a good one? What would he want for you?'

'Colin wouldn't want me to do it,' she admitted, a frown creasing her brow.

'There's no hurry to make a decision, so have a think about it.'

'OK.'

Jess hoped she would decide not to see him. 'Is there someone I can call for you? Your parents, maybe?'

'No!' The denial was instant and accompanied by a vigorous shake of her head. 'I can't.' Taking a tissue from the box on the table, she blew her nose. 'No one knows about Colin and me.'

Jess let it go for now, not wanting to pressure the girl or distress her further, hoping instead to build rapport and a level of trust that would enable her to help if she could.

'Can you tell me your name?'

The girl fiddled nervously with the chain around her neck, suddenly clutching it before tucking it inside her blouse and doing up the top button, as if to hide it. Before Jess could consider the odd behaviour, the girl shifted nervously, her gaze darting around the room.

'Marcia Johns,' she finally offered, barely above a whisper.

'Thank you, Marcia.' Jess smiled, accepting the name, even though she was unsure at this point whether or not it was genuine. 'Would you like to talk about Colin?'

A firm nod greeted the suggestion, and although tears shimmered in her eyes, a wobbly smile curved her mouth, revealing how pretty she could be. 'Yes, please. Is that OK?'

'Of course. I'd like to hear about him. When did you meet?'

'Over a year ago when I started my summer job,' she explained. 'Colin worked nearby. He was three years older than me, and never in a million years did I imagine him noticing *me*. Tall and handsome, with dark hair and blue eyes and a gorgeous smile, he was the one all the girls wanted. I'm shy and overweight and always fade into the background,' Marcia continued, revealing low self-esteem. She shook her head, as if in wonder, and gave a little laugh. 'When Colin began spending time with me, I couldn't believe it! There were all these thin, pretty girls chasing after him but he kept saying it was me he wanted, that he saw the real me inside. That I was kind and smart and funny, and he loved me the way I was.'

What a lovely young man, Jess thought, seeing how Marcia lit up talking about him. And what a terrible tragedy that his life had been cut so short. Sensing Marcia's need to talk, she encouraged her to continue.

'We were going to get married when I finished school and got a full-time job,' she said, toying with the friendship ring that encircled the middle finger of her right hand, no doubt a gift from him, Jess thought. 'His father died when he was twelve, and his mother when he was sixteen, so Colin had to look out for himself. He was much more responsible and steady than the boys I knew at school. There was never much money, but that didn't matter. We spent all our time together, walking on the beach, having picnics, watching DVDs or listening to music at his flat, talking for hours. Talking about everything. For the first time I felt as if someone really knew me and understood me.'

'Don't you feel that at home?' Jess probed, hoping to find out more about Marcia's background.

'Not really.' She gave a casual shrug, but it obviously mattered to her. 'We're a big family. My parents are busy working and caring for us all, and my brothers and sisters are all outgoing and active, and so much more

attractive than I am. They all have the family colouring.
I got the eyes but my hair is dead straight and mousy
blonde. I'm interested in books and music, not sports. I
don't understand them and they don't understand me. I
know they love me,' she added, wiping away the twin
tears that tracked down her rounded cheeks. 'They just
don't *see* me. Everything is so hectic and noisy. I don't
think they notice whether I'm there or not.'

'But Colin noticed.'

'Yes. Yes, he did.'

Jess understood how special and important the young
man must have made Marcia feel, boosting her confidence and setting her free from the shadow of her
vibrant family. Marcia might be very young, but she
had a sensible head on her shoulders and for her, her
relationship with Colin had been a close and genuine
one.

Marcia pulled her shoulder bag on to her lap and rummaged inside for a moment before producing a couple
of photos and handing them across.

'Thanks.'

Jess looked down at the first picture, seeing a very
handsome young man dressed in jeans and a black leather jacket, wavy black hair brushing over the collar. The
blue eyes were startling, full of intelligence, humour and
kindness, his smile adding to the impression of warmth
and friendliness. The second picture, of Marcia and
Colin together, banished any lingering doubt about the
full extent of this young girl's relationship with Colin.
No one seeing the two young people together could
question their feelings. Their happiness and love shone
out, and the expression of devotion on Colin's face as

he looked at a laughing Marcia brought a lump to Jess's throat.

'They're lovely. Thank you for showing me,' she murmured, handing the pictures back.

Marcia looked at them for several moments before tucking them carefully back in her bag. She sobbed, pressing a hand to her mouth, despair in her eyes.

'What am I going to do?' Rocking back and forth, tears flowed in earnest once more. 'Colin was my whole life. I love him so much. And I need him. He can't be gone. He *can't*. It isn't fair. Oh, God… Why? *Why* has this happened? What's the point in anything if Colin isn't with me?'

As she tried to comfort the girl, Jess wished she had answers to explain the cruel and senseless loss of a life. Fresh anger built within her at the driver who had thoughtlessly climbed behind the wheel of his car, his selfish actions shattering two young lives. He should be made to see Colin's lifeless, damaged body, and witness the terrible grief Marcia was suffering. What words could she possibly offer the girl that didn't sound trite?

A knock at the door announced the arrival of Ellen and provided a welcome distraction. 'May I come in?'

As Marcia nodded and mopped her tears, Jess met the kindly nurse's gaze, seeing the sympathy and sorrow in her eyes.

'I have Colin's things for you, love,' Ellen said, setting a black leather jacket on the seat beside Marcia, the same jacket Colin had worn in the photos.

Marcia drew the jacket into her arms, closing her eyes and burying her face in the wear-worn leather. 'I saved up for ages to buy this for his birthday. It smells of him,' she whispered, clutching the familiar garment more tightly to her and rubbing one cheek against it.

A lump in her throat, Jess exchanged a glance with Ellen. Maybe having Colin's jacket would bring Marcia some comfort and familiarity in the difficult times ahead.

'Here are the photographs and the other things Colin had with him,' Ellen said, holding over a large padded envelope.

Refusing to let go of the jacket, Marcia took the envelope with her free hand. 'Thank you, it means a lot. And thanks for being so kind to me.'

'You're welcome, my love.' Suppressed emotion made Ellen's voice huskier than normal. 'I'm so sorry.'

After Ellen had left them alone once more, Jess allowed Marcia some quiet time. While she waited, she took a page from her notebook and jotted down some information for the girl to take away with her.

'I don't like to think of you going home alone, Marcia. You've had a horrible shock. Are you sure I can't call your parents? Or I could arrange for someone here to take you home,' Jess suggested, willing to drive her there herself, but Marcia was withdrawing and shaking her head.

'No. No, I don't want that.' She took another tissue and mopped her eyes. 'Thank you. I'll be all right.'

Jess didn't believe it for a moment, but she couldn't force her and she didn't want to break the tentative trust between them. All she could do was encourage Marcia to keep in touch.

'You can contact me here at any time, Marcia,' she told her, adding another telephone number to the list. 'I've also given the details for the Samaritans. If you need to talk to anyone in confidence, day or night, you can call them. I volunteer once a week, usually on Friday evenings, but you can talk freely to anyone.'

'OK.'

Jess was relieved as Marcia took the sheet of paper, looked it over, and then tucked it into her bag, suggesting she might actually use it and not toss it into the first litter bin she came across.

'I'd really like to know how you are. And if there's anything I can do…' She let the words trail off, not wanting to nag.

The sound of her pager intruded. Smothering her frustration, Jess checked the display before glancing around the room and discovering there was no telephone.

'I've taken up too much of your time,' Marcia murmured, beginning to gather her things together.

'No, no, it's fine, honestly.' Jess smiled and told a white lie. 'I'm not in a hurry. I just have to reply to this. If you don't mind waiting, I'll just pop into the next door room to use the phone. I'll be back in a jiffy.'

Jess found a phone and made the call. She doubted she'd been gone more than a minute, but by the time she returned, Marcia had gone.

'Damn it!'

Upset, she rushed down the corridor and back into the busy casualty department, asking a couple of nurses and the clerks at the desk if they had seen Marcia come though, but no one had noticed her. Not even the security guard by the main doors. It brought back Marcia's own words…she faded into the background and no one saw her.

Cursing the appalling timing of the interruption, Jess went outside, hoping to catch a glimpse of Marcia, but it was hopeless. The sense of disappointment was huge. She couldn't bear to think of Marcia alone with her grief, unable and unwilling to seek the comfort of a family who loved her but seldom had time for her.

An image of Marcia and Colin before the tragedy, so happy and in love, fixed itself in her mind. Why did awful things happen? She could make no sense of the cruelty that had befallen two lovely young people. She swallowed, blinking back tears.

'Jessica, are you all right?'

Gio's voice behind her had her spinning round in surprise. 'What are you doing here?'

'I was in A and E and saw you run outside.' The expression in his blue eyes, so warm and intimate, robbed her of breath and held her captive as he raised a hand and with exquisite gentleness removed a salty bead of moisture suspended from her lashes, his fingers brushing her cheek. His voice turned even huskier. 'I was worried about you.'

Everything in her screamed at her to lean into his touch, craving what she had denied herself for so long, but reality intruded, the instinct for self-preservation ingrained. She jerked back, feeling the colour staining her cheeks as Gio regarded her in silence, speculation, concern and a frightening resolve in his eyes.

'Tell me what's wrong,' he invited as they headed back to the hospital.

Sighing, Jess gave him a brief summary of what had happened, unable to prevent her emotion from showing. 'It was just awful.'

'I'm sorry.' He shook his head, murmuring what sounded like a curse in Italian. 'Josh was talking about the accident in the canteen.'

Back in the room where she had spoken with Marcia, Gio remained with her, increasing her sense of awareness. 'I feel as if I failed her,' she admitted.

'Of course you didn't,' he chided gently.

'I don't know.' With another sigh, she gathered up her things. 'I'm even more sure now that Marcia Johns is not her real name.'

'Definitely not.'

The edge of amusement in Gio's voice had her head snapping up. There was nothing remotely funny about the situation. But before she could remonstrate with him, he shook his head and pointed to something behind her. She turned round, noticing for the first time the information posters on one wall of the room.

The 'infomercials' were sponsored by well-known drug companies and 'Marcia' had been clever enough, despite her distress, to cobble together a false name on the spur of the moment, using parts of two words from the company name emblazoned in large letters on one of the posters. Jess cursed herself for having been so thoroughly duped. She was also disappointed that the girl had felt the need to deceive her.

'She had her reasons, and I'm sure they were personal to her and nothing to do with you.'

Jess knew Gio's words were offered by way of consolation, but they did little to ease her upset and concern. 'Marcia' would remain in her thoughts and she would worry about her unless and until she had any further news of her. She could only hope that at some point the girl would use one of the contact numbers she had given her and get in touch.

'I know how much you care,' Gio said now, scarily attuned to her thoughts. 'You would not be so good at your job if you didn't, but you cannot carry the burden of everyone's problems on your shoulders, Jessica.' He stood in front of her, tipping her chin up with one finger until her gaze met his. 'Who is there for you?'

She felt branded by the contact and once more she stepped back to break it, resisting the urge to press her free hand to the spot that still tingled from the soft touch of his fingertip. This was ridiculous! She needed to give herself a stern talking to. Squaring her shoulders, she headed for the door.

'I'm fine,' she told him, injecting as much firmness into her voice as possible.

'You are here at all hours, taking on the burden of everyone else's problems,' he continued, refusing to let it go. 'Who listens to yours?'

Frightened that his perceptiveness and caring were chipping away at the defences that had protected her these last four years, she laughed off his question and repeated the words she used as a mantra to convince others...and herself. 'I'm fine!'

He took her by surprise—again—politely opening the door for her and following her out. So grateful was she that he had let the subject drop, she was not adequately on her guard.

'Where are you going now?' he asked.

'Hmm...' Jess frowned, trying to remember what had been on her agenda before the call had come in for her to attend A and E.

'If you have a few minutes to stop off at my office, I have some things to discuss with you.'

Although she would sooner have parted company there and then so she had time to re-erect her barriers against him, she was relieved he had focused back on work matters. Cursing her weakness and the voice in her head that tormented her about her vulnerability to this man, Jess found herself assenting to his request.

'All right.'

'Thank you.'

His smile of satisfaction made her uneasy. What had she agreed to? And why did she feel he'd set her up and she'd fallen for it—as she feared she had for him—hook, line and sinker?

CHAPTER FIVE

'COME this way.'

Jess found herself ushered into Gio's office, his hand at the small of her back sending a charge of electricity zinging through her. He had a disturbing habit of touching her. As he closed the door, Jess took the opportunity to put some much-needed distance between them. The room was by no means small but, confined in it with Gio, it seemed claustrophobic and she felt an urgent need for the comfort of her own personal space.

'What I am about to reveal to you is strictly confidential, Ms Carmichael. You do realise that?' he asked, his expression sombre...but for a tell-tale glimmer of mischief in his tanzanite-blue eyes.

Jess had no idea whether he was serious, or whether he was toying with her. Why did just being in the same room with him make her feel so off kilter and peculiar? She didn't like it. What she most wanted was to escape.

'Jessica?'

She jumped, continually unnerved at the way he spoke her name, his husky, accented voice far too intimate and intoxicating. But it was the light touch of one finger on her forearm that brought her inbuilt flight response into action again as she stepped back, distracted by the way all her nerve-endings were fired into life. Startled, she met the intense blueness of his gaze, seeing the curiosity, knowledge and masculine appreciation that lurked in his eyes. She didn't want anyone interested in her or asking questions about her, least of all this man who posed a unique and definite danger.

'What's confidential?' she queried, intrigued and yet nervous.

'Apart from my secretary, no one knows about this. I'm trusting you, Jessica.'

'Yes, of course.' She agreed without hesitation. It was asked of her, in one way or another, every working day, either by a patient, relative or colleague. And very little surprised her. 'What is it?'

Gio moved to his desk and beckoned her closer. She edged forward, watching as he opened the bottom drawer of his desk, pulling it back with frustrating slowness, building her suspense as centimetre by centimetre the contents came into view.

She'd been wrong to believe he couldn't surprise her. Her eyes widened in astonishment as she found herself staring at a drawer full to the brim with...

'Chocolate!'

Gio couldn't help but laugh aloud at Jessica's stunned reaction. 'What is your poison? Plain or milk? With or without nuts?' he asked, taking a selection of bars from the drawer.

'I don't eat much chocolate.'

'But you like it,' he prompted, hearing the waver in her voice. 'You must do...given the delicious scent of your hair and your skin.'

His words brought a bloom of colour to her porcelain cheeks. But it was the longing in her eyes that betrayed her sweet tooth. And then her pink tongue-tip peeped out to moisten the sensual curve of her lips, causing his body to react in such an immediate and blatant way that he drew back in shock.

'Treat yourself,' he encouraged, thankful that she appeared unaware of his response to her and, as he waited for her to make her selection, struggled to get his mind and body back under control.

'OK.' She took a small bar of milk chocolate with a hazelnut praline centre. 'Thank you.'

'Good choice,' he murmured as she moved away.

Taking a bar of dark chocolate with almond for himself, he put the rest away and closed the drawer. Sitting down, he opened his chocolate, his gaze remaining on Jessica as she inspected the expensive high-class packaging, noting the moment realisation dawned.

'*Cioccolato Corezzi?*' She looked up, stunning green eyes wide with interest. '*You* make this chocolate?'

'My family do. My paternal grandfather began the company over fifty years ago, and Papá and Mamma have grown it from a small specialist business with one shop in Turin into what it is today—one of Italy's most famous hand-made chocolate houses.'

'You're understandably proud of them.' She smiled, snapping off a square and popping it into her mouth, nearly killing him as those mesmerising eyes closed and a blissful look transformed her face as she savoured the flavours he knew would be bursting on her tongue. 'Oh, this is *amazing*!'

'Thank you.' Her opinion was important to him and her enthusiasm made him feel warm inside.

Snapping off another square, she laughed. 'No, thank *you*!' she insisted, before popping the chocolate into her mouth to savour the taste as before.

It was the first time he'd heard her laugh. It was a warm, throaty, infectious sound and he wanted to hear it often. Frowning, he acknowledged just how involved he was becoming.

'Did you never want to follow in your parents' footsteps?' she queried after a moment, perching on the edge of his desk, stretching her skirt across the pleasing curve of womanly thighs.

'No,' he answered, his voice rough. Clearing his throat, he sat forward. 'It was never an option, and my parents knew it wouldn't have suited me. Besides, I would have eaten all the profits!'

Taking a bite of his chocolate, he enjoyed another of her throaty chuckles.

'You must have lorry loads of it delivered, judging by your drawer!'

Having her relax enough to tease him was an unexpected pleasure, as was listening to the softness of her accent. He wondered how she had come to be in Cornwall, so far from home, but he refrained from asking...for now.

'Now you know my secret,' he said, keeping his tone light and teasing. 'It's only fair you tell me one of yours, no?'

The change in her was immediate and, while he regretted her withdrawal and the loss of their rapport, he was intrigued by her reaction and eager to find out its cause. Her whole body tensed, as if she was closing in on herself. Sliding off the desk, she turned away, but not before he had seen the hurt and loneliness she worked hard to hide. Stepping across to the window, her shoulders lifted as she breathed in a slow, deep breath. Finally, she turned round, popping the last piece of chocolate in her mouth and scrunching up the wrapper.

'I'm not very interesting, and I don't really have any secrets,' she told him with a manufactured smile, not meeting his gaze.

Oh, but she most certainly did. He knew it. And he was determined to uncover them and understand what she was anxious to hide. Behind the façade she presented to the world, the real Jessica was far from fine.

'I ought to be going,' she announced, picking up the collection of items she had with her all the time in the hospital.

'What *do* you carry around in there?' he asked with a mix of interest and amusement.

Her voice sounded strained now, all traces of the fun Jessica reined in and back behind her protective wall. 'I have my notebook and diary,' she began, looking down at the pile in her arms.

Gio listened as she told him about the information sheets, details of various diseases and injuries and their treatments, names and contacts for self-help groups and a welter of other things people might need. Her mobile phone, like her pager, was either attached to her waistband or in her pocket, depending on the clothes she was wearing. He suspected Jessica used the things she carried as a barrier, a shield between herself and others. He wanted to know why. The list of questions he had about her continued to grow.

Disappointment speared inside him as Jessica moved towards the door. 'Thanks for the chocolate.'

'Any time. I'll tell my secretary you have free access

to my secret drawer.' He smiled, drinking in his fill of her while he could. 'See you later. And try not to worry about your girl.'

'I'll try. Bye.'

The door closed softly behind her. At once the room felt different…and he felt lonely without the vibrancy of her presence. *Dio*. A week ago, if anyone had told him he'd be attracted to another woman, he would have believed it impossible. But Jessica had shaken him to his foundations—and out of the darkness that had enveloped his life for the last five years.

'Megan, are you all right?'

'Yes.' It was a lie, but she managed a smile for Jess. 'I'm sorry, I was miles away.'

Her friend sent her an understanding smile. 'Josh?'

'Yes,' Megan repeated, a deep sigh escaping.

It had been a huge shock to discover that Josh had joined the St Piran's trauma team back in the spring. Megan had assumed he was still in London. Wished he *was* still in London. Working with him when she was on call to A and E from Paediatrics was difficult and she had found it harder still since little Toby's funeral.

'He wants to talk,' Megan confided, her recent confrontation with Josh in the canteen still fresh in her mind. Why did he want to rake over the past? Did he think she didn't live with it every day of her life?

'Would talking to Josh be such a bad thing?'

Megan's stomach churned in response to Jess's softly voiced question. Her friend knew there was past history with Josh, but Megan hadn't divulged any details. She had never told anyone what had happened. She felt too guilty, too confused, too stupid, too hurt.

'What's the point?' Bitterness laced her voice but she was unable to soften it. 'It's over. Done. What good would be served stirring it up eight years on?'

'Perhaps *you* need to talk as much as Josh thinks *he* does,' Jess suggested, confusing her more.

Megan frowned. 'What do you mean?'

'It's clearly still causing you heartache. Things are unresolved in your own mind.' Jess paused a moment, her dark green gaze direct. 'Forget Josh and his reasons for wanting to talk. Think about yourself. Do *you* have questions that need answering before you can put things behind you once and for all?'

Too many to count, Megan allowed silently, one hand unconsciously moving to press against the flatness of her belly, a wave of pain rolling through her at all that was lost—all that Josh had taken from her. The thought of facing him after eight years was too scary to contemplate.

'Maybe, but—' Megan broke off, uncertain and indecisive.

'But?' Jess probed gently.

'Seeing him again hurts so much and has brought back so many difficult memories.' She bit her lip, ashamed that she had been so foolish over Josh—and that part of her remained drawn to him, despite everything that had happened. 'I'm so angry with him, Jess. And with myself. Yes, there are things I want to know, but I'm not sure I can cope with what he has to say.'

'Only you can decide if finding out what you need to know will help you find peace with the past.'

Megan nodded. Her friend's words made sense. She just wasn't sure what to do. The fact that Josh now had a picture-perfect wife, aside from causing her added pain and distress, complicated things even more. Although the body language she had witnessed between him and his beautiful wife, Rebecca, suggested that things might not be right in Josh's marriage, he *was* married, so having contact with him beyond the professional was inappropriate.

'It scares me, Jess.'

Her words whispered from her as she faced the awful truth—underneath the pain, anger and betrayal, a spark of the elemental chemistry still burned. She was as vulnerable to him as she had always been.

'Emotions are complicated and the dividing line between love and hate can be wafer thin.' Jess's pager sounded and she glanced at it, a faint blush colouring her cheeks. 'Sorry, Megan, I have to go.'

'Problems?'

Jess shook her head. 'It's time for the neurosurgery case meeting. Gordon Ainsworth and, um, Gio, asked me to attend,' she explained, gathering up her things. Pausing, she smiled. 'Think things over. If you need to talk, you know it will remain confidential between us.'

'Thanks, Jess.'

'Take care, Megan. And good luck.'

Megan watched the other woman walk away, her vibrant auburn hair restrained in a plait. Recalling her friend's blush, and thinking about the electric atmosphere she had noticed whenever Jess and Gio were together, she wondered if something was brewing there. It would be wonderful to see Jess happy. She was so private, and always seemed so alone. Megan shook her head, realising how alike they were. She respected Jess, and trusted her, and she knew how lucky she was to have her to talk to.

Unfortunately, her friend couldn't tell her what to do. No one could. Decisions about Josh, and whether to face the past, were hers alone.

Gio stepped into the warmth of the August evening. Dusk was falling, and he glanced up at the darkening sky, expelling a sigh. He'd been called in earlier that Saturday evening after Josh O'Hara's concern had grown about a man who had collapsed while on an outing to the beach with his wife. Further tests, including CT and MRI scans, had revealed that the man had a tumour growing in his brain, affecting his optic nerve and sensory centre. Surgery was scheduled for Monday.

The man and his wife would benefit from Jessica's input. He'd speak with her on Monday. Which was nearly thirty-six hours away and too long to wait, especially as he hadn't seen her since the previous afternoon, when she had attended what would become a regular Friday meeting for the neurological unit. Her presence had been beneficial to the team—but distracting for him on a personal level. He shook his head. Until a few days ago he hadn't *had* a personal level.

Confused that his life had turned upside down, he walked towards the almost deserted consultants' car park. The previous night had been the first when they'd not met up for an end-of-the-day chat. Jessica had been unable to come because she volunteered for the Samaritans and spent several hours there each Friday evening. He wasn't surprised. Once more she was devoting her time to other people's problems. Was it a way of avoiding her own?

In the car, he leaned back and rested his head, reflecting on how long and lonely the weekend was becoming without Jessica. He swore softly to himself. What a sorry state he was in. Part of him rebelled. He didn't want any new woman in his life. Or so he had thought until Jessica. Now he couldn't stop thinking about her or wanting to be with her. He wanted to learn her secrets and encourage the real Jessica out from behind her defensive wall. Was he the only one to notice the loneliness and hurt that lurked in the depths of her beautiful green eyes?

Starting the engine, he reversed out of his parking space, his gaze straying to the psychology building.

'What the hell?'

He braked, letting the powerful engine idle as he observed the light that shone from Jessica's office window. The rest of the building was in darkness. Had she forgotten to switch off the light the day before? He saw a flicker of movement inside and cursed. Jessica was here? *Now?* Returning his car to its parking space, he switched off the engine, climbed out and locked the door.

As he walked towards the building he reflected on Jessica's odd behaviour and her reluctance to let him see inside her office. He'd brushed it off as a quirk, but her furtiveness made him certain that something more was going on and he couldn't let this go.

Frowning, he remembered when he'd visited her office. She'd rushed home to meet her insurance company's assessor and he'd forgotten to ask why. Was something seriously wrong?

The outer door of the psychology building was locked, but his swipe card and ID code gained him access. Relocking the door, he made his way through the darkened foyer and down the corridor to Jessica's room. It was uncharacteristic for him to be impolite but, not wanting to give her time to shut the door in his face, he checked to see if it was unlocked. It was. He gave a sharp rap and swung the door open, astonished at the scene that greeted him.

Jessica, bare-footed and dressed in a pair of cotton shorts and a sleeveless tank top, which emphasised her voluptuous curves and set his pulse racing, was sitting cross-legged on a blow-up mattress on the floor. A pillow and a few items of bed linen were folded at one end. For the first time, he saw her hair in all its heart-stopping glory as it fell around her shoulders, the curtain of copper-red and burnished chestnut curls enveloping her in a halo of fire.

But she was not alone. Her companions held him transfixed and momentarily speechless. Two small, playful kittens frolicked around her, Tabby balls of fluff on stubby legs and paws that looked too big for them. His gaze returned to Jessica. The smile had frozen on her face and panic was setting in.

Determined to discover what was going on, but not wanting to alarm her, he closed the door and crossed to her before she had time to get up. He dropped to his knees, sitting back on his heels, smiling as the kittens investigated him, sharp claws digging into his thighs as they used him as a climbing frame.

Gently, he slid a palm under each warm, rounded little body, lifting them close for a better view, seeing the similarities and differences in what were clearly siblings' faces. He loved animals, and would have surrounded himself with them, but Sofia had been allergic to several kinds of animals, making pets impossible.

Thinking of his beloved wife, taken from him so devastatingly five years before, brought the familiar pain and he closed his eyes, rubbing his face against the two fluffy animals, feeling the dual purrs vibrating against his hands.

Gio opened his eyes and focused on Jessica, who sat little more than a foot away, shocked to silence, a whole mixture of emotions chasing themselves across her expressive green eyes. Turning the kittens so they were facing her, he held them against his chest, enjoying their softness and the feel of their heartbeats.

'What are their names?'

His question apparently threw her because she stared at him for several moments as if expecting him to launch into an interrogation. She bit her lip, diverting his attention to the tempting swell of her mouth. As she sucked in a breath, his gaze rose to clash with hers once more.

'Th-that's Dickens,' she finally informed him, her voice unsteady and her hand shaking as she pointed to the kitten in his left hand, which had a dark face, pink nose and round green eyes, not unlike her own in colour.

'And this one?' he asked of the kitten in his right hand, which had slanting, almond-shaped eyes in a darker shade than its sibling's.

'Kipling.'

She looked lost and alone so he handed Dickens to her, and she clutched him close as if needing the comfort.

'They are favourite authors of yours?'

Jessica nodded, her curls swaying like dancing flames. 'Partly. But also for their characters. They're very mischievous and inquisitive. With him,' she continued, pointing to the kitten cradled in his hands, 'I kept thinking he's just so naughty, just so cute, just so everything, and so I thought of Kipling and his *Just So* stories.' She was still tense, but a smile tugged her mouth as she looked at the kitten she held. 'This one was into everything and I was always asking what the dickens he was up to. The names stuck.'

'How long have you had them?'

'About six weeks. Their mother was an unknown feral stray who had a litter in the barn on a farm near my cottage,' she told him, relaxing a little. 'Flora, who lives there, and who is a nurse at the doctors' surgery in Penhally, isn't sure what happened to the mother, but the kittens were abandoned and Flora took care of them. She couldn't keep them all and was looking for homes for the others. I took these two.'

'What happens to them during the day?' he asked, intrigued how she had organised things.

'They stay with Sid Evans—he's the hospital handyman.' Gio nodded, confirming he knew of the man. 'He lost his wife recently and I've spent some time chatting to him,' Jessica continued, although he was unsurprised to learn of her kindness. 'He was very down and told me he wasn't allowed pets at his flat. So I asked the hospital management if he could have the kittens in his work room during the day and they said yes.' A warm smile curved her mouth. 'Sid loves having them.'

'I'm sure he does.' He admired her even more for her thoughtfulness. He also suspected that Jessica had set things up so that Sid felt valued, believing he was doing her a good turn. He was sure the hospital management didn't know where the kittens spent the night. 'How long have you been camping here?'

His question, getting to the core of the issue, had her tensing up again and she ducked her head, her hair falling forward, hiding her face.

'Talk to me,' he encouraged softly. With one finger beneath her chin, he urged her to look up again. 'What's going on, Jessica?'

Very conscious of Gio's touch, Jess trembled. The pad of one finger, that was all, and yet her whole body felt alive, charged and vitally aware of him. It was so long since she'd been touched…at least before this week when Gio had done so several times, stirring up desires she'd managed to banish for the last four years. But she had to quash the yearnings Gio had reawakened because he—like everyone else—was out of bounds. Steeling herself, she drew back enough to break the physical connection, concerned how much she missed the contact.

In shock from Gio's sudden arrival, fear built now that one of her secrets, albeit the least monumental and important of them, had been discovered. She didn't want to tell him anything but how could she bluff her way out? Even if she could excuse the kittens, the damning evidence of the makeshift bed was impossible to explain away.

'Jessica?'

'I, um, recently moved into my cottage,' she began shakily, unsure how much to tell him. 'The storm ten days ago destroyed the roof, causing water damage and the electricity being shut off. I tried to say there anyway…'

'Dio! With no power and no roof?' he exclaimed, muttering something uncomplimentary in Italian.

Jess lowered her gaze. 'It was only one night. I was

concerned for the kittens,' she explained, failing to add that not only had it been miserable with no electricity or hot water but that she'd been spooked in the isolated cottage with no security.

'So you've been staying here since then?'

'Yes,' she admitted with reluctance.

She couldn't help but be mesmerised by the way Gio continued to stroke Dickens, his fingers sinking into the soft fur. The kitten was enjoying it if his purrs were anything to go by. It made her think dangerous and never-to-be-allowed things…like how it would feel to have Gio's fingers caress *her* body from top to toe. She had no doubt she'd be purring, too.

Looking down lest he read anything in her eyes, Jess struggled to push her wayward thoughts away because no matter how much she may crave his touch, it wasn't going to happen.

'Why here, though?' Gio's voice reclaimed her attention. 'Why not stay at a hotel…or with friends?'

She fudged an answer, mumbling about the need to keep the kittens with her and everywhere being fully booked at the height of the season, because no way was she going to tell him the truth about the sorry state of her finances or that she didn't *have* any friends. Not the kind she could stay with, anyway. To explain either would involve the impossible—revealing what she could never reveal…*why*.

Why she had crashed and burned so badly…

Why her life had changed so drastically and irrevocably four years ago…

And why she was now counting the cost in so many ways, not just financially but professionally—hence her change of career and re-training in her mid-twenties to become a counsellor—and socially—keeping people at a distance and denying herself the closeness, emotional or physical, she had once enjoyed as a normal part of life. Nothing about her life these last four years had been normal. But she'd succeeded, she was coping...or had been until Gio had arrived, bringing home all she had lost and making her yearn for things she could never have again.

'It's only for a short while.' She crossed her fingers, hoping that was true. 'The insurance company have agreed to the repairs and the builders are starting work next week. As soon as possible, I'll move back in.'

'You can't stay here and live like this until then, Jessica,' he protested, clearly upset about the situation.

'It's not so bad,' she countered, trying for a carefree smile. 'I don't have any choice.'

'Of course you do.'

His words and the determined tone of his voice made her nervous. 'What do you mean?'

'As of now, you're moving in with me.'

the question.

CHAPTER SIX

UNOBSERVED, Gio leaned against the doorjamb and watched as Jessica carried out some graceful Tai Chi movements. She was dressed in a loose T-shirt, shorts that left shapely legs bare from mid-thigh down, and a pair of trainers, her vibrant curls restrained in a pony-tail. He never tired of looking at her. Taking a sip of his coffee, he waited for her to finish her routine.

It was the August bank holiday weekend and they both had two days off. Jessica had been in his house for two weeks. She'd protested, but there had never been any question in his mind about where she should stay. He couldn't let her camp in her office. She'd wanted to pay rent, he'd said no, but they'd compromised and she made a contribution towards food and supplies.

She'd also set rules. No touching. And nothing more than a platonic friendship. He'd agreed. Sort of. Temporarily. If setting them and keeping things on a friendly footing was what Jessica needed to begin with, he would play along. For now. That she'd felt the need to make rules at all proved she felt the same electric awareness he did.

He was using the time to gain Jessica's trust and continuing to get her used to his touch. He stopped the moment she withdrew or showed signs of disquiet. As the days went by, it was taking her longer to step away. He had yet to discover why she struggled so hard to deny the attraction.

Having coaxed her and the kittens home that Saturday night, the next day they had driven to her cottage. He'd grown up bilingual thanks to his parents and his American-born maternal grandmother, but, however fluent he was in English, he swore best in Italian and he'd unconsciously reverted to his native language as he surveyed the state of Jessica's home. It had been far worse than he'd imagined.

Built of stone and sitting in an isolated spot surrounded by untended land, the large cottage was single storey. The thatched roof and rotten rafters had collapsed inwards, wrecking several rooms beneath, letting in the rain and rendering the place uninhabitable. He'd seen the promise, had visualised the picture-book traditional cottage as it would be when it was finished, but that Jessica had tried to stay in what was little more than a ruin had astounded him.

Turning round, he'd seen the pained expression on Jessica's face, and realised the effect his rant was having on her. Reverting to English, he'd gentled his tone and closed the gap between them. His nature was to touch, to hug, to comfort, and it had been difficult to stop himself from drawing her into his arms.

Slowly he'd raised one hand and cupped her cheek, marvelling at the peachy softness of her skin. 'I'm sorry. I was not shouting at you, just at the state of the place and knowing someone would sell it to you in such a perilous condition.'

Some of the tension had drained from her, and for

a second she'd leaned into his touch. He'd brushed the pad of his thumb across the little hollow between her chin and her mouth, watching as her lips had parted instinctively and her eyelids lowered in response. She hadn't actually purred like one of the kittens, but her reaction had been unmistakeable. He'd so wanted to kiss her, but the moment had ended as she'd withdrawn into herself, turning her head away to break the contact.

'If the cottage had been in better condition I couldn't have afforded it,' she'd told him. 'I knew the roof was dodgy...' She'd given a wry laugh as she'd looked at the blue sky visible between what remained of the rotten rafters. 'I didn't expect it to cave in with the first storm.'

He'd never had to worry about money, and he knew how lucky he was, never taking things for granted. The business had made his family wealthy and money cushioned many blows. Except grief. Nothing eased the pain of that, but at least he'd been in a position to fund the trust in Sofia's name and help other people. He hated to think of Jessica struggling to make ends meet, and wondered why she had apparently sunk every penny she'd had into such a run-down, if potentially lovely, cottage, with no money left over to furnish it...or why she hadn't stayed in a hotel when she'd been forced to vacate it. Why had she been so insistent on buying outright rather than taking a small mortgage or personal loan to leave her some working capital?

For now Jessica and the kittens were living with him. Having been alone for five years, he'd been nervous of her moving in but it felt scarily *right*. They fitted. As this was the first time he'd been attracted to another woman, he'd struggled with feelings of disloyalty. Something

Sofia would chastise him for, having made it clear she didn't want him to remain alone.

Living with someone revealed so much about them and unearthed little ways and habits previously unsuspected and which could be irritating out of all proportion. So far he'd not discovered anything annoying about Jessica but there were several things that intrigued and amused him. One was the collection of assorted vitamin and dietary supplements she had stacked at one end of the kitchen worktop. He had no idea what they were for or why she felt she needed them. She was fastidious about washing up any of the crockery or cutlery she used, sorting them into a neat pile separate from his.

'Do you have a hygiene fetish?' he'd asked with a chuckle that first weekend, but his humour had rapidly faded given her reaction.

'No, of course not.'

The words of denial had been accompanied by a forced, hollow laugh, but it had been the unmistakeable hurt mixed with alarm and embarrassment in her eyes that had grabbed him.

'I didn't mean to upset you,' he'd apologised softly.

'You haven't.'

It had been a lie, he knew it. Just as he knew that something about what he had said or how he had said it had stung her.

The more he observed about her, including her anxiety at touching and being touched, the more he wondered if she'd experienced a bad relationship. Had someone criticised her, controlled her or, what he most feared, hurt and abused her?

Jess pivoted on one leg, turning her body in his direction, and he stifled a laugh when she spotted him, her eyes widening in surprise as she missed her step and stumbled momentarily before regaining her balance.

'Hi,' she murmured, embarrassment now predominant in her olive green eyes.

'Morning.' He straightened as she approached him warily, always keeping that extra bit of distance. 'Are you done?'

The fingers of one hand tucked stray wisps of hair back from her face. 'Just about. Why?'

'I have something to show you. Come with me.'

'Where are we going?' Jess asked as Gio drove away from the house.

'I can't tell you.'

She frowned at his unsatisfactory response. 'Why not?'

'Because then it would not be a surprise, would it?' he reasoned with calm amusement.

With no information forthcoming, Jess rested back in the luxurious seat of the sleek sports car. She hated to admit how much of a thrill she got each time she rode in it. As Gio turned out of the drive and onto the B-road that hugged the coastline on its route to St Piran, Jess glanced across the fields to the house she had been living in for the last fortnight. How could she feel so comfortable and yet scared at the same time?

The house sat atop the cliff as if carved from the bedrock and perfectly suited its Cornish name, *Ninnes*, 'the isolated place'. At first glance it suited Gio, too—wild, remote, alone.

'It's very impressive,' she'd murmured when she had first seen inside the architect-designed property. It didn't feel like a home. Clinical, cold, unlived in, it was like a set from an interior design magazine.

'Now tell me what you really think,' Gio had invited with a smile. 'It is soulless, no? A show-house, not a home,' he added, mirroring her own thoughts. 'The agent instructed to rent a place for me must have imagined someone moving from London would like it.'

'And you don't?' she'd asked, relieved this was not what he would have chosen for himself.

'No. But it gives me time to find something I *do* want and at least I have a roof over my head in the meantime.'

A laugh had burst from her at his unintentional choice of words and the expression on his face as the reason for her reaction dawned on him...she was there because she currently did *not* have a roof over hers!

Judging by the tone of his tirade when he had seen the state of her cottage, it had been worse than he'd expected. Had the property been in better condition, it would have been way beyond her budget, even with the unexpected legacy that had allowed her to step onto the housing ladder. But she had fallen in love with the place, and its parcel of neglected land that would allow her to have more animals and grow her own produce.

That Gio had seen the potential in the cottage had pleased her, and telling him about her plans for the place had diverted him from his questions about her reasons for not taking out a mortgage or personal loan. Either would have enabled her to get on with the renovations and furnishing the house straight away, but when she had looked into funding she had been asked questions about herself that she'd no wish to answer—and which may have meant she'd have been turned down anyway. She couldn't explain that to Gio without explaining *why*. And that was impossible.

So she had succumbed to Gio's arguments and the shameful temptation of moving in with him. Dickens and Kipling were in heaven. She was halfway between heaven and hell. They'd settled into a routine, their friendship becoming closer every day. Contrarily, his agreement to her rules and conditions had brought an inner stab of disappointment, though she knew friendship was all they could ever share.

Her hormones raged in protest, and she had to fight her attraction to him. Keeping people at a safe distance had become ingrained within her these last four years, but Gio was breaching her defences. He made her want things she could no longer have, reminding her of broken dreams and abandoned hopes.

'Jessica?'

'Mmm?' She blinked as Gio's voice impinged on her consciousness. 'Sorry, did you say something?'

He chuckled. 'Several times, but you are living with goblins! That is the saying, yes?' he added as she stared at him blankly.

'Sorry?' she repeated, confused for a moment before realisation dawned. 'Oh! You mean away with the fairies! No, I was just thinking.' A flush warmed her cheeks. No way could she tell him where her thoughts had really been.

'We are here,' he said now, switching off the engine.

They were at the harbourside in St Piran, Jess discovered, scrambling out of the car before Gio could come round and offer a hand to help her. The less she touched him, the better. He took some things from the car, including a picnic basket, handing her a canvas bag with towels, spare T-shirts and some sunscreen. Apprehension unsettled her. She hadn't realised this was a day's outing.

Her gaze feasted on the sight of him dressed in deck shoes and shorts that left well-defined muscular legs bare from mid-thigh downwards. His torso was encased in a white T-shirt that emphasised the tone of his skin and hugged the contours of his athletic body. Jess bit her lip to stop a sigh of appreciation from escaping

'Have you been on a boat before?' he asked, guiding her towards a jetty along which several very expensive-looking craft were moored.

'Only a car ferry.'

His throaty laugh stole her breath. 'This isn't quite the same.'

Jess gathered that as he halted by a huge, gleaming, red-and-white speedboat. 'Oh, my.'

She gazed at the boat in awe, excitement mounting as she anticipated what it would feel like to ride in the kind of jet-powered boat she'd seen offshore racing on television. The name *Lori* was written on the side and she wondered at the significance.

'My one indulgence…apart from my car,' he told her with a touch of embarrassment.

'It's beautiful.' She smiled, imagining the thrill of speeding across the waves. 'How long have you had it?'

Relaxing, as if relieved at her reaction, he smiled the rare, special smile that reached his eyes, banishing the shadows that often lurked there and trapping the breath in her lungs. 'About eighteen months. I could not get out often when I was in London and she was moored on the south coast, but I hope to use her often here.'

Gio climbed aboard with practised ease, set down the items he was carrying and turned to help her. Jess swallowed. Adopting avoidance tactics, she gave him her bags instead of her hand.

'I can manage,' she told him, cursing the way he quirked an eyebrow and watched with amusement as she scrambled inelegantly over the side.

To her surprise, the luxury powerboat had a small but fully equipped cabin below, with a tiny kitchen, a minuscule washroom and a seating area that converted into a sleeping space for three people. They'd have to be very friendly, Jess thought. After putting the picnic items in the fridge, they went back outside and Gio collected two life-jackets from a locker.

'Are these necessary?' Jess asked as he handed one to her.

'Absolutely.' He fastened his in no time. 'I would never take risks with your safety.'

She knew that. They might not have known each other long but she trusted him implicitly. It was herself she worried about, she thought wryly as she struggled with the life-jacket, huffing with frustration as it defeated her.

'Here,' Gio chuckled, closing the gap between them. 'Let me help.'

'It's OK...'

Her protest fell on deaf ears as he took over. Did he need to touch her that much? Or so slowly and intimately? And he was far too close—so close that every breath she took was fragranced with his musky male scent, weakening her resolve and tightening the aching knot in the pit of her stomach. She couldn't stop breathing so she closed her eyes and tightened her hands into fists, praying for the exquisite torture to be over and reminding herself why she couldn't succumb to temptation. He was taking longer than necessary, surely, the brush of his fingers burning her through the fabric of her T-shirt.

'All done.'

His voice sounded huskier than usual and she opened her eyes to find herself staring directly into his. A tremor ran through her at the sensual expression he made no attempt to mask. Her body craved his touch, making it difficult for her to keep her distance, to step back now as she knew she must.

As if anticipating her retreat, he released her and moved away, but not before he dropped a kiss on the tip of her nose. Confused, Jess remained motionless for several moments. The tip of her nose felt warm and tingly…nothing to do with the late August heat and everything to do with the brush of his lips on her skin.

Why had he done that?

Why had she let him?

Panic welled within her. Maybe it would be best if she got off the boat now, before she did anything even more stupid. But while she was wrestling with indecision, considering her options, Gio effectively removed them by untying the moorings and firing the boat into life.

He settled her in the padded horseshoe-shaped seat adjacent to his, then he was manipulating the controls, inching the boat into the main harbour towards the open sea. The twin engines throbbed with leashed power, straining for freedom. Despite her uncertainties, a new burst of excitement coursed through her.

'I hate to confine your incredible hair, but you might want to tie it back—or I can lend you a baseball cap,' Gio said as the harbour entrance approached.

Taking his advice, she accepted the cap he offered, pulling her untamed curls back into a ponytail before feeding it through the slot in the back of the cap. The brim helped shade her eyes from the August sunshine.

'Hold on.'

Jess felt her heart thudding with excitement as they reached open water and gained speed, going west along the coast from St Piran. The sea was calm but the bow of the boat rose up and rode the crests and troughs. Gio opened the throttle and a whoop of joy escaped her. She felt free, truly understanding how he felt and how this blew away tensions and stresses.

'This is incredible!' She laughed, raising her voice so Gio could hear her above the noise of the engines, the whoosh of the wind and the sound of the boat hitting the water. She tilted her head back and closed her eyes, savouring the sun on her skin, the occasional salty spray and the sense of speed. 'It's amazing! I love it.'

Lying face down on a towel stretched out on the sand in the secluded cove they had discovered, Jessica stretched and sighed. 'I could get used to this.'

Gio smiled. She sounded sleepy and contented fol-lowing their exhilarating morning flying across the waves. They had travelled miles, moving from the bay in which St Piran stood, through Penhally Bay and past the village of Penhally itself, with its horseshoe-shaped harbour and the rocky promontory at one end, off which,

Jessica had told him, lay the wreck of an old Spanish galleon.

They had headed part of the way back before finding their cove. After a swim, they had enjoyed their picnic lunch. As Jessica relaxed, he finished his apple, his gaze straying over her deliciously curvy figure. She had pulled her shorts on over her one-piece costume but that didn't spoil his view. Everything male in him responded to her voluptuous femininity. And her hair continued to captivate him. Freed from the cap, it seemed alive in the sunlight, the strands fanning across her shoulders like tongues of fire.

Her delight at the boat made Gio glad he'd brought her. He'd had doubts. He'd never taken anyone out with him before. Time on the boat was guarded jealously. It was his escape, his retreat, his guilty pleasure, and he'd been worried...not that Jessica wouldn't enjoy it but that having anyone with him would detract from what he gained being alone on the water. The desire for Jessica's company proved how fully she had breached his defences in the weeks since they'd met. Today he'd discovered that sharing the boat with her made the experience better than before.

'Why is your boat called *Lori*?'

Jessica's softly voiced question made him tense. She was looking at him through those sexy green eyes, and he dragged his gaze free, staring out to sea. Maybe it was time to tell her about Sofia. If he wanted Jessica to trust him and share the secrets that held her back from relationships with people, then he had to trust her, too. Which meant placing his broken heart in her hands. He cleared his throat, the emotion building before he even begun to speak.

'Lori was my wife's nickname,' he began, hit by a wave of memories. 'In Italy it is common to shorten someone's surname to use as a derivative. Sofia's maiden name was Loriani…to friends she was Lori. At school everyone called us "Lori and Cori".' A smile came unbidden. 'We used the names for each other into adulthood.'

Jessica's smile was sweet, interest and understanding in her eyes. 'That's lovely. You'd known each other a long time?'

'Since we were six.'

'Six?' she exclaimed with surprise. 'Wow!'

'Sofia's *mamma*, Ginetta, came to work for my parents,' he continued. 'She lived in, originally caring for the house—and me—while my parents worked long hours with the business. Ginetta rapidly became indispensable, and she and Sofia were soon part of the family.'

Gio paused and took a drink of water. 'Sofia and I were the same age and were friends from day one. We scarcely spent a day apart. Many people believed we'd go our separate ways with time, but it never happened. It wasn't something we planned.' He frowned, trying to find the best way to explain. 'We just never wanted anyone else, you know?' Jessica nodded and turned more towards him. 'We married at eighteen. I did my medical training and Sofia trained to be a teacher. Throughout everything we remained best friends.'

'Soul mates,' Jessica added, her voice husky.

'Yes.'

Leaning back on his elbows, enjoying the feel of the sun against his skin, he found himself telling her all kinds of stories as happy memories flowed so quickly it was difficult to catch hold of them.

'We were in no hurry to start a family of our own. Being together was all we wanted. We thought we had time...but it ran out,' he added, choking on the words.

'What happened, Gio?'

Jessica's whispered query took him back into the darkness. Voice thick, he told her of the moment they had found out that Sofia was dying.

'It is ironic, no, that Sofia should be struck down by the kind of brain tumour I now operate on often?' He heard Jessica's shocked gasp, aware that she was sitting up but too lost in his thoughts to stop now. 'Sofia's tumour was inoperable. It was virulent and resistant to treatment, claiming her quickly.'

What he didn't add aloud was how guilty he felt. And that he couldn't forgive himself for being unable to save her, tormenting himself as he relived those terrible weeks...to the signs he must have missed and failing to catch the tumour early enough to make a difference. His head knew it wasn't true, Sofia's doctors had told him time and again that it wouldn't have made a difference, but still he wondered and beat himself up over his failings.

'Gio, you're not in any way to blame.' Jessica was closer, he could feel her behind him, feel the kiss of her breath against his shoulder as she spoke, her voice gentle but firm. He heard the emotion she was keeping in check as she continued. 'It is too unspeakably cruel, for Sofia and for you.'

'I wish I had her courage. She faced death with the same warmth, bravery, humour and gentleness of spirit with which she embraced life. I was at her side every second of her brief but futile fight, and I was holding her hand when she took her final breath.'

His colleagues and the staff who had cared for her had left him alone with her. For the first time in his adult life, he had wept—for Sofia and for himself. And then he had shut down a significant part of himself, closing off his heart because it was the only way he could cope with going on alone. As he had somehow emerged from the blackest of days after her loss, he had thrown himself into his work, into making himself better, and in trying to stop others dying the way Sofia had.

'Life was nothing without her. We'd been inseparable for twenty-one years. I felt lost, cast adrift,' he admitted, the emotion catching up with him.

'Gio…'

Jessica came up onto her knees behind him and wrapped him in her arms, shocking him. Full, firm breasts pressed against his back and, as she rested her head on his shoulder, he felt her tears against his skin. As he drew in another unsteady breath, it was fragranced with the subtle aroma of her chocolate-scented shampoo and body lotion. Drawing on her comfort, he raised his hands, finding hers and linking their fingers.

'You worked so you wouldn't think,' she said, her voice throaty with emotion.

'Yes.' She understood, he suspected, because she did the same, focusing on other people's problems to escape her own.

'And the trust you told me about…'

'I set it up in Sofia's name, funding research, raising money to provide scanners and equipment for hospitals around the world and providing information and support for those struck down by neurological conditions, especially tumours.'

'Sofia would be so proud of you.'

'She would also be kicking me for not getting on with life,' he added wryly.

'But you have,' Jessica protested. 'You did what you needed to do for you and you've helped countless others through very difficult times.'

Her generosity touched him. And he savoured the closeness and physical contact, hoping Jessica would not suddenly remember her no-touching rule and take flight.

He took a deep breath, feeling calmer, telling Jessica of his discovery of the album Sofia had made of their lives, packed with photos and letters and memorabilia from childhood, through their wedding and to their last days together. He treasured it. It gave him solace, made him grateful that she'd been his life, but it also made him grieve for what would never be. Sofia was the only woman he had ever loved, the only woman with whom he had ever *made* love. In the last five years his bed had felt too big and cold and lonely, but nothing and no one had ever tempted him.

Until Jessica.

As Gio fell silent, Jess thought over all he had told her, feeling devastated for him and his wife. Many times she had wondered about the woman who had claimed Gio's heart. Sofia. She envisaged a glamorous, beautiful woman with a model-like figure. Whatever she had looked like, Sofia had been lucky to win Gio's love, devotion and loyalty. And cruelly unlucky to have been taken from him at such a young age.

Gio's fidelity and love for Sofia was in stark contrast to the thoughtlessness and infidelity shown by Duncan, Jess's ex-fiancé and the man who had changed her life for ever. Discovering Duncan had been unfaithful on too many occasions to count had been hurtful and shocking enough. Being eight weeks away from the wedding she had dreamed of for so long had made it worse. The wedding had never taken place. And the dream would now never come true for her.

There were so many things Duncan had taken from her, including her trust in people. And herself. Her life had changed beyond recognition. Her fiancé—*ex-fiancé*, she corrected with the anger and bitterness that had never left her—had seen to that.

The thought of never being close to anyone again was depressing, so she kept busy and absorbed helping others so that she had no time to think of herself. So she understood Gio's need to lose himself in work after such a heart-wrenching loss. That he blamed himself was terrible, and yet driving himself as he had meant he had given hope, care and fresh chances to his patients. Patients he tried so hard to save as he had not been able to save Sofia.

Her situation was different but the outcome had been similar. A lonely life devoting herself to caring for others. Now and again, in a weak moment, a stray thought crept in. A yearning for intimacy. Not even sex…just a need to be held and cherished. As she and Gio were holding each other now.

The reality of it was a shock. She'd acted on instinct in response to his pain, forgetting the need to keep distance between them. Now, pressed against him, her arms around his shoulders and their hands locked together, she battled the awareness and desire that were coursing through her.

How she wished she could satisfy the urge to bury her face more fully into his neck and breathe in his scent…the earthy aroma of man mixed with the subtle but arousing fragrance of his soap and warm, sun-kissed skin. It was crazy! But everything in her was drawn to him on some basic level. She couldn't give in to it. To do so would involve telling him her secrets and she couldn't do that. If she did, he would run in the opposite direction, just as everyone else in her life had done when they'd found out. She was tarnished, spoiled goods, untouchable. And she would do well to remember that when she indulged in any foolish notions about Gio.

Drawing in one last breath of his intoxicating, delicious scent, her desire for him threatening to melt her bones and turn her resolve to dust, she began to withdraw.

'I'm sorry, I shouldn't have done that,' she apologised, disconcerted when he kept hold of her hands.

'I'm not sorry.' He allowed her to place only a small distance between them before shifting so he was facing her. 'Thank you.'

Jess shook her head in confusion. 'I didn't do anything.'

'Yes, you did. You listened, you understood. You cared,' he added huskily, setting her heart thudding.

Knowing she was in big trouble, Jess sucked in a ragged breath, unable to drag her gaze free from the intensity of his. 'W-what are you looking at?' she finally asked, the electric tension increasing with every passing second.

'Your eyes.'

Jess frowned. 'What's the matter with them?'

'Nothing. They're beautiful.' He smiled, seeming closer than ever. 'This is the first time I've noticed the little specks of silver-grey in them.'

'Really?' Was that her voice sounding so breathless and confused?

'Mmm.' Blue eyes darkened as they watched her. 'I've meant to ask before…what is the gemstone in your earrings? They're the same shade as your eyes.'

Again he had thrown her and she tried to focus on his question and not on the affect of his nearness. 'Olive apatite. My grandmother had a passion for gemology and she gave them to me for my twenty-first birthday,' she told him, thinking with sadness and gratitude of the woman who had died the previous winter and whose unexpected legacy had enabled her to buy her cottage.

'They're perfect for you,' Gio told her, the approval and intimacy in his voice making her tingle all over.

Jess couldn't help but shiver as Gio ran the pad of one thumb along the sensitive hollow between her chin and her lower lip. She couldn't prevent her lips parting in response. It took a concerted effort not to sway towards him. Instead, Gio moved, oh, so slowly leaning in until warm supple lips met hers. Jess jumped. One of his hands still held hers and her fingers closed reflexively on his.

He tasted of things sinful, things long denied her but which she could know again if only she let go. Could she? Dared she? What if she did? How would she put the lid back on the box again afterwards? More than anything she wanted to forget common sense.

But she couldn't.

Gathering all the strength and willpower she could

muster, she turned her head away, breaking the spell. She heard his soft sigh, his smothered exclamation of regret and frustration, but she hardened her resolve. It was for the best, she told herself over and over again, hoping that repeating the mantra often enough would make her believe it. But the thought of telling him the truth made it easier.

The truth.

Her secret.

The one that hung over her like the sword of Damocles. Nothing could happen without him knowing—and once he knew, he would reject her anyway. Like everyone else. She valued his friendship too much to risk spoiling everything by giving in to a moment of madness, one she knew had no future to it.

'Jessica...'

'Please, Gio, don't,' she begged before he could continue. 'I can't. I'm sorry.'

His disappointment was clear, but he smiled, running one finger down her cheek. 'It's OK. I'm not giving up on you but there is no hurry. When you are ready, you will tell me...whatever it is.'

Jess had no reply to that, unable to imagine a time when she could ever reveal the truth to him.

'Friends, remember?' she said now, moving away and helping him pack their things ready to return to the boat for the journey home.

She'd told Gio to remember the rules, but she had been as guilty as him of ignoring them. With the boundaries becoming more and more blurred all the time, who most needed the instruction to behave...Gio or herself?

CHAPTER SEVEN

'MEGAN?'

Josh O'Hara looked at the fragile form of the woman who had caused much of the mental and emotional turmoil that had plagued him since he'd arrived at St Piran's and discovered her here. A blast from the past. One with which he'd never come to terms.

She turned around, her gaze scanning the A and E staffroom, and a frown formed as she realised they were alone. He felt uncertain and awkward as the silence stretched between them. They had been tiptoeing around each other for weeks now. He had questions that needed answers, but attempts to confront the past had been futile…meeting with hostility and denial.

Yet despite the dark cloud that hung over them, when Megan, as registrar on call, had come to A and E from Paediatrics, they'd worked well together and been attuned to each other. Now he had a rare window of opportunity to talk to her alone.

'Have you been in Cornwall all the time?' he asked, daring to venture onto dangerous ground.

Her gaze flicked to his and away again. 'Pretty much.'

At least she'd answered rather than walking out or telling him to back off. 'How is your grandmother?'

'She died three years ago.'

'I'm sorry.' Damn it, could he say nothing right to this woman? 'I know what she meant to you.'

Her small smile was tinged with sadness. 'I owe her everything.'

She'd told him once how her parents had been killed in a road accident when she'd been four and her grandmother had raised her. She'd not been in the best of health and Megan had been caring for her while going through medical school.

With Megan in a more conciliatory mood, he risked asking more of the questions that plagued him. 'Why here, Megan?'

'My grandmother lived in Penhally when she was young and she wanted to come home before she died. It seemed as good a place as any to be,' she finished, sounding so lost and alone that his heart ached for her.

He'd forgotten her grandmother's connection with Cornwall. Or had he? Was that why, when Rebecca had suggested leaving London, Cornwall had been the first place he had thought to go? Had he, some place deep in his subconscious, made the connection with Megan?

He remained as affected by her as he'd always been. The past would never go away. Neither could he change it. But he craved answers.

'I know you don't want to talk, and I won't ask again if that's what you choose, but I need to know, Megan—' He broke off, capturing her gaze, his heart in his mouth. 'Was the baby mine?'

He saw her shock and the pain his question caused as

she reeled back, anger replacing the hurt in her eyes. 'Of *course* it was yours. Don't judge me by *your* standards. *I* didn't sleep around.'

'Why didn't you *tell* me?' he demanded, his own hurt and anger rising with the confirmation of what he had known in his heart all along.

'How could I?' she threw back at him, her voice shaky with emotion. 'When was I meant to tell you? You refused to talk to me. And what good would it have done? What would *you* have done? You'd made it clear I meant nothing to you. You wouldn't have welcomed fatherhood…you never wanted children. Just as you rejected marriage—although *that's* changed in the last eight years.'

Pain and bitterness rang in her tone. Her accusations hurt…the more so because he recognised the truth in them. He *had* behaved badly. He'd been anti-marriage—for himself—and he'd never wanted children. Something he'd made clear to Rebecca from the first, and the reason why he was refusing her latest demands for a baby.

But he didn't want to think of Rebecca now. His thoughts were in the past. He'd had a right to know eight years ago. Hadn't he? Megan's challenge rang in his ears. What *would* he have done? He wasn't sure but it would undoubtedly have been the wrong thing. Avoidance of the truth. Running away. He'd been good at that. But knowing it *had* been his lifeless son he'd once held in his arms was devastating.

'You denied me any chance of making those decisions for myself.' The depth of his emotion shocked him and his voice was choked. 'You gave me no chance to say goodbye to my son.'

'You have a nerve. What chance did *you* give *me*

when you tossed me aside?' Tears gleamed on her lashes. 'You took my baby from me, Josh. And with him any chance of me having another child.'

'God, Megan. Those weren't my decisions.' His tone softened as her pain sliced through him. She looked more fragile than ever and he fought the urge to comfort her—something he should have done eight years ago.

Eight years…

He was plunged back to that terrible night when A and E had been in chaos following a multiple crash involving a coach of schoolchildren. He'd been a junior doctor facing something far beyond his experience as the paramedics had brought in a woman in the throes of a miscarriage and haemorrhaging terribly. Discovering it was Megan had thrown him.

'The obstetrician/gynaecologist did what was necessary to save your life. There wasn't even time to transfer you to Theatre.'

The possibility of Megan dying had been real. The surgeon had pulled the tiny baby from her body and given it to him. He'd stared at the lifeless form, too premature to survive, trying to work out dates with a brain that refused to function. A nurse had taken the baby away, and he'd been drawn back into the emergency procedure, assisting as the surgeon had made the decision to take Megan's womb.

'I asked him—*begged* him—to leave you hope for the future, but he was adamant there was no other way to stop you bleeding to death. What else could I have done?' he appealed to her, his stomach churning as he relived that awful night.

'I don't know.'

Tears ran down her cheeks and his heart, for so long

encased in a protective coating of stone, threatened to break at the depth of her sorrow and pain. He'd pushed the memories into the background, unable to deal with them. Megan had been living with them every day. He felt guilty, confused…

'What did you call him?' he asked, knowing he was tormenting them both but needing to know.

'Stephen.' Her voice was rough. 'After my father.'

'Thank you for telling me.'

They stared at each other, fighting the past, the pain, the memories—and the chemistry that, eight years on and despite all that had happened, still bubbled below the surface.

The sound of his pager announcing an incoming emergency cut through the tense silence, swiftly followed by the ring of Megan's pager, bringing their conversation to an end. Although he now had confirmation about the baby, a sense of unfinished business still remained.

Eight years ago he had known that Megan was different, had sensed she was dangerous to him. And he'd been right. The night he'd let down his guard had been the most amazing of his life. He'd told Megan things he had never told anyone else, and she had touched a place inside him in a way no other woman ever had. It had scared him. And he'd done what Megan had accused him of. He'd blanked her, keeping as far from her as possible because she'd burrowed under his skin.

If only he had been mature enough to know what he knew now. That the sort of connection he had found with Megan was rare. Not just the incredible physical passion that had overwhelmed them both but the deep mental and emotional union he'd experienced with no one but her. By the time he'd realised what he could have had and all he had thrown away, it had been too late.

He'd wobbled. Briefly. Then he'd gone on, focusing on his career and rapid advancement. Four years ago he'd met Rebecca and they'd seemed to want the same things, including no children. He'd cared about her, he'd been lonely and enjoyed having her to come home to. She'd wanted the doctor husband and the lifestyle. He'd convinced himself it was for the best, not the same as he'd had with Megan but safer.

Things had been wrong long before they'd left London. Bored, Rebecca had changed the rules, deciding she wanted a child. But as Izzy had said weeks ago when her daughter had been born, a child couldn't hold a bad marriage together and shouldn't be brought into the world for the wrong reasons. He wouldn't have a baby he didn't want with a woman he didn't love and who didn't love him.

Seeing Megan again, he saw with terrible clarity what he had thrown away, and he wished with all his heart that he had done things differently when he'd had the chance. As they walked down the corridor to the main A and E department, it occurred to him that he had still not asked Megan one of the questions that had been bugging him all along.

'Why *did* you stay the night with me, Megan?'

Her sharp intake of breath was audible, but she pushed through the swing doors into the busy department, bringing further discussion to an end. As he was directed to Resus, Megan was called to a treatment cubicle and she walked away from him without a backward glance. He had no more idea what to do about her—and his feelings for her—now than he had in the past. She was an itch under his skin that wouldn't go away, affecting him in the same unique way she had done eight years ago.

'Is there anything else I can do for you?' Jess asked, sitting beside the bed of the woman with whom she had spent a considerable amount of time over the last few days.

Faye Luxton, in her early seventies, had come in for a standard knee replacement but had suffered a severe bleed in her brain during her operation and had woken in Intensive Care to find her world turned upside down. She'd been handed over into Gio's care and, just days ago, he had needed to operate on a second bleed to remove a clot and also to put a coil around a small aneurysm that had threatened to enlarge and cause even greater problems.

Unfortunately, the damage already caused could not be reversed, although the numbness and weakness down one side of her body and her difficulty speaking were improving. Faye could still have a good quality of life, but she would no longer be able to live alone or care for herself and her animals.

With no family, Faye faced the horrible necessity of selling her much-loved home and moving into an assisted-care facility. Jess had helped support her when Social Services had come to discuss the options.

Faye had faced everything with courage, but had been distressed at times as she tried to come to terms with the drastic changes in her life. Jess had done all she could, helping Faye deal with the emotional upset.

'You've done so much.' Her speech was slow and

slurred, but clearer than it had been. 'I wouldn't have coped without you.'

'I'm sure you would. You have such a strong spirit, Faye. You've been a joy to care for and a real inspiration, too,' Jess assured her.

'I agree.'

Gio's voice sent a prickle of awareness along Jess's spine and she looked round, her gaze clashing with his as he strode through the door, his senior registrar, a couple of junior doctors and the ward's charge nurse trailing in his wake. Jess was all too conscious of Gio close beside her chair, blocking her exit, his leg and hip pressing gently against her, as he greeted Faye warmly.

'I'll step out,' Jess offered, making to rise.

'Can Jess stay?' Faye asked, looking unsettled.

Gio smiled at their patient. 'Yes, of course.'

Jess subsided back onto the chair as his hand came to rest on her shoulder. Although his attention was focused on the medical team updating him on Faye's condition, his hand lingered, and Jess felt the fire in her blood as his touch warmed her through the fabric of her shirt. His fingers gave a gentle squeeze before he released her and reached out for Faye's notes.

They were halfway through September and while they'd been on their best behaviour since their bank-holiday outing in the boat, Jess was finding it difficult to ignore the electric buzz of attraction that intensified with every passing day. But she valued their friendship too much to risk losing her head and doing anything stupid.

They'd been out on the boat twice more and she loved it. Much to her amazement, Gio had also been teaching her how to drive it. The thrill had been so huge it had even managed to take her mind off his body pressed close to hers—and the divine male scent of him—as he'd helped her work the controls.

The tragedy of his wife's death still affected her and she remained shocked at the way she had acted on instinct in response to his grief. It had scared her. With Gio it was too easy to forget the hard lessons of the last four years.

Curious, Jess had steeled herself to ask Gio more about Sofia a couple of nights ago. Gio had brought out the album Sofia had made when she'd known she was dying, creating a story of their lives in words and pictures, and Jess had choked up all over again at the incredible bond they had shared and the cruel way they had been parted.

Sofia had been a surprise. Rather than being model thin and styled to perfection, she'd been small, curvy and very much the girl next door, possessing the kind of fresh-faced natural beauty that could never be faked and that shone through because of the person she was, in her laughing dark eyes, her smile and her obvious love for Gio. And his for her.

The photos of Gio and Sofia in their teens, so much together, so right for each other and so in love, had reminded Jess of Marcia and Colin—another young couple who had been ripped apart by terrible tragedy, and one she hadn't been able to get out of her mind.

'How are you feeling, Faye?' Gio asked, sitting on the edge of the bed and taking her good hand in his.

'I'm frustrated my body won't do what I want it to. I can't even tell you properly.' Faye shook her head. 'I can't imagine life away from my home and without my animals. I'm thankful for all you've done for me, but knowing things will never be the same is difficult.'

'Of course. It's hard enough to recover from surgery without having to come to terms with such unexpected changes. Things seem overwhelming, yes?' he sympathised, stealing Jess's heart as he took a pristine handkerchief from his pocket and wiped the elderly lady's tears with gentle care.

'Yes, exactly.' Faye visibly relaxed, soothed by Gio's attention. 'I'm old and set in my ways.'

Gio gallantly protested, making her smile. 'You're doing well and we will all do everything we can to ensure you regain as much strength and capability as possible.' The air locked in Jess's lungs as his gaze flicked to her. 'Jessica is here to help make the transition as trouble-free as possible.'

'I'm so worried about my animals, but Jess is marvellous,' Faye confided to Gio. 'If other arrangements can't be made to keep them together, she's promised she'll care for them herself.'

A blush warmed Jess's cheeks as Gio looked at her, his expression unreadable.

Gio talked with Faye awhile longer before rising to his feet. His entourage exited ahead of him but he lingered, and Jess excused herself from Faye, worried about his reaction to the animal thing.

'I was going to tell you, Gio. The workmen are making good progress on the cottage, and I'll arrange to have the fences dealt with. If the animals have to be moved before I'm back home, I'll ask Flora if she has room for them until I'm ready,' she rushed to reassure him. 'I don't expect you to house them or anything. I—'

Her rushed words were silenced as Gio pressed a

finger to her lips. 'Stop apologising.' Blue eyes twinkled with amusement and something else she couldn't discern but which made her warm and tingly and a little bit scared. 'I would have been surprised had you *not* offered to step in.'

'Oh...'

He glanced each way along the corridor, his tone conspiratorial as he leaned closer to her, making her quiver with awareness as his warm breath fanned her face. 'Shall I tell you a secret?'

She nodded, unable to answer, hardly able to breathe, fighting every urge within her to touch him, hug him, kiss him.

'I was going to make the same pledge to Faye myself.'

Jess blinked, his nearness robbing her of thought. 'You were?'

'I was.'

Jess felt mesmerised, her skin aflame as he ran one finger down her cheek. The suddenness of an alarm further along the corridor had her snapping back, conscious of where they were. Disconcerted by his touch, she stepped away. There was nothing she could do to escape the non-physical connection, the electrically charged one that bound her ever more tightly to him.

Gio's hand slowly dropped to his side and she swallowed as she met his gaze. He smiled, the full-on smile that stole her breath. 'I must go,' he said, glancing at his watch. 'We'll drive out to Faye's after work to talk with her neighbour and decide what is best to be done. OK?'

'OK.'

Jess watched as he strode off to join his team. How

was she going to cope when she moved back to her own cottage with the kittens? Gio had become far too important in her life.

'Stop the car!'

Gio reacted instantly to Jessica's cry, startled when she opened the door and scrambled out before they'd come to a stop. Cursing in Italian, he parked safely at the side of the road and climbed out in time to see Jessica running along the pavement and disappearing from view around a corner. Concerned, Gio jogged after her. What was earth going on?

They were in the centre of St Piran, on the way home following their visit to Faye's smallholding. Enquiries to several rescue centres had proved futile, which left them bemused and amused to find themselves foster-parents to a motley collection of animals. There were more than Gio had anticipated. He'd wanted animals, yes, but he hadn't imagined taking on so many in one go! Jessica's enthusiasm had swayed him, though.

Now, along with Dickens and Kipling, their menagerie included a donkey, two Gloucester Old Spot pigs, three sheep of mixed heritage and several assorted chickens. Faye's neighbour would care for them in the short term until the fencing at Jessica's cottage, and the necessary movement licences, were arranged. Gio didn't want to think about Jessica moving out—he had ideas but it was too soon to discuss them—but whatever happened between Jessica and himself, he intended to share the cost and responsibility for the animals.

Rounding the corner, he saw Jessica walking back towards him, her shoulders slumped, her steps reluctant as she kept pausing and looking behind her.

'What's going on?' he asked as he joined her.

She looked up, olive-green eyes despondent. 'I saw Marcia.' Again she scanned the crowds along one of St Piran's main shopping streets.

'The girl who gave you the false name after her boy-friend died?' he asked, frowning at her nod of confirma-tion. 'Are you still fretting about her?'

'Yes.'

She tried to carry everyone's problems on her own shoulders. 'Jessica...'

'I saw her, Gio. She looked so alone, so lost. The girl I met was prettily plump and well groomed,' she told him, clearly upset. 'She's put on weight and hasn't been taking care of herself. Her skin was grey and her hair lank and unstyled.' Again she met his gaze, and his chest tightened at the expression in her eyes. 'I can't help but worry about her.'

'You have a special empathy with people. But you can't solve everyone's problems, *fiamma*,' he advised her, the endearment—meaning flame in Italian—slipping out without conscious thought.

'I know that, but—'

As her defensive words snapped off, Gio cupped her face. 'Marcia knows where you are. If she needs you, she'll contact you in her own time. Everyone comes to terms with grief in their own way. Believe me, I know.'

Fresh tears stung Jessica's eyes as Gio's words hit home, pain for him mingling with her anxiety for Marcia. 'I'm sorry.'

'There's nothing to apologise for.' His smile was gentle, as was his touch.

Jess bit her lip, fighting the temptation, the *need*, to step closer, to press herself against him and be hugged… held in those strong arms. 'I'm OK,' she lied, stepping back and manufacturing a smile.

'Jess!' A female voice called her name and she looked round, smiling as she saw Kate Althorp approaching. 'Hello, my love.'

'Hi, Kate, how are you? And how is Jem?' She had spent many an hour talking with the older woman, especially when her son had been badly hurt in a car accident earlier in the year.

Kate's smile was free from the shadows Jess had seen there in the past. 'Jem's made a wonderful recovery. Thank you. And we're all well.'

'I'm so glad.' She was painfully conscious of Gio beside her and, when Kate looked at him expectantly, Jess had to introduce them. 'Kate, this is Gio Corezzi. He's a neurosurgeon and joined St Piran's in August,' she explained, her gaze flicking to him and away again. 'Gio, meet Kate Althorp. She's a midwife at the surgery in Penhally.'

Jess watched as the two shook hands and exchanged pleasantries, noting how Kate glowed when faced with Gio's natural charm and humour.

'What Jess has modestly left out, Gio, is how wonderful she has been to me,' Kate told him. 'She not only helped me a year ago when I had a scary brush with breast cancer, but she was an absolute rock when my son, Jem, broke his pelvis five months ago.'

'I didn't really do anything,' Jess murmured with embarrassment.

Kate waved her protest aside. 'What nonsense! I couldn't have got through it all without you, life was so difficult,' the older woman insisted, deepening Jess's blush and her discomfort. Kate smiled up at Gio. 'Jess is one in a million.'

'Yes…I know.'

Jess opened her mouth then closed it again, unsure what to say in response to Gio's husky words.

Kate chuckled, a twinkle in her brown eyes. She glanced at her watch and sighed. 'I'm afraid I have to run. There's so little time before the wedding and I have a million things to do. You are coming, aren't you, my love? I so want you to be there, it would mean so much to me. Bring Gio,' she added with a wink.

As Kate hurried off, Jess turned to walk back towards the car, but Gio surprised her, catching her hand and leading her in the opposite direction. 'This way.'

'Where are we going?' she asked, all too conscious of the way her fingers curled naturally with his.

'You're going to need a dress for the wedding and, as Kate said, there isn't much time.' He headed in the direction of one of St Piran's classy boutiques. 'We can take care of it while we are here.'

Jessica tried to dig her heels in. No way could she afford anything from that kind of shop. 'I'm not sure if I'm going to go,' she admitted, pulling on his hand.

'Not go?' He halted, an eyebrow raised in query as he looked at her. 'Why ever not?'

She attempted a careless shrug. He'd known about the wedding—the invitation had been propped on the mantelpiece in his living room for some time—but now he'd met Kate, it was more difficult to explain. It was one thing interacting with Kate at the hospital and quite another to move things into a social context. Jess didn't do social. Telling Gio that she felt too shy and nervous to go to the wedding on her own sounded far too pathetic.

'Kate wants you to be there,' he pointed out.

'Yes, but—'

'But nothing.' Gio forestalled further protests, the smile that curved his sexy mouth doing peculiar things to her insides.

'Gio,' she protested as he started them walking again.

'I'm going to buy you a frock for the wedding, to which I shall be honoured to escort you,' he informed her, shock rendering her temporarily compliant as he guided her along and halted outside the door of the boutique.

'Gio, you can't buy me a dress!'

'Of course I can!' He tweaked the tip of her nose between finger and thumb of his free hand.

Gazing at him in confusion, her skin tingling from his touch, she swallowed, all too conscious that this man was getting far too close. The walls she had constructed for her own protection felt increasingly vulnerable. And she was scared. Scared that if she continued to allow Gio to breach her defences and become more than a platonic friend, she would end up breaking her heart all over again.

And this time she might never recover.

CHAPTER EIGHT

IT WAS wonderful to see Kate so happy. Sitting with Polly d'Azzaro and a heavily pregnant Lucy Carter, in the garden of the beautiful granite-built barn a few miles outside Penhally that was now Kate's home, Jess watched the older woman mingle with her guests. She had a broad smile on her face, her brown eyes were alight with joy, and Nick, her new husband, was never far from her side.

St Mark's, Penhally's small church, had been bursting at the seams as people had come from far and wide to attend Nick and Kate's wedding. Nick's grown-up children from his first marriage had been there to support their father and give their blessing to Kate. And Kate's eleven-year-old son Jem, who had only recently discovered that Nick was his real father, had recovered well enough from his broken pelvis to proudly walk his mother down the aisle. A lump had formed in Jess's throat as Jem had stood with his half-brothers and -sister, watching his mother marry his father, publicly acknowledging him and making them one big united family at last.

Nervous about attending the party, Jess would never have come alone. Having Gio there made her feel better.

When they'd arrived at the barn, anxiety had gripped her as she'd faced the prospect of socialising with so many people. Unconsciously she'd moved closer to Gio. A moment later her right hand had been enveloped in his left one. Far from flinching away, or reminding him of the no-touching rule, her fingers had linked with his and held on tight.

Now, several hours later, after endless chat and laughter, an informal buffet, complete with hog roast and lashings of champagne, the dancing was soon to begin. Having enjoyed things more than she'd expected to— although she'd lost count of the number of times she'd explained she and Gio were just friends—the prospect of the live band and dancing into the evening was making her tense.

Jess's gaze strayed to Gio, who was deep in conversation with Polly's husband, Luca. Both Italian and with similar tragedies in their pasts, the two men had much in common. Luca was also Jess's GP.

'Gio's very handsome,' Polly commented, following the direction of her gaze.

'Mmm.' Jess hoped her murmur of agreement sounded noncommittal, even though her heart did somersaults every time she looked at him. He was always stunning but in his suit and tie he looked like a matinée idol. 'We're just friends.'

Polly's blue eyes were filled with understanding. 'That's a shame.'

'It's for the best.' Jess's words emerged as a whisper and, however much she wanted to deny it, even she could hear the regret in her voice.

'Is it?' Polly's smile was kind. As a fellow GP at Penhally surgery, Jess knew the other woman was speaking both as a doctor and a woman. 'Are you sure, Jess?'

She nodded, glancing at Polly before her gaze was drawn inexorably back to Gio. 'Yes.' Although it was getting harder and harder to believe it.

Before Polly could say any more, Nick and Kate passed on their way indoors to prepare for the first dance. Nick looked on with an indulgent and contented smile as Kate hugged Polly, whom, Jess had discovered, was Kate's god-daughter.

'We're so glad you and Gio came, Jess, and thank you so much for your lovely gift and the beautiful words in your card,' Kate told her, linking her arm through Nick's. 'You're looking gorgeous today.'

'Thank you,' Jess murmured, taken by surprise.

She was wearing the dress Gio had insisted on buying at the boutique in St Piran. Sleeveless and deceptively simple, it fell to her knees, highlighting her curves, the shades of teal and peacock green bringing out the colour of her eyes and highlighting the rich reds in her hair, now drawn back in a ponytail. She felt guilty for giving in to temptation—and Gio's persuasion—but the instant she had put the expensive dress on, she'd fallen in love with it. The desire and appreciation in Gio's eyes when he'd seen her in it had set her blood zinging in her veins.

'Enjoy yourselves,' Nick instructed with a benevolent smile before leading Kate away.

Gio and Luca returned, bringing non-alcoholic fruit punch with them, which both she and Polly accepted gratefully. She met Gio's gaze, her stomach muscles tightening at the expression in his intense blue eyes, her hand not entirely steady as she sipped the ice-cold drink.

Jess was about to tell Gio that she'd like to leave before the dancing began when Luca's twin daughters came running towards them. She'd been shocked when she'd heard how their mother had died giving birth to them. Now four and a half, they were adorable, so alike in looks but so different in character. It was the bolder, more outgoing Toni who arrived first.

'Mummy Polly?' she asked breathlessly.

'Yes, darling?'

'Rosie wants to know if she can have more cake.'

'Does she?' Jess saw Polly's lips twitch as she saw through the ruse. 'You can tell Rosie she can have a piece if she wants one.'

Toni's eyes widened and her mouth formed a silent O as she realised what had happened and tried to work out what to do about it. Gio and Luca both chuckled. Toni glanced round at her sister and then looked pleadingly up at her father, who hid his grin by taking a drink. The little girl's anxious gaze returned to Polly.

'Would *you* like another piece of cake, too, Toni?' she queried, unable to contain her amusement.

'Yes, please!' The relief on the child's face was so funny they all laughed.

'All right,' Polly agreed. 'You can both have one more *small* piece each.'

The little girl leaned in and kissed her stepmother soundly on the cheek. 'Thank you!'

As Toni ran off to join her quieter sister, Jess experienced for the first time the pressing weight of regret that she would never know the joy of motherhood. She hadn't thought of it much before. She'd never felt a maternal yearning, neither had she and Duncan ever discussed having a family.

Now, seeing the twins, she couldn't help but wonder what Gio's children would look like…although any idea of *her* ever being with him was pure fantasy. But it hit home that this was one more thing Duncan had taken away from her.

Gio was aware of the change in Jessica but was unsure of its cause. She put on a smiling face, but a light had dimmed in her eyes. He wanted to know what had happened. Unfortunately this was neither the time nor the place to ask. He was proud of her. She'd been nervous and uncomfortable about the party, even before she had clung so tenaciously to his hand when faced with the throng of guests. But she'd gradually relaxed, especially when the d'Azzaro family had taken them under their collective wings.

He'd enjoyed himself, too. Much of that had been simply being with Jessica, but he'd also been pleased to meet Luca. Discovering that Luca's life had mirrored his own in many ways had given him much to think about, especially seeing how Luca had been able to move on to find love and happiness with Polly.

'It wasn't easy,' Luca had told him. 'For so long I lived only for my girls. I'd not even looked at anyone else after Elaine died and I never expected to love again. Then I met Polly.' His smile and tone of voice had revealed his emotion more than words. 'I'm so lucky. And grateful. Don't close your heart and mind to possibilities, Gio,' he'd advised, his dark gaze straying to where Jessica and Polly had been sitting. 'You have the chance for something special. Jess deserves the best. She's not someone to be toyed with.'

The warning had been gently given, but it was a warning nonetheless. Luca and Polly not only viewed Jessica with affection, they were also protective of her. Gio wondered what his compatriot knew but was unable to reveal because of patient confidentiality.

After the live band struck up, Nick and Kate taking the first dance, most of the guests took to the floor. Jessica, however, refused all offers. It was Luca who eventually managed to get her on her feet, and Gio was shocked by the rush of envy and possessiveness that washed over him. Luca was happily married and had no designs on Jessica, but Gio hated to see her in anyone's arms but his own.

'Would you mind dancing with me, Gio?'

Polly's request took him by surprise. 'I'd be delighted,' he agreed politely, although the only person he wanted was Jessica.

'Don't worry, it won't be for long.' Polly, a pretty blonde and tiny, smiled up at him. 'Luca's giving Jess a pep talk.'

'A pep talk?' Gio frowned. What was Luca saying to her? And why?

Polly glanced across to where her husband and Jessica were dancing. 'Be ready to take over when Luca gives the signal.'

Puzzled but intrigued, Gio did as he was bidden, eager for the moment they would swap partners and he would have Jessica in his arms at last.

'It's good to see you happy.' Luca smiled, holding Jess lightly and allowing her to determine the personal space she was comfortable with. 'Gio's a nice guy.'

'We're just friends,' Jess said for the umpteenth time. Her protest produced a teasing chuckle. 'Right!'

'We *are*.' Jess sucked in a ragged breath and tried not to keep staring at Gio. Worst of all, she struggled to banish the ridiculous jealousy that swept through her as he danced with Polly. 'I can't get involved with anyone, Luca, you know that.'

Luca's expression sobered and he steered them to a quiet corner where they wouldn't be overheard. 'I know nothing of the sort. You can have a normal relationship, Jess. I gather Gio doesn't know?'

'No.' A shiver rippled through her. 'He'd run a mile— like everyone else—if he did.' She hated the bitterness in her voice but the lessons of the last four years had been learned the hard way. 'Gio's still grieving. Even were he not, no man would want someone like me.'

'You're wrong, Jess. And you're doing Gio a big dis- service,' he cautioned, his words forestalling a further protest from her. 'Give him a chance. He cares about you and knows what a wonderful woman you are. If he reacts as you fear, then he isn't worthy of you. But what if he understands? Think of all you then have to gain.'

Jess bit her lip, caught in an agony of indecision. She didn't want to lose what she already had and she didn't dare to believe she could have more.

'Don't condemn yourself to a lifetime alone. I nearly did. I was so fearful of being hurt again, but my life is so enriched thanks to Polly. Think about it,' he added, guiding her back onto the dance floor. 'It might sound like a cliché, but none of us knows what the future holds so live each day to the fullest and allow yourself to love and be loved.'

It sounded simple when Luca put it into words, but Jess knew it was anything *but* simple in reality. So distracted was she that she didn't notice Luca steering her towards Gio and Polly, but in the next moment she found herself in Gio's arms as Luca reclaimed his wife. Oh, hell! She hadn't intended dancing at all, and certainly not with Gio because of the temptation when she was near him. But she couldn't make a scene in front of everyone.

She held herself stiffly as he drew her closer, his touch, his scent, the feel of his body brushing against hers having a potent affect on her. One dance wouldn't hurt, would it? One moment out of time to enjoy being in his arms, forgetting why she had to be strong?

As she relaxed, giving up the fight, Gio drew her closer, making her even more aware of him, her body instinctively responding to his nearness. When the music ended, she sighed and made a half-hearted effort to draw away.

'Stay. Please.' The throaty warmth of his voice stripped her of any remaining willpower and common sense.

The tempo slowed and Jess found herself pressed far too intimately against him, her arms winding round him of their own volition. His fingertips brushed the bare skin between her shoulder blades, exposed by the V back of the dress, making her burn with a rush of desire. She was oblivious to everyone else, focused only on Gio, every sense heightened and attuned to him.

He bent his head, the warmth of his breath caressing her neck, the brush of his faintly stubbled jaw against her sensitive skin incredibly erotic. She'd never expected to be held again, let alone dance in public. Emotion threatened to overwhelm her and, to her horror, tears stung her eyes. She buried her face against his chest to hide them…from him and anyone else.

Revelling in this opportunity to hold Jessica properly for the first time, Gio breathed in her unique womanly scent mixed with the familiar hint of chocolate that clung to her hair and skin. Hair and skin that felt super-soft beneath his fingertips.

He was conscious of her heightened emotions, although he doubted she was aware of the way she was clinging to him. Determined not to rush or scare her, he held her, swaying to the music and waiting for her to relax, welcoming the moment she gave up whatever inner battle she was fighting and melted into him. She felt so right in his arms, her curvy body a perfect fit for his.

'Ready to go home?' he asked some considerable time later as they stepped outside to get some fresh air. He wanted her to himself, relishing these moments when he felt closer to her than ever.

She tipped her head back and looked up at the night sky. 'Yes, please.'

After saying goodbye and gathering up their belongings, they drove home in good spirits and were greeted by two sleepy kittens, who stirred long enough to be cuddled. As Jessica settled them again, he went through to the kitchen.

'Hot chocolate?' he asked, smiling at the look on her face.

'Lovely!'

'I'll make it for you the proper Italian way. None of this powdered cocoa with water in a microwave.' He gave an exaggerated shudder of disgust, making her laugh.

'And what is the proper Italian way?'

He took a large bar of *Cioccolato Corezzi's* finest dark chocolate from his stash in a kitchen drawer. 'You must begin with real chocolate. Once melted, you add a little sugar and some milk, bring it to the boil and stir. Some people make it so thick it is like a mousse and has to be eaten with a spoon,' he explained as he broke squares of chocolate and dropped them into a bowl, the satisfying snap a sign of its high quality. 'I prefer it liquid enough to drink, although I keep the teaspoon to reach the last drops!'

'It sounds sinfully delicious.'

It was Jessica who was sinfully delicious. Looking at her fired his blood and stirred his body. Waiting for the water to heat, he leaned his hip against the worktop and watched as she sat at the counter, trying to undo the barrette clasp that held her ponytail in place. Something was stuck and as she muttered to herself, making him smile, he stepped in to help.

'May I?'

Before she had the chance to refuse, he moved behind her, feeling her tense as his fingers set to work. Within moments the clip was free. Unable to resist temptation, his fingers burrowed into the fiery mass of curls that tumbled around her shoulders.

'You have beautiful hair,' he told her, hearing the roughness in his voice.

She gave a shaky laugh. 'I used to hate it.'

'No! It's amazing. Silky soft.' He leaned closer and caught the scent of her chocolatey shampoo. 'And you smell so good.'

'Gio...' Her voice sounded husky and sensual.

The sexual tension increased, electricity crackling between them. Jessica slowly slid round on the stool until she was facing him, olive-green eyes dark with awareness and unmistakeable desire.

His breath caught. 'I *have* to kiss you,' he whispered roughly.

A tremor ran through her but she didn't move away. His hands fisted in her hair as he closed the gap millimetre by millimetre, his heart thudding a rapid tattoo. Finally, their lips met. He felt heady with excitement and yet incredibly nervous as he kissed her for the first time.

They were both tentative, finding their way, learning, savouring, exploring, but the passion quickly flared out of control. Jessica's lips parted and he tilted his head, deepening the kiss. She tasted like heaven. Sweet and sensual, and so addictive. He couldn't get his fill of her. Tongues met, stroked, tempted, and he heard her soft, needy whimper as she clung to him. One hand left her hair and he wrapped his arm around her waist, drawing her into him as he stepped up between her parted thighs. She wriggled closer, pressing herself against him.

Jessica was with him, taking and giving, meeting and matching the blaze of passion that flared so intensely between them, demanding more. Gio was all too aware when instant panic set in and she began to withdraw. With a sharp cry she pulled away from him, clearly distressed.

'What is it, *fiamma?*' he asked between ragged breaths, confused and concerned as tears spilled from eyes full of torment. 'What's wrong?'

She shook her head. 'I'm sorry. So sorry. I can't do this.'

Before he could respond, she pushed away from him, slipped awkwardly off the stool and ran. He heard her footsteps on the stairs and, moments later, the sound of her bedroom door closing. What the hell had happened? Running an unsteady hand through his hair, he took a moment to gather himself together and get his body, so unused to the fiery passion that had ignited between them, back under control.

No way could he leave Jessica in such a distressed state. He wanted to know what had gone wrong, but more important was his concern for her well-being. After checking the house was secure and the kittens were settled, he finished making the hot chocolate and carried two mugs upstairs, anxious about what he might find. Taking a deep breath, he knocked on the door.

'Jessica?'

There was silence for several moments, a silence that hung so heavily around him that he could hear each beat of his heart. 'Yes?' The word was so soft that had he not been listening so intently he would not have heard her.

Cautiously, he opened the door. Dressed now in un-flattering but comfortable pyjamas, Jessica was sitting in the middle of the bed, her arms wrapped around herself as she rocked slightly to and fro. She looked so lost, vulnerable and scared that his heart, which he'd thought could never feel anything again, squeezed with pain for her...and such deep affection and longing he didn't dare examine the emotions too deeply.

'May I come in?' His heart was in his mouth as he waited for her decision.

She didn't meet his gaze, but finally she nodded. He

sat on the edge of the bed, careful not to crowd her. He handed her a mug, noting that her hands were shaking as she reached for it, but she cupped it in her palms and sipped, a soft sigh escaping as she savoured the thick, chocolaty treat.

Gio followed her lead, hoping she would begin to relax. She even managed the ghost of a smile when he handed her a teaspoon so she could copy him and capture the final bits of chocolate.

'Good?' he asked, nearly having heart failure as her tongue peeped out and she licked the remains of chocolate from her lips.

'Amazing.' Her voice was still soft but sounded stronger. Popping the spoon in the empty mug, she handed it to him. 'Thank you.'

Gio set the mugs aside, feeling a growing tension now the moment had come to seek answers to some questions.

'Jessica, we need to talk.' Once more she wrapped her arms around herself, lashes lowering to hide her expression, but not before he had seen the fear in her eyes. 'I need to know. I know you guard your personal space and avoid being touched. At first I thought it was me, then I noticed it was the same with everyone. Including your clever ruse using all that stuff you carry round the hospital so you can avoid shaking hands.'

The blush that brought colour back to her too-pale cheeks was confirmation that he was right.

'My imagination is running away with itself. I'm scared to ask but...has someone hurt you in the past?' He could hardly get the words out but knew he had to. 'Were you raped or abused?'

'No.'

The denial was firm and he knew she was telling the truth. The relief was *huge*. But there was still something major and important. He knew it. She looked so alone, and the despair and hurt in her eyes tore him apart.

'May I hold you, Jessica...please?'

She raised her head and met his gaze. What she was searching for, he had no idea, but whatever it was, she apparently found it as, after the longest time, she bit her lip and nodded. The air trapped in his lungs was released in a rush of relief. He moved onto his knees and edged towards her, needing the physical contact as much as she did. When he was as close as could be, he sat back on his heels and drew her into his arms with infinite care, cradling her tense and shaking form against him.

As she gradually began to relax, she rested her head against his chest. With one hand he stroked the unrestrained glossy copper-red curls as they tumbled with abandon around her shoulders.

'Can you talk to me now?' A breath shuddered out of her in response. Her casual shrug belied the tension that poured from her and the tremble he felt ripple through her whole body. 'Jessica?'

'I don't know. I...'

The whispered words were husky with emotion and he sought to discover the cause of her hesitation and reluctance. 'What worries you, *fiamma*? Do you think I won't understand? Do you fear it will change how I think of you and feel about you?'

'I know it will,' she responded, the humourless laugh and bitter edge to her voice speaking volumes.

'Listen to me,' he instructed gently, seeking the words to reassure her. 'I don't know what experiences you've had with other people, but *nothing* you tell me will make me turn away or reject you.' Whatever route their relationship eventually took, he was unable to envisage any circumstance that would change the basic friendship and bond that had formed so quickly but so intensely between them. He dropped a kiss on the top of her head. 'Trust me. I won't let you down.'

The sincerity in Gio's voice was beyond question but Jess still hesitated. He might believe *now* that nothing would make him reject her but would he feel the same when he knew?

She recalled Luca's words. He'd advised her to give Gio a chance, pointing out that only by confiding in him would she discover the depth of his friendship and the kind of man he really was. Deep in her heart she knew. And she *so* wanted to believe. But her former friends and colleagues had turned her away and her family had disowned her.

The last few weeks with Gio had been the happiest she had known for such a long time and she was terrified that revealing the truth about herself would change for ever the nature of their friendship, maybe even end it. She didn't want to lose what she already had, but every day things were becoming more complicated because her heart and emotions were ever more entangled and it was no longer enough just to be his friend.

Those moments in the kitchen when she had allowed herself to wallow in the pleasure of being touched, followed by the most explosive and incredible kiss she had ever known, had proved that. He had breached her defences so completely and she'd been so lost in Gio and her desire for him that she'd forgotten why she shouldn't have been doing it. Reality had hit like a thunderclap and she'd run. They'd crossed the boundaries of friendship now. And in reaching for more, would she destroy what she already had?

She wouldn't know the answer unless she did as Gio asked and trusted him. Cocooned in his embrace she felt safe and protected and, for the first time in over four years, she didn't feel alone. She sucked in a deep breath, inhaling the warm musky-male scent of him that had become so familiar. And arousing. Drawing back just far enough, she looked up and met his steady, intensely blue gaze. While the arm supporting her cuddled her close, his free hand caught one of hers, raising it to his mouth and pressing a kiss to her palm before he entwined their fingers, linking them and giving her his support.

'I don't know where to start,' she admitted with a nervous laugh, feeling sick inside now the decision was made and the moment had come to share her shameful secret.

'Take your time. I'm not going anywhere,' he promised. 'Is it something that goes back to the time before you came to St Piran?'

'Yes. It started just over four years ago when I was still in Scotland,' she admitted, closing her eyes as the memories flooded back. She paused, unsure if she could continue, but Gio's support and strength gave her the courage to face what had to be faced. 'I was working in a hospital there,' she explained, ignoring for now the information about her former career. 'I was living with my fiancé, Duncan. He was my first and only proper boyfriend. I was happy. I thought I had everything I wanted, and I was busy planning the wedding, which was only eight weeks away.'

* * *

As Jessica gathered her thoughts, Gio struggled with the unreasonable jealousy that assailed him at the knowledge she had been in love and about to be married, already disliking the man she spoke of without knowing any more about him. But he hid his reaction, needing to give her all his understanding now that she had done him the honour of trusting him. He couldn't—wouldn't—let her down.

'Did Duncan work at the hospital, too?' he asked, keeping his tone neutral.

'No. He worked for a company that supplied equipment and aid for relief charities out in the field and his job took him all over the world. He was away a lot. I missed him, but I supported what he did.'

He was unsurprised by her selflessness and the sacrifices she'd no doubt made. 'It's not easy maintaining a relationship long distance.'

'No.' Another shiver ran through her and he tightened his hold, wanting to protect her from the hurt she was reliving. 'I hadn't been feeling well for a while,' she continued, and his concern for her increased. 'There was nothing specific I could put my finger on, and I put it down to the pressures of work and the excitement and lack of sleep as the wedding drew closer. Duncan had to take several trips away during those weeks and so everything fell to me. A colleague noticed how off colour I was and suggested I see a doctor. I didn't think anything of it, but because I wanted to feel right for the wedding, I made an appointment to see my GP.'

Gio felt his gut tightening with the premonition that something dark and of huge importance was about to be revealed. Looking into green eyes shadowed with fear and pain, it was the dart of shame that confused him. He raised their joined hands, pressing a kiss to her fingers.

'What happened, *fiamma*?' he prompted.

'My GP didn't think there was anything serious going on, but he organised some tests to be on the safe side. And…' She halted, her voice breaking, tears shimmering on long sooty lashes.

Gio steeled himself for whatever was to come. 'And?'

'The results came back.' A sob tore through her, ripping him to shreds. 'It t-turned out that D-Duncan hadn't been the f-faithful, loving fiancé I'd imagined,' she continued, the words stuttering through her tears. 'He'd slept with countless women during his trips abroad and thanks to him I h-have a lasting legacy. The tests, unlike Duncan, didn't lie. I…' Again she broke off, drawing in a shuddering breath, her fingers instinctively tightening on his as she raised her head, tear-washed eyes bleak. 'Gio, I was…*am*…HIV positive.'

CHAPTER NINE

'*Madre del Dio*.'

The words escaped on a whisper of breath when all
Gio wanted to do was rage and swear at the man who
had done this to Jessica. He listened as she told him how
she had been diagnosed with a seroconversion illness
and although it was not his branch of medicine, he knew
enough to understand that this was often the first sign
of illness people had after they had been infected, when
the body first produced antibodies to HIV.

'I had many of the usual symptoms…a fever, aching
limbs, headache and a blotchy red rash…which could
have been linked to a variety of conditions,' she explained, the matter-of-fact tone of her voice belied by
the shadows in her eyes. 'It was such a shock and not
something I had ever anticipated.'

'Of course not. You trusted the man you were about
to marry,' Gio reasoned.

She nodded, and he tightened his hold as a fresh
shudder went through her. 'I must be a really bad person
because I can't forgive him—not just for what he did to
me but I keep thinking about the unknown number of
other women out there he infected, as well, and what

they might be going through. I can't even feel sorry that he was diagnosed, too,' she whispered.

'No, no, no! You are not remotely a bad person! How can you think that?' Gio swore in Italian, wishing he could let Duncan know what he thought of him. 'You are an amazing woman, Jessica. Even struggling to come to terms with what has happened to you, through no fault of your own, your thoughts are still for other people. You have the generosity of spirit to worry about the women with whom your ex-fiancé—' he stumbled over the word, choked by his anger and disgust at the man '—had been unfaithful.'

'It wasn't their fault. I've no doubt he lied to them, too.'

'And now,' he made himself ask, needing to know so much but anxious not to stress her more, 'how are you? Are you taking medication?'

'I'm OK. And I'm not taking medication yet,' she told him, and the relief was immense. 'I have regular tests to monitor my CD4 cell count, which gives an idea of the strength of my immune system. And a viral load test, which can tell how active HIV is in the body. It's only if those levels reach a certain point that medication will be necessary. It's a big step to take because once started, you can't stop. I go to London twice a year to see a specialist,' she added, surprising him.

'Why London?'

'I went there first when I left Scotland. I trust Mr Jackson. When I moved to Cornwall, he agreed to keep seeing me.' Her smile was tired but brought some life back to her eyes. 'And I have Luca and the other doctors at the Penhally surgery who take care of day-to-day things.'

Gio was relieved she had someone so good caring for her. 'Was there no one giving you support at home? What about family and friends?' he asked, taken aback by her derisive, humourless laugh. Unease curled inside him.

'I was stupidly naïve and assumed that in this day and age people would be more informed and understanding,' she began with a shiver, shifting so that she was resting against his chest. 'But they weren't. I was so shocked by the negative reactions. Some people blanked me, some were openly hostile and abusive, making a big fuss if I touched them in any way, refusing to drink from a mug or eat off a plate I might have used in the canteen. Not one so-called friend or colleague stood by me.'

As he listened to Jessica outline some of the things people had said to her and what she had put up with once her diagnosis had become known, Gio's anger rocketed. It was disgraceful that people should be so ignorant and prejudiced. And it was hardly surprising after her experiences that she'd been stripped of her confidence, her self-esteem and her trust in people.

'My family were worse.'

'What happened, *fiamma*?' he asked softly, fearing her answer.

'Shocked and upset, I went home and told them the news. My father has always been a dour, strict man with rigid opinions. He disapproved of me living with Duncan before the wedding. He said...' Her fingers tightened on his and emotion turned her voice husky as she continued. 'He said it was all I deserved for living in sin, that I had brought shame on the family, and he disowned me. He turned me out with all my belongings and told me never to contact them again. He even had me barred from visiting my grandmother, who was bedridden in a nursing home by then. She was the only one who cared. She left me the money that helped me buy my cottage, but I never had the chance to see her again before she died and tell her I loved her.'

Her words ended on a sob and the tears she had been choking back escaped. She tried to pull away from him but he drew her trembling frame more fully against him and, wrapping her protectively in his arms, he held her tight, keeping her safe as she cried out the hurt and anger. After everything Duncan had done, and the reaction of those she'd considered friends, the cruel rejection by the family meant to love and care for her must have been the ultimate betrayal and almost impossible to bear. Thinking of her alone and scared tore him apart.

He guessed she'd been bottling up the emotion for a long time and now it had been set free, like opening a dam and allowing everything backed up behind it to gush out. As he cradled her, he struggled to come to terms with the truth, the reality, the consequences...and with what her life must have been like these last four or more years.

His own eyes were moist and his heart hurt as he tried to comfort her while the storm ran its course. So many things now made sense. Her reluctance to touch and be touched, the absence of any close friendships, the lack of trust and the little habits at home like the supplements and washing her things separately. No wonder she had looked so hurt when he'd teased her about having a hygiene fetish. He smothered a groan. After all she had been through since being diagnosed, it was understandable she had developed a range of coping mechanisms.

When Jessica finally calmed, he eased back and cupped her face in his hands. Olive-green eyes were framed by tear-spiked lashes while her flawless, translucent skin was devoid of colour. Concerned for her, he dropped a light kiss on lips that still trembled.

'Don't go anywhere. I'll be back in a couple of minutes. OK?'

Her nod was weary, almost defeated. Reluctantly, he released her. He didn't want to leave her, even for a moment, but he had a few things to do. When he returned, having undressed as far as his boxer shorts, prepared his bedroom with jasmine-scented candles and turned down the bed, she was sitting motionless where he had left her, her eyes closed.

'Jessica?'

Long lashes flickered then he was staring into her eyes. She blinked, her gaze skimming over him, a flush bringing some warmth back to her pale face. Her reaction amused him, momentarily easing his concern for her.

'Hi.' He smiled as she swallowed and dragged her gaze back to his. 'Are you OK?'

She nodded, remaining silent until his next moved shocked her out of her torpor. 'Gio!' Her cry escaped as he scooped her off the bed and lifted her in his arms.

'Hold on,' he instructed.

'What are you doing?' Despite her protest, she wrapped her arms around his neck. 'Gio, I'm far too heavy.'

'Nonsense.'

He carried her from the room, only pausing long enough for her to switch out the light. Walking down the corridor, he went into his bedroom, set her gently on the bed and drew the duvet over her before walking round the other side and sliding in beside her. To his surprise and delight, she turned into his arms and burrowed into him. He stroked the glossy curls that spread across his chest, each indrawn breath fragranced with a teasing hint of her scent.

'Gio…' Her voice was soft and sleepy, and it still held the lingering legacy of the emotions that had ravaged her just a short while ago.

'Shh,' he soothed, relishing the feel of her feminine curves and the softness of her skin. 'It's very late and you've been through a lot. Sleep now. I'll keep you safe.'

It was Sunday afternoon and the closer they got to home, the more nervous Jess became. She knew what was going to happen. She wanted it. And yet she couldn't help but be as scared as she was excited. Gio, too, seemed preoccupied and edgy as the electric tension continued to build between them.

She thought back to the night before and everything that had happened after their return from the wedding and the most incredible kiss she'd ever experienced. Telling Gio how her life had been turned upside down following the HIV diagnosis had been so difficult, but he had been amazing, his supportive reaction in marked contrast to those she had encountered in the past. But now her shameful secret was out, nothing would ever be the same between them again.

Spending the night in Gio's arms had been wonderful. For the first time in a long, long while she hadn't felt alone. And she wished she could wake up with him every morning, especially if it meant experiencing the delicious caress of his hands and his lips on her bare skin.

'I want more than anything to make love to you,' he'd told her, the throaty roughness of his voice resonating along her nerve-endings. 'I have since the day I first saw you, and I've wanted you more each day since.'

'Gio,' she'd murmured in confusion, hardly daring to believe that the truth hadn't put him off. He may have held her through the night, but...

'Nothing you have told me changes anything—I only marvel more at what an incredible woman you are,' he'd continued, his words bringing a lump to her throat. 'Unfortunately, right now I have no protection.'

She had masked her disappointment. 'OK.'

'But we can improvise.' The tone of his voice and his sexy smile had sent a tremor right through her. 'We can't make love fully now but I want to bring you pleasure and show what a special and desirable woman you are.'

And bring her pleasure he had. Oh, my! A shaky little breath escaped, warmth stealing through her as her body tingled at the memory of his kisses and caresses. How delicious to wake up like that every day. But she knew it was a fantasy. She was getting too far ahead of herself.

They'd spent the day doing normal things at the house, having a late breakfast and playing with the kittens before going to see how things were progressing at her cottage. The main supporting structure had been replaced and the thatcher was well on the way to creating a beautiful new roof.

Knowing that the cottage would soon be habitable again and discovering that Gio had arranged for the fields to be cleared and the fences renewed in readiness for Faye's menagerie had brought mixed emotions. Pleasure at seeing the cottage come back to life. Surprise and gratitude at Gio's generosity. But anxiety at the knowledge she would soon have to leave his house— and him. What would happen then? Gio was adamant about sharing responsibility for the animals but how would that work? And what did it mean for them?

Next, they'd spent a couple of hours on the boat, speeding across the waves. She'd felt so close to him and, now her secret was out, she hadn't had to fight to avoid physical contact. Gio had taken every opportunity to hug and kiss her. But her nervousness had returned when they had stopped at the supermarket on the way back to the house and condoms had been added to the items in their basket.

Feeling jumpy and on edge, not at all sure what to do or say, Jess helped Gio put the shopping away and then played with Dickens and Kipling for a while before feeding them. As they curled up to sleep in a tangle of limbs, she felt even more anxious.

'I think I'll go and have a shower,' she murmured, feeling as gauche and awkward as a teenager.

Gio looked up and smiled. 'OK.'

He appeared so calm that had he not bought the condoms she would have wondered if she had dreamed everything that had happened when she had woken up that morning. And what she was anticipating would happen later. Unsettled, she went upstairs and, after undressing and tying up her wayward curls to keep her hair from getting wet, she stepped into the shower, welcoming the feel of the hot barbs on skin that still felt alive and sensitive from the caresses of Gio's hands and mouth.

Eyes closed, she tipped her head back and reached

out a hand for the chocolate-scented cleanser she loved to use, a squeal of shocked surprise escaping as, instead of encountering the plastic tube she was expecting, her fingers met male skin. Every part of her trembled as he stepped up behind her, the front of his body pressing against the back of hers, making her supremely aware of his arousal.

She heard the snap of the top on the tube she'd been reaching for and a moment later felt the touch of hands that were slick with foamy cleanser. He began at her shoulders, working slowly and sensually down her back, lingering at her rear before sweeping down her legs in long, caressing strokes that turned her knees to jelly. One arm wrapped around her waist in support, and she leaned back against him, feeling boneless and on fire as he turned his attention to the front of her.

Jess bit her lip to prevent herself crying out as he devoted time to her breasts, the exquisite torture almost too much to bear. It had been so long since she had been touched like this…and yet *never* like this because the kind of explosive passion and intense desire she shared with Gio was way beyond anything she had ever experienced before.

When she thought she would expire from the pleasure of his touch, Gio turned the cleanser over to her and allowed her the same freedom to explore and enjoy his body. She turned round on legs that felt decidedly unsteady, the blood racing through her veins as she drank in the sight of him. It was impossible not to be struck by the masculine beauty of his body, the broad shoulders and the perfectly toned muscles of his arms and torso that made her mouth water. A brush of dark hair in the middle of his chest cast a shadow on olive-toned skin, tapering to a narrow line that her gaze avidly followed down over his abdomen and navel to where it nested the potent symbol of his maleness.

She refocused on his handsome face, seeing the needy desire, which mirrored her own, in his deeply blue eyes. Feeling both shy and bold at the same time, she began her own lingering caress of his body, working the foamy, chocolate-scented suds across his skin, hearing his in-drawn breath and feeling the tremor and ripple of muscle as he reacted to her touch.

With an impatient exclamation his hands closed on her upper arms, drawing her back up and into a searing kiss. She clung to him, kissing him back with equal ardour, savouring the feel of wet warm skin under her hands and the sexy, sinful taste of him in her mouth. They were both breathing heavily by the time they broke apart. Gio snapped off the water before reaching for a towel and wrapping her up in it. With evident impatience he briskly ran another towel over himself. Tossing it aside, he took her hand and led her down the corridor to his bedroom, her legs so rubbery she didn't think she could walk.

Some of her anxiety returned as she entered the room with him and saw the huge bed standing ready and waiting, the duvet turned back, the generous pillows plumped up. She knew how luxurious and incredibly sexy the gunmetal-grey sheets felt against her skin. And within moments she was experiencing them again as Gio gave her a gentle rub down with the towel before removing it and tumbling them both into bed.

Excitement and tension vied for prominence. She could feel the heat of his body even though he wasn't quite touching her. Smiling, he gently removed the pins from her hair and fanned the tresses out on the pillow.

'Do you think you are the only one who is nervous, *fiamma*?' he asked, his throaty, accented voice sounding even more sexy than usual.

Surprised, she met his gaze. 'You're nervous, too?'

Her question was met with a wry laugh. 'I listen to some of the young doctors talking in the scrub room and the canteen, discussing their conquests, and I realise what an oddity I must seem for having slept only with Sofia.'

'Then I'm odd, too, because I've only ever had one relationship before,' she told him. 'And, to me, the fact that you have never been the kind of man to sleep around is a major strength, not a weakness. You are loyal and true. And you haven't played Russian roulette with your own health or anyone else's.'

She thought of Duncan, of how he had cheated on her, and his cavalier disregard for himself, let alone her or the other women. Gio was a treasure and it was the very quality he considered an oddity that made her trust him. Had he been another Duncan, she would never be here now, on the cusp of giving herself to him in the most elemental of ways.

As if by instinct, they moved in unison to close the last of the gap between them, and the instant he touched her, the instant her lips met his, the doubts that had seemed so real for a moment dissolved into nothing. They needed no words because their bodies talked for them. Jess found she couldn't formulate a single coherent thought as Gio continued what he had begun that morning and in the shower, devoting his time and attention to her.

Every touch, every kiss, every caress of his fingers and brush of his lips and tongue built the pleasure layer by layer. She writhed against him, her body turning molten as his mouth worked down the column of her throat, setting every nerve tingling and every particle of skin on fire. He trailed down the valley between her breasts, bypassing flesh that yearned so badly for his attention and continuing down to her navel. She hadn't known she was so sensitive there but the tantalising, teasing quest of his teeth and tongue had her body arching up to meet him, seeking more.

She must have spoken the word aloud because he chuckled, the huff of warm breath against her skin a subtle and teasing caress of its own. She moaned as he finally turned his attention to her breasts, the perfect pressure of his fingers driving her crazy.

'Gio, please,' she begged, craving the touches he teasingly denied her.

Relenting, his teeth gently grazed one sensitive nipple before his tongue salved the delicious sting. Then he sent her to the stratosphere as he took the peak into the warm cavern of his mouth. When she thought she couldn't bear it a moment longer he released his prize, turned his attention to its twin and began the exquisite torment all over again.

Impatient, her eager hands traced the muscular contours of his shoulders before working down his back, urging him closer. She wanted to explore and savour him as he was doing to her, but she was so close to the edge she couldn't wait a moment longer to know the joy of being united fully with him.

He took a moment to protect them and she pleaded with him not to wait any longer as he moved to make them one. She arched up to meet him, wrapping her legs around him, gasping his name at the delicious sensations as her body welcomed his and, finally, they were one.

'Jessica…'

'Yes. Please, Gio. Don't stop.'

She had never experienced anything as magical and special as making love with Gio. It was incredible, earth-shattering and she never wanted it to end. He murmured to her in Italian as they moved together in a rhythm as old as time. She abandoned herself to him completely, as he did to her, and the mix of exquisite tenderness and fiery passion she found with him was a devastating combination.

When the inevitable moment arrived, Jess clung to him, burying her face against him, breathing in his musky scent, calling his name as they drove each other over the edge to a shattering release. As she spun out of control, she didn't care if she never came down to earth again, just so long as she was with Gio.

Gio gazed at Jessica's sleeping form, the wild fire of her hair tossed across the pillow and a couple of tell-tale little marks on her otherwise flawless, silky-smooth skin following the intensely passionate night they had shared. It had been the most incredible experience, beyond any-thing he had imagined. And it had scared him.

He wasn't sure at exactly which moment during their sensual night together it had happened, but he had sud-denly known with surety and not much surprise that he loved her. It may have happened far more speedily but, as with Sofia, they had begun as friends first and fore-most. He and Sofia had been children and their emotions

had evolved slowly, whereas with Jessica the friendship
and the desire had hit in tandem.

The pain of losing Sofia had nearly killed him and
he'd never imagined wanting another woman again.
Then he had met Jessica. He not only wanted her in
every way but he liked and respected her as a person and
valued the special friendship they shared. So why was
he feeling so unsettled? Things had happened so fast,
he had fallen so deep so quickly and he knew that if he
tied himself to her and anything happened, he would
never recover a second time.

Could he take the risk on Jessica's health? All he
knew was that he couldn't face the prospect of burying
another woman he loved. It was a possibility he couldn't
ignore when making a decision that would affect both
their futures.

Waking up alone had been unnerving and when she
went downstairs and found Gio making coffee in the
kitchen, Jess's unease increased. He greeted her with a
smile, but she sensed a change in him. He was on edge,
distant. And when he backed off physically, moving
away when she would have stepped in for a hug, a cold
chill went through her.

'What's wrong?' she asked, fear building as he failed
to meet her gaze.

'Nothing. I...'

'Gio?'

He ran a hand through his hair, a characteristic sign
of agitation. 'I'm just not sure what to think about this.
It's all happened so quickly.'

'You regret it.' Her heart sank.

'No! Of course not. Neither of us was expecting

this. The connection was there from the first and our friendship is special and important to me,' he explained, his expression sombre, and Jess sensed a 'but' coming. 'But—' Jess allowed herself a humourless smile '—maybe we should slow things down, take some time. I'd never considered having a new relationship. I'm not sure I'm ready. Especially after what happened with Sofia.'

Everything in her screamed in protest. 'I see.'

'I need to be sure, Jessica. Not of you but of me. Losing Sofia nearly killed me and I can't go through anything like that again,' he finished, emotion heavy in his voice.

The awful thing was that she understood. She couldn't argue against his words and the chance of something happening was greater with her with the HIV hanging over her head than it was with another woman. Wrapping her arms around herself, she tried to hold everything together, to not let him see how deeply the rejection had wounded her. Because that was what it felt like. And in that moment, the truth hit home with devastating force... she loved him. In every way and with every part of her being.

Gio had said their friendship was important and apparently he considered things would go on as before, but Jess felt as if part of her was dying inside because friendship was never going to be enough now.

'I'm going to Italy at the weekend for my parents' fortieth wedding anniversary,' he reminded her, thrusting his hands into the pockets of his jeans.

Her heart breaking, Jess struggled to keep her voice as normal as possible. 'My cottage should be ready by then, so I'll move out.'

'I didn't mean that.' He frowned as if her leaving was not something he had considered.

'Living here was only meant to be temporary,' she pointed out, knowing she couldn't stay with him and not *be with* him. 'It's for the best.'

His frown deepened, confusion and disappointment mingling in his intensely blue eyes. 'If that's what you want.'

It wasn't what she wanted at all, but she didn't see how she could do anything else if what she really wanted—Gio himself—was not an option.

The next few days were like purgatory, and by the time Friday arrived, Jess was at breaking point and not at all sure how much longer she could hold on. Pretending to accept Gio's decision to return things to a platonic footing had involved the performance of her life. She hadn't been able to sleep, lying in a bed a short distance down the corridor from him, wanting more than anything to be in his arms. But it wasn't going to happen and the sooner she faced that and rebuilt her battered defences, the better it would be.

He went to Italy on the Friday and, after the loneliest night in the house without him, Jess tried to hold back the tears as she packed her things into her car and then put Dickens and Kipling into their basket for the short journey to her cottage. The kittens would miss Gio almost as much as she would, she reflected sadly. He'd been so good with them. She choked back the emotion as she recalled the way he had lain on the floor, chuckling as the two growing kittens had romped over him. And the time she'd come in late one Friday night after her session of volunteering at the Samaritans to find Gio lying asleep on the sofa, the kittens curled up on his chest in a tangle.

Feeling numb inside, she secured the house and drove away from it, wondering if it was for the last time. However much she hurt, she couldn't blame Gio. She knew how devastating Sofia's death had been and it was understandable that he was wary of embarking on another relationship, especially with someone like her. She was well at the moment, and she would do all she could to stay that way. As Luca and her specialist, Mr Jackson, frequently told her, there was no reason why she couldn't live into old age with very few problems at all. But anyone would be wary of taking on that uncertainty, especially someone who had experienced what Gio had.

No, Gio was not to blame. It was her own fault. She'd hoped for too much…had dared to dream and to believe in the impossible. Now she had to pick up the pieces because fairy-tale, happy-ever-after endings didn't happen to people like her.

'Why did you stay the night with me?'

It was one of the things Megan had most dreaded Josh ever asking and it had played over and over in her head since the day in A and E when they had done the unthinkable and faced their past.

Aside from not wanting to acknowledge the truth to herself, she certainly didn't want to tell *Josh* the answer to his question. To admit that she had been drawn to him from the first moment she had seen him and that, despite his reputation, she had yearned for him for years like some lovestruck teenager was beyond embarrassing.

Between medical school and caring for her grandmother, she'd had no time for a social life, so going to a party on New Year's Eve had been a real treat. Wearing an exquisite dress, her hair and make-up done, she'd felt like Cinderella. Only she'd been granted a bit longer before the spell had been broken…not at midnight, for her, but lunchtime the following day.

For the first time, Josh had approached her. Given his undivided attention, she'd melted like an ice cube under the noon sun. He'd made her feel special. Surprisingly, they had talked and talked, and she'd found him so much *more* than she had ever expected. He'd been funny, he'd listened as if what she'd had to say had mattered, he'd sympathised about her grandmother, and he had confided in her, too. The night had ended in the inevitable way, the sexual chemistry and tension between them impossible to resist.

Megan closed her eyes and tried to push away the painful memories. She had believed in her heart that what they had shared had been more than one night. Much more. Or she never would have gone home with Josh in the first place. They'd connected. On every level. She hadn't imagined it. And it *hadn't* just been the sex, amazing as that had been. She knew Josh had been spooked by their closeness as he'd freely admitted that he'd revealed things to her that he'd never told to anyone else. He'd told her she was different. He'd been so genuine. And she'd believed him. Had *wanted* to believe him. So badly.

They had finally, reluctantly, parted but only after Josh had made love to her one last time and had made her promise to meet him that evening. It had been noon when she had rushed home to her grandmother feeling a mix of guilt and euphoria. The hours with Josh had been the most amazing of her life and she hadn't been able to wait to see him again. So when he had stood her up, failing to meet at the agreed time and place, she had been confused and upset.

When she had finally seen him several worrying days later, he had blanked her completely, laughing with his friends, ignoring her as if their night had never happened. She'd been devastated. Even now she could remember how she had felt…used, cheap, stupid, incredibly naïve and very, very hurt.

Megan shivered in reaction as the memories of that lonely, frightening time and what had followed over the next months flowed through her. Ashamed, she had withdrawn and hidden herself away. And then she had discovered that she was pregnant. And *so* scared.

Weeks later she'd experienced a searing pain and had remembered nothing until she had woken up in hospital to learn that Josh had been part of the team who had not only taken away her baby but had performed a hysterectomy, depriving her of ever becoming a mother. She'd been devastated, the sense of loss and grief overwhelming.

Eight years on, listening to his explanation and seeing his own emotion had given her much to think about. The hurt remained, both at his rejection and at the loss of her baby. But while there was much she was still angry with him about, she no longer blamed him for the miscarriage or the lengths taken to save her life.

Despite their past and all that lay between them—including the very real presence of his wife—the chemistry remained. When they worked together in A and E, they often knew what the other was thinking or doing without the need for words.

She knew he was out of bounds. She knew what had happened the last time the chemistry had led her astray. And she couldn't forget the way Josh had rejected and betrayed her. So discovering that she was still vulnerable to him, still drawn to him and still unable to get him out of her mind, frightened her.

If she showed the slightest weakness she feared what might happen. And only heartache would lie ahead. She had learned her lesson the hard way the last time round. So why did she have the terrible feeling that history was going to repeat itself?

CHAPTER TEN

LATE on Sunday afternoon Jess walked along the surfing beach east of Penhally's harbour, lost in thought. It
had been another beautiful day, but the air was cooling
as the sun began its slow descent towards the horizon.
Pushing her hands into the pockets of the floaty skirt
that fell to her knees, Jess sighed. There was no escaping
her thoughts. Thoughts that were stuck in one place and
refused to budge. With Gio.

He would be back tonight and tomorrow she would
see him at work. She wasn't sure how to continue pretending that nothing had happened or behave normally,
accepting they could only ever be friends. *Could* she
be friends when she wanted so much more? It was a
question that had pounded in her head all week and she
still didn't know the answer. All she did know was that
she had missed him terribly and faced with a choice of
never seeing him again, then, as sad and pathetic as it
sounded, any part of Gio was better than no Gio at all.
Even if she was dying inside. Because she had fallen in
love with a man who had experienced such heartache
that he couldn't take a risk on someone whose future
could be as uncertain as hers.

As she neared the end of the promontory on which

the lighthouse, coastguard office and St Mark's church stood, she heard shouting and laughter, and looked up to see a couple of teenagers messing about on the rocks. She was about to turn round and retrace her steps back along the beach when the tone of the teenage voices changed and she watched in horror as one of the boys lost his footing and crashed face down amongst the rocks.

Jess ran towards the scene of the accident, as did a few other people who were further away on the beach and up on the promontory. The teenager's friend was now silent and standing motionless in shock and terror as he gazed down at his stricken comrade. Reaching the rocky outcrop, and glad she was wearing trainers, Jess began to climb.

The lower rocks were slippery, and several times she lost her own footing, resulting in umpteen cuts and bruises, but she kept going as rapidly as she could, fearing what she would find when she reached the boy. Moving towards him, she misjudged a step and fell heavily. Pain seared through her foot, leg and side, and she felt the hot stickiness of blood flowing down her calf. Ignoring it, she limped and scrambled awkwardly the rest of the way to the boy.

His injuries were worse than she'd feared. Frightened eyes stared up at her, and she struggled to mask her shock so as not to distress him further. His face had borne the brunt of his fall and, along with a lot of bleeding and considerable soft-tissue damage, she could tell that his jaw, nose and one cheekbone were all broken.

Instinct took over as she did a quick assessment. There were no other apparent injuries but that hardly mattered because there was one serious, immediate and life-threatening problem…the boy was finding it increasingly impossible to breathe.

'Has anyone called an ambulance?' she shouted to the small crowd that was gathering on the rocks above her.

'Yes,' someone called. 'ETA at least twelve minutes.'

Jess swore. They couldn't wait that long. 'I need a sharp knife—preferably a scalpel. And something like a small piece of tube, or a drinking straw. Anything narrow and hollow. He can't breathe and I have to help him,' she shouted up.

'The lighthouse and coastguard station both have full first-aid kits. I'll get one of those,' the man called down to her.

'Please hurry! There isn't much time.'

Hoping the man understood the urgency, and that the kit would contain the things she needed, Jess returned her attention to the boy and tried to talk soothingly to him as she continued her assessment. With all the blood, fragments of bone and the rapidly swelling tissues around his face, there was no way she could clear or maintain an airway. It was no surprise when he began to panic as he failed to draw oxygen into his lungs and started to lose consciousness.

It seemed an eternity before the man reappeared above her and began the dangerous climb down. His exclamation of shock when he saw the boy was understandable but Jess didn't have time to do anything but take the first-aid kit from him. She winced at the shaft of pain in her side as she dragged the heavy bag close, but she pushed her own discomfort aside and opened the kit, giving heartfelt thanks that it was an extensive and well-stocked one.

Gathering together the things she needed, she told her unknown companion what she was doing. 'I have to create an opening in his throat so he can breathe. We can't wait for the ambulance. What's your name?'

'Charlie.'

'I'm Jess. I...' She paused and sucked in a breath. 'I'm a doctor,' she told him, speaking aloud the words she had not used for four years. 'Have you got a mobile phone, Charlie?'

'Yes, right here.'

'Phone 999 and tell them we need the air ambulance, too,' she requested, knowing that if what she attempted was successful, the boy would need to get to hospital as fast as possible.

As Charlie made the call, Jess focused on the task ahead. Nervousness gripped her. Shutting out the comments from the small crowds on the rocks above her and the beach below, she steadied herself and called on all her former training. She was scared, but she'd done this a few times before. She could do it now. She had to if the boy wasn't to suffocate before the ambulance arrived. Closing her eyes, she did a quick mental run-through of the emergency procedure she had never expected to be called on to perform again.

After using an antiseptic wipe on the boy's throat, she draped some gauze around the site and then she took out the sterile, single-use blade that was in the kit. She had no local anaesthetic available, but with his consciousness level low he probably didn't need it. Unsure how aware he was, she told him what she needed to do, talking through it as much to steady herself as him.

With the fingers of one hand she felt for the correct spot on the throat and, with her other hand, made a small vertical incision through the skin. Identifying the cricothyroid membrane, she made a horizontal cut through it, careful to ensure that she didn't damage the cartilage. With no proper tracheal spreader available she had to improvise again, and she used the handle of a small knife she found in the kit, inserting it into the incision and turning it so that it created a small passage. Already there was a life-saving flow of air in and out as the boy's lungs inflated and reinflated.

'Could you cut me some strips of tape, Charlie?'

As he obliged, Jess cut a piece of plastic tube to the right length and, with great care so as not to damage any cartilage or the vocal cords, angled it and slid it into the makeshift passageway. It was a temporary measure but it would keep the boy alive and his airway open until the paramedics arrived. Taking the strips Charlie handed her, she secured the tube in place.

'Well done, Jess!' Charlie praised when she had finished, giving a thumbs-up to the crowd on the promontory and beach, who broke into spontaneous applause.

Jess sat back and let out a shaky breath. 'Thanks.'

It had only taken two or three minutes to complete the procedure and yet she felt weary and quite unsteady. Taking the boy's hand, she continued to monitor his breathing, relieved that he was awake. She gently wiped away the blood from around his eyes—brown eyes that were now open again and staring at her with a mix of relief and fright and pain.

'The ambulance will be here very soon,' she reassured him, rewarded when his fingers tightened on hers.

He was going to need an excellent maxillofacial surgeon for reconstruction, Jess reflected, her thoughts interrupted by the sound of an approaching siren, and relief flowed through her as the ambulance arrived. Charlie moved the first-aid kit out of the way, then showed the paramedics the best way down the rocks. Jess recognised both men, who greeted her by name, their surprise evident as she debriefed them and they realised the role she had played in events.

Things passed in a blur after that. Charlie left, but Jess remained where she was, answering the occasional question but mostly watching the paramedics work. It wasn't long before they were joined by the medics from the air ambulance and she had to give her debrief over again. Once the boy was stabilised, volunteers were needed to help extricate the stretcher from the difficult location, but before long he was off the rocks and on his way to St Piran's in the helicopter.

'Now, then, Jess, our heroine of the day, what about you?' Stuart asked, squatting down in front of her while Mark cleared up their things and invited the more nosy and persistent onlookers to disperse.

'Me?' Jess frowned. 'I'm fine.'

He chuckled. 'I hardly think so, love. You're pale as a ghost and your leg is a mess,' he pointed out.

'I'd forgotten all about it,' she admitted, so focused had she been on what she needed to do.

'You were a bit busy, weren't you?' His grin was infectious. 'Are you hurt anywhere else?'

'Just some cuts and bruises. I bashed my side and twisted my foot when I fell. It's nothing. I'll clean up at home,' she assured him, anxiety setting in at the prospect of either Stuart or Mark treating her.

Pulling on a fresh pair of protective gloves, Stuart sat back and looked at her. 'That's a deep cut, Jess. You've lost a fair bit of blood and it's going to need stitching. And that's without getting the other things checked out.'

Her anxiety increasing, Jess bit her lip. She wished she could dismiss her injuries and refuse treatment, but looking at her leg she could see that the wound was bad and not something she would advise anyone else to try and take care of alone. As the adrenalin that had sustained her while waiting for the ambulance wore off, her foot and her ribs were also becoming increasingly painful and she feared she might have broken at least one bone. All of which meant she was going to have to tell Stuart the truth.

Fighting back an uncharacteristic welling up of tears, she sucked in a ragged breath. 'Stuart, I…' She hesitated, frightened what would happen when he knew.

'What's wrong, Jess?' he prompted, his concern evident.

'You need to double-glove,' she told him, her voice unsteady, her lashes lowering so that she wouldn't see the expression on his face. 'I'm HIV positive.'

A few seconds of silence followed and she felt sick as she waited for the inevitable reaction to her admission. An errant tear escaped and landed on her cheek. It was Stuart's hand that reached out to wipe it away and she glanced up, wide-eyed with surprise to see nothing but understanding and compassion in the forty-year-old father-of-three's hazel eyes.

'Don't you worry, Jess, love. We'll take good care of you.'

His kindness and easy acceptance, so at odds with

her earlier experiences—apart from Gio, of course—
brought a fresh welling up of emotion. As Stuart set
about dressing her leg, Jess struggled to push thoughts
of Gio to the back of her mind. She wished more than
anything that he was there with her now. But he wasn't.
She was on her own. Just as she had been these last four
years.

Before she knew it, they were setting off on the
thirty-minute drive from Penhally to St Piran, arriving
a long time after the air ambulance had deposited their
casualty. Stuart and Mark were wonderful, as was Ben
Carter, into whose experienced, caring and understanding hands they delivered her.

Supportive and reassuring, Ben guarded her confidentiality and refused to make an issue of her status.
By the time she had been X-rayed—thankfully there
proved to be no breaks—and returned to A and E to
have the deep cut on her leg stitched, her other cuts and
grazes cleaned and a supportive bandage put on her
swollen, painful foot, she was feeling tired and woozy.
The antibiotics and pain medication she'd been given
didn't help.

Dismissing the nurse who had waited with her, Ben
drew up a chair, sat down and sent her a warm smile. 'I
know you wanted news. The boy's name is Will. He's
in Theatre and has the best of chances, thanks to you.
You saved his life today, Jess. Care to tell me how you
did it?' he asked, signing off her notes and closing the
file.

Her defences lowered by all that had happened, not
just with Will and her own injury but the deep pain of
Gio's rejection and withdrawal, she found herself pouring the whole story out to Ben.

'Surgery's loss is St Piran's gain,' he told her a while later when her flow of words had ended.

'Thank you.'

'Does Gio know? Do you want me to call him?'

The two questions brought a fresh threat of tears. 'Yes, he knows,' she admitted, trying to steady her voice before she continued, forcing out the words. 'But don't call him. He's in Italy. And we're just friends.'

'Friends?' Ben raised a sceptical eyebrow.

'You heard about his wife?' she asked. When Ben nodded, she continued. 'He's not ready for a new relationship. Even if he was, it's too much for him to take on someone like me.'

'I wouldn't give up on him too quickly, Jess.'

She appreciated Ben's kindness but she had little hope left in fairy-tales. Resting her head back, feeling very tired, she sighed. 'Can I go home?'

'Not for a while, especially as you'll be on your own once you get there,' he added brushing aside her half-hearted protest.

A knock on the door curbed further conversation and senior staff nurse Ellen came in. Although she smiled, it was clear that something was bothering her and, before she closed the door, Jess heard the sound of some sort of commotion going on somewhere in the department.

'I'm sorry to interrupt,' Ellen apologised. 'Ben, we have a problem out here. Can you come?'

'Yes, of course. Rest here for a while and try not to worry about anything, Jess. I'll be back shortly to see you,' he promised, giving her hand a squeeze before pushing back the chair and rising to his feet.

'Thanks, Ben.'

'Is there anything I can get for you, love?' Ellen

asked, taking a moment to fuss with the sheet and pillows and make sure she was comfortable.

Feeling tired and washed out, Jess managed a smile. 'No, thanks. I'm fine.'

As they left the room, leaving her alone, Jess closed her eyes. It was one thing to tell her not to worry, but she was finding it impossible when her thoughts were fixed firmly on Gio. Despite thinking she could never trust a man again, in such a short time she had fallen irrevocably in love. But he couldn't feel the same about her and now, when she most needed his arms around her, he wasn't there. Ben had told her not to give up, but why would Gio want someone who was living with a condition that could change at any moment and drastically reduce her life expectancy, causing him to lose someone else?

She'd taken a huge risk, opening her heart and allowing Gio into her life, and all too briefly she'd experienced a piece of heaven before it had been ripped away from her again. She had no idea what the future held in store. After years of uncertainty, she had found a place where she felt at home and could settle. Was that now all to change because of Gio?

As much as he'd enjoyed his couple of days back home in Italy, and especially celebrating his parents' fortieth wedding anniversary, Gio continued to feel edgy and unsettled. For once it was nothing to do with returning to a place that reminded him of Sofia. His disquiet was all due to Jessica. Within hours he would be flying back to the UK and driving to the house he had shared with her in St Piran these last weeks. Knowing that she wouldn't be there made that return a dismal prospect.

'Something is troubling you, *figlio*.'

Gio looked up as his father joined him on the terrace and he gave a wry smile, unsurprised by the older man's insight. 'I'm fine, *Papà*.'

'Tell me about his woman.'

'What woman?' Gio prevaricated, shifting uncomfortably.

'You said you might be bringing a friend this weekend,' he reminded, 'but you came alone.'

'I might have meant a male friend.'

His father chuckled. 'You might. But you didn't. My guess is that you were referring to the woman who has been staying with you. The woman responsible for bringing you back to life these last weeks, bringing laughter and happiness back to your eyes.'

Gio sighed, somewhat stunned by his father's words. And by the realisation, the truth, of how much Jessica had changed him in the short time he had known her. He leaned against the railing and gazed out at the familiar Piedmont countryside. It was home—and yet now his heart felt as if it belonged elsewhere.

'Gio?'

Turning round, he pulled up a chair next to his father. 'I think I've made a big mistake, *Papà*.'

It had not been his intention to unburden himself, but now he found himself telling his father all about Jessica—and his dilemma.

'*Figlio*, you have never lacked courage. Do not start doubting yourself and your feelings now,' his father advised when he had finally run out of words.

'What do you mean?' Gio asked with a frown, running the fingers of one hand through his hair.

'Tell me,' his father asked, leaning forward and

resting his elbows on his knees, his gaze direct, 'would you have forgone the life you had with Sofia if you had known in advance that you would lose her when you did?'

A flash of anger flared within him at the question. 'Of course not!'

'That is what I thought.' His father smiled and although his tone gentled, his words lost none of their impact. 'Yet now you risk throwing away this second chance for love and happiness because you fear that you will one day lose Jessica, too.'

'Papà...'

His father gestured with one hand to silence him. 'Jessica is clearly a very special woman and she has become very important to you. You love her, I can see it in your eyes and hear it in your voice when you speak of her, and yet you're holding back. I know the pain and heartache you suffered when Sofia died. We all miss her. What you had together was so rare and so special. Few of us are blessed with that kind of happiness *once* in a lifetime, let alone *twice*,' the older man pointed out with a shake of his head.

In the brief pause that followed, the words sank in and Gio reflected on just how lucky he had been. He looked up as his father rested a hand on his shoulder and continued.

'We are all going to die at some time. What is important is what we do with the time we have. You have made us so proud, *figlio*, not only with your career and the work you do in Sofia's name but also because of the person you are. From all you have told me of her, your Jessica is a rare woman, and not one who would ever now trust herself to a man lightly. Yet she has trusted herself to *you*. Are you going to let her down? Are you going to let fear turn you away from love and the many years you could have together?'

The questions hit him full force, shocking him, but his father had not yet finished with him.

'Sofia would be so angry with you, Gio. She wanted you to live, to be happy, to love. Now you have found someone worthy of you, someone who has brought so much to your life. Don't throw that away, *figlio*,' he pleaded softly. 'You have our blessing, and Ginetta's, too,' he added, referring to Sofia's mother, who remained part of their family. 'You deserve new love and happiness. So does Jessica. Follow your heart…go back to the place that has become your home and show the woman who has given you so much the kind of man I know you to be.'

Hours later everything his father said still resonated in his head. It was early on Monday morning but he had given up trying to sleep. He had driven past Jessica's cottage before coming home from the airport but her car had not been there and it was clear no one was in. When he had also been unable to reach her by phone, unease had set in. Where was she?

Now he stared out of the window, seeing nothing but the darkness. There was also darkness inside himself. The house had felt cold and stark and lonely without Jessica, as he had feared it would. And so had he. All the joy and fun and warmth had left it with her departure. A departure he could blame on no one but himself.

He pressed one palm to the hollow ache in his chest. He had been so blind, so stupid. How could he have ever believed that he could live for the rest of his life in a vacuum? He hadn't been living at all, only existing. It was Jessica who had brought meaning back to his world again and had made him want to embrace life in every way.

Leaning his forehead against the coolness of the glass, he reflected on his mistakes. He had coaxed and cajoled Jessica into trusting him, caring for him, opening up to him. He'd taken what she had given him without properly considering just what it must have taken for her to trust, and exactly what that trust meant. She had shown such courage, while he had got cold feet. In doing so he had behaved as abominably as her ex-fiancé, her family and her former friends and colleagues had. How must Jessica be feeling now? *He* felt lower than low when he forced himself to consider what his withdrawal, his insistence that they could have nothing but friendship, must have done to her.

Dio!

How was he going to put things right?

Because he could see now with startling clarity that all his father had said was true. And he thought of Luca, who had been through a similar kind of loss as his own and who'd had the courage to let love back into his life again. He was a doctor, Gio chided himself. He knew that Jessica could fall ill tomorrow—but equally she could live a long and normal lifespan, keeping fit and well. Given the right care and precautions, even having a healthy child free of HIV was not the impossibility she believed it to be. Whatever she wished, he would support her all the way.

No one knew what the future held in store, just as his father and Luca had said. And facing the rest of his life alone was no longer the answer he had once thought. He could not guard himself from hurt without denying himself all the joys. And he knew now, after such a short time without Jessica, that he didn't want to waste any more time alone. Whether they had five years or fifty years, he wanted to share every moment with her. If she would forgive him and allow him a second chance.

Jessica had trusted him in the most elemental way and he had let her down. The knowledge cut him to the quick. In the face of her bravery he had been nothing but a coward. Were he to be lucky enough to win her back, he would spend the rest of their lives together proving to her that she was loved and cherished. Going downstairs, he made coffee and stepped outside into the coolness of the pre-dawn air, lost in his thoughts.

Along with the album Sofia had made of their lives had been a final letter for him. He carried it with him always, with her photo, next to his heart. He knew it word for word as she told him how much she loved him, that every moment had been worth it because they had been together, how she respected him and supported him.

'You must go on with your career, Cori, and with your life. Grieve for me, but not for too long. We have been so blessed and had so much more in twenty-two years than many people have in a whole lifetime. I know you, *amore mio*. And I beg you to move on, not to stay alone and sad for the rest of your life. I want you to be happy, fulfilled, cared for. You have so much love to give. Open your heart, Cori. For me. I will always be with you and will always love you. Look up at the night sky and the brightest star will be me smiling down on you, wishing you the best of everything and for a special woman to love you as I love you.'

His throat tight with emotion, he turned his gaze up to

the sky, finding the brightest star. He thought of Sofia's words, of her wish for him, her blessing, and realised he was letting her down by refusing to accept all life had to offer him. Had their places been reversed, he would have wanted the same for her…that she would find someone to care for her, who would make her happy. And his courageous, spirited Sofia would grieve, would never forget, but would face life with her customary bravery. Just as Jessica was doing in her own way, making a whole new life for herself after being so badly betrayed and left to cope with the devastation alone. He owed it to Sofia, to Jessica and to himself to step back into life.

He looked back at the star, opening his heart, knowing Sofia would always be there, that he would never forget and would always love her, but that there was room and a special place for Jessica, too. It was time. For a moment it seemed as if the star glowed even brighter, filling him with a sense of peace. As dawn broke, the stars fading as the sky slowly lightened, bringing a rosy glow to the magnificent Cornish coastline, Gio knew what he had to do.

CHAPTER ELEVEN

'OH, MY GOD.' Jess felt her whole world shattering into tiny pieces as she stared in horrified disbelief at the local newspaper. This couldn't be happening. 'How? Why?'

Ben sat solemn-faced beside her, appearing tired and drawn, as if he hadn't slept in the hours since she'd last seen him. 'I'm sorry, Jess. We tried to stop it.'

Fighting back tears and a terrible sense of doom, she re-examined the lurid headline emblazoned in large letters across the front page...

HOSPITAL HEROINE HAS HIV!

The night was a blur. She'd fallen asleep in A and E, knocked out by the medication and emotional exhaustion. 'We don't normally have staff sleeping in the department overnight but we made an exception for you,' Josh had teased her when he'd checked her over before the night shift ended.

When Ben had come back on duty, she'd discovered that the disturbance he'd been called to had been caused by Kennie Vernon, a reporter on the *St Piran Gazette*, known as 'Vermin' for his unpleasant methods and his motto of never allowing the truth to spoil a good story.

She'd met him once when he'd delved unsuccessfully into the background of a patient in her care, and he'd left an unfavourable impression. Short and stout, his greasy black hair worn in a narrow ponytail, he had a goatee beard, beady brown eyes and a shifty nature.

'One of the bystanders in Penhally overheard you telling the paramedics about the HIV and informed Kennie. The bastard ran with that angle of the story.' Ben's anger and disgust were evident. 'He came poking around A and E. I threw him out. You were sleeping, so Josh and I decided to keep you here. We didn't want you going home alone or risk you running into Kennie.'

Jess wrapped her arms around herself, unable to stop shaking. 'What am I going to do?'

'You told me about the appalling way you were treated when you were first diagnosed, but that isn't going to happen here,' he reassured her, but she lacked belief.

'Right.'

Ben took her hand. 'You'll be surprised, Jess. I'm not, because I know you are loved and respected. There may be one or two idiots, but ninety-nine percent of the hospital are supporting you. We've had endless calls sending you good wishes and they're continuing to come in.'

Jess didn't know what to say.

'We took the liberty of making some arrangements on your behalf,' he continued, and nervousness fluttered in her stomach.

'What arrangements?'

'Flora wanted to help. She said she held a spare key for your cottage in case of an emergency?' Jess nodded, trying to take everything in. 'Knowing you'd worry, she's picked up your kittens and will look after them for as long as you need.'

'Thank you,' she murmured, surprised but relieved.

'Your car remains where you left it in Penhally, so you'll need a lift to pick it up, but Megan met Flora at your cottage and collected some things you might need.'

Fresh tears pricked her eyes. For someone who seldom cried, she could have filled a swimming pool this last week. She didn't ask, but the person she most wanted to know about, and to see, was Gio. He'd be back from Italy. He might even be in the hospital, she realised, glancing at her watch, shocked by the time. What would he think? She felt sick with worry.

When Ben left, Jess gingerly slipped out of bed, thankful for the adjacent shower room that meant she didn't have to wander down the corridor in the unflattering hospital gown she was wearing. After a wash, she sat on the bed, feeling emotionally and physically battered as she wondered what to do.

'Where is she?'

Jess heard Megan's anxious question from outside and someone's voice mumble in reply. She barely had a moment to compose herself before her friend rushed in, her face pale and tears spiking her eyelashes. Without uttering a word, Megan dropped a carrier bag on the bed and wrapped her in a hug.

'You silly, silly girl,' she admonished, halfway between a laugh and a sob. 'Oh, how I wish I'd known. I can't bear to think of you going through this alone.'

Megan's acceptance and support was overwhelming. Jess began to explain, her voice shaky and whisper soft, when Brianna arrived. She looked as worried and upset as Megan. And, like Megan, Brianna's first instinct was to hug her.

With her friends giving the caring support she had never expected to know, Jess told them what she had told Gio—about Duncan, her diagnosis, the prejudice, ignorance and discrimination she'd encountered, and being disowned by her family. They were all crying by the time she had finished.

'I'd have been scared witless doing an emergency cricothyroidotomy,' Megan admitted when the talk moved on to the incident on the rocks and Jess's former career. 'I'm in awe at what you did.'

Brianna hugged her again. 'We all are. You're amazing, Jess. How far through your training were you?'

'I'd qualified and had begun a trauma rotation when I was diagnosed. I wanted to be a surgeon but was advised to find another career.'

'That's awful,' Brianna stated.

'It is,' Megan agreed. 'But it explains why you're so knowledgeable and able to explain things to patients when we don't have time. Do you miss it?'

'At first I was devastated. I attended an HIV support group and someone there suggested I think about counselling,' she told them, sharing things she'd told no one but Gio. 'I could continue helping people but without physical contact. I enjoy what I do and wouldn't change it now.'

'What about Gio?' Megan asked softly.

'He wants friendship, that's all.' It didn't become any easier with repetition. 'I understand why after he lost his wife. And it isn't as if I have anything to offer him.'

'Stuff and nonsense!' Brianna exclaimed, her Irish accent stronger than usual.

It hurt too much to talk about Gio so Jess changed the subject and reflected on the damage the newspaper article might have caused. The nightmare was real, the secret she had guarded was now public knowledge, and she feared the consequences. She was mulling over what to do when Ben returned.

'I'd rather you had a couple of days off and rested that leg, but sitting at home alone won't be good for you.' He frowned, deep in thought. 'We can look out for you here at the hospital. Just be sensible and don't over-stretch your side. And keep your foot up as much as possible. I've brought you some pain medication. Come and see us if you're not feeling well or you have problems with the wound.'

Jess took the tablets and smiled. 'OK. Thanks, Ben, you've been wonderful. How's Lucy?'

'About to pop!' he said, making them laugh. 'She's fed up and excited. We can't wait for the baby to arrive.'

Jess noticed Megan's and Brianna's smiles dimmed and both had pain in their eyes. She suspected her friends carried secrets and had been hurt in the past, and she wished there was something she could do to help them.

After Ben had given her a hug and final instructions, he returned to work. Megan and Brianna had to do the same but, before leaving, they arranged to meet up for lunch. Before heading to her office and what could be an uncomfortable chat with her boss, Jess changed into the clothes Megan had collected for her and went up to the ward to check on Will, anxious to know how he was. She felt nervous and unsure of the reception she would receive from colleagues and patients.

* * *

Driving to the hospital, Gio joined the queue at the traffic lights, his gaze straying to the pavement outside the newsagent's shop. His heart threatened to stop as he noted the headline on the local paper. Pasted onto a sandwich board for all to see, it shrieked out at him…

HOSPITAL HEROINE HAS HIV!

He swore furiously in Italian. There was little doubt to whom the headline referred. What the hell had been going on while he'd been in Italy? Anxious for Jessica and desperate to find out what lay behind the headline, he waited in frustration as the lights changed and the traffic moved forward then made his way as fast as he could to the hospital.

Dread clutched at him as he parked his car and hurried inside. One of the first people he saw was Ben, who gave him a brief résumé of events and then showed him the newspaper. While he felt deep concern for her well-being and fury at the thoughtless reporter, he was also full of pride at the way Jessica had saved the young man's life.

'Thank you for taking such good care of her,' he said now, shaking Ben's hand. 'Where is she?'

'She left here about five minutes ago and was going to visit Will in Intensive Care before going to her office.'

'Thanks,' he repeated.

Ben nodded, holding his gaze. 'Jess needs you, Gio,' his friend told him, and he knew he deserved the hint of chastisement that had laced the words.

'I need her, too,' he confided, earning himself a smile. 'I won't let her down again.'

Determined, he set off to find her.

* * *

'May I sit down?' Josh asked, taking advantage of the rare opportunity of finding Megan sitting alone in the canteen.

'OK.'

The agreement was grudging, but at least she *had* agreed and hadn't told him to go away. He set down his mug of coffee and pulled up a chair.

She looked at him, a small frown on her face. 'You look tired.'

'Is that a polite way of saying rough?' he teased with a wry smile, running the palm of one hand across his stubbled jaw, intrigued by the flush that brought a wash of colour to her pale cheeks.

'No, I didn't mean that.'

'I've just pulled an extra couple of night shifts and needed the caffeine fix before going home for some sleep. I'm back on days tomorrow,' he explained, savouring the hot, reviving drink.

What he didn't tell her was that he'd been doing extra shifts to avoid having to go home. Things were becoming more and more untenable with Rebecca and he didn't know what to do about it. They had grown further apart than ever. He had tried to encourage her to get out of the house, to take up some kind of voluntary work or hobby if she didn't want to get a job. Anything to give her something else to focus on instead of sitting at home working out ways to try and persuade him to change his mind about having a baby.

He wasn't going to change his mind. Ever. What he hadn't told Rebecca was that he had once teetered on the brink of fatherhood—unknowingly and no more willingly as that may have been at the time. He took another drink, his gaze fixed on Megan. Since talking to her and hearing once and for all that her baby had been his, he'd been able to think of little else.

Hearing in words the reality that he had held his tiny, lifeless son in his hands had hit him far harder than he had ever expected. And it had only made him more certain that having a baby with Rebecca was the wrong thing to do in so many ways, for him, for her and, most importantly of all, for any resulting child.

Setting down his mug, he folded his arms and leaned on the table, watching as Megan spread honey on a granary roll. 'How's Jess?'

'A bit sore. Very upset about the newspaper report. That beastly man,' she growled, echoing his feelings and those of everyone he knew.

'Poor Jess. No one needs that kind of thing.' He shook his head. 'I think people are more stunned at discovering she's a qualified doctor and saved that boy's life than anything else.'

Megan licked sticky honey off her finger, a simple gesture but one that nearly stopped his heart and brought a wave of all-too-familiar desire—the same desire he had always felt for her and her alone.

'Megan...'

'Don't, Josh, please. I—' Her words snapped off, her expression changing as she looked beyond him. He sensed her complete withdrawal, but before he could ask what was wrong, she spoke again. 'Your wife is here.'

He swore under his breath, looking round and seeing Rebecca standing just inside the entrance of the canteen. As always she looked picture perfect. Expensively dressed, polished, outwardly beautiful...and completely out of place.

'Megan,' he began again, returning his attention

to her, not at all sure what he wanted to say, still so confused and churned up inside, knowing only that he resented Rebecca's intrusion.

'Just go, Josh.'

After a moment of indecision he rose to his feet, spurred into action as Rebecca spotted him and began to close the distance between them. After an inadequate word of farewell, he left Megan and worked his way between the tables towards Rebecca and the exit.

'What are you doing here?' he asked, taking her arm to steer her out of the canteen, irritation shooting through him, compounded by the tiredness of two long night shifts.

She made her customary pout. 'You said the garage wouldn't have your car ready until this afternoon, so I thought I'd surprise you and pick you up.'

'I told you there was no need.'

They walked in silence towards the exit. A silence that spoke volumes about the physical, mental and emotional distance between them. They had nothing to speak about, nothing left in common. They didn't talk any more. He wondered if they ever had. One thing was certain…he could never share with her the jumble of emotions that continued to rage within him about Megan and about Stephen, their lost son.

'You! Ms Carmichael. Or Dr Carmichael…whatever your name is!'

Leaving Intensive Care after visiting Will, who was making good progress, and having been thanked by his grateful parents who had seen the newspaper report but were just relieved that their son was alive, Jess halted.

Her stomach churned as she turned to face the man whose angry voice had bellowed her name.

She'd been overwhelmed by the support she'd received from colleagues, many of whom had made a point of stopping her on her walk from A and E to Intensive Care. Now she was forced to encounter someone who sounded far from friendly.

The man was short and stocky with a ruddy complexion and a receding hairline. His heavy footsteps pounded on the floor as he strode determinedly towards her. Nervous, Jess heard the familiar ping that announced the arrival of one of the lifts, accompanied by the soft whooshing sound as the door opened. Unfortunately the lift was too far away for her to use it as an escape route.

'It's outrageous that you are allowed to walk around this hospital so close to vulnerable patients,' the man stated loudly, making her cringe with embarrassment. 'I don't want you anywhere near my wife.'

As the man continued his tirade, his language becoming ever more abusive, Jess was very aware that they were drawing a crowd. People walking the corridors stopped to see what was going on, while others emerged from nearby wards and offices. No one intervened. She was on her own.

Alarmed and humiliated, Jess stepped back, only to find her path blocked as she came up against something solid and strong and warm. Before she could even draw breath and absorb the fact that Gio was really here, one of his arms wrapped around her, across the front of her shoulders, drawing her against his familiar frame, making her feel protected.

'That is enough, sir.' Gio didn't raise his voice and

yet his words rang with such authority and steely command that her detractor at once fell silent. 'You have no business abusing any member of hospital staff at any time, and even less so when your information is wrong and you are speaking from ignorance.'

'But—'

'But nothing. Jessica is a highly valued and respected colleague. Her status is no one's business but her own and she poses absolutely no danger to anyone else,' he stated firmly, his hold on her tightening as she relaxed into him, drawing on his strength. 'Yesterday she saved the life of a young man who would have died had she not been there. For her courage and her selflessness she deserves gratitude and praise, not the ill-informed comments and judgemental attitudes of people who do not know what they are talking about.'

Jess remained speechless with amazement as Gio launched into his defence of her, declaring his support of and belief in her. But even when the man who had challenged her had been silenced and walked away by Security, she discovered that Gio had more to say, uncaring of their audience of colleagues, patients and visitors who remained.

'I am so proud of you, Jessica, and so sorry that I was not here for you when you needed me,' he declared, gently turning her round and cupping her face in his hands. She stared into intense blue eyes, every part of her shaking. 'I love you. I want to marry you and spend the rest of my life with you...if you will have me and forgive me for being so stupid this week and letting you down.'

Jess barely heard the gasps of delight and whispered comments from the people around them. All she could see, all she could hear, all she cared about was Gio, the man who had changed her life in such a short time, who believed in her and accepted her and who had just announced his love for her to the world.

'If I'll have you?'

She didn't know whether to laugh or to cry! So she did both. At the same time. He was everything she wanted. All she wanted. After the last few days of pain and uncertainty, thinking she could never have more than his friendship, she could hardly dare to believe this was true. For now, a wave of love and joy swamped the doubts that still lingered within her. Uncaring of where they were, of her painful side and throbbing leg—even of providing more gossip fodder for nosy Rita—she wrapped her arms around his neck, welcoming the instant response as his own arms enclosed her and held her close.

'I love you, too,' she managed through her tears.

As he swept her off her feet and into a passionate kiss, she dimly heard the whistles and whoops, the calls of congratulations and the spontaneous round of applause. She kissed him back with equal fervour and with all the emotion, love and thankfulness that swelled her heart.

After what had seemed the longest of days, and when he finally had Jessica to himself, Gio could not banish the flicker of unease that nagged at him. Concerned for her well-being and her injuries, he had brought her home to her cottage and insisted she rest while he cooked them a meal. She had eaten it, but she had grown quieter and quieter as the evening progressed. Now, as she paced the living room, her limp evident, he could bear the suspense no more.

As she passed within reach of his armchair, he caught her hand and drew her down to sit on his lap. A deep sigh escaped her and although she didn't pull away from him, she was far from relaxed.

'What is wrong, *fiamma*?' he asked, scared that she was having doubts and changing her mind. 'You are so restless. Talk to me.'

'I can't thank you enough for what you did today. It was horrible and I didn't know what to do.' For a moment she hesitated, her gaze averted, then she sighed again and looked at him, revealing the shadows in her olive-green eyes. 'Then you were there and made everything right.'

So why did he suddenly feel that things were now wrong? His heart lurched in fear. 'Jessica…'

'I won't hold you to it. I'll understand if it was something you said on the spur of the moment because of the circumstances,' she told him in a rush, her voice shaky.

'You won't hold me to what?' he asked, genuinely puzzled.

Long lashes lowered to mask her expression and her voice dropped to a whisper. 'Marrying me. You don't have to.'

'You don't want me to?'

'Yes. No. Not if you don't want to.'

She frowned in confusion and he felt bad for teasing her, but now he could see to the root of her worries, it felt as if a huge weight had lifted from his shoulders. He understood her doubts. He deserved them after the way he had behaved. But this, he hoped, he could deal with.

'Look at me.' He cupped her face with one hand,

drawing her gaze to his. 'It is true I had not planned on asking you to marry me in such a way, with so many people listening. But at the time a public declaration seemed right.' Uncertainty remained in her eyes. 'Can you pass me my jacket?'

'OK.'

He held her steady as, her frown deepening, she reached out to retrieve the jacket of his suit, which he had discarded and left draped over the arm of the adjacent sofa.

'Thank you.' With his free hand he checked the pockets until he found what he needed. 'The timing and the setting may have been unplanned, but I meant every word I said.'

He heard her indrawn gasp of surprise and she looked at him with a mix of warring emotions in her eyes. 'Gio?'

'I'm not surprised you doubted me. I deserve that after the terrible way I behaved last week,' he told her, pressing a finger to her lips to silence her protests. 'It needs to be said, *fiamma*. I was wrong. I knew how badly other people had treated you and yet I allowed my own momentary fears to rise up and my withdrawal, timed with my trip to Italy, must have felt like another rejection of you. I am so sorry.'

'Don't.' She caught his hand, their fingers instinctively linking together. 'I understand. And I don't blame you.'

'You should.'

She shook her head, her loose hair shimmering and dancing like living fire. 'No. You went through so much with Sofia. I knew you were scared of going through anything like that again. And, let's face it, the odds could be less good with me.'

'I do not care about odds, Jessica, I care about *you*,' he insisted. 'I never imagined that I could fall in love again, that I would ever know happiness and peace again, but my life changed for the better the moment I met you. Thanks to you I stopped existing and started living again.'

'Gio,' she whispered, her eyes bright with unshed tears.

'Please, I need to say this.' He drew her hand to his mouth and kissed it. 'I hate that I hurt you, that my withdrawal left you so lonely and uncertain. You deserved so much more from me and, if you will let me, I'll spend the rest of our lives proving to you how much I love you and that I'll never let you down again.' He paused a moment, sucking in an unsteady breath, his heart thudding against his ribs. 'I came back from Italy knowing what an idiot I had been and knowing what I wanted and needed to do. Events overtook us, and my plans went awry.'

Eyes wide with disbelief and hope, she bit her lip, her fingers clinging to his. 'What plans?' she managed, and he could feel the tremble running through her.

'My plans to be with you alone, like this, to beg your forgiveness and to ask you properly to be my wife.' Holding her gaze, he released her hand and reached into his pocket once more, drawing out the box. 'I bought this in Italy. For you. I meant all I said this morning, I just meant to say it in private! So the timing may have been wrong, but the question was heartfelt and genuine, not something I made up on the spot.' He placed the little box in her hand. 'Jessica, I love you. I want to spend the rest of my life cherishing you, being your friend and your lover. Please, will you make me the happiest and luckiest of men and marry me?'

'Yes. Yes, yes, yes!'

Jess felt as if her heart had swollen so full of love and joy that it would surely stop beating. All day doubts had nagged at her, but now her fears had been allayed as Gio had laid his own heart on the line for her. Again. Her vision blurred by tears, her fingers shaking so badly she could hardly make them work properly, she did as he encouraged and opened the jeweller's box.

'Oh, my,' she gasped. 'Gio!'

'You like it?' he asked nervously, and she laughed through her tears that he could doubt it.

She gazed down at the gorgeous ring. Set in platinum were three stunning olive apatite stones that exactly matched those in the earrings her grandmother had given her and which she wore every day. The three stones were set on a slight angle with the shoulders of the ring overlapping each side, each sparkling with a row of tiny diamonds. It was the most divine ring she had ever seen. She didn't dare imagine how much it had cost but it was not the monetary value that mattered, it was that Gio had chosen something so special, with such care, knowing what it would mean to her and giving it to her with love.

'It's beautiful,' she murmured huskily as he took it from the box and set it on her finger. 'Perfect. Thank you.'

'You are perfect and beautiful.'

He cupped her face, bestowing on her the gentlest and most exquisite of kisses. Jess sank into him, wrapping her arms around him, wondering how she had ever been lucky enough to know such happiness. As the passion flared between them, healing the past, uniting them heart and soul and full of promise for the future, she gave thanks for this very special man.

'I love your home,' Gio told her softly as they lay in bed later that night, replete after the physical expression of their love and togetherness. 'I feel at peace here,' he continued, filling her already overflowing heart with new joy as his feelings mirrored her own. 'Any day the fences will be ready and our menagerie will come home.'

'I thought maybe you'd arranged for that to be done so I'd leave your house and move back here,' she admitted softly.

'No!' He sounded so shocked she couldn't help but laugh, secure now in his feelings and her own. 'That was not why at all,' he insisted. 'It was to make you happy but also, selfishly, because I wanted to come here and to care for the animals with you. Can this *be* our home, *fiamma*? Can we bring this beautiful shell back to life together and make it ours for ever?'

'Yes, please!'

Snuggling into his embrace, she smiled into the darkness, knowing that they shared the same vision, not just for this place that would be their home but for their future. However long they were blessed with they would share together. And with the friends and colleagues who had shown them so much support and understanding.

It was not just the cottage that had been a shell that would be brought back to life. She and Gio had been shells, too. They had each been alone, rocked and ravaged by the events that had turned their lives upside down. But fate had brought them together…two people who had needed each other so much. They had found their place. Had found each other. And together they had found the sunshine, new hope and a fresh joy of living.

Safe in Gio's arms, Jess felt truly at peace, secure in a love, a friendship and a happiness that neither of them had ever expected to know again. They had been granted second chances and they had found their rightful place in this special part of Cornwall.

It had been a difficult journey but, finally, she was where she was meant to be…with Gio.

ST. PIRAN'S: DAREDEVIL, DOCTOR...DAD!

ANNE FRASER

To Rachel and Stewart – my personal on-call doctors – and to Megan Haslam, my supportive, patient and all round fabulous editor.

CHAPTER ONE

ABBY sank onto the sofa transfixed by what was happening on the TV screen. At the end of a rope, a man was being lowered out of a Royal Navy helicopter. Abby held her breath as the figure swirled precariously in the buffeting wind. She had put on the TV to catch the weather report but now she couldn't tear her eyes away from the drama unfolding in front of her.

Beneath the helicopter a boat was listing dangerously to one side, obviously in serious trouble. The reporter covering the story was telling the viewers that the Royal Navy rescue service had been called out to the stricken vessel. 'The family of four were on a sailing trip when they got into trouble off the Cornish coast. Heavy seas pushed their boat onto rocks and it is now taking on water rapidly. We have heard that the helmsman took a heavy blow to his head and is unconscious. His wife, who radioed for help, and their two young children, are still on board.'

Although the newscaster's expression was calm, Abby could detect suppressed tension in her voice. 'The helicopter crew has only a short time to get everyone off before the boat sinks. We understand that there is a doctor helping from the Royal Cornwall Air Ambulance Service.'

The man at the end of the winch dropped onto the listing boat, unhooked himself from the line and slithered his way across the deck. Within minutes he was being lifted back on board the helicopter, with two small figures attached to him like clams.

He swiftly dropped down to the boat again, retrieving another person from the stricken yacht. Heart in her mouth, Abby leaned forward. The injured skipper was still on the boat! Could he be rescued before the yacht sank, taking him and his rescuer along with it? If he had a head injury, as the newscaster was suggesting, then it would be dangerous to move him. But what other option was there? To leave him would be unthinkable.

The downdraught from the helicopter whipped the sea into a frenzy. Nearby, a coastguard rescue boat was making valiant attempts to approach the yacht but the heavy waves were preventing it from getting anywhere close. Abby squeezed her eyes closed. She could hardly bear to watch.

'A second man is being lowered onto the boat.' The newscaster's voice dropped to a whisper. 'We understand he's a doctor.'

Abby opened her eyes. Sure enough, she could just make out the letters on the fluorescent jacket of the second man.

The line attached to the helicopter was swinging wildly as the pilot struggled to keep the aircraft level. The small boat rose up to meet the man on the end of the winch then dropped away again. The figure swung first to the right then to the left as the deck kept veering away. Abby knew there was a real possibility that the rescuers might lose their own lives in the attempt to reach the injured skipper.

Suddenly the doctor was on the deck. Quickly he

released himself from the harness and the line was reeled back into the helicopter.

Almost unable to breathe, Abby watched him pick his way across the slippery deck, almost losing his balance as the boat shifted wildly in the heavy seas. Moments later another man dropped down from the helicopter, this one with a stretcher. Abby lost sight of the first man as he disappeared from view. Had he slipped overboard?

While she'd been watching, Emma had come into the room. Seeing Abby staring at the screen, she unplugged herself from her MP3 player and sat down next to her.

'Is that what you're going to be doing?' Emma asked. 'In your new job?'

'Sometimes,' Abby admitted. Although she hoped to hell she wouldn't be involved in anything quite as dangerous as what was going on in front of her. It was one thing being trained to be winched up and down from a helicopter in calm conditions—this was something altogether different.

Emma looked at her wide-eyed. 'Cool,' she said.

Thankfully her daughter didn't seem to appreciate the danger the men were in. That was good: Abby didn't want Emma worrying about her.

It seemed like hours but it could only have been a few minutes before the stretcher, now loaded with the injured skipper, was being attached to the winch. Abby knew the danger was far from over. The yacht was sinking rapidly. She was amazed that it had managed to stay afloat as long as it had.

Then the men with the stretcher were being lifted back onto the helicopter. As soon as they were on board the aircraft swung away. Seconds later the boat tipped up and with a final surge was engulfed by the waves. Any sooner and it would have taken the three men with it.

'I understand the mother and two children have been taken to hospital where they are being treated for hypothermia and shock,' the reporter continued. 'At this time we have no details about the condition of the skipper except that he is stable. But right now we can give you a live interview with some of the men involved in the daring rescue.'

The drama over, Emma went back to her music and left the room. Before Abby could switch the television off, the camera panned out slightly, revealing two men. One, a man in his fifties, was wearing the jumpsuit of the Royal Navy, the other the fluorescent jacket of a rescue doctor. Both men were smiling broadly, as if what they had just done had been exhilarating—and no more dangerous than a routine training exercise.

But as the camera zoomed closer, it was the younger man, the doctor, that made Abby's heart leap in her chest. Underneath his five-o'clock shadow there was something disturbingly familiar about his hooked nose and wide grin. But before Abby could get a better look at him the camera, frustratingly, focussed solely on his colleague.

'I have Sergeant Lightbody with me, who was the winchman involved in the rescue,' the reporter said.

The older man shifted slightly, looking uncomfortable to find himself on TV.

'Sergeant Lightbody,' the newscaster continued, 'can you tell the viewers at home what it was like out there today? From what I could see, it seemed that you just managed to get the victims off the boat in the nick of time.'

Sergeant Lightbody looked even more ill at ease. 'It was certainly a little breezy out there. I guess it was one of the more difficult situations we've been involved in for a while.'

'A little breezy? A bit of an understatement, surely? If you and your men hadn't been able to get these people off, it could've ended in tragedy. That all the family members survived is testament to the skill and courage of your team.'

'It's what we do.' Sergeant Lightbody shrugged. 'Anyway, if it hadn't been for Dr MacNeil here, we might not have got the skipper off without further injury—if at all.'

The camera shifted to the younger man. He was shaking his head. Despite the hat pulled low on his brow, shadowing his eyes, Abby realised with a jolt that she did recognise him. She didn't need to check the photograph she had kept for all these years to know that Dr MacNeil was Mac—her dead sister's lover and Emma's father!

Her legs shaking, Abby got up and retrieved the remote then froze the screen. She was breathing rapidly as she studied the fuzzy picture. It was him! He was older, yes; there were faint smile lines on either side of his mouth and radiating from the corners of his ice-blue eyes. He had filled out a little, and his hair was shorter, although still sun-bleached at the tips. Still, she would know that wide smile and glinting, expressive gaze anywhere.

She pressed the remote and the picture moved again.

'Dr MacNeil, could you tell us what happened back there? I understand you work with the Royal Cornwall Air Ambulance team. Is this just another typical day for you?'

Abby's heart was pounding so hard she could almost

hear it. She had found Mac! And not just found him, she was actually going to be working with him. She sank back down on the sofa as her legs threatened to give way beneath her. Thank God Emma had left the room. She would have known immediately that something was wrong, and right now Abby needed to make sense of what she was seeing.

Mac grinned into the camera. Unlike Sergeant Lightbody, he seemed completely at ease. 'Not exactly a typical day but, yes, the Royal Cornwall Air Ambulance teams up with other rescue services when required. We believe that having immediate medical attention on the scene can often make the difference between life and death.'

'Even if it means putting your own life at risk?' The stunning blonde reporter was almost whimpering with admiration.

'I'm pretty certain the Royal Navy wouldn't let anything happen to me,' Mac replied lightly. 'Besides, they are the real heroes. They do this sort of thing day after day. If it wasn't for the pilot of the helicopter and his team, we would have never been able to get to the casualties.'

Abby still couldn't believe what she was seeing. It was ironic, really. Abby had tried desperately to find this man years before without any success, and now he was here, in Penhally, and she'd be working with him!

Incredible to think that the reason they were here in the first place was because Emma didn't have a father.

A few months ago, just before Emma's eleventh birthday, Abby had asked her whether she wanted to invite her schoolfriends over for a party. To Abby's horror, Emma had burst into tears. When she'd eventually managed to calm her down, Emma had admitted that the children at the school had been ostracising her for the last couple of weeks. Only her best friend had still talked to her.

'But why, darling? Has something happened? You used to have loads of friends.'

Between tears and sobs of anguish Emma had explained that one of the girls had started taunting her about not having a dad.

'I told them that of course I had a dad,' Emma had said, indignant. 'So they asked where he was. When I told them I didn't know, they made fun of me. They said that I was lying or else I must be a rubbish daughter that my dad didn't want to know me. I tried to ignore them but they kept coming after me, saying these horrible things.' She'd looked up at Abby, her blue eyes swimming with tears. 'I know you're not my real mum, Mum.' She'd smiled, realising what she'd said. 'I mean, you're my real mum, but not my birth mum. But you've never told me who my father is. Why doesn't he care about me? Why *hasn't* he ever come to see me?'

Abby's heart had ached for her child. Although, as Emma had put it, *she* wasn't her biological mother, Emma was hers in every way that counted. She couldn't love her more had she given birth to her, and Emma being her twin sister Sara's child simply made the bond closer.

'I want to know who my dad is,' Emma had continued quietly. 'All the other girls at school know who their dad is, so why can't I?'

Abby had looked into the stormy blue eyes that were so like Sara's and a lump had formed in her throat. She'd known only too well how Emma had felt.

'My darling, he probably doesn't even know you exist.'

'How can he not know? How could my real mum not have told him?'

Abby winced before she'd begun speaking. 'Sara was very happy you were going to be born. I guess she didn't want to share you.'

The truth was that Sara hadn't wanted Emma's father to know about the pregnancy. At least not until she discovered that she was going to die. It was only then that she told Abby that Emma's father was Mac, the windsurfing instructor they had met while on holiday in Mykonos. When Emma was just three months old Abby went back to the Greek island to try to track him down, but it was hopeless. The summer season was over, and the visitors as well as the instructors had long since packed up and left. No one could tell her anything about Mac. Who he was or where he'd gone.

Before Sara died, Abby promised she would raise her daughter as her own. She had kept that promise and even though it hadn't always been easy, Abby had no regrets. Emma brought such joy to her life.

'I don't want to stay at that school, Mum. Please. Can't I go to a different school when I go to secondary?'

'It's not that easy, sweetie. Here in London it's difficult to find a good school within walking distance. Let me try and sort things out with the school first.'

But despite several visits to the school, the bullying continued. It both angered and saddened Abby to see Emma withdraw more and more into herself, so when Abby saw an ad for an experienced paramedic for the Royal Cornwall Air Ambulance Service, after talking it over with Emma, she decided to apply. Cornwall would be perfect for them. It was near the sea and would suit Emma's love of the outdoors much better. They were both thrilled to leave London and its sad memories behind. Abby had promised Emma that as soon as they were settled in their new home and she in her job she would continue the search for her father. Little did Abby know then that fate was going to throw them directly in his path, sooner than either of them could possibly have imagined.

Abby retrieved the tattered holiday snap from the sideboard drawer. It had been taken on the last night of her and Sara's holiday on Mykonos and Abby studied it for what must have been the hundredth time. It was a group photograph, taken on the beach. Mac had his arm draped around Sara, who was laughing up at him. She herself was at the end, a solemn figure with mid-length hair, her eyes hidden behind sunglasses. She doubted if Mac had even been aware that she was there. They had been introduced, of course, but his glance had slid almost immediately straight past Abby to her much more glamorous and fun-loving sister.

She turned to stare at the TV again, almost expecting him to reappear. She still had a week of training to complete before she started her job, so she had some time to think before she came face to face with Dr William MacNeil.

What was she going to tell Emma?

What was she going to say to Mac when they met?

What the hell was she going to do?

CHAPTER TWO

ABBY'S stomach fluttered nervously as she stepped into the base of the Royal Cornwall Air Ambulance Service. Although she had been a trained paramedic for almost twelve years, this would be an altogether different experience. She would be *flying* to rescues and despite the intensive training she had just undergone, she worried how she would cope with being lowered from a helicopter, particularly in gusty weather. But she was here now and those concerns paled into insignificance in comparison to her anxiety about meeting Mac again.

Ever since she'd seen him on television she'd been agonising over what to do. What if he was married and had a family of his own? What if Mac didn't want to know about his daughter? That hurt would be too great for the little girl. In which case should she even tell Emma that Mac was here? Did she have the right to keep the truth from Emma?

In the end she decided she wouldn't say anything to Emma until she'd had a chance to suss Mac out for herself. After all, a bad father was worse than no father at all.

The air ambulance leader, who had interviewed Abby when she'd applied for the job, met her at the door. Paul was in his early fifties with an easy smile and a relaxed and welcoming manner.

'Abby, we've been looking forward to you joining us,' he said. 'Did you enjoy your training? The course leader spoke highly of you.'

The course leader might have spoken highly of her, but that meant zilch. How she would cope in a real-life rescue would be what counted.

'What do think of Penhally Bay?' Paul continued.

'It's lovely. I haven't had too much time to explore yet—what with the course, getting my daughter settled into school and all the unpacking. But I promised Emma that on my first day off we'll have a proper look around.'

'It's a great place for a child to grow up,' Paul said. 'My kids have long since flown the coop, but they come back whenever they can. Is Emma liking Penhally High? Mine went there and they loved it. I can't imagine it's changed too much.'

Abby nodded, managing a small smile. If nothing else, their move here had been the right thing for Emma, at least as far as her new school went. Although her daughter had only been at Penhally High for a short while, she had quickly made new friends and already seemed much happier and settled.

So she was here to stay, and if life had thrown her a curve ball by flinging her directly in Mac's path, so be it. There was no going back. But until she decided what, if anything, to tell him, she would play her cards close to her chest.

Nevertheless her heart was pounding uncomfortably at the thought of meeting him again. Would he recognise her after all these years? It was unlikely. Her appearance had changed quite a bit and he hadn't paid her much attention twelve years ago. He had been far too caught up in her twin sister, the glamorous, effervescent Sara.

'Come up to the office and meet everyone,' Paul interrupted her thoughts. 'They're looking forward to meeting you.'

Her legs like jelly, Abby followed him up a steep flight of steps and into a large room where a number of people were chatting and drinking coffee.

Immediately her eyes were drawn to Mac. He was sitting, his long legs stretched out in front of him, his arms cradling the back of his head as he chatted to a colleague. Like most of the others in the room, he was dressed in an orange jumpsuit, but his was unzipped almost to the waist, revealing a dazzling white T-shirt underneath. There was no disguising his powerful build and Abby felt as if a bird were trapped in her chest.

'Everyone, I'd like you to meet our latest recruit, Abby Stevens,' Paul introduced her.

This was the moment she had been dreading. Would Mac remember her? Would he recall Sara's last name? Had he even known what it was? Although everyone turned to look at her, Abby was unable to stop herself from watching Mac's reaction. Blue eyes narrowed for a moment as if she had triggered a memory, but then he grinned and jumped to his feet. His eyes swept over her body.

'I'm Dr William MacNeil. But everyone calls me Mac.' His grip was firm and to her dismay it felt as if she had touched a live wire. Abby withdrew her hand quickly and turned to greet the other members of the team but not before she'd seen Mac's puzzled frown.

Abby forced herself to concentrate as she was

introduced to the others in the room. Apart from Paul, there were two paramedics, Mike and Jim, a pilot—an older man called Greg—as well as Lucy, another doctor, and Kirsten, whose job it was to take the calls and keep in touch with the ambulance throughout the rescue. They all smiled welcomingly.

Instinctively Abby knew she would enjoy working with this group of people—with one possible exception.

'Would you mind showing Abby around, Mac?' Paul asked. 'I have some paperwork to attend to and Lucy and Mike have just popped in to give us a report on yesterday's callout.' Paul turned to Abby. 'I'll see you all later.'

'A car accident on the coastal road,' Lucy explained as Paul left the room. She was small and plump with bright, intelligent eyes. 'The driver was going too fast for these roads and hit another car head on.'

'Any fatalities?' Abby asked.

'Surprisingly not. Luckily the oncoming car managed to swerve in time. The fire brigade had to use the jaws of life to get the driver out. It took hours and we had to keep him ventilated by hand. He's still on the critical list, but he's damned lucky to be alive.' Lucy glanced at her watch. 'Time for me to go!' She held out her hand again. 'It's good to have another woman on board, Abby. Kirsten and I get a little overwhelmed by all the testosterone around here, don't we, Kirsten?'

Kirsten grinned back. 'Don't let Lucy kid you—she's a match for the guys any time.'

Abby glanced across at Mac, who had remained silent throughout the exchange. He was studying Abby as if she puzzled him.

'Hey, have we met before?' he asked.

Abby's pulse beat even faster. Although she and Sara hadn't been identical twins there had been similarities between them—hazel eyes, straight noses and curvy mouths. But Sara had cropped her hair short and bleached it platinum blonde for their Greek holiday. In contrast, Abby had kept her shoulder length caramel hair tied back in a ponytail and at that time had worn glasses. The two sisters could hardly have looked more different and unsurprisingly Mac had barely glanced at Abby back then. Even if he did recognise her, this was hardly the time or place to tell him about Sara and Emma. Not that she had decided *what* to tell him.

She forced a smile. 'I don't think so.'

He lost the frown and grinned at her. 'You're right,' he said, lowering his voice. 'I would have remembered you. I don't tend to forget beautiful women.' He winked at her.

'And unless you're losing it, they don't tend to forget you either. That's what you mean,' chipped in Lucy. She turned to Abby, her eyes twinkling. 'Watch out for our Mac here. We love him to bits, but he's a heartbreaker. Luckily I'm too old for him and Kirsten's already taken.'

'You know I'd take you to dinner any day of the week, Lucy. Just say the word.' Mac grinned back.

'Ah, if only,' Lucy sighed theatrically. She picked up her handbag. 'I'm out of here.'

'Me too,' Kirsten said. 'I've got work to do around here!'

Left alone with Mac, Abby felt as if she had a coiled spring somewhere in her chest. He was still looking at her through half-closed eyes as if she puzzled him. 'Dr

MacNeil,' she said stiffly. 'I think we should get on with that tour, don't you?'

Again there was that heart-stopping grin. 'Call me Mac. Everyone else does.'

Mac stood back to let Abby go in front of him. He whistled under his breath as he watched the way her bottom swayed as she walked. On anyone else the orange uniform tunic top and matching trousers would have been unflattering, but it could have been tailor made for Abby. And, even apart from her figure which looked as if it had been designed with him in mind, she was a stunner. A man could drown in those eyes and as for the high cheekbones, emphasised by the hint of colour his remarks had brought to her cheeks, he had dated models who would scratch their eyes out for bone structure like that. Even the spattering of freckles over her nose didn't detract from her beauty—if anything, it made her cuter. He had already checked the third finger of her left hand. No wedding ring. Good. This was going to be interesting.

Mac had only just started showing Abby the little office where Kirsten and her small team fielded the calls when the telephone rang.

Kirsten held up a finger, asking for silence. They listened as she entered a few details into the computer.

'Try not to worry, love. We'll have someone there as soon as possible. Stay on the phone while I talk to the doctor.'

She swivelled around in her chair until she was facing Abby and Mac.

'I have a lady on the line. She's thirty-four weeks pregnant but thinks she's gone into early labour. She can't get herself to the hospital because she's on a farm and her husband is away with the car.' Kirsten covered the mouthpiece with her hand. 'She also tells me she has placenta praevia and was due to be admitted for a Caesarean section in a couple of weeks.'

'Where is the farm?' Mac asked. Gone was the laconic man of earlier. In his place was someone who was entirely focussed.

Kirsten pointed to a map. 'Over here.'

'What about the local road ambulance?' Abby asked.

Kirsten shook her head. 'It's at least an hour away on these roads and, besides, the woman—she's called Jenny Hargreaves—says the track to the farm is pretty impassable for anything except a four-by-four. We've had some heavy rain over the last fortnight.'

'We need to get her to the maternity unit as fast as possible,' Mac said. 'Okay, Kirsten, get Greg to fire the 'copter up and tell Jenny we're on our way. Is there anyone with her who can help? A friend? A neighbour?'

Kirsten shook her head. 'She's on her own, apart from her nine-year-old son.'

'Get him on the line and keep him there. Then phone St Piran's and bring them up to speed. Could you make sure we have an incubator for the baby on board, too? C'mon, Abby. I guess you're on. Let's go and get kitted up.'

As Abby raced after him down the steps and into the cloakroom where their gear was kept, she ran through what she knew about placenta praevia. And what she did know didn't make her feel any better.

'Not good news, is it?' she said as Mac passed her a jacket.

'Tell me what you know about the condition.'

'Placenta praevia is where the placenta is lying in front of the baby, blocking the birth canal. I know it can cause massive, even fatal bleeding if left untreated. If she's already in labour, we don't have much time.' Although they had covered complications of childbirth in their training, until Sara it hadn't crossed Abby's mind that it could really happen. Now she knew better. Please, God, don't let this first call end in disaster.

'Do we have an obstetrician on call?' she asked.

'At St Piran's. Kirsten will patch us through as soon as we're airborne. There's no time to wait, though.' Mac stopped for a moment and rested his hands on her shoulders. He looked directly into her eyes. 'Are you going to be okay?' His look was calm, reassuring. Everything about him radiated confidence and Abby relaxed a little.

'Sure.' She kept her voice light. 'All in a day's work.'

They piled into the helicopter and lifted off, heading towards the coast.

'ETA twenty minutes,' Greg's voice came over the radio. 'It's a bit breezy where we're heading so it might get a little bumpy.'

'Do you think we'll be able to put down?' Mac asked.

'There's a good-sized field behind the farmhouse, but I guess it depends on how soggy the ground is. We won't know until we get there.'

Abby and Mac shared a look.

'Have you ever done an emergency section before?' Abby asked. If they couldn't get mother and baby to hospital, it would be their only chance. But such a procedure would be tricky even for a qualified obstetrician in a fully equipped theatre. Her heart started pounding again. Confidence was one thing, but did Mac have the skill needed to back it up?

'I have.' He leaned across and flashed Abby another wicked grin. 'But don't worry, I have every intention of letting the obstetricians do it.' He held up a finger and listened intently.

A quiet voice came over the radio. 'Hello, Mac. Dr Gibson here. What do we have?'

'A thirty-four-weeker with placenta praevia who has gone into early labour. Control has her son on the phone. Mum tells him she thinks her contractions are coming about five minutes apart. The mother's name is Jenny Hargreaves. She tells us she was due to be delivered by section at St Piran's so you should have her case notes there.'

There was a short silence. Abby guessed Dr Gibson was bringing up Jenny's record on her computer screen.

'I'll make sure neonatal intensive care is standing by and that we have a theatre ready. How long d'you think before you'll have her here for us?'

'Another ten minutes until we land. If we can. Say another ten to examine our lady and get her loaded and twenty back. Do you think we'll make it?' Again there was that easy smile as if this was just another everyday callout.

'If anyone can, you can,' came back the reply. 'But if she's gone into active labour she could be bleeding massively and you may have to section her there and then. It won't be easy.'

'Hell, whoever said anything is easy in this job? But trust me.' He turned and winked at Abby. 'If I can get her to you without having to section her, I will.' He flexed long fingers. 'Been a long time since I did one of those.'

'Good luck,' Dr Gibson said calmly.

A short while later they reached the farm. To Abby's relief the pilot had been able to find a spot to land. The helicopter rotors had barely slowed when Mac hefted the large medical bag over his shoulder.

'Okay, we're on. Remember to keep your head down.' Abby took a deep breath, sent a silent prayer towards heaven, and followed him out of the helicopter.

Mac sprinted towards the farmhouse, carrying the medical case that weighed at least ten kilos as if it were nothing. Abby ran after him, doing her best to keep up.

A child with wide, frightened eyes was waiting for them by the doorway.

'Please hurry, my mum is bleeding,' the boy said.

This was the worst possible news. Jenny being in labour was one thing, but they had banked on having enough time to get her to hospital. If she had started bleeding it meant that the placenta was beginning to detach. As it did, the baby's life support system became compromised and the life of the mother was in jeopardy. It would have been dangerous enough in hospital, but all Abby and Mac had was some morphine and basic equipment. It wasn't good. Abby's heart jumped to her throat.

Mac paused by the doorway and hunkered down so that he was at eye level with the boy. He placed a hand on the child's shoulder.

'What's your name, son?'

'Tim.'

'It's going to be all right, Tim, I promise. Now, if you could take us to your mum, we'll look after her.'

Whatever Tim saw in Mac's eyes seemed to reassure him. He nodded and led them inside the farmhouse and into a bedroom. On the bed, a woman lay writhing with pain. She was pale and her eyes were stretched wide with fear.

Abby and Mac rushed to her side.

'Jenny, isn't it?' Mac said as he laid the medical case on the floor. 'I'm Dr MacNeil and this is Abby Stevens. We're going to do everything we can to look after you and your baby.'

Abby felt Jenny's pulse.

'Over one hundred and thready,' she told Mac as she unwrapped the stethoscope from around her neck.

'How long have you been bleeding? And when did the contractions start?' Mac asked.

'I just started bleeding a few minutes ago. The contractions started about an hour ago. I phoned the hospital and they said they would get an ambulance.' Jenny reached out a hand and squeezed Abby's fingers hard. 'You have to save my baby. Please. You've got to help us.'

'We are going to do everything possible,' Abby replied with what she hoped was a confident smile.

She checked Jenny's blood pressure. As expected, it was low. Jenny was already bleeding heavily.

'I'm just going to give you some fluids through a needle in your vein,' Mac explained as he swabbed a patch of skin near Jenny's elbow. 'Then we're going to get you onto a stretcher and into the air ambulance, okay?'

'What about Tim? I can't leave him here by himself. My husband isn't due back until tomorrow morning.'

'Is there a neighbour we could call for you?'

Jenny shook her head. 'We only moved here a couple of months ago. I don't know anyone yet. I've been so busy getting ready for the new baby.'

'In that case, Tim can come in the helicopter with us. How about it, Tim?' Mac turned to the little boy who had remained by the door, taking everything in with wide eyes.

'Wicked,' he said. Now adults were taking control, the colour had returned to his face.

Mac finished setting up the drip.

'Okay, Jenny. The helicopter's just outside waiting to take you to hospital. We're going to get you on board as quickly as we can.'

Jenny clutched her stomach as another contraction took hold. 'Just get me to the hospital,' she said through gritted teeth. Then she forced a smile and turned to her son. 'Tim will help, won't you, love?'

Tim's terror had disappeared. Whether it was because they were there helping his mother or whether it was the excitement of the helicopter ride, Abby didn't know or care. All that mattered was that the boy was calm. It would help Jenny and give them one less thing to worry about.

Abby draped a blanket round her patient before strapping her into the stretcher. As they carried her outside, Abby tried not to wince when a contraction gripped the mother and she squeezed Abby's fingers with ferocious strength.

Please let her hang in there, Abby prayed silently. At least until they got her to hospital. She slid a glance at Mac. Nothing in his demeanour indicated that at any time they could be dealing with a life-and-death scenario. Was he really as calm as he appeared?

Inside the helicopter they attached Jenny to the on-board monitoring equipment and pumped fluids into her. Abby checked the fetal heartbeat again. So far so good.

As soon as they had Jenny settled and the helicopter was heading towards St Piran's, Mac raised his thumb to Tim. Greg had given the boy a helmet and earmuffs to deaden the noise.

Tim returned the salute, unable to hide his excitement.

Abby slid a glance at Mac as he leaned over Jenny. He puzzled her. Everything about him contradicted the image of him she had held in her head for the last twelve years. Whenever she'd thought about him, she'd imagined an ageing Lothario chatting up young women on the beach under the pretext of teaching them how to windsurf, not this caring and utterly professional doctor.

Even if it was obvious from his behaviour when they'd met as well as Lucy's comments that he still was a blatant flirt she liked the way he had taken the time to reassure Tim.

Her thoughts were interrupted as the helicopter touched down on the hospital landing pad. Abby breathed a deep sigh of relief. They had made it!

'Stick close to me,' Mac said to Tim after removing the young lad's helmet.

The helicopter's rotors hadn't even stopped when the hospital staff were there to take charge of Jenny. The transfer was quick. Mac and Abby updated the hospital staff as they ran next to the trolley with Tim following closely behind.

'Thanks, guys. We'll take it from here,' the doctor Mac had addressed as Dr Gibson said.

They watched as Jenny disappeared from view.

'C'mon, Tim. Why don't we get you a drink or something?' Abby offered, knowing that now the excitement of the helicopter journey was over the boy would start fretting again. 'And in the meantime we can try and get your dad on the phone and either me or Dr MacNeil here will speak to him. How does that sound?'

'Sounds okay. When can I see Mum?'

'Not for a little while,' Abby said. 'But while Dr MacNeil is speaking to your father, I'll find somewhere where you can wait.'

Tim's face crumpled. 'I don't want to stay on my own. I want my dad.'

Abby felt terrible for the little boy. If something happened to her, she'd hate for Emma to be left alone. But what could they do? They had to get back to the air ambulance base. There could be another call at any time.

But Mac seemed to have his own ideas. 'Tell you what,' he said. 'When I speak to your dad, I'll suggest you come back with Abby and me to the air ambulance headquarters. How about it? You could have a look around see all the stuff we use. We have some cool things we can do with our computers. I'll let the staff here know where we are and as soon as they have any news about your mum they can let us know. What do you say?'

Tim's face brightened. 'Could I? No one will mind? I promise I won't get in the way.'

Once more, Abby was pleasantly surprised. Mac could easily have left the child here. After all they had done their job and Tim wasn't their responsibility. She really had underestimated him. Nothing about him made sense. Her head was beginning to ache. Right now she would have given anything for some time on her own to think, but she had promised Tim a drink while they waited for Mac to speak to his father and do the handover.

Spotting a vending machine against the wall inside the A & E department, Abby scrabbled in her pocket for some change and fed it into the slot. To no avail— the wretched machine stubbornly refused to part with its goods. Banging with the flat of her hand against the side had no effect either.

'Here, let me help.' A woman who looked as if she had stepped out of a magazine came across. She fiddled with the machine and a can rolled out.

'It just takes a certain knack.' She held out a mani-cured hand. 'You must be new. I'm Rebecca O'Hara, my husband Josh is one of the A & E consultants.'

'Abby Stevens. First day with the Air Ambulance Service.'

'Pleased to meet you, Abby. Where are you from? I can tell by your accent that you're not from here.'

'I've been living in London for the last few years.'

'London?' Rebecca looked wistful. 'Don't you miss it?'

'I love it here,' Abby said honestly. She glanced across the room to where an anxious Tim was wait-ing for her. Although she had the distinct impression Rebecca wanted to chat, Abby didn't like to leave the boy any longer than she had to.

Just then Mac appeared. 'Oh, hello, Rebecca.' He smiled. 'If you're waiting to see Josh, I'm afraid he's up to his neck with patients at the moment.'

Rebecca looked dejected. 'I'll have a cup of coffee with the nurses while I'm waiting.'

She turned back to Abby. 'Lovely to meet you.

Perhaps we could have a coffee some time?' And then with a flutter of slim fingers she headed towards the staffroom.

Back at base, no one seemed particularly surprised to see Tim. Mac gave him the promised tour after which he settled Tim in front of the computers and started explaining how the system worked.

A little while later, Dr Gibson phoned to say that they had sectioned Jenny and although she had lost a great deal of blood, she and her new baby son were going to be fine. Tim was ecstatic about having a brother, but as it was going to be a couple of hours before Jenny would come around properly from the anaesthetic, they decided to keep him with them a bit longer. Tim's father was on his way to the hospital.

'I'll drop Tim back at the hospital later,' Mac said to Abby. 'I'm due to do some teaching there this afternoon.'

Abby raised an eyebrow.

'I keep my hand in at the hospital when we're not busy. It helps keep me up to date and it only takes me a couple of minutes to get back here if we get a call-out.' He smiled. 'You don't fancy a drink later, by any chance? I can tell you all about Penhally.' His expression was teasing, his eyes glinting.

Abby was horrified to feel a tingle run down her spine. Damn it! Why did she have to find him so damn sexy? Even sexier and better looking than twelve years ago. And the fact that he had a caring side made him all the more attractive. What was she thinking? There was no way she could be attracted to her dead sister's ex-lover; it was too weird. What was more, she had to remember that Mac was the type of man for whom flirting was as natural as breathing. It didn't mean anything. Wasn't the way he'd treated Sara evidence of that?

He was looking at her, waiting for her reply, certain she would say yes. He was so supremely confident she would love to turn him down. And she would have, if it wasn't for Emma. Her antennae, honed by years of being let down by men just like him, were on red alert. Of all the men in all the world, why did she have to be working with him?

Despite every nerve cell in her brain telling her to keep her distance from this man, for her daughter's sake, she needed to learn more about him. Emma was going to a friend's after school and wouldn't be home until seven. Abby made up her mind.

'I'll tell you what,' she said. 'I like to go for a walk after work. You can join me if you want.' She shrugged. 'It's up to you.' Smiling to herself as she saw the look of surprise in his eyes, she whirled on her heel, ignoring the feeling that two blue eyes were watching her speculatively.

Mac watched Abby's retreating back until she was out of sight. He would have bet a hundred bucks she had been about to turn him down, and her acceptance had taken him by surprise. Not that a walk was what he had in mind and not that he would have let one refusal put him off. In fact, it would have heightened the excitement of the chase. He tried to ignore the unpleasant feeling lurking somewhere deep down that felt uncomfortably like shame. Should he really be going after Abby? Although she intrigued and excited him, there was a certain wariness about her that suggested she had been hurt before, perhaps badly. And then there was the odd way she had kept looking at him during the callout. For someone as experienced as she was supposed to be there was an edginess about her that, while not quite alarming him, concerned him a little.

There was something else about Abby that was niggling him. He could have sworn he had met her before, but he had to be mistaken. He might have been with a lot of women in his life, but he would never have forgotten someone like her.

What was her story anyway? Not that it really mattered. He liked women, enjoyed their company and had a lot of respect for them, but he had no intention of having a long-term relationship with one. Once they made demands on him, he couldn't help but lose interest. But he was getting way ahead of himself. This was simply a walk with a colleague, albeit a beautiful one. What was the harm in that? Nevertheless, however much he tried to dismiss the feeling of unease, he couldn't quite shake it. A sixth sense he had relied on all his life was telling him that something extraordinary had arrived in the form of Abby Stevens and he wasn't sure he liked the feeling one little bit.

CHAPTER THREE

MAC was leaning against the side of a four-by-four, looking relaxed, when Abby eventually emerged at the end of her shift. After changing out of her jumpsuit, she had taken a few moments to put on some lipstick and brush her hair. She told herself that she wasn't preening herself for Mac, it was simply that she needed the confidence of make-up as well as the time to get her thumping heart rate under control. But she knew deep down that wasn't the whole truth. Wasn't there just a tiny part of her that liked it that he had made it clear he was attracted to her? She dismissed the thought immediately. This wasn't about her. It was about Emma.

Mac was wearing a pair of faded jeans and a white T-shirt under a well-worn leather jacket. His teeth flashed in a wide grin when he saw her. Surely it was anxiety over what she had to tell him that made her stomach flip?

He opened the passenger door of the Jeep with a flourish.

'There's an interesting cliff walk about ten minutes' drive from here. There's a fantastic fish restaurant nearby. We could have something to eat after our walk and I'll drive you back here so you can collect your car.' He paused. 'Unless you want to leave your car at your house? I could follow you home and we could leave from there. Where is it you live, anyway?'

Something in the way his eyes were glittering made Abby wonder if he was imagining an ending to the evening that included him and her in bed together. Little did he know there was a greater chance of hell freezing over.

'I'm renting a cottage in Penhally Bay while I look around for a place to buy. But I'd rather follow you in my own car. And as for supper...' she shook her head '...sorry, I have other plans.' A walk was one thing, a meal à deux quite another.

Mac frowned and Abby felt a small stab of triumph. He was clearly a man who was used to getting his own way. Well, he'd find out soon enough that she liked having her way, too.

She followed his four-by-four, uncomfortably aware of the anxiety that was coiling in her chest. He had no idea about the bombshell she was soon going to be dropping into his life. For a second she felt sorry for him, but only for a second. Emma was the only person who mattered in this whole sorry mess.

The sun was slipping lower, streaking the sky with gold, but it would be light for another hour or two. There was still a hint of warmth in the air, and the earlier wind had subsided. It was a perfect October evening, with just a hint of summer still.

The hordes of tourists had long since left and there was only one other car in the car park as they parked their cars side by side.

'The walk I had in mind is a couple of miles each way,' Mac said. 'That's not too far for you, is it?'

'I like walking,' Abby said. 'As long as I'm home for seven.'

She had to walk rapidly to keep up with Mac's long strides. He glanced down and checked his pace so it matched hers.

'How are Jenny and the baby doing?' she asked. As promised, Mac had taken Tim back to the hospital where his father had been waiting for him.

Mac frowned. 'Last I knew, mother and baby were doing fine. Why, did you hear something?' There was no mistaking the concern in his eyes.

'No, I haven't heard anything.' Abby said. 'I just thought you might have popped in to see her when you were at the hospital.'

Mac looked puzzled. 'Why would I do that?'

'Don't you follow up on your patients? Aren't you curious to know how everything turned out?'

He shook his head. 'I treat them, look after them as best I can, then let the hospital staff do their bit. All I care about is giving the best treatment I am capable of. I don't see the point in getting too involved with patients. We have to know when to let go, so we can move on to the next one.'

Abby was dismayed. Once again it seemed she had got this man wrong. Could he really be as disinterested in his patients as he seemed? Abby couldn't imagine not following up on her patients. Most of the time, out there on a rescue, she formed a strong bond with the people whose lives depended on her. It was part of who she was.

'So tell me, what brings you here, to Cornwall and Penhally Bay in particular?' Mac changed the subject. 'Someone mentioned you'd been working with the London ambulance service for the last eleven years. What happened? Did you get tired of the big city?'

Anxiety raced along her spine. It was the perfect

moment to tell him about Emma, but she wasn't ready. Not yet. Not until she knew more about him. Once she told him there would be no going back.

'My daughter needed a change of air,' Abby said evasively. 'And I needed a change of scenery.'

'You have a daughter? I didn't know.' He sounded surprised...and regretful.

Abby suspected he wouldn't have been so keen to ask her out if he'd known she had a child. Most of the men she had dated in the past had reacted the same way. They all backed off when she told them and if they didn't, her refusal to put them before Emma usually made them give up on her sooner or later. And that was fine. She didn't need or want a man in her life who couldn't accept Emma. Not even this one. *Particularly* not this one.

He flicked his eyes to her left hand again. 'You don't wear a ring so I'm guessing you're not married.'

'I'm a single mum.' Let him make of that what she would. He would know the truth soon enough. First she had some questions of her own.

'What about you? I assume you're not married?'

'Nope. Not the marrying kind, I guess.'

'Children?' Abby held her breath as she waited for his reply.

'No, none of them either. Not the father kind.'

Little did he know.

'How long have you worked for the air ambulance?' Abby asked.

'Two years. I completed my specialist training in anaesthesia, then I did a course in medical emergency retrieval in Glasgow. But unfortunately the surfing conditions aren't great there, so when I found they were looking for a rescue medic here, I jumped at the chance. It means I can kite board when I'm not working.'

So his sport was as important as his job. Maybe more so. Abby was disappointed. Minute by minute she was having to revise her opinion of the man who was Emma's father.

'Although I can tell you're Scottish from your accent, it doesn't sound very Glaswegian,' Abby probed. The more she knew about this man, the better.

'I was brought up on Tiree. It's an island off the west coast of Scotland. I lived there until I went to medical school in Glasgow when I was eighteen. I don't go back to Tiree very often.' His mouth tightened and as Abby glanced at him she could have sworn she saw anger behind his eyes, but it disappeared so quickly she couldn't be sure. Did Mac have secrets of his own?

She was about to question him further when he stopped in his tracks. She followed his gaze to see what had caught his attention. To their left, close to the edge, a man was pacing frantically up and down, shouting a boy's name.

'Something's wrong,' Mac said. 'I'm going to take a look-see.'

As Mac called out, the man turned to them, relief evident under his panic.

'It's my son,' he said. 'I can't find him! One minute he was here, and then the next he was gone. I only meant to close my eyes for a minute, but I must have dropped off. You've got to help me find him. He's only eight.' The man's eyes were darting around while he was speaking.

Mac placed a hand on his shoulder. 'Stay calm and tell me everything. What's your name?'

'Dave. My son's called Luke.'

'Where did you last see Luke?'

'He was over there.' The man pointed behind him.

'He wanted to go down to the beach but I told him there was no path. I said I'd take him there tomorrow. Oh, my God. What if he tried to go down by himself and fell?'

'Have you phoned for help?'

'No, I haven't had time. I've been too busy looking for him.'

Mac's eyes raked the side of the cliff. Something caught his attention and he stopped and sucked in a breath. Abby followed his gaze. Near the edge, a piece of the cliff had broken away. From the look of it, it had only happened very recently. Seeing the troubled look in Mac's eyes, she knew he was thinking the same thing. There was a good chance the boy had got too close to the edge and slipped over. If they were right and the boy had fallen, he could be badly hurt, or worse.

'Abby. Phone 999 and get them to alert the coastguard and the rescue services. Dave, I'm just going to have a look over this cliff and see if I can see him. You stay back, okay?'

Abby touched Dave's shoulder reassuringly as she used her mobile. It was still possible the boy had wandered off and was nowhere near the cliff but they couldn't take the chance.

Mac walked close to the cliff then dropped to his stomach to peer over the edge. 'I think I can see him,' he called. 'Is he wearing a red jacket?'

Luke's father rushed forward. Mac jumped to his feet and barred his way.

'You have to stay back,' Mac warned. 'The edge here is already unstable. If you come any closer you could slip or a bit of the cliff could crumble and fall on your son.

'I'm going to climb down there and see how he is, okay?' Mac added quietly.

'Shouldn't we wait for the rescue services?' Abby said. 'The operator said they shouldn't be more than ten minutes. If you go down there, you could fall, too.'

Mac dug in his pocket and pulled out his car keys. He tossed them to Dave. 'Dave, go back to the car park. My car is the Jeep. In the boot you'll find a red medical case, a rope and a yellow jacket. Could you fetch them?'

Dave hesitated and Mac gave him a gentle push. 'Go! It's the best way to help Luke. Be as quick as you can.'

As soon as Dave had set off at a run, Mac turned back to Abby. 'We don't have time to wait for help.' While he was talking he had removed his jacket. 'I'm going to go down. When Dave returns I might need you to lower my medical bag on the end of the rope. Okay?' He moved towards the cliff.

'Shouldn't you at least wait for the rope?' If Mac fell they would have two victims to rescue. Even in her anxiety, the irony wasn't completely lost on her. She had just found Emma's father. If he fell now, Emma might never get to know him.

Mac turned around and grinned. 'Hey, I was brought up near cliffs. Never met one yet I couldn't beat. I'll be okay. As soon as you hear the rescue 'copter, let off a flare. Keep Dave occupied by telling him to search for a good place for the helicopter to land.'

Before she could protest further, he disappeared over the edge.

Abby's heart banged against her ribs. What was Mac thinking? Although if it had been Emma down there, she would have gone herself. Fear of heights or not.

She tiptoed over to the edge, following Mac's earlier

example, and lay flat on her stomach and peered over. Although Mac was picking his way carefully down the cliff he was moving faster than she would have thought was safe. From this vantage point she could see that although the cliff was steep, it didn't fall away as sharply as she'd thought. Relief swept through her. Perhaps Luke had a chance.

As Dave returned with the bag, rope and Mac's fluorescent jacket she became aware of a whooping sound in the distance. Shielding her eyes against the sinking sun, she could just about make out the large yellow shape of a Sea King helicopter. Thank God! They would have proper equipment and hopefully a way to get both Mac and Luke up.

'Come on.' She jumped up and shouted across to Dave. 'We need to find a decent landing place to direct the pilot to land.'

'How is my son? Could you see him? Is he okay?'

Abby moved towards open ground and yelled back over her shoulder. 'Mac will be with him in a few minutes. He's a doctor. He'll do everything he can to help Luke.'

Without waiting to see whether Dave was following or not, she raced over to the flat piece of ground. It was just about big enough for the helicopter to land and thankfully the previous days' rain had run away, leaving it solid underfoot.

Abby waved Mac's jacket and immediately the helicopter headed in their direction. Dave was standing behind her, looking lost and terrified. She summoned up a smile. 'I promise you, your son is in good hands.' And she believed it. 'Stay back until they land, then tell them everything. Okay? I'm going to lower the medical bag down to Mac.'

She ran back to the cliff edge and dropped on to her front again. Mac was at the bottom now and kneeling next to the prone figure of the boy. At least he had made it down in one piece. But Mac couldn't risk moving the child on his own. If Luke had survived the fall, there was every chance he had serious neck and head injuries and any movement could mean the difference between a full recovery and life in a wheelchair.

Mac glanced up and gave her a thumbs-up. Luke must still be alive. She tied the medical bag to the rope and lowered it down but it snagged on the jagged rock face. The incline may have helped Mac reach the boy, but it was hampering her efforts to get the bag down to him. Almost crying with frustration, she was only vaguely aware of a hand touching her shoulder. She looked up into calm green eyes of a crew member from the helicopter.

'Miss, you have to stand away from the edge.' Before she could protest, the man took her arm and raised her to her feet. 'We'll take it from here.'

'Mac—Dr MacNeil—is down there with the boy. Mac's a doctor with the air ambulance. He needs his bag.'

'Mac, as in Daredevil Mac?' A broad smile spread across the man's craggy face. 'Well I'll be bug—blown. We know him well, and if he's onto it, everything will be A-okay. Don't worry, I'll get the bag down to him.'

Pulling the case back up, the man, whose name badge said Roberts, took it and ran back to the helicopter. Seconds later the Sea King took off again.

Abby joined Dave, knowing that for the time being there was little she or the anxious father could do. She hooked her arm in his as they watched the helicopter hover over the cliff. A couple of tense minutes passed before a figure, clutching a stretcher and the medical bag, was lowered from the side of the helicopter. Abby's heart thudded painfully. In many ways she would have preferred to be down there helping. This waiting was worse than anything.

Minutes crawled like hours. Then suddenly the crewman came back into view. He was holding onto the stretcher, which now contained a figure. Immediately after the winchman and the stretcher were pulled on board, the helicopter lowered the rope again and after a few moments Mac appeared above the top of the cliff. He, too, was pulled into the waiting Sea King.

Instead of flying off, the helicopter landed again. Abby grabbed Dave's hand and ran towards it. Roberts had barely pulled her and Dave in before the helicopter banked away. Roberts passed her a helmet with a radio attached.

With a brief word to Dave to stay where he was, Abby hurried over to Mac, who was bent over the stretcher.

'He has a compound fracture of the femur. I can't rule out internal injuries and of course we have to suspect head and spinal injuries. I've given him IV morphine for the pain.'

Mac attached his patient to the pulse oximeter while Abby checked Luke's vital signs.

Although Luke's blood pressure was low and his pulse elevated, and he wasn't out of the woods yet, he was a very lucky boy. His leg would take time to heal and would have hurt like crazy before the morphine took effect, but as long as he didn't have internal injuries he'd probably be able to leave hospital in a week or two. Abby shuddered when she thought what might have happened if she and Mac hadn't come across Dave when they had. She was even more confused about Mac than ever. He had risked his life for Luke, he had been thoughtful with Tim, yet he had made it clear that he didn't believe in getting involved with patients. Which one was the real Mac?

Luke tried to sit up, but Abby pushed him gently back down.

'Dad?' he asked. 'Where's my dad?'

Abby beckoned to Dave to come forward. Anything to help the child stay calm was good.

'He's right here,' Abby said gently. She moved away slightly so Luke could see his father. Both father and son started to cry. 'Dave, you need to move away again so we can work on your son, okay? Try not to worry, I'm sure he's going to be okay.'

When they touched down at St Piran's the staff from A & E were waiting for them.

'Status update?' the A & E consultant, bearing the name badge Dr Josh O'Hara, asked. Abby had only the briefest impression of dark hair and deep blue eyes before Luke was rushed inside.

Abby, her part in the drama over, went in search of Dave. He would be desperate for news of his injured child. She found him sitting outside Resus, his head in his hands.

She tapped him gently on his shoulder. 'Dave.'

He looked at her with red-rimmed eyes. He tried to speak, but couldn't. He shook his head, almost as if he were too scared to ask after his son.

'How is he?' he managed after clearing his throat.

Abby sat next to him and took his hand in hers.

'I think he'll be fine, Dave. It was good we found him when we did, and that we were able to start giving him medical treatment straight away. All that will make a big difference to his recovery.'

They sat in silence for a moment. 'Is there anyone I
can call for you? Luke's mother? She'll need to know
he's in hospital.'

Dave took a deep shuddering breath. 'She's dead.'
He buried his face in his hands. 'She died from breast
cancer six months ago.'

'I'm so sorry,' Abby said.

Dave's eyes were bleak. 'She'd never forgive me if
I let something happen to our child. I promised her I'd
look after him and I fell asleep. What kind of father am
I?'

'You're human. It can be difficult, bringing up a child
on your own. You can't watch them all the time.'

Dave raked a hand through his hair. 'But I fell asleep!
I've been working overtime so I could afford to take
Luke away on holiday. So he and I could spend more
time together. He needs something to cheer him up. The
loss of his mum was a terrible blow. To both of us.' Abby
was only dimly aware of Mac coming to stand next to
them. 'And I could have lost him, too.'

'You've not lost him,' Mac said quietly. 'He's got to
go to Theatre to get his leg pinned where it was broken,
but he's going to be fine.'

'He's going to be okay?' Dave said almost as if he
didn't dare allow himself to believe what Mac was telling him. The relief in Dave's eyes brought a lump to
Abby's throat.

'Yes, he is. I promise you,' Mac said firmly. 'You can
see him for a few moments before he goes to Theatre,
if you like.'

Dave sprang to his feet. He clasped Mac's hands in
his. 'How can I ever thank you? I know you put your
own life in danger and I'll never forget you for that.

Either of you.' Without giving them a chance to reply, he rushed away to see his son.

'Another satisfied customer,' Mac said wryly. 'Perhaps he'll take better care of his son after this.' He rubbed a hand across his chin. 'What the hell was he thinking? Having a nap while his eight-year-old played near a dangerous cliff. Some people just shouldn't have children.'

Abby rounded on him. 'He's doing the best he can. Do you know he only fell asleep because he's been working all hours to give his son a holiday? Luke's mother died recently and Dave has been doing the best he can to care for him. Being a single parent isn't easy. We all make mistakes. It's just by the grace of God, most of the time, things turn out all right.' What the hell did Mac know about being a parent, the demands, the worry?

Mac held up his hands as if to ward off her words. He looked stunned and contrite. 'Hey, I had no idea.'

'You shouldn't be so quick to judge, Mac. As the saying goes, you don't know what a person's life is like until you've walked in their shoes.'

Mac narrowed his eyes, his expression unreadable. 'I have no intention of ever walking in his shoes, as you put it.' The clouds cleared from his face. 'But I didn't know his circumstances,' he said. 'If I had, I wouldn't have been so quick to make assumptions.' He smiled ruefully. 'I stand corrected.'

Their eyes locked and Abby's heart somersaulted. She had the strangest feeling that he knew every thought that was rattling around her confused brain. Dismayed, she pulled her eyes away from his searching gaze and glanced at her watch. She had to get back for Emma, but her car was still miles away where she had left it when she and Mac had set out on their walk.

Mac caught her look of alarm. 'What is it?'

'I need to get home,' she said. 'Like now. But my car's on the other side of Penhally, still in the car park.'

'Mine, too,' Mac glanced up as Josh emerged from Resus.

'Know where I could borrow a car, mate?' Mac asked.

Josh dug in his pocket and fished out a set of keys. He tossed them at Mac, who caught them.

'Take mine,' Josh said. 'Just make sure you bring it back in one piece.'

'Hey.' Mac pretended to look offended. 'Don't I always?'

Josh raised an eyebrow. 'You know it's only a matter of time if you continue to drive like the devil.'

'I only drive fast when I'm on my own. And when the road allows. Your car will be perfectly safe.' Mac turned to Abby. 'I'll drop you off at your house then collect your car.'

Abby wasn't at all sure she wanted to be in a car with Mac after hearing Josh's comments, but she did have to get home. Emma was too young to be left on her own, even for a short while. 'What about yours?' Abby protested.

'Don't worry about mine. It's not a problem. I can get it any time.'

Inside Josh's car, Abby glanced at her watch again. She should make it before Emma. With a bit of luck.

'You did a brave thing back there,' she said as they drove down the narrow lanes in the direction of Penhally Bay.

Mac grinned at her and her pulse scrambled. He was having the strangest effect on her. As if she didn't have enough to contend with. Leftover adrenaline, she told herself.

'As I said before, it was a piece of cake. Where is your house?'

Abby gave him the address and he nodded. 'I think I know where you are.'

'But don't you think you were a little reckless?' Abby persisted. 'You could have been killed, or fallen and then we would have had two bodies to rescue.' *And Emma wouldn't have a father, suitable or unsuitable.*

Mac slid her a glance. 'Where's the fun in life if you can't take risks?' he said. 'You might as well be dead if you don't. And, anyway, I knew I could climb down to him. Believe me, it wasn't nearly as dangerous as it looked. At least, not for me. Free climbing is one of my hobbies.'

Abby frowned. She didn't like the sound of this free climbing, whatever it was.

'Which means what exactly?'

'It's a form of climbing where you don't use ropes. Great fun.'

Oh, dear Lord. Emma's father was an adrenaline junkie who didn't seem to care whether he lived or died. Could it get any worse?

'Oh, and by the way,' Mac said, following her pointed finger, as he pulled up in front of the small two-up, two-down where she and Emma lived. 'You owe me a date. And one thing you should know about me is that I always collect my debts.' His diamond-coloured eyes locked onto hers and once again Abby had the strangest feeling he could see into her soul.

The blood rushed to her cheeks. It was as if someone had lit a fire just below her skin and it was smouldering away. Any minute now she'd go up in a puff of smoke.

She was out of the car almost before it had come to a complete stop. So far none of this was going the way she'd planned.

Shortly after Mac left, Emma came running into the cottage and flung herself down on the sofa. She beamed happily at Abby.

'Hey. I gather you had a good time?' Abby asked.

'It was great. A few of the other girls came over and we had the coolest time trying on each other's clothes and make-up. Not one of them asked me anything about my dad. I don't think they care at all.'

'Those girls in your other school were the exception, Emma. They just had to make themselves feel good by putting you down.' She ruffled her daughter's hair. Whatever happened with Mac, they had made the right decision coming here. In the last few weeks Emma had changed back from the subdued, under-confident girl she had become in London to the lively fun-loving kid she had always been before that.

Emma jumped up from the sofa and hugged Abby fiercely. 'You're the best mum in the world,' she said.

Abby's heart twisted. All she had ever wanted was to give Emma the security and love she and Sara had never experienced. There was nothing she wouldn't do for Emma. Not even risk losing her to her father. If that father could make her happy. What she was not prepared to do now that Emma was just getting back to her bright usual self was risk her daughter being rejected. Abby knew only too well how that felt.

'Sara loved you as much as I do. You'll never forget that, will you?'

'I know. You tell me that almost every day.' Emma looked sad for a moment. 'I really wish I could have known her.' But in the way kids did, her face brightened almost immediately. 'At least I have you to tell me all the stories about her. I love hearing the ones about how you both kept getting into trouble. They make me laugh.'

'Yes, but, remember, I only tell you some of these stories as a warning about how easily you can get into trouble.' Abby was stricken. What if Emma tried to copy some of the pranks she and Sara had got up to? It didn't bear thinking about.

Emma grinned. 'You are so easy to tease, Mum. I get you every time.'

'Why don't you have your shower while I get supper ready?' Abby suggested. 'Then afterwards there's a movie on TV we can watch together.' Mac would be back any minute with her car, and she wasn't ready for child and father to meet.

And that wasn't the only thing she wasn't prepared for, Abby admitted to herself as she set about preparing supper. She hadn't expected to find herself reacting to him the way she did. The way her heart kept misbehaving every time he was around wasn't just down to her anxiety about Emma and was an unwelcome complication in a situation that was already complicated enough. Damn it, why did he have to be so infuriatingly gorgeous?

As she'd hoped. Emma was still in the shower when Mac arrived with her car. In her haste to have him gone before Emma came downstairs, she practically grabbed her car keys from his hand. All this emotional turmoil was exhausting. She knew she couldn't keep father and daughter apart for ever. Sooner or later, she would have to tell them the truth.

CHAPTER FOUR

BACK at work, Mac didn't mention another date. Abby wasn't sure if she was relieved or offended. For her second shift, she worked with Lucy, attending a car accident as well as a child with breathing difficulties. Although she enjoyed working with Lucy, she had to admit she was disappointed that she wouldn't always be working with Mac. She told herself it was simply because she was trying to figure him out and nothing to do with the fact she felt alert, more alive somehow, when he was around.

Every now and again she would look up to find his eyes on her. He would grin as if he'd caught her out and she would look away quickly, terrified in case he noticed the blush stealing up her cheeks.

'What do you say we go for a walk down on the beach?' Abby suggested to Emma one day after work. Although it was after five, it was unseasonably warm for October.

'Great. Can I go swimming?' Emma asked, and before Abby could reply she was off upstairs to her small bedroom. Emma had to be constantly on the go.

Abby fetched her own costume from the bedroom opposite Emma's. She slipped into her bikini before pulling on a long, silky cardigan to cover her until they

got to the beach. Their rented home was tiny, having
once been a fisherman's cottage. It had a sitting room
and a small kitchen downstairs and two bedrooms upstairs with a small bathroom separating them. Abby
would have preferred something bigger, but her salary
as a paramedic didn't stretch very far. After rent and
food, anything left over went on clothes and outings
for Emma. Sometimes it was a struggle to make ends
meet, but if the alternative had been not having Emma
in her life, Abby knew it was no contest. Over the years
she had scrimped and saved until she had some savings
in the bank. Enough to put a deposit down on a small
house when they found the right place. At least here in
Penhally they had a chance of getting on the housing
ladder. In London, it had been impossible.

'I'm ready. Let's go,' Emma called to Abby.

The beach was a ten-minute walk from their house.
Although the tourists were away, the sun still warmed
the air and there were plenty of locals making the most
of the last few warm evenings.

As they walked, Emma asked Abby about her job.

'I love it. The rest of the team seem really nice. I
went on my first rescue on Monday with one of the
doctors. We managed to get a woman to hospital so her
baby could be born safely. We also had to rescue a boy
who had fallen down a cliff. Being here has different
dangers from those in London. Ones that you might not
even think about. So, please, Emma, you need to be very
careful when you're out with your friends.'

'You worry too much, Mum. Nothing will happen to
me.'

Abby smiled at her daughter. 'I know it won't. And
I know I'm a worry wart. But just promise me you'll

always be careful.' She couldn't bear it if anything happened to her.

'I might be a pilot when I grow up,' Emma said, dismissing Abby's fears. 'I think I would like flying off to help people in trouble.'

Trust Emma to be drawn to that kind of career. The little girl loved nothing better than taking on anything that was exciting. It struck Abby that she shared at least one trait with Mac. The worst possible, in Abby's opinion. How many more would there be? 'You can be anything you like, darling. As long as you stick at school and do your best.'

Emma stuck out her tongue. 'C'mon, Mum. I'll race you to the sea.' And with that she was off, long legs flying across the sand and her blonde hair streaming behind her. Abby laughed and raced behind her daughter, her heart feeling as light as it had for as long as she could remember.

The shore was busy with people either walking their dogs, playing ball games or paddling. To one side, in an area cordoned off, were the surfers, windsurfers and kite boarders. Abby had watched them once or twice before, impressed at their skill.

The wind down at the shore was gustier than it had been at the cottage and the surfers were taking full advantage of the substantial waves. Further out, where the waves were even bigger, was a kite boarder. Abby and Emma stopped paddling to watch as the boarder let his parachute pull him into the air. There was a collective gasp from other people who had stopped to watch as he somersaulted in the air before landing perfectly on the water. He caught the wind in his parachute to propel him across the water, faster than Abby had ever seen anyone move without the use of an engine. Just as she thought he was going to crash onto the beach, he flipped in the air again, this time landing so he faced in the opposite direction. Abby had never seen anything quite as graceful before. Although the figure was tall, well over six feet, his movements in the air were almost balletic.

'I want to learn how to do that,' Emma said, her eyes wide with admiration. 'It looks so cool.'

Over my dead body, Abby thought grimly. It was far too dangerous. But she didn't say anything. Experience of her headstrong daughter had taught her that the more Emma was told not to do something, the more she wanted to do it. In that way she was very like Sara.

'I think you have to learn to surf or windsurf first, before you can move onto something like that,' Abby said mildly. With a bit of luck it would take Emma years to master the basics. And by that time she would have forgotten her interest in kite surfing.

The kite surfer was racing back towards the shore. When he was only a metre or so away, he turned his board sideways and jumped off. He seemed to have given up for the day.

As he walked up the beach, Abby's breath caught in her throat. It was Mac. He shook the water from his hair before peeling his suit down to his waist. Abby sucked in her breath. His chest was as muscled as she'd remembered, the six pack of his abdomen even more defined than twelve years earlier. All at once a memory of the first time she had seen him came flooding back.

It had been the first full day of their holiday on Mykonos and Abby had been looking forward to relaxing in the sun with Sara. The last few years had been tough. Since their mother had more or less evicted them from the family home, Sara's behaviour had become wilder and wilder. Although Abby had trained as a paramedic, Sara had not found a job she'd wanted to do for more than a few weeks. More interested in partying than working, Sara had lost more than one job for failing to turn up for work after a late night. Abby had hoped that their holiday would give her a chance to talk to Sara and make her see that sooner or later she had to settle down.

As they'd made themselves comfortable on their sun-loungers, Abby's attention had been caught by a tall windsurfing instructor who had been giving lessons to a group of beginners on the beach close by. His height alone would have caught her attention, but his tanned and toned physique had made him stand out like some Greek god. His sun-bleached hair had reflected the sun and when he'd grinned, which had been often, his eyes glinted. Abby had never seen anyone whose presence had been so immediate before and her stomach had flipped. He must have felt the intensity of her gaze as he'd looked up from what he was doing and, catching her eye, had winked with a wide smile. Abby had blushed and dipped her head.

Sara had noticed and followed her gaze to where Mac had returned his attention to his class and had been demonstrating how to move the sail on the board in order to catch the wind.

'Now, that's what I call hot,' Sara said appreciatively. 'I think I've just signed up to windsurfing classes.' Not having a shy bone in her body, Sara sauntered over to join the group, and that was more or less the last Abby saw of her for the rest of the holiday. Instead of the girly chats Abby had envisaged, from that moment Sara spent every spare minute with Mac, leaving Abby to amuse herself.

* * *

Abby was forced back to the present as Mac noticed them standing on the beach and walked up to them. He smiled widely.

'Fancy meeting you here,' he said to Abby. His eyes glinted as they lingered on her bikini-clad figure and Abby resisted the impulse to wrap her arms around her body to shield herself from his appreciative gaze.

'We were watching you out there. Pretty impressive.' Abby's heart was in her throat. This wasn't how she'd planned father and daughter would meet.

'Yes. It was really wicked,' Emma piped up.

He turned his gaze to Emma and raised a quizzical eyebrow at Abby.

'This is my daughter, Emma. Emma, this is Dr William MacNeil, my colleague.' *And your father.*

'I'm pleased to meet you, Emma,' Mac said with a tip of his head.

'How did you learn to do that?' Emma said, unable to hide her admiration.

'Many, many years of practice.'

'Could you teach me?'

'Emma,' Abby said warningly. 'I don't think it's fair to ask.'

Mac caught Abby's eyes over the top of Emma's head.

'Why not? I'd have to teach you how to windsurf first. And I could teach Abby, too.' He raised a challenging eyebrow.

Emma's face lit up. 'Would you? That would be amazing! My dad was a windsurfer. Mum, would that be okay? Please say yes.'

Abby suppressed a groan. Emma's dad was a windsurfer right enough. This one standing in front of them. And here he was, offering to give lessons to the child he had no idea was his daughter. Under any other circum-stances, Abby would have smiled. In many ways, this was exactly what she had hoped for. Daughter and father getting to know each other, but it was all happening too fast. Abby hated to refuse Emma anything, but she *had* to tell her and Mac the truth before they met again.

'We'll see. But the weather's going to start getting colder soon and then it will be winter. Perhaps it would be better to leave it until next year?' she hedged.

'But that's ages away,' Emma protested. 'I can wear a wetsuit. That'll keep me warm, won't it, Dr MacNeil?'

'Let's just see how we get on. You might decide you hate it after a go or two and that's okay. Not everyone sticks it out.'

'I will. Mum always says I stick to everything once I make up my mind, isn't that right?'

Abby ruffled her hair. 'It's true.'

'Okay, then. How about next Saturday? If the weather holds. I can pick you and your mum up.'

Emma squealed with delight before remembering she was trying to be cool these days. She clamped her hand over her mouth. 'Can I, Mum? Please say yes.'

Abby hated to refuse Emma anything and right now she couldn't think of a single reason to say no. She could always cancel the lesson later. If she had to. She shivered as the sun dropped below the horizon. 'Okay, but we'd better let Dr MacNeil get on. And I should be getting supper ready.'

'Why don't I take you girls out for something? My treat,' Mac suggested.

Behind Emma, Abby shook her head at him. The last thing she wanted right now was to have these two spending time together. At least, not until she had told them the truth.

Emma's face dropped. 'I said I would go round to Sally's house to watch a film. Her mother said she'd order pizza in for us.'

'In that case…' Mac grinned at Abby '…there's no reason why we can't go, is there?'

Abby wanted to refuse, but now that Emma and Mac had met she knew she had to speak to Mac. Putting it off would just make it harder.

'I'll have to drop Emma off at her friend's and get changed first,' she said.

'No problem. I need to go home, too. What about if I pick you up in an hour's time? We could go to the restaurant I mentioned the day we went for a walk.' Without waiting for a reply, he picked up his sailing gear and walked away, whistling.

CHAPTER FIVE

ABBY was breathing so fast that too much oxygen was making her knees weak. She would have to find the words to tell Mac that Emma was his daughter. And after that she would have to tell Emma. There was no way she could let this windsurfing lesson go ahead without both of them knowing who the other truly was.

Emma chatted about Mac and kite boarding all the way back to their little cottage. 'I can't wait to learn how he does that. How long do you think it will take me to learn? I can't believe you're working with someone as cool as him. Just wait until I tell my friends.'

Abby ached for her child. Even before knowing Mac was her father, Emma was clearly starstruck. And Abby couldn't blame her. But the very things that made him an exciting figure were the very things that could make him totally unsuitable as a father. For the umpteenth time, Abby wondered if she were about to make a dreadful mistake. Now Emma had met Mac, she'd be even more devastated if Mac wanted nothing to do with her. Whichever way Abby looked at the problem, there was no obvious right answer.

After dropping Emma off at her friend's, Abby jumped into the shower. Then she attacked her wardrobe, pulling out one outfit after another before discarding them on the floor. She told herself she wanted to look good because she needed the confidence to face Mac with her news.

Eventually she settled on a pair of dark trousers and a deep red silk blouse. A slick of dark eye shadow and the merest hint of lipstick completed her make-up. She brushed her hair until it shone and left it loose around her face, studying herself critically in the mirror. Her eyes were bright, and two spots of bright colour on her cheeks stood out against her pale skin. Suddenly she had to laugh. When Mac saw her, no doubt he would think it was the thought of going out with him that was making her look like an over-excited schoolgirl. She had to relax. Cool, calm and collected was what the occasion demanded and she knew only too well how to do cool, calm and collected. She must never let herself forget, not even for a second, that Mac was Emma's father. That fact alone made him totally out of bounds.

Hearing a knock on the door, she ran downstairs, grabbing her raincoat from the peg beside her door.

Mac smiled broadly at her when she opened the door. He had changed into dark jeans and a white shirt, which accentuated his tanned skin and the dazzling blue of his eyes. A shot of electricity ran up her spine. Despite the warning signals her brain was firing at her, her body clearly wasn't listening.

Tonight he was driving a low-slung sports car instead of the Jeep. Abby looked at him questioningly.

'The Jeep's my day car,' he said carelessly. 'This one I save for night-time. What?' He laughed, catching her look. 'I like cars. You know—boys' toys.'

He drove the same way he did everything else—fast, but with total concentration. Thankfully he slowed down on the narrow coastal roads where visibility was limited.

Nevertheless, Abby found herself gripping her seat and pumping an imaginary brake pedal as if she could slow him down.

He caught her doing it, and grinned wickedly, but he slowed the car down even further.

'Isn't it beautiful?' Abby pointed to the horizon where the sinking sun was turning the sea red. Despite the way her heart was hammering, the sight had a calming effect on her. Abby relaxed into her seat. Why *did* he have to be so attractive? She had thought he was the sexiest man she'd ever seen the first time she'd ever set eyes on him, and she still thought that. Boy, she should have got out more.

'I find everything about it beautiful,' Mac said slowly, turning his head to look at her. 'Quite stunning.'

She couldn't think of a reply, let alone force the words past a throat suddenly as dry as dust. Thankfully moments later they drew up outside a quaint-looking building. It was single storey with thick stone walls. It had been built close to the sea and as Abby stepped out of the car she gasped with pleasure. Stretching before her, as far as the eye could see, was the ocean. It was bluer than Mac's eyes and crests of white tipped the waves, which boomed like thunder as they crashed onto the shore.

Mac came to stand beside her. 'You like?' he asked, his ready smile back in place. 'See that little cove down there?' He pointed to a sandy area to Abby's left. 'That's one of my favourite places to go kite boarding.'

'You mean you surf out there? Where all those rocks are? Isn't it dangerous? Not to say foolhardy?'

Mac's grin got wider. 'Safe is boring.'

Abby craned her neck to see down to the bay. As far as she could tell, there was no path down.

'How do you get down there? I don't see a path.'

'There isn't one—that's part of the attraction. It means I always get the place to myself.'

'So how do you get to it? By boat?'

'Sometimes. Sometimes I climb down. It's more fun. It's not really that difficult—as long as you know what you're doing. One day I'll show you.'

Abby shivered at the promise behind the words. He was making it clear he found her attractive and that he expected to see more of her. Soon he would learn that it was probably going to happen, but not for the reasons he thought.

His daredevil attitude worried her. What if Emma found her father only to lose him in some reckless escapade? She was beginning to appreciate where her daughter had got her own love of risky sports from. She'd always assumed it was from Sara, but now she knew it was from both her parents. It didn't bode well for the future. She shivered again.

'You're cold. I'm sorry. Let's get inside.' He sniffed the air. Wood smoke mingled with the scent of the sea. 'Smells as if they have a fire going inside. We're early enough to grab a table that's near the fire and also has a view of the sea.'

Abby was glad he'd put her shiver down to the cold. She was already beginning to dread telling him about Emma. What if he refused to accept she was his daughter? If he did, at least this way Emma would never need know. At least, not until she was eighteen and perhaps by then she'd be able to deal with her father's rejection. But she was getting way ahead of herself. Unlikely though it seemed, perhaps he'd be pleased to find he had a child. He had been good with Tim and Luke. There was only one way to know for sure and no point in putting it off any longer.

Nevertheless, she waited until they had ordered. Mac was looking at her with the same air of puzzlement that he had shown when they'd been first introduced.

'I can't get it out of my head that we've met before. We haven't, have we? You know…' He had the grace to look embarrassed. 'No, of course we haven't. As I said, I would have remembered you.'

Abby took a deep breath. 'I lied that first day at work. We have met before. Almost twelve years ago. On Mykonos.'

Mac's frown deepened and he looked at her intently. 'Mykonos? I was there as a windsurfing instructor, but I don't… Wait a minute. I do remember you. Your hair was shorter and you wore glasses. But of course. You were there with your sister, Sara.' He leaned back in his chair and whistled. 'You've changed.'

To her fury, Abby blushed under his frank admiration. Of course he hadn't remembered her. Nobody had ever given her a second glance. Not when Sara had been around. Sara had been confident, keen to meet new people and to try out new experiences. She had thrown herself into life almost as if she'd known she wasn't long for the world. Abby had always taken on the big sister role, even though she'd only been the elder by a couple of minutes, and had never minded always being in Sara's shadow. All she'd ever wanted had been for Sara to be happy.

Abby opened her handbag and pulled out the photograph she'd put in it. She handed it to Mac. 'That's my twin, Sara. Non-identical, obviously. You have your arm around her shoulder. The one at the end is me.'

'I remember now. Hell, I haven't thought about that

summer in years. Imagine you carrying that photo around all this time' He looked at her, his dark brows drawing together. 'Why?' He half smiled. 'Don't tell me you had a crush on me and I didn't know. If so, I'm sorry. One thing's for sure, no one could fail to notice you now.'

Once again he sent her a look that gave her goosebumps and infuriated her at the same time. Did the women he knew really fall for that kind of patter?

'How is Sara?' he continued, grinning. 'If I remember correctly, your sister knew how to have fun! Has she settled down? Sorry. That was a stupid question. Of course she has. She must be what, thirty—thirty-one?'

'Sara's dead,' Abby said bluntly.

There was no mistaking the shock on Mac's face. 'Dead! I am so sorry. When? What happened?'

'She died just over eleven years ago. About nine months after the holiday where you met.' It still sent a stab of pain through Abby whenever she had to say the words. Would she ever get used to it?

'I can't believe it! She was so full of life.' He pushed his half-eaten food away. 'I liked her very much. She was a lovely person.' Clearly he hadn't fully grasped the implication in her words.

'So fond of her you never tried getting in touch after she left?' Abby couldn't keep the bitterness from her voice. Mac had taken advantage of her sister. He had used her. Although they had both been young, he must have known that there had been a chance Sara could fall pregnant. Or had he simply not given a damn?

'Hey, I did try to get in touch, once or twice,' Mac said. 'But the phone number she left with me was never answered.' He leaned across the table, his eyes unfathomable. 'We were both young. We both accepted it was a holiday romance. Nothing more.' He placed his hand on top of Abby's. She snatched it away. Whether it was because she was still angry with him or whether it was because his touch sent little sparks of electricity shooting up her arm, she didn't want to think about.

'How did she die?' he asked softly. 'Was it an accident?'

This was the hard part. This was where she had to tell him about Emma. But suddenly she couldn't. Not yet.

'Could we talk about something else?' she asked softly. 'Even though it's been years, it still hurts too much.'

Mac was immediately contrite. 'Sure.' He leaned back in his chair and studied her intently. 'Tell me about you. How come you ended up here? Penhally is quite a change to London.'

How could she explain the change without mentioning Emma?

'I'd rather talk about you,' she said evasively. 'When we met back on Mykonos you were a windsurfing instructor. It was a bit of a shock to find you are a rescue medic.'

Mac grinned. 'Yeah, well. Back then I'd just graduated and I wanted one summer off before I started my first house job. I was fortunate. I managed to get an instructing job every summer while I was a medical student. It helped pay the bills.' For a moment his eyes darkened and he lost his ready smile. Then just as quickly the grin was back in place. 'If I couldn't be a doctor, I probably would have been a professional windsurfer. Luckily I got into medical school. Better pay and much more satisfying.'

He paused as a couple took a table close by. 'Tiree has an international reputation for some of the best surf in the world. I couldn't grow up there and not do a watersport of some description.'

'Don't tell me that's what brought you to Penhally Bay.' She didn't even attempt to hide her incredulity. What kind of doctor took a job because of the surfing conditions?

He looked amused. 'Partly. Glasgow is a great city, but I couldn't live in a place I can't kite board regularly. But I also came here because there was an opening for a medic in the air ambulance service. The job here is exactly what I always wanted.'

'You love it, don't you? The excitement and the danger. I saw the rescue you did with the family on the boat on television. You risked your life to save those people. Just as you did with Luke.'

Mac grinned again. 'It's part of the job. But you're right. I feel more alive when I battle the elements—beat the odds. But what about you? Do you think you'll cope? It must be different from what you've been used to.'

How deftly he had turned the conversation away from himself again.

'Some of it does frighten me. Especially the thought of being lowered by a winch in blustery conditions. I think it has something to do with being a mum. You know that you have a child waiting for you at home. Someone who needs you to be around for a long time, and it makes you think twice about taking risks.'

'I wouldn't know about that.' Although he smiled, a shadow crossed his eyes. 'One of the benefits about being single is that I don't have anyone who needs me. Luckily.' Abby suspected she was being warned. *Don't expect too much. I'm not in it for the long term.*

So far nothing Mac had said was what she wanted to hear.

Sensing that Mac was about to ask about Emma, Abby added quickly, 'What about your parents? Brothers? Sisters?' It wasn't just that she wanted to keep the conversation away from Emma for the time being at least, she was intensely curious. She told herself it was purely because Mac's family would be Emma's family, too.

It was as if the shutters had come down. Mac's blue eyes grew cold and distant.

'I'm an only child. I have no idea who or where my father is,' he said shortly. 'My mother still lives in Tiree. I see her when I can.'

Abby felt a tug of sympathy—and recognition. Whenever she was asked about her parents, she gave pretty much the same reply. Her father had disappeared after she and Sara had been born. He had never come back to see his daughters and the only contact they'd ever had with him had been the odd birthday card. He had died years ago, and their mother had only thought to tell Sara and Abby long after the funeral had taken place.

'But let's not talk about the past.' Mac leaned forward. 'It's the here and now that matters. I want to know more about you.'

'And the future?' Abby persisted. 'Doesn't that matter?'

Mac grinned and narrowed his eyes speculatively. 'The only thing about the future that interests me right now is when you're going to come out with me again.'

Abby returned his look coolly. Her brown eyes were reproving, almost accusing. Mac could have kicked himself. He should have known the usual direct approach wouldn't work with this woman. Instinctively he knew that Abby was someone who would expect to be courted slowly and seriously. But he didn't feel like taking things slowly with Abby. If he could have taken her home with him tonight and made love to her, he would have without a moment's hesitation.

And he didn't do serious. Abby was a woman with a child. A mother, and a protective one at that. Everything he had learned about her so far told him that she wasn't the kind of woman to have casual affairs. Why, then, was he ignoring the alarms bells that were jangling in his head?

The faint scent of her perfume drifted across at him and before he could stop himself he leaned across the table and took a lock of her thick caramel hair between his fingers. It was heavy and silky. He swallowed a groan as an image of Abby naked beside him, her hair touching his skin as she leaned over to kiss him, flashed into his head. He knew without a shadow of doubt he would never be satisfied until he had this woman in his bed.

A range of emotions he couldn't quite place crossed Abby's face. He would bet his life, though, that she felt the attraction, too.

'But the future does matter, Mac. So does the past.' She fiddled with her napkin. 'Emma…' she started. 'Sara…' She took a deep breath. Some of the colour had left her face.

'Sara died following childbirth. She developed an infection a few days after she delivered Emma. The doctors did everything they could but it was no use.' Her enormous brown eyes swam with unshed tears.

'After Emma was delivered?' Mac echoed. 'I thought Emma was your child.'

'She is. But I'm not her birth mother. Sara was. After she died, Emma came to live with me.'

Mac was puzzled. Why was she telling him this? It did explain, however, why there was no father in the picture. Despite everything he'd just told himself, he couldn't help feeling glad.

'Sara delivered Emma nine months after she returned from Mykonos.' Abby caught her bottom lip between her teeth.

Did she have any idea how cute she looked when she did that?

'Mac, Emma is your daughter.'

Emma? His daughter? At least he thought that was what Abby said. He must have misheard.

'Did I hear you correctly?' he said. He hoped to hell he hadn't.

'Yes. I didn't know at first. Sara wouldn't tell me who the father was, although, given the timing, I had my suspicions.'

'So she might not be mine?' He heard the relief in his voice.

'She didn't tell me it was you until she knew for certain she was going to die. Then she confirmed what I had suspected all along. You were the father.'

Mac felt as if he was in a nightmare. He couldn't have a daughter. It was impossible. God knew, he didn't want one. He would make a terrible father anyway. His mind was racing. Admittedly, Sara and he had spent almost the whole fortnight together and, yes, they'd had sex. Neither of them had ever pretended that what they'd shared had been anything more than a holiday romance. And he remembered he had asked about contraception. He hadn't been such an idiot as to have unprotected sex. Although Sara had insisted she was on the Pill, they had used condoms, too. In his twenty-one years he had hardly been a saint and he hadn't taken chances with anyone's sexual health. So how could she have fallen pregnant? But then it came back to him. There had been one evening after a beach party when they'd both had too much to drink and they hadn't used condoms. It had never crossed his mind that Sara could have become pregnant. He forced himself to focus on what Abby was saying.

'When Emma was three months old, I went back to Mykonos to try and find you, but it was no use. You were gone. All I knew was that you were called Mac. I asked around, but nobody could tell me anything that would help me trace you.'

'That summer was my last of teaching windsurfing. After that I was too busy doing my house jobs. I didn't need the money or, more to the point, have the time.' He still felt dazed. 'You can't be sure she's mine, whatever Sara told you.'

'Think about it, Mac. Sara had no reason to lie. If she had wanted to, she could have told you she was pregnant, but she didn't. It was only when she knew she was going to die that she told me. And that was only because she knew that one day Emma would want to know something about her father. Possibly find him.' She paused. 'But if you still have your doubts I'm sure we can arrange a DNA test.' Although that wasn't what she wanted. Emma would be hurt to find out that the father she so desperately wanted had needed proof that she was his daughter.

'I think that might be a good idea.' Mac stumbled to his feet. He had to get out of there. He needed time to think. He saw his life changing in front of his eyes. A father!

'Mac, I know this has been a shock to you. It was to me when I realised I would be working with you. At least, in my case, I've known about you for years.'

'Does Emma know? That I'm her father, I mean?'

'She knows that her father is out there somewhere. She doesn't know it's you. Not yet. I thought it was only fair to talk to you first.'

'Will you tell her?'

'Yes. She desperately wants to find her father.' Abby reached out and touched him on the hand. 'Mac, please sit down. I can't think with you standing over me like that.'

Reluctantly Mac did as she asked. He owed it to Abby to hear her out, however much he didn't want to believe what she was telling him.

'The reason I took the job here was because Emma was being bullied at her school in London. You know how cruel kids can be. When they found out that Em didn't know who her father was they started teasing her. They wouldn't even come to her eleventh birthday party. Things just got worse from there.'

Ouch. Mac remembered only too well how that felt. Growing up in a small community, as he had done, it had been exactly the same for him, but at least he'd had his windsurfing. Out on the waves he'd been able to forget everything. Besides, his skill on the board had made him a bit of a hero in the other children's eyes. But their teasing had still hurt. He felt a rush of sympathy towards Emma. And anger. How dared those children pick on a little girl about something that was out of her control? If he had them in front of them right now, he'd be tempted to bang their heads together.

'If it turns out I am Emma's father, I won't deny her,'

he said. 'I'll do what's right. Provide financial support, whatever you need.'

Abby's eyes flashed with anger. 'Financial support isn't what is needed, Mac. Emma and I manage fine. What Emma needs is far more complicated than that. As soon as she knows about you she is going to want a relationship. Can you give her that?'

Right now, Mac had no idea.

Mac got to his feet again. 'I'm sorry, Abby, I just don't know if I can do what you're asking. I never wanted to be a father. I don't have the first clue about being one. There's a good chance I'll be rubbish at it. Emma is probably better off without me.' He jammed his hands into his pockets. 'I need time to think about this. Decide what to do.'

'Don't think too long, Mac. I have to tell Emma that I've found you.' She got to her feet, too. 'You said you'd take her windsurfing next Saturday. Whether you show up or not is up to you.'

He could see the determination in her calm nut-brown eyes.

'But let me warn you. If you do decide to get involved with her, it's not something you can back out of later. You're in it for keeps. Make no mistake, Mac, if you hurt my child, you'll have me to reckon with.'

CHAPTER SIX

MAC let himself into his flat and flung his car keys on the table. He had dropped Abby back home and they had sat in silence the whole of the journey. He was still reeling from what Abby had told him. There he'd been thinking he had been doing nothing more than taking a beautiful woman out to dinner. Now it seemed as if he was father to that woman's daughter!

He thought back to when he had seen Emma on the beach. She was tall—like him. And she had blue eyes— like him. But was that enough to go on?

He crossed over to his full-length windows and stared out to sea. How could his life have changed so dramatically in just a matter of hours? The last thing he wanted, or needed, was an eleven-year-old daughter. Why hadn't Sara told him she was pregnant? He felt a grudging respect for the woman who had given birth to his child. She had known how much his medical career had meant to him. She had also probably known, he admitted ruefully, that back then he had not been up to being a father. But was he up to it now?

The wind had risen, whipping the sea against the rocks. He wished he was out there, challenging himself against the elements. It was so much easier than dealing with the bomb Abby had thrown at him.

He poured himself a whisky and swirled the amber liquid around the glass. Memories of his own childhood came rushing back. The endless stream of men his mother had brought home, insisting that he call them Dad. He had refused. And just as well; none of them, except Dougie, had lasted more than a couple of months. Mac had got on with him. It had been Dougie who had given him his first second-hand board and Mac would have considered calling him Dad, but eventually Dougie had left, too, driven away by his mother's excessive demands. She had blamed Mac. Told him that he had ruined her chances of finding happiness. No wonder he had learned to windsurf. The time on the waves had been his only relief from his bitter, resentful mother. That, and school. As soon as he'd been able to, he had left home, supporting himself through medical school by taking out loans and teaching windsurfing. It had been hard. There had been too many times when he'd had to choose between buying a textbook and eating. But he'd survived, learning to depend on only himself. No wonder he'd never let anyone get close to him and so far it had worked out exactly the way he wanted. He was living the perfect life. A job he loved, this flat, mountain biking, free climbing and kite boarding whenever he could, and dating the kind of women who seemed happy to fit in around his other pleasures.

Until now.

He took a swig of his whisky, letting the liquid roll around his tongue. His life was going to be turned upside down. But what if Sara had been wrong? What if Emma wasn't his child? He had to know for certain one way or another. If she was his, he wouldn't abandon her. He couldn't do the same thing to a child, his child, as his father had done to him. At least Emma had Abby. An image of hazel eyes and a warm smile floated in front of his eyes. She was the opposite of the women he normally went after. She was serious, warm, caring and fiercely protective. He knew instinctively she would be like a tigress when it came to protecting her daughter. Abby, he was sure, would never have told him he was Emma's father if she hadn't been certain of it herself. She had taken a risk telling him and she knew it. Sighing, he placed his empty glass on the table and reached for the phone. He had to see Abby and arrange the DNA test after she had a chance to tell Emma. The sooner he knew for sure that Emma was his, the better for all concerned. But deep down he was getting used to the idea. Already he felt something strange, a sense of protectiveness towards the young girl who Abby claimed was his child.

Abby finished tidying the kitchen while listening to Emma's excited chatter. It was so good to see the little girl back to her usual self.

'Emma, I need to talk to you about something,' Abby said when Emma drew breath. 'Why don't I make us a cup of cocoa and we can take it in to the sitting room and chat there?'

When they were settled, Abby turned to Emma.

'You know how we spoke about your dad? Remember I told you I tried to find him when you were very little?'

Emma nodded and waited for Abby to continue.

'Well, I've found him.'

'Where? Who is he? How did you find him? Did he come looking for me?' The hope in Emma's eyes made Abby's heart stumble.

'He couldn't look for you, sweetie, because he didn't

know about you. I kind of found him by accident.' Abby took a deep breath. There was no going back now.

'You know Dr MacNeil? The man we met on the beach? He's your father.'

Emma looked stunned. 'Dr MacNeil? I thought you said my dad was a windsurfer.'

'Well, he is. We saw that down on the beach, but he's also a doctor. He taught windsurfing as a way to put himself through medical school.'

A slow smile crept across Emma's face. 'That's so cool. Does he know? Did you tell him? What did he say?'

Abby smiled at Emma's excitement. 'Yes, he knows. I told him.' Abby leaned across and took Emma's hand in hers. 'It was a bit of a surprise to him. He had no idea that your mother had even been pregnant. I guess it'll take him a little time to get used to the idea he has a daughter.'

Emma's brow puckered. 'You mean he doesn't want me.'

Abby took the mug from Emma and placed it on the coffee table, before pulling her daughter into her arms. 'Of course he'll want you. He just needs time to get to know you better. You and I have always known that you had a dad out there somewhere, but this has all come as a big surprise to him.'

'Is he still going to take me windsurfing?'

'I'm not sure. Em, don't get your hopes up too much. Remember when we've spoken about this before, we always said that even if we found your father, he might not want to be as involved as you might hope.'

'I don't care,' Emma said fiercely. 'I know I've always got you.' She sat up, her brows furrowing. 'This won't make any difference to us, will it? I mean, you'll always be my mum, won't you? He can't take me away from you, even if he wants to, right?'

Abby had wondered the same thing herself. When Sara had died, Abby had thought about adopting Emma officially, but it hadn't seem to be necessary. The social services had been more than happy to leave Emma in her care. Surely, and Abby thought this was unlikely, even if Mac did want to have Emma with him full time, no one would give him custody?

'I don't think that's going to happen. You're my daughter and no one is ever going to take you away from me. Look, let's take this one day at a time. You and Mac can get to know each other and we'll take it from there.'

Emma nodded. 'At least the kids won't be able to tease me about not having a father any more.' She hugged Abby. 'I can't wait to meet him properly. What's he like? Tell me everything you know.'

Emma was too excited to go to bed and she and Abby talked into the night. Abby brought out all her old photos of Sara and repeated the stories of their childhood that Emma could never get enough of. Finally she was able to persuade an exhausted but happy Emma to go to bed. Looking down at her sleeping child, Abby made a vow: Dr William MacNeil would not be allowed to cause her daughter so much as a moment's pain.

Early the next morning, there was a knock on the door. Abby opened it to find Mac standing there, an uncertain smile on his face.

'Can I come in?'

Abby was glad Emma was still in bed, catching up on sleep after their late night.

She stood back to let him in.

He brushed past her and started pacing her small

sitting room. He only managed a couple of strides in each direction before he had to turn round.

'Have you told her?' He hadn't even said hello.

'Yes. Last night.'

'How did she take the news?' He seemed nervous, uncharacteristically unsure of himself.

'She was thrilled. I warned her that I didn't know what you were going to do about it.'

'I'm not going to ask for a DNA test,' Mac said abruptly.

'Oh? Why not?' Had he made up his mind that regardless of whether it could be proven Emma was his child, he still didn't want to know? Abby's heart gave a sickening thud. It would be hard telling Emma, but perhaps it was for the best. In that case, either Mac or she and Emma would have to leave Cornwall. It would be too cruel for Emma to be reminded daily that she had a father who didn't want her.

'I don't want a DNA test because it's not fair to Emma. You say she's my child. The dates fit. She looks like me. If I insist on a DNA test, how will that make her feel? I know that if I were in her shoes, I would think that my father was trying to prove I wasn't his. No child deserves to be put through that.'

'So what are you saying, Mac? I'm afraid you're going to have to spell it out.'

'Look, I don't know what sort of father I'll make, but I'm going to give it my best shot. You and Emma will just have to be patient with me. Can you do that, Abby? Can you accept I can only do the best I can? That it might not be good enough?'

Abby was relieved he wasn't insisting on a DNA test. But as far as what kind of father he would be? Well, that was up to him. It wasn't as if she could go and pick him up a set of instructions from some kind of parent supermarket.

'Just promise me you'll do the best you can,' she said softly.

He sighed. 'You're going to have to help me here, Abby. As I said, I have no idea how to go about being a father. I mean, what do I do?'

He looked so different from his usual confident self that Abby's heart melted a little.

'I think taking her windsurfing is a good start,' she said. 'That way you and Emma can get to know each other without it seeming forced and unnatural.'

'I can do that. What else?'

'Let's just take it day by day, Mac. Learning to be a father takes time.'

'Tell Emma I'll see her on Saturday.' And with that he turned on his heel and was out the door as if the devil himself were after him.

CHAPTER SEVEN

Mac took a gulp of his beer as he waited for Josh to emerge from the changing room. It had been a good match, even if it had been closer than Mac would have liked. Shortly after Mac had started working on the air ambulance crew, Josh had invited him to join the five-a-side football team that many of the staff at the hospital played for. In the end, their team had just pulled the match out of the bag. Mac was pleased. He hated to lose.

'I got one in for you,' he told Josh when he appeared, gesturing towards the pint he had placed on the table.

After the match, the team would have a quick pint and usually talk about work. For various reasons tonight it was just him and Josh who'd stayed for a drink. Everyone else had had reasons to rush away, but although Josh was married he never seemed in a hurry to leave after the game.

Mac knew little about Josh's personal life. He had met his wife, Rebecca, once or twice when she had dropped into A & E to see her husband. Mac had got the impression that Rebecca was a little lonely. The life as a wife of a consultant could be like that, especially if, like Rebecca, she didn't work. Another reason to stay footloose and fancy-free, Mac decided—except he wasn't, not any more.

'How's Rebecca?' Mac asked. 'Does she like living here?'

Josh studied his pint glass as he twirled it around in his hand. 'I think Rebecca is more of a city girl. She misses being able to pop into the shops any time she pleases.'

'Yet she agreed to move here?' Mac said.

'It was too good an opportunity for me to miss. Hopefully in time Rebecca will make friends. Although it's difficult when she doesn't work. Not having children doesn't help either. If we had kids, she'd probably meet some mothers down at the school gates.'

'If you're planning on having some, I wouldn't leave it too long. How old is Rebecca? Thirty-three? Thirty-four?'

Josh frowned. 'Thirty-four. But we always agreed they weren't part of the plan.'

The expression on Josh's face darkened for a moment. What's going on here? Mac thought. But whatever it was, it was none of his business. Josh and Rebecca's private life had nothing to do with him.

'Anyway, what about you? I guess you're not the father type either. Or haven't you met the right woman yet?'

Mac shifted in his seat. Served him right. He had started this conversation. Besides, people were bound to find out sooner or later.

'Er… Actually, it turns out I am a father,' he said. The words sounded strange, still unbelievable.

Josh's eyebrows shot up. 'You kept that quiet. A bit of a dark horse, aren't you?'

'I only just found out myself.' If it were possible,

Josh looked even more astonished. But he said nothing, simply waited for Mac to continue.

'It's complicated,' Mac said. 'You know our new paramedic, Abby Stevens?'

'She's the mother of your child?' Josh's eyebrows couldn't go any higher.

'No. She's the aunt of my child. Emma, my daughter, is the result of a relationship I had with Abby's twin—years ago.'

'I think you're going to have to be more explicit,' Josh said, leaning back in his chair. 'Go on, I'm all ears.'

Mac wasn't used to talking about himself, but he had to tell someone. Perhaps thinking out loud would help. So, hesitantly, between sips of beer, he told Josh the whole story.

'And you had no idea Sara was pregnant?' A shadow crossed Josh's face, making Mac wonder, but he kept his thoughts to himself.

'None. It never crossed my mind.'

'And you believe Abby?'

'If you knew Abby better, you'd know that's a daft question. She's not the kind of woman to lie about something like this. She's totally upfront. With Abby, what you see is what you get.'

Josh raised an eyebrow again. There was a hint of a smile at the corner of his mouth. Mac wanted to tell him that he was mistaken, that there was nothing between him and Abby, but he knew his protests would only increase that amused look in Josh's eyes.

'Besides, it is entirely possible. The timing works out. And I was young at the time. Not always as responsible as I should have been.'

Josh's frown deepened. Did he disapprove? Surely Josh must have behaved in ways he now regretted when he had been a medical student. But perhaps Josh had been sensible enough always to take precautions. As medics, they knew better. Or, at least in his case, should have known better. But, damn it, he wasn't asking Josh for his approval. 'Shortly before she died, Sara told Abby I was the father and I can see no reason why Sara would lie. Besides, Emma has my eyes. I don't think there's much doubt.'

'So what are you going to do about it?'

'No idea, Josh. It's not as if I planned to be a father. I'm pretty sure I'll make a rotten one. But I can't turn away from my responsibilities. I told Abby that I'll spend time with Emma. I'm going to teach her to windsurf. At least I can do that.'

Josh looked thoughtful. He put his glass down on the table and leaned forward. 'You know, Mac, sometimes life deals us a hand we never wanted, or expected. We get one chance at grabbing what's in front of us. If we don't take it while we can, it might be a mistake we end up regretting for the rest of our lives.'

Something in his voice made Mac wonder if he was speaking from personal experience, but before he could decide whether to probe further, Josh went on. 'If I were you, I would think very carefully before you turn away from something that might turn out to be the best thing that's ever happened to you.'

'It sounds as if you know what you're talking about,' Mac said.

'Let's just say, if I had a particular time over in my life, I might have made different choices.' Josh picked up his and Mac's empty glasses. He nodded in the direction of the bar. 'Fancy a refill?' he asked.

On the way home Mac thought about what Josh had said. There was a mystery there, he was sure of it, but he respected his colleague too much to speculate on what it could be. If he wanted him to know, he'd tell him. As far as his advice about Abby and Emma went—that was different. He had promised Abby that he would get to know Emma and he had never gone back on his promise. But the thought still scared him witless. What did he know about being a father? He hadn't exactly had a good example himself. Unless it had been how not to be a father. His father had walked out on him and his mother without a backward glance. Walking out of the marriage had been one thing, but abandoning your only child had been quite another.

He swallowed his anger. It was no use thinking like that. What he did have to think about was *his* child. Whatever the future brought, however much he hadn't planned on having a child and however much disruption that might bring to the life he had carved out for himself, there was really no choice. He was Emma's father and he wouldn't—couldn't—abandon her.

CHAPTER EIGHT

THE next couple of days were busy, and Mac and Abby were seldom alone together, for which Mac was grateful.

He was still getting used to the fact that he had a daughter and almost as strange was that Abby was the mother of his child. For the first time in his life he was confused by his feelings for a woman.

He liked working with Abby. He admired the way she was with the patients: calm, assured but gentle, as if they really mattered to her.

They had the usual callouts to walkers with broken ankles that turned out to be badly twisted, and a couple of car accidents that thankfully turned out to be less serious than initially thought. When there wasn't a callout, the team went over rescue procedures and updated each other with new medical developments. Mac was careful to treat Abby like simply another member of the team.

It wasn't easy. He'd come to recognise the habit she had of biting her lip whenever she was anxious, and more than once he had to stop himself from leaning across and brushing a lock of hair from her eyes. He could hardly keep his eyes off her. He loved the way her mouth curved and her eyes lit up when she was pleased about something and he resented the way he kept imagining what it would be like to feel her mouth on his. Okay, so she was beautiful and sexy and warm but now he knew about Emma, Abby was out of bounds. He already had one commitment he had never expected and he didn't need another.

It was just after lunch on Wednesday when they received a call to attend a woman who had been thrown off her horse and then trampled. The only information they had to go on was that the woman was unconscious and in a field with no road access. The call had been transferred to the RAF, which was sending out a Sea King so that the medics could be winched down to the casualty if necessary

Within minutes Abby and Mac were being flown towards the injured woman.

'This could be nasty,' Mac said into his radio. 'If she's unconscious, it'll be difficult for us to be sure just how badly injured she is.'

'In that case, don't we treat her as if she has a spinal injury?' Abby asked.

'The most important thing is to keep her breathing,' Mac agreed. 'And not to make things worse.'

Ten short minutes later they were hovering over the accident site. A man was standing next to the woman, waving a brightly coloured jacket to get their attention.

'As we thought, there's nowhere to put down, I'm afraid,' the pilot said. 'It's too marshy. You're going to have to be winched out.'

Mac glanced at Abby and was surprised to see a flash of fear in her eyes.

'Are you okay?'

Abby nibbled her lip. 'It's the first time other than

training that I've had to winch down. I'm just a little nervous.'

'Tell you what,' he said. 'Seeing there is someone on board that can lower us both, why don't we go down together? That way we can get down quicker.' It wouldn't really make much difference timewise, but going down in tandem would make Abby feel better. It was the first time she had revealed a less than certain side to her and it made him feel unusually protective. Whether it was because she was the mother of his child or because this woman engendered feelings he had never experienced before, he didn't want to think about. He much preferred to think it was the former.

Mac stood and attached the winch to the harness they always wore in the helicopter. Although she was determined not to show it, Abby was relieved he'd be going down with her. She was intensely aware of the touch of his hands on her legs and hips as he tested the buckles.

The last few days he had been polite but distant towards her. When she'd asked him whether he still intended to take Emma windsurfing, he'd looked surprised. 'I don't go back on promises, Abby,' he'd said. 'Especially not to a child.'

They were lowered over the side, pressed together, one of Mac's arms holding her close. This was almost worse than going down alone. Her fear disappeared under her awareness of his hard, muscular body touching every inch of hers. She raised her head to look at him and he winked. She wasn't sure whether she was glad or disappointed when they touched the ground and Mac released them from the winch. All she knew was that her body felt as if it was on fire and that the blood was whooshing in her ears.

Mac raced to the fallen woman, leaving Abby to follow in his wake.

He crouched down beside her, feeling for a pulse. Then he used the small torch they all carried in the top pockets of their jumpsuits to shine a light in her eyes. Abby's heart sank when she saw that only one pupil reacted to the light.

'How long since it happened?' Mac asked the man who had stayed with her.

'I don't know, but not long before I found her. She cantered past me a few minutes earlier. I lost sight of her but then I saw her horse galloping away without a rider, so I knew something had happened. I telephoned for help immediately.' He looked at his watch. 'About twenty-five minutes ago. So I would estimate it's been approximately half an hour since she fell.'

'Has she been conscious at all? Have you moved her, Mr...?'

'Fox. No, I know you're not supposed to. I had some medical training when I was in the army. I just checked that she was breathing.'

Abby slipped a neck brace out of her bag. Although the head injury was their primary concern, they had to assume until they knew otherwise that the victim had a spinal injury, too.

Mac nodded and working together they slipped the brace round the fallen woman's neck and an oxygen mask over her face.

Then they strapped the rider's legs together to make the transfer to the helicopter. With Mr Fox helping, they slipped the two halves of the stretcher underneath her.

Mac was winched into the helicopter with the stretcher and a short time later the line was dropped again. Her heart thudding, Abby attached herself and gave the thumbs-up signal to be lifted. She could hardly ask Mac to leave their patient and come back for her. But to her relief the upward lift was okay. Having done it on the way down with Mac had helped. Abby knew that from now on she would never again worry about that part of the rescue, and she had Mac's thoughtfulness to thank for that.

Back in the helicopter, Mac had already attached their patient to the onboard monitoring system and was gently feeling her abdomen. As he did so, Abby noted some swelling just below the woman's ribs. She glanced up at Mac, who was shaking his head and looking worried.

'Damage to the spleen?' she asked.

He nodded. 'The sooner we get her to hospital the better. If she has ruptured her spleen she'll need surgery as soon as possible. I'll radio ahead and let them know so they can have the surgeons and a theatre standing by.'

The next ten minutes were tense as Abby continued to monitor the woman's vital signs and neuro observations. Her pulse was rapid, making the possibility of a ruptured spleen more likely. Mac helped Abby put up a drip. Giving the injured woman fluids would help keep her stabilised in the short term.

Abby sighed with relief when the helicopter landed gently on the landing pad at the hospital. As before, they were met by the A & E team. There was no time for introductions as they wheeled the woman straight into Resus and Abby stepped back, allowing the A & E team to take over. As they carried out their own assessment, Mac relayed what he and Abby had done so far.

'I think you're right about the ruptured spleen, Mac,' the dark-haired emergency consultant who had loaned them his car told them. 'Could I have a portable ultrasound over here, please?' While the A & E consultant prepared to scan the victim's abdomen, Mac was checking her reflexes. 'Right pupil still blown,' he said. 'I suspect a subdural haematoma, Josh. We should get the neurosurgeons down here to have a look.'

'I'm here.'

Abby whirled around to see a Latin-looking man enter the room. He crossed over to the trolley and Mac stepped aside to allow him to examine the rider. By this time the resus room was crowded. Apart from Dr Corezzi, the neurosurgeon, and Josh, there were several other people in the room, all occupied with the patient.

Mac passed an endotracheal tube down the woman's throat.

'Okay, let's get her to Theatre. The spleen *is* ruptured so she's going to need that fixed, too,' Josh said quietly. Despite his calm voice, Abby knew they were worried. A few moments later the woman was being wheeled out of the room to Theatre.

The emergency over, Josh and Mac peeled off their gloves.

'That was close,' Josh said. 'It was a good thing you were there, Mac. It makes a difference knowing in advance what we might be dealing with. This is exactly the type of case where having a doctor attached to the ambulance service makes a difference.'

'You're right. But whether a few successful cases will persuade the powers that be that having a full-time doctor attached to the service makes financial sense is a different story. She still might not make it,' Mac replied. 'But at least she has a chance.'

Mac glanced over at Abby, seeming surprised to see her still standing there. 'I couldn't have done it without

Abby. Abby, this is Dr Josh O'Hara, one of the A & E consultants here. Josh, this is Abby, our new paramedic, who has joined us from the London service.'

Josh grinned. 'We're lucky to have you.'

Abby took in his dark hair and ready smile. He was very good-looking, but for some reason he did nothing to her pulse. Unlike Mac. Unfortunately.

'Have you had a chance to look around St Piran's, Abby?' Josh asked.

Abby smiled. 'Not yet. There hasn't really been time. But I'd really like to go to the special care nursery. I have a patient there I'd like to see.'

'I have to pop into ITU,' Mac said. 'Josh, if you're not busy, perhaps you could take Abby up to Special Care? I'll meet you there in five.'

'Sure. No probs. I'll just let the nursing staff know where I am. I can introduce you to whoever is on duty at the same time, Abby.'

There were too many faces for Abby to take in, but everyone welcomed her warmly. She couldn't help but notice that Josh caused quite a stir in the department. There were several wistful looks in his direction of which he seemed oblivious. After they left the department, Josh took Abby upstairs to the SCBU. A nurse met them as they entered.

Josh introduced Abby. 'Abby was the paramedic who helped Mrs Hargreaves when she went into labour. She wanted to say hello and see how the baby's getting on.'

'Mum is with the baby now and they are both doing fine. It would have been a different story if you and Dr MacNeil hadn't got them here so quickly.' She peered over Abby's shoulder, as if expecting to find Mac standing behind her. She looked disappointed to find he wasn't. The nurse pointed to a cot near the middle of the room. 'They're over there if you want to go over.'

'Is Dr Phillips on duty?' Josh asked.

'Megan? Yes. Isn't she always? She's in the staffroom, catching up on paperwork.'

Josh looked at Abby. 'That's where I'll be if you need me. Mac should be along shortly.'

Abby found Jenny sitting by the cot, gazing down at her baby. As soon as she noticed Abby, her face broke into an enormous smile.

'How's he doing?' Abby whispered, peering into the cot. A tiny infant lay in it, his nappy almost taking up half of his small body. There were a few lines snaking from his tiny hands and feet, but he was breathing on his own. That was a good sign.

'He's doing okay. They think I'll be able to take him home in a week or two. And it's all thanks to you and Dr MacNeil. The staff say that if I'd been any later getting to hospital I might have lost him—or died, too. I don't know how to thank you enough.' Her voice cracked slightly. She had been through a very stressful experience and was bound to still be worried.

'You don't have to thank us. It's our job. I'm just thrilled that it all worked out okay.' Abby held out her arms and Jenny passed her sleeping child to her. Abby breathed in the particular blissful scent of baby.

Jenny was looking at something over Abby's shoulder. Abby turned round to find Mac standing there, looking at them. Jenny smiled and waved him over.

Mac approached them slowly, looking as if he'd rather be anywhere else than there.

'Dr MacNeil, I'm so glad I caught you. I wanted to thank you personally for saving my baby. And for taking care of Tim. I know he had his brave face on, but he was truly terrified until you came along.'

Mac shuffled his feet, looking uncomfortable. 'As I'm sure Abby told you, it was nothing. All in a day's work. How is Tim anyway?'

'He's at school today. His dad will bring him up later. He's totally besotted with his little brother. He kind of feels that he almost helped deliver him. He was a bit embarrassed when he first heard I was pregnant—you know how young boys can be about that sort of stuff— but now he couldn't be prouder.'

Just then Josh approached them, accompanied by a woman with russet hair and fine, delicate features.

'Abby, this is Dr Megan Phillips—one of the paediatric registrars,' Josh introduced her.

'Hi, Abby. I've heard all about you from Mrs Hargreaves here. I understand that it's thanks to you our latest miracle baby is doing well,' Megan said.

'Would you like to hold him, Dr Phillips?' Jenny asked. 'And seeing as you're all here, I might take the opportunity to pop to the bathroom.'

But Abby was surprised when Megan blanched. Instead, Josh stepped forward and took the tiny infant in his arms, cradling him with practised ease.

'Hey, Josh,' Mac teased. 'Looks like you're a natural after all. Are you practising for when you and Rebecca have kids? The nurses in A & E tell me that's all she talks about when she visits the department. You'd better make the most of the next few months. One of these days you'll be up to your ears in nappies.'

'Not me, I'm afraid,' Josh said lightly.

Abby saw Josh and Megan exchange a look. It was brief, the merest glance, but the paediatric registrar's face went even whiter. If she hadn't known Josh was married to Rebecca, Abby would have sworn there was something between the two doctors. But perhaps her own situation was making her hypersensitive. That was all.

As soon as Jenny returned Megan made her excuses. 'I'll be back to check on this little one in a while,' she told the happy mother. 'But if you'll excuse me, right now I have other patients to look in on.' She smiled, but Abby could see it didn't quite reach her eyes. After a brief nod at the two men, she left the ward.

'I should be getting back to A & E,' Josh said, handing the baby back to his mother. 'So if you'll excuse me, too? Abby, it was good to meet you. I'm sure we'll meet again soon.'

'We should go, too, Abby,' Mac said.

'No problem. If someone could just point me in the direction of the bathroom first? It was lovely to see you again, Jenny. And your baby. We don't always get the chance to catch up with our patients, so when we do, it's a real pleasure.'

'Thank you both, again.' She gazed down at her sleeping child, who was just beginning to stir. 'Looks like he's ready for a feed.'

'The bathroom's just outside the swing doors, Abby,' Mac said. 'I'll meet you downstairs.'

Abby found the bathroom. To her surprise Megan was leaning against the basin, her face streaked with tears. Concerned, Abby moved towards her and touched her on the arm.

'Megan? What's wrong?'

Megan managed a wan smile and leaned over the sink to splash her face with water. 'Don't mind me. I'm just having one of those days.'

'Are you sure there's nothing I can do?'

Megan reached for a paper towel to pat her face dry. 'No, really. But I'd appreciate it if you kept this to yourself. It doesn't seem too professional for the doctor to be found crying in the bathroom.'

'We all have our moments,' Abby said, 'when stuff gets on top of us.' She paused. 'Look, I'm new here and I haven't really met many people yet, and I'm always up for a bit of adult female company. Why don't you come over for supper one night?'

Megan smiled. She really is beautiful, Abby thought. But her eyes are so sad. Something was bothering her and it was more than just an off day, Abby would have staked her life on it.

'I would like that,' Megan said.

Abby wrote down her address and mobile number and passed it to Megan.

'Phone me?'

'Sure,' Megan said, pocketing the number. But somehow Abby didn't think she would.

CHAPTER NINE

ABBY woke early on Saturday morning to find that Emma was up before her. That in itself was unusual. She normally had to call Em at least twice before she could get her out of bed. Even more unusual was the smell of toast drifting from the kitchen. Moments later Emma appeared by her bed, carrying a tray with tea and buttered toast.

'Hey, what's this?' Abby said, sitting up and taking the tray.

'I woke up really early. I couldn't stay in bed so I thought I'd make you breakfast for a change.'

Emma's eyes were bright with excitement and it worried Abby. Perhaps she shouldn't have told her about Mac? Maybe she should have waited to see how the relationship developed? What if after today Mac backed away from having anything to do with his daughter? Abby knew the rejection would break Emma's heart. But what was the alternative? Lying to Emma? One way or another her daughter would have found out about Mac. Maybe not straight away, but eventually. And then how would she have felt about Abby keeping the truth from her? That would have been worse. One of the things Abby had always promised Em was that she would never lie to her.

Emma was dressed, with her long blonde hair, so like Sara's, tied back in a ponytail. She crept into bed beside Abby. 'When do you think he'll be here?' she asked.

Abby glanced at her watch and groaned. It was only six-thirty.

'Not for a little while. I think he said eight.'

'What if he doesn't come?' Emma asked anxiously.

'He'll come,' Abby promised. Or he'll have me to answer to, she thought grimly. But somehow she knew that once Mac had made a decision he would stick to it.

'Are you coming, too?' Emma asked.

'Do you want me to?'

'I think so,' Emma said.

'Then I will.' Abby tossed the bedclothes aside and jumped out of bed. 'But there is no way I'm going to try windsurfing. The sea's far too cold for me.'

Emma grinned up at her. 'Don't be such a wuss. We'll be wearing wetsuits. Come on, Mum. You have to give it a go. It'll be fun.'

'We'll see,' Abby said evasively. 'Right now, I need a shower.'

Bang on eight o'clock there was a knock on the door. Abby opened it to find Mac standing there, looking almost as nervous as Emma. He had a bunch of flowers in his hand. 'I brought these for Emma,' he said. 'To be honest, I didn't know what the form was for meeting one's daughter officially for the first time.'

Abby smiled. 'She'll be delighted. I don't think anyone's given her flowers before.' She took the bouquet from him. 'Emma!' she called out. 'Mac's here.' As she stood aside to let Mac into the small hall she added, 'I think Mac is best at this stage, don't you?'

Mac nodded, craning his neck to look behind her.

'Hi, Mac,' Emma said from behind her.

'Mac brought these flowers for you. I'll put them in water before we go, shall I?'

Emma's smile lit up her face. 'Flowers. Wicked. Thank you, Mac.'

Mac bowed slightly in acknowledgement. 'It is my pleasure. Have you got your costume and something warm to put on after your lesson? We'll be warm enough while we're moving, but when we get out of the water, you might get cold.'

Emma nodded. 'Mum's already been through all that. She's coming, too. She said she might even try it herself.'

Mac raised an eyebrow. 'Good for her.' He paused. 'Did you know I taught Sara how to windsurf?'

Emma nodded again. 'Mum told me. She said that's how you and my real mum met. Was she good at it?'

Abby's heart cracked a little. Emma was so desperate for any titbits about Sara. Abby had told her as much as she could about her, leaving out the bits about Sara's wild side, concentrating on the warm, fun-loving side of Sara. The only reason Sara had taken windsurfing lessons had been to get to know Mac. As far as Abby knew, once Sara and Mac had become an item, Sara had given up windsurfing, preferring to sit on the beach and watch.

'She wasn't bad.' Mac grinned. 'But she didn't take the lessons for very long.' Abby was grateful to Mac for his tactful answer. 'I have a feeling you're going to take to it.'

Ten minutes later they were on the almost deserted beach, and only the real die-hard surfers were out on the waves. While Emma was getting changed, Mac popped into one of the surfing shops that hired out equipment and returned with a couple of wetsuits. 'I brought one for you,' he told Abby, 'in case you do give it a shot. 'I'm just going to get a beginner's board for Emma then we'll be set.'

Abby was getting the distinct impression she wasn't going to be allowed off the hook.

By the time Emma appeared, wrapped in her towel and shivering in the cool morning air, Mac had organised a board for her. He handed her a wetsuit and helped her into it.

'Okay, this first bit we do on land. Abby can join in without getting changed. All she needs to do is slip off her shoes.'

Just as she'd suspected, Abby thought ruefully. There was no getting out of it. She undid the laces of her trainers and removed her socks. The sand squirmed pleasantly between her toes.

'Okay, Emma. Pop onto the board. I'll show you how you lift the sail and how to balance yourself. Then we'll have a go on the water.'

Emma got the hang of the basics pretty quickly. 'It will be more difficult in the sea,' Mac warned, 'but so far I'm impressed. Now, Abby, how about you having a go?'

Reluctantly, Abby stepped on the board and, following Mac's instructions, tugged on the sail to try and lift it. It was harder than she had expected. Determined to do it, she pulled with all her strength and almost toppled over when the sail whooshed up towards her. But Mac had anticipated her losing her balance and she felt strong hands circle her waist, steadying her. The feel of his hands cupping her waist sent all kinds of sensations shooting through her body and she prayed neither he nor

Emma noticed the heat that rushed to her face. The last thing she wanted or needed was to have such a physical reaction to this man and, even worse, for either of them to notice.

Mac remained behind her, close enough for every cell in her body to be acutely aware of him. His breath tickled her neck as he placed his hands over hers, showing her how to hold the board. She was getting more and more flustered. Abruptly she let the sail fall back to the ground and stepped off the board. She knew she had to put some physical distance between her and this man.

'That's enough for me for the time being,' she said, trying to keep her voice light. 'I think Emma's dying to get out on the water.'

Mac looked at her and the way his eyes danced told her he knew exactly why she had jumped off the board. His mouth twitched. 'Okay, then. Let's go, Emma.'

Abby found a rock and watched as Emma clambered onto the board and valiantly tried to pull the sail from the water. It took several attempts, but with Mac helping her she eventually got the sail up and started to move out towards the open sea. She must have surprised herself as she immediately let go of the sail and fell into the water. Even from a distance, Abby could see the flash of Mac's white teeth as he threw his head back and laughed. In response, Emma splashed him. Relief coursed through Abby. It really was the perfect way for Emma and Mac to get to know each other. From what she could see, the initial awkwardness of earlier had passed. It was early days, of course, but at least it was the right start.

After an hour, Abby was getting chilled despite having a cup of coffee from the flask she had packed. Emma had managed to get up on the board and move

a little distance before falling off. Abby knew she must
be getting tired and, sure enough, a few minutes later
Emma and Mac, both grinning widely, made their way
to shore. Emma flopped down beside Abby, her cheeks
flushed and her eyes sparkling. 'That was so good.' She
looked up at Mac, who was detaching the sail from the
board. 'Can we do it again? Soon? Please?'

'Sure thing. But I think you should get changed now.
I don't want you to get cold.'

As Emma hurried away to get dressed, Abby looked
up at Mac. He really was gorgeous. No wonder Sara had
fallen for him hook, line and sinker. She found herself
wondering about him. How come a man as cute and as
eligible as he was hadn't been snapped up? But perhaps
he had. For all she knew, he had been married at one
time.

'I think she enjoyed that,' Abby said.

Mac looked after Emma's retreating back. 'She could
be very good, you know. She has natural balance and,
more importantly perhaps, seems hugely determined to
succeed. Is she like that in everything?'

Abby didn't attempt to hide her pride. 'She's a wonderful girl, Mac. She gives everything she does her best
shot. I know her drive and determination will take her
far in life.'

'And a lot of that must be down to the way you
brought her up.' Mac's eyes glittered and once again
Abby felt her body tingle in response.

'I hope so. But she has a lot of her mother in her,
too.'

When Mac raised an eyebrow, a shot of anger coursed
through Abby. She would not have this man making
judgements about Sara. Okay, so Sara had been pretty
wild, but she'd also been kind and loyal.

'Sara was a good person, Mac,' Abby said quietly.

Mac opened his mouth as if to reply but Emma, dressed in jeans and a thick woollen jumper, arrived back.

'Can we have something to eat now? I'm starving!'

The tension disappeared as they all laughed. 'It's not even ten o'clock yet, Em,' Abby protested.

'But it's ages since I had breakfast.'

'I swear I don't know where she puts it all,' Abby told Mac. 'She eats like a horse but is as thin as a rake.'

'At least she eats,' Mac said mildly. 'And she's still growing.'

'Mum says I'm going to be tall.' Emma looked shyly at Mac. 'I must take after you. How tall are you anyway?'

'Six foot three, or something like that. I'm hungry, too. What do you say we grab a burger?'

Abby frowned. 'I don't really like Emma to have junk food,' she said primly.

'I don't think one will hurt,' Mac protested.

Abby felt her hackles rise. One day as a father and already he was interfering. But she swallowed the angry words that rose to her lips. She was being overly sensitive. Why spoil the day by falling out over something as ridiculous as a burger? Nevertheless, she would have to speak to him and make it clear that as far as Emma was concerned, it *was she* who made the decisions.

'On the other hand,' Mac went on smoothly, 'there is a café up the road a little that does great home-made soup and sandwiches. And they have the best hot chocolate, too. Why don't we go there?'

'Whatever,' Emma said. 'I don't mind.'

Inside the café, Mac and Emma tucked into their soup and sandwiches while Abby nursed a mug of coffee.

She listened as Emma fired questions at Mac, and Mac replied with much the same answers he had given Abby. Nevertheless, there was a reticence, a carefulness about his replies that made her think he wasn't being totally candid. But why should he? No doubt he was, quite sensibly, feeling the way with his new-found daughter.

'Can I meet my grandmother?' Emma asked.

'Tiree is a long way from here,' Mac said evasively. 'But maybe one day.'

'Have you got brothers and sisters?'

'Only me, I'm afraid.'

Emma looked glum for a moment. Abby knew that part of her fantasy about finding her father was the hope that she'd discover a whole load of aunts, uncles and cousins at the same time.

But it wasn't long before her natural cheerfulness re-emerged.

'Did you always want to be a doctor?'

'For as long as I can remember,' Mac replied. 'What do you want to be when you grow up, or haven't you decided yet?'

'Not really decided. I might be a pilot or a vet.' She looked thoughtful. 'Or a doctor like you who rescues people. It looks fun.'

'Yeah, it can be fun, but it can also be a little scary at times.'

Emma's eyebrows shot up. 'I don't think you find anything scary.'

Oh, dear, Abby thought. One day in and already Emma had found a hero in Mac.

Mac flicked a glance at Abby and smiled. 'I find lots of things scary,' he said. Then he changed the subject. 'One of the other things I like doing is mountain biking. How do you fancy coming with me one day?'

'Oh, I'm not sure about that,' Abby interrupted before she could help herself. 'Can't that be pretty dangerous?'

Mac narrowed his eyes at her. 'It can be dangerous crossing the road, if you're not looking where you are going,' he said mildly. 'The important thing is to weigh up the risks, decide how you can best protect yourself then go for it.' Abby had the uneasy feeling he wasn't just talking about mountain biking. 'It's good for kids to test themselves. I believe it stops them from taking risks in other ways. Anyway, I'll only take Emma on gentle slopes and make sure she's wearing all the right gear to protect her.'

Once again he was challenging her authority as a mother and Abby didn't like it one bit. Keeping her voice level, she stood up. 'I'll think about it. Emma, it's time for us to get back. We need to go shopping for groceries.'

'Oh, do we have to?' Emma said. 'Can't I stay with Mac?'

Before Mac could say anything, Abby shook her head. 'I'm sure Mac has something planned for the rest of the day, and I would really like your help with the shopping, Em.' It was a pretty poor excuse, but Abby wanted Emma to get to know Mac slowly. Give them both time to let the relationship develop.

Reluctantly Emma got to her feet. 'Thanks, Mac. It was great.'

'We'll do it again next weekend, if you like,' Mac promised. 'And I'll try and work on Abby about the mountain biking thing.'

Emma smiled happily and Abby knew she was too late. Emma had found exactly the kind of father she had always wanted.

CHAPTER TEN

THE next few weeks flew past. Abby looked at a couple of cottages that would have been perfect for her and Emma—if the price hadn't been out of her reach. Mac and Emma had developed a routine, seeing each other a couple of times a week—either to go windsurfing or mountain biking. Abby's heart still leaped every time she saw Mac, but she tried to make sure they were never alone. He didn't ask her out again either. She didn't know whether to be pleased or disappointed. All she did know was that it was better this way. Much, much safer.

As the weather became more unpredictable, Mac had agreed with Abby, much to Emma's disappointment, that the windsurfing had to stop—winter was on its way.

'I don't mind getting cold,' Emma had protested. 'And I'm just getting the hang of it.'

'You're doing more than getting the hang of it.' Mac had grinned. 'I've rarely had a pupil that's taken to it as quickly as you have. But it's not just the cold. The waves are getting bigger now, and neither your mother nor I want to risk anything happening to you.' He ruffled Emma's hair as the child glowed with pleasure at his praise.

Abby was relieved. Although she trusted Mac not to let Emma do anything outside her capabilities, there was a recklessness in both father and daughter that frightened her. They were both risk-takers.

'But we can carry on mountain biking?' Emma asked. 'I like that, too.' Abby reluctantly capitulated and agreed to let Mac take Emma.

'As long as it doesn't get too wet, yes. And as soon as spring arrives, we can go windsurfing again.'

Emma wasn't prepared to give up without a fight. 'Are *you* going to stop kite boarding?'

Mac laughed again. 'When you learned to windsurf in Tiree, as I did, a little cold and big waves don't put you off.'

Emma started to protest, but Mac cut her off. 'I promised Abby that I won't let you do anything dangerous and I'm sticking to that promise, okay?'

Seeing the easy way Mac dealt with Emma, Abby was pleased. Despite her concerns, Mac seemed to be developing a real bond with his daughter. Emma's confidence was growing by leaps and bounds. Abby had one concern, though. She knew how much Emma wanted to impress her newly found father and she wouldn't put it past her to do something outside her comfort zone to impress him. But there was little she could do about that. She would just have to trust Mac.

Over the last couple of weeks Abby had been on several callouts with Mac. He was always calm and very efficient. Every day she was learning to respect him more and more. But that wasn't all. Every day she was finding herself more and more attracted to him, and not just physically. She was learning that he had an easygoing nature and that nothing ever fazed him. She often found herself wondering why he had never married.

This morning Mac came in looking tired.

'Late night?' Kirsten teased. 'Some woman keeping you up?'

Abby caught her breath as an unfamiliar stab of jealousy hit her in the solar plexus.

Mac shook his head. 'I wish.' He smiled. 'No, I was called late yesterday afternoon. There was a nasty accident on one of the main roads. Two fatalities, I'm afraid.'

'But you saved one,' said Mike, who had walked in in time to hear the last of the conversation. 'I heard it was a real touch and go.'

Mac pulled his hand through his hair. 'I had to intubate at the scene. It wasn't easy, even with the fire brigade giving me some light to work with—and some shelter. The rain was pretty torrential. But, yes, the driver of the second car is going to be okay. I just wish we could have done something for the occupants of the other car, but it looks like they died on impact.'

Everyone hated hearing about death, even if they knew it came with the job. Abby was a little surprised to hear the sadness in Mac's voice. He usually gave away very little of himself.

'I ended up staying at the hospital until the small hours. I wanted to make sure before I left that the man pulled from the car was stable.'

He caught Abby's eye and smiled. 'I think it's important we follow up on our patients. Don't you, Abby?'

Abby smiled back. It seemed that Mac was breaking his no involvement rules in more ways than one.

Except with her, that was. He was always friendly when he collected and returned Emma.

'Anyway,' Mac said, 'back to work. Anything on the board?'

'Shouldn't you be at home, catching up on your sleep?' Abby asked.

Mac shrugged his shoulders. 'I'll be fine. We doctors learn very early on to do without sleep. A gallon of coffee and I'll be fine.' He must have noticed that Abby was far from convinced. 'Honest.' He held up two fingers. 'Scout's honour.'

While he'd been talking Abby had spooned some coffee into a mug and added water from the recently boiled kettle. 'Drink this,' she ordered.

As Mac sipped his coffee, the radio came to life and everyone stopped talking. They could only hear Kirsten's side of the conversation, but the look on her face told them it was a bad one.

'We have a pregnant woman who has gone off the road. The road ambulance and fire brigade are there, but they're requesting assistance from us. She's complaining of severe abdominal pain and they have no idea what they are dealing with. The fire brigade is cutting her out of her vehicle at the moment.'

Mac jumped to his feet, every trace of tiredness banished.

'Okay, Abby. Let's go.'

'Mac has called from the air ambulance. They are bringing in a pregnant woman from an RTA with severe abdominal pain,' Josh told the assembled A & E team. 'Would someone page the obstetric and paediatric registrar, please?'

'I'm on it,' the senior nurse said, turning away and picking up the phone.

Josh pulled a hand through his hair. He was tired. Spending so much time at the hospital, putting in extra hours, was taking its toll.

But you don't need to, an insistent voice whispered in the back of his mind. The department copes well when you're not there. He knew the real reason. It was more and more difficult to spend time at home with Rebecca, pretending. Some time soon he would have to face the reality of the situation, but for now it would have to wait.

Minutes later he was called to Resus to see his patient. Mac and Abby were by her side.

'Who have we got here?' he asked.

'Mrs Diane Clifford,' Mac replied calmly. 'Twenty-four weeks pregnant and has been having right-sided abdominal pain for the last six hours. She was driving herself to hospital when she blacked out and crashed. No obvious injury from the accident. We're going to have to leave you guys to it, I'm afraid. We have another call to go to.'

As Mac and Abby left, Josh smiled reassuringly as he palpated his anxious patient's abdomen. 'Don't worry, Diane. We'll get to the bottom of this.'

He glanced up as Megan swept into the room. As usual she looked every inch the calm professional, her dark hair neatly swept back from her face, her expressive eyes already taking in the scene.

'You called the paediatric registrar?' she said, acknowledging Josh with a faint smile before introducing herself to the woman on the bed. 'I'm Dr Phillips,' she said softly. 'We're going to get your baby attached to a monitor so we can monitor the heartbeat. Is that okay?'

Diane's frightened eyes darted from Josh to Megan.

'Do you think there's something wrong with my

baby?' She reached out and grabbed Megan's hand. 'Don't let me lose my baby.'

Pain flickered in Megan's eyes before she rearranged her expression into her usual professional mask. Anyone else would have missed it, but for Josh it was plain to see. Damn it. Why did it have to be Megan who was called to this particular case?

'Dr Phillips, could I have a word?' he said, indicating that Megan step outside the cubicle with him. 'Diane, the nurse is just going to get you attached to the monitor while I have a quick chat with Dr Phillips here. Is that okay?'

Diane nodded silently and Josh followed Megan outside the cubicle. They moved away so they weren't overheard by their patient.

'What are you thinking, Josh?' Megan's voice was calm and steady, but she couldn't quite hide the anxiety in her eyes. He knew her too well.

'It could be three or four things. Appendicitis, premature labour or an abruption. But I don't really believe it's appendicitis.'

Megan sucked in a breath.

'You could get someone else to take over,' Josh said gently.

Megan's eyes flashed. 'No, I couldn't. Josh, you have to stop treating me as if I were made of china. I'm here now and Diane is my case.'

'She's twenty-four weeks,' Josh continued. 'I hope to God we don't have to deliver her.'

Megan bit her lip. 'We both know a twenty-four-weeker doesn't have much of a chance. We'll give her steroids just in case. But if you need to deliver, we'll do the best for the baby.'

Josh wanted to reach out and touch her. The need

to comfort her was so strong he had to lock his hands behind his back.

'Okay. We'll do an ultrasound. See how the baby's doing when we get the CTG result. After that we'll make a decision. I'll give you a shout if we need you.'

But before he could turn away, Megan grabbed his arm.

'I'm staying,' she said. 'If she has an abruption you might have to deliver her without waiting for the obstetric team. But have a look at her ovaries. A cyst could present in much the same way.'

He nodded. He hoped she was right.

Everyone waited anxiously while Josh ran the ultrasound probe over the injured woman's abdomen. He looked up and smiled.

'There's a ten-centimetre cyst on the right where the pain is.' He caught Megan's eye. 'Good call, Dr Phillips. We were right to wait.'

They both knew they were far from out of the woods but at least it wasn't premature labour and it wasn't an abruption. It was still serious and Diane had to be taken to Theatre immediately. But at least this was one woman who wasn't going to lose her baby. Josh explained to Diane that the cyst had probably become twisted on its stalk, cutting off the blood supply to the ovary and resulting in severe pain.

Megan blinked rapidly. 'I better go and get changed. They'll need a paediatrician standing by in Theatre, just in case.'

Then she smiled. God, he loved her smile. It seemed to start somewhere deep inside her until her whole face lit up. Once more he felt a pang of regret so deep it hurt.

Why couldn't things have been different between them? How in God's name had he made such an almighty mess of his life?

CHAPTER ELEVEN

ABBY was surprised to find Mac waiting for her when she emerged from the building after changing into her civvies.

'Are you okay?' he asked, his eyes searching hers.

Abby nodded. 'I am now. It got a bit hairy there for a while. I always get really anxious when the victim is pregnant.'

Mac smiled slowly and his eyes creased at the corners. Abby's heart lurched. How could anyone look so cool and sexy after all they had just been through? She was sure she looked as if she'd done a couple of rounds in the boxing ring. It felt like it anyway.

For a moment Mac looked directly into her eyes and what she saw there made her heart start pounding again. The world started spinning around her.

'How about you and Emma coming out for dinner?' he asked.

Abby struggled to control her breathing. What she was feeling was nothing more than a delayed reaction to the rescue.

'Normally we'd love to, but Em is going around to a friend's after school. Maybe another time?' She was pleased to hear that her voice was steady, betraying nothing of her inner turmoil, and she thanked the years of practice she'd had of keeping her feelings hidden.

'We could go on our own.' He smiled at her. 'Go on, say yes. I don't know about you, but every time I go on a rescue, I get hungry.'

There wasn't any reason to refuse as far as she could see, except for her reluctance to be alone in his company a moment longer than she had to. Every time she was near him, her body kept behaving in the strangest way. On the other hand, what harm could it do? It wasn't as if she could avoid being alone with Mac for the rest of her life. Not when they worked together and not when they shared Emma. Emma would be having supper at her friend's and Abby had planned on warming up soup to have with a sandwich. She hardly saw her daughter these days. Emma was either going round to see friends, or staying on at school for hockey practice, or out with Mac. But although she missed spending time with her, she knew it meant her daughter was happy and settled. It was natural for Emma to want some independence, and it was a sign that she was continuing to develop her confidence, knowing that Mac and Abby were there if she needed them.

'Unless you'd like to have supper at my place?' she said. The moment the words were out of her mouth, she regretted them. Although the thought of an evening alone with Mac excited her, it unnerved her, too.

'Home cooking? How could I refuse?'

Too late. She could hardly retract the invitation now.

'It won't be very fancy, I'm afraid. You might regret it.'

'Let me tell you, Abby, for a man who lives on takeouts and microwave meals when I'm not eating out, the thought of home cooking is irresistible.'

'Okay, then, you're on. Why don't you come home with me now? It'll save you a trip to your flat and back.'

'Sure thing. I'll stop off on the way and pick us up some wine, shall I? Red or white?'

'White. Although I'm not much of a drinker, so you might be drinking most of it yourself.'

'Give me half an hour?'

By the time Mac knocked on the door, Abby had rummaged around in the fridge and found enough to make a stir-fry. As she'd told Mac, supper wouldn't be fancy, but with the soup it would be adequate. She hoped she had enough. A big man like Mac was bound to have a healthy appetite. Although there wasn't an inch of flab on his muscular frame, given all the exercise he did, he was bound to need calories.

'Wine—and some olives,' Mac said, proffering his purchases to Abby. 'I didn't know if you liked them, but I took a chance.'

'Love 'em. Why don't you pop the wine in the fridge? You don't fancy lighting the fire while I finish supper?' Abby gestured to the open fire with a nod of her head. 'You'll find everything you need there.'

By the time the meal was ready, the fire was burning cheerfully. There was no room in the tiny house for a kitchen table, so Abby set two places on the coffee table in front of the fire.

'Sorry,' she apologised. 'I guess it'll be slightly awkward for you, but as you can see there isn't a lot of space.'

Mac looked around the small sitting room-cum-kitchen.

'I don't know,' he said. 'It's kind of cosy. But you know, if you and Emma need something bigger, I'll be happy to chip in.'

'We manage fine,' Abby said, more sharply than she'd intended to. 'I'm looking for something bigger to buy once we're sure where we want to live.' She didn't add that it was nigh on impossible on her salary, but she guessed she didn't need to.

'It must have been a struggle sometimes, bringing up a child on your own,' Mac said quietly. 'I wish Sara had told me. I would have done something to help.'

Abby shrugged. 'If you knew Sara, you'd know she had her pride. I guess when she found out she was pregnant the baby was the first thing she'd ever had that was truly hers. All through her pregnancy she refused to tell me who the father was. She said it wasn't important. She only told me about you right at the end.' Despite her best efforts her voice cracked. Mac put his fork down and laid a hand over hers.

'Tell me about her. Although we spent those two weeks together, all I really knew about Sara was that she had a great sense of humour and a genuine love of life.'

Abby placed her knife and fork on her plate and leaned back on the sofa.

'To understand who Sara was you have to know something about our upbringing. Our mother—well, I guess you can say she wasn't the maternal type. When Sara and I were eighteen she told us it was time to leave home.'

'Go on,' Mac said quietly.

'I think my mother thought we got in the way of her

life. Men weren't that interested in a woman with two children.'

She sneaked a look at Mac and was surprised to see anger in his eyes.

He smiled but his eyes remained bleak. 'My mother was the same.'

'Sara and I set up home together, if you could call it that. We didn't have much money, but we got by.'

'What about your father?'

'We never really knew him. He left when we were three and didn't come back.'

'Like mine,' Mac muttered. 'Except he didn't wait until I was three. He was off the minute he knew my mother was pregnant.'

Abby's heart ached for him.

'Anyway, Sara went a little off the rails when we left home. It's like she thought she was unlovable, and who could blame her? If your own mother doesn't want you, what does that say about you?'

'And you? How did you feel?'

'I was different from Sara. I decided that it was my mother's problem and I would find a way of proving to her that I could make it on my own. All through our childhood, I was the responsible one.'

Abby picked up a cushion and clutched it to her chest. Despite her words she had been hurt by her mother's rejection. It still hurt. 'I trained as a paramedic. I discovered I was good at it. Sara, though, couldn't find anything she really wanted to do.' Abby blinked the tears away. She had tried everything to get her sister to believe in her own self-worth, but Sara just wouldn't—couldn't—believe it.

'When we were twenty-one I had saved up enough money to pay for a holiday in Mykonos for both of us.

I thought two weeks of sunshine, together, would bring us closer again. I had hoped that I could really talk to Sara. Convince her it was time she made something of her life.'

'And then she met me. I can't imagine you were best pleased.'

'Then she met you,' Abby said softly. 'I have never seen her so lit up. I think she fell in love with you the moment she set eyes on you.'

'She spent most of the holiday you had planned together with me,' Mac said.

'Yes. It wasn't exactly the way I had thought it was going to be. But I couldn't deny her her chance. It had been a long time since I had seen her so happy.'

Mac groaned. 'I had no idea. I was so wrapped up in myself then, all I knew was that there was this beautiful woman who wanted to be with me. And I guess meeting me then falling pregnant was the last thing Sara needed. But how come I never noticed you?' He touched Abby briefly on her cheek. 'You are just as beautiful.'

'I wasn't back then. I was so much shyer than Sara. Anyway, the holiday wasn't a total disaster. I left Sara to it and took a ferry to the Greek mainland. I visited the Temple of Poseidon, and the Acropolis in Athens. Even if Sara had not been...' she paused '...occupied, she wouldn't have come with me. So I guess she got the holiday she wanted and I did, too. It was just a shame we didn't have the time I wanted to get closer to each other again.'

Abby smiled. 'I was happy for her. Those two weeks were the happiest I'd ever seen her. Instead of that vague sadness and emptiness that seemed to have followed her most of her life, it was as if she'd found something.

Something that made her believe in herself.' Abby looked at Mac. 'I know I have you to thank for that.'

'When did she tell you she was pregnant?'

'About three months after we returned from Mykonos. After we came back she was quieter, almost serene. I don't know...as if she'd found peace. I asked her if something had changed, but she just smiled. Then for a bit she was different again. Anxious and withdrawn. After a while, when she started showing, she told me she was going to have a baby. She said she hadn't told me at first because she hadn't been sure she was going to keep it.

'As you can imagine, I was stunned. I guessed the father must be you, but when I asked her she wouldn't say. She said it wasn't important. I didn't know how the three of us were going to cope, but Sara was so happy.'

Mac was listening intently.

'I wanted her to tell the father, even if she wouldn't tell me. I thought whoever it was had a right to know. But she refused point blank. She said the baby was hers and nobody was going to have any say about how she brought up her child. During her pregnancy she started a degree with the Open University. I could see she was determined to make a future for herself and the child and she knew I would always be there for her. Our own mother, of course, wasn't the slightest bit interested.'

'But she did tell you that I was the father—eventually.'

Abby squeezed her eyes closed.

'When she knew that she wasn't going to live to look after Emma, yes, she gave in and told me.'

The memory of those last few days were burnt into Abby's mind. At first everything had gone as planned and Sara's labour, although long, had resulted in a healthy baby girl. When Abby had seen her sister holding her child, it had been a moment of such joy Abby couldn't have felt prouder even if she had been the mother instead of Sara. Not even their mother's disinterest in the birth had blighted those first few days. After all, she and Sara had each other and however difficult and challenging the next few years would be, together they would be there for Emma, be their own little family. Then Sara had developed an infection and had been admitted to ITU. Even then, Abby had never suspected for one moment her sister might die. But Sara had got steadily worse. She hated thinking about it. Her sister, lying in ITU, pale and listless, and for once Abby had been totally unable to help her.

'Abby, I don't think I'm going to make it,' Sara had whispered, her face flushed with fever.

'Don't say that. Of course you're going to be okay.'

Sara smiled wanly. 'Somehow I knew deep inside that this was too good to last.'

Abby reached for her hand and squeezed it tight, trying to transfer all her strength to her failing sister.

'You can't die, Sara,' Abby cried. 'Emma needs you. I need you.'

'I'm not strong like you. You'll be okay.' For a moment strength returned. 'Look after Emma for me, promise. Don't let anything bad happen to her. I want her to know she's cherished and loved.'

'I promise, Sara. But you mustn't talk like that. You're going to be okay.'

'Hey, I thought I was the optimist.' Sara managed a smile. She struggled to speak. 'Remember Mac? Back on Mykonos? He's the father. I'll leave it to you to decide whether you want to tell him or not. Whatever you decide to do is okay with me.'

Shortly after, with Abby holding her hand, Sara had slipped into a coma. She never came round and died a few days later.

Tears fell as Abby repeated the story to Mac. She was barely conscious of his arm slipping around her shoulder and pulling her close.

'I'm so sorry,' he said. 'You must miss her. If I had known, I could have helped.'

'I tried to find you when Em was a few months old. But I knew nothing except that you were called Mac and taught windsurfing. I took Emma with me back to Mykonos to try and find you but the season was over and the resort closed down. I phoned their main office, but they refused to give me any details of the staff who worked there.' She shrugged. 'There was nothing more I could do, so we just came home.'

Suddenly conscious that she was in his arms, Abby pulled away. Her heart aching, she crossed to the fire and added a log. A sudden flurry of sparks crackled in the hearth.

'So you brought Emma up on your own. It couldn't have been easy. What about your mother?'

'She wasn't even there when Sara died. She had gone on holiday. Said she needed the break.' Abby couldn't keep the bitterness from her voice. 'To be fair, she couldn't have known Sara was going to die.'

'But you must have warned her? When Sara was admitted to ITU?' The anger in Mac's voice was almost palpable. How could anyone understand how a mother could stay away from her child when she needed her?

'She came back in time for the funeral,' Abby said. 'Then, unbelievably, when she held Emma for the first time, it was almost as if Mum changed before my eyes. She became besotted with her grandchild, in a way she never had been with her own daughters. Maybe it was different. There was no responsibility involved. She could have all the good times with Em without the bad. And maybe it was guilt. Guilt that she hadn't been there for Sara when she'd needed her most. Who knows? But she does love her granddaughter. She helped with child care when Emma was little so I could work. So people can change. And I'm glad. I've always felt it was important Emma knows who her family is. She's had little enough of them—until now, that is.' She forced a smile. 'But enough about that. What about your parents?'

This time it was Mac who shifted uneasily. 'My family isn't any better than yours, I'm afraid. If anything, they could be worse.'

Abby looked at him. He was studying his feet as if he could find answers there. She waited for him to continue.

'My mother sounds very much like yours. I also never knew my father. I sometimes wonder if my mother did. I was an only child and she made it clear from early on I was nothing but a nuisance.' He looked up and Abby saw the pain in his eyes. 'I spent as much time away from her as I could. She made it clear she didn't expect much from me, but I knew I wanted more from life. When I wasn't outside in the sea or on the hills, I was in my room studying. I was damned if I was going to give her the satisfaction of turning out the way she expected me to. I was lucky, I won a scholarship to medical school, and the rest is, as they say, history.'

'Do you see her?'

'I go back to Tiree once a year. She's not getting any younger. Whatever she is, she's still my mother.' He sent her a half-smile. 'You and I have a lot in common after all.'

'Does she know about Emma?'

'I phoned her. I thought she'd like to know. Perhaps she's mellowed or perhaps she's lonely, but she's asked to meet her.'

'Have you mentioned it to Emma?'

'I thought I should run it past you first.'

'Maybe we could all go?' Abby suggested.

'I'd like that.'

There was silence for a moment. 'I don't want Emma to grow up without a father. I told myself I would never have children, but now I have, I want her to know I'll always be there for her. Don't ever take her from me, Abby.'

Abby walked across the room and crouched by his side. She touched his face lightly.

'What makes you think I will? I want her to know her father, too.'

He touched her lips with a finger. 'Emma is lucky to have you as a mother.'

For a moment their faces were only inches apart. Abby could feel his breath on her skin, almost feel the warmth radiating from him. He smelled of wood smoke and earth. His eyes, drilling into hers, were as blue as the sea. Her heart was thudding so loudly she thought he must be able to hear it. Gently he slid his hand behind her neck. The feel of his fingers on her skin sent tiny shots of electricity fizzing through her.

She didn't know if he pulled her towards him or whether she was the one to make the move, but suddenly they were kissing. Softly at first, almost exploring each other's mouths, and then, as desire lit a flame in her belly, she was in his arms and he was kissing her as if his need for her was all-encompassing. No, no, no, a voice was shouting in her head. Don't do this. Nothing good can come of this. But her body wasn't listening. She could no more pull away from him than she could have walked across the desert.

Without knowing how it happened, they were lying on the sofa, their bodies pressed along the length of each other.

'Abby,' Mac whispered into her hair. 'Beautiful, sweet Abby.'

What was she doing? What were they doing? Apart from anything else, Emma would be back any moment. Reluctantly, Abby disentangled herself from Mac's arms and slid out of his grasp. Her heart was beating like a train and her breath was coming in short gasps. Mac reached for her again but she stepped away from his outstretched arm.

'This is so not a good idea,' she said.

'Why not? I think it's a very good idea.' His eyes darkened like the sea before a storm.

'Emma could come back any minute. I don't want her finding us in a clinch.'

'In a clinch?' The smile was back. 'Is that what you call it?' Laughter rippled under his words.

'Whatever.' Abby smoothed her hair with her hands. 'Nevertheless, if Emma walked in now…'

'Call it what you will, I think it's a very good idea.' He sat up and before she could move, his hand shot out lightning fast and caught her by the wrist, pulling her down on his lap. He buried his face in her neck, his lips touching her in places she hadn't even known, until now, had nerve endings.

She moaned softly. Being here with him felt so right. It had been so long since she'd been held. But she forced herself to push him away. There was no way she could think with him nibbling her neck.

'No, Mac. We can't. We have Emma to think about.'

Mac frowned at her. 'Emma?'

'Yes. Can't you see? If we start something, it'll give Emma all the wrong ideas. Besides, what if we fall out?' She held up her hand to stop the words he was about to say. 'It could happen, you know it could. How will it be for Emma then?'

Mac's frown deepened. 'I wasn't really thinking of a relationship. Hell, Abby, I wasn't really thinking at all. You must know I find you attractive. What's wrong with two adults…er…enjoying each other's company?'

Abby had to laugh. He was doing such a good impersonation of a well-known, ageing movie star. 'Seriously. Mac. Think about it. Don't we have enough to be getting on with? Trying to work out a way to co-parent Emma?'

Mac drew his hand across his face in a gesture Abby was beginning to know well. He looked so disappointed Abby almost changed her mind. Almost.

Mac stood up. 'Perhaps you're right,' he said, reaching for his jacket. He stopped and looked at her intently. 'Right now, Abby, you're holding all the cards.'

And before she could ask him what he meant, the door closed behind him with a gentle click.

CHAPTER TWELVE

BACK at his own house, Mac paced the floor. He still
couldn't believe how much his life had changed in the
last few weeks. It had been a shock finding out that he
had a daughter, and the last thing he had expected was
to feel the way he did about Emma. He found he was
looking forward to spending time with her. She was so
like him with her love of adventure.

And like Abby, too.

Over the last few weeks he had found himself drawn
to Abby in a way that he had never been drawn to a
woman before. It wasn't just that she was sexy, in that
way that only a woman who had no idea of her own
beauty could be, but it was her loyalty, her strength of
character, her kindness that drew him. It couldn't have
been easy bringing up a child—his child—on her own,
but she had done it without a second thought. And she
had made a good job of it.

But it was different now; he could help. Be there for
Emma and Abby. Help financially. He thought about the
little house they were renting. It was barely big enough
for one, let alone two of them. And here he was in this
spacious flat with more space than he knew what to do
with. Perhaps he should ask them to move in with him?

Immediately he dismissed the idea. It was crazy. Abby

would never agree. The thought of sharing his home with Abby made the blood rush to his head. Seeing her every day. Her sleeping just a short distance away would drive him crazy. He'd never be able to keep his hands off her. And that way lay madness. She was right. What if they started something and it didn't work out? Having a child was one thing, but having a permanent relationship with a woman quite another. He didn't do relationships. If he started something with Abby it would, like all his other relationships, end sooner or later. And when it did there would be hard feelings and recriminations. There always were. No matter how often he warned the women in his life that he wasn't in it for the long haul, they never really believed him. They always thought they would be the one to change him. And if he gave in to his need to have Abby, what then? When it came to an end she might stop him from seeing Emma. He was surprised at how much the prospect alarmed him. Now he had got to know his daughter, he couldn't imagine a life without her.

And what if Abby met someone else? He didn't want that either. The thought of her in another man's arms made his blood boil. But if she did, what if she moved away and took Emma away from him? As it stood, he could do nothing to stop her. And what if that man treated Emma like his mother's boyfriends had treated him? As if she was a nuisance they could do without?

He pulled a hand through his hair. Now he had found Emma he was damned if he was going to let anyone take her away from him again.

The days sped by as winter approached. Abby kept her eyes open for a house for Emma and herself, but so far nothing remotely affordable had come onto the market. Abby knew the only realistic option for her and Emma would be to buy something in serious need of refurbishment, and she didn't have the time for that, or a small modern flat, and she didn't have the heart for that.

Emma and Mac continued to spend time together and had developed an easy teasing camaraderie. Often they would gang up on Abby, once forcing her to join them mountain biking. Although she had gone along with them, one experience of being soaked to the skin and terrified out of her mind had been enough. She had refused point blank to go again. Some evenings Mac would drop in and they would play Scrabble or play games on Emma's computer console, the latter usually causing Mac and Emma to share a laugh at Abby's expense. Abby didn't care. She treasured those evenings. It was the family life she had never known.

One Saturday, Mac turned up at the cottage with a big smile on his face. Although it was cold, the rain had stopped and the sun was doing its best to cast some sunshine their way.

'You're looking pleased with yourself,' Abby said as she stood aside to let him in. 'But if you're looking for Emma, I'm afraid she's gone into the town with some friends from school.'

'It's not Emma I'm looking for. I have something I want *you* to see.' His eyes were sparkling with barely suppressed excitement.

'Oh, and what could that be?'

'I'm not saying. You have to come with me. Go on, grab a jacket.'

Mystified, Abby did as she was told. Mac was waiting for her in his Jeep.

'Where are we going? Come on, give me a clue.'

'No way. You're going to have to wait and see.'

They followed the road out of Penhally, heading in the general direction of St Piran's. But then Mac turned off and headed inland. A little while later, still refusing to answer Abby's questions, he turned up a steep track and came to a halt.

'We're here,' he said.

'Here? And where's here?' From where they were standing, Abby could see the coastline in the distance. Otherwise they were on a small bit of land surrounded by trees on the sides facing away from the sea.

'This little piece of land I'm standing on is for sale. Remember the boy we rescued from the bottom of the cliff? Dave, his father, came to see me. He wanted to thank us all personally. Anyway, to cut a long story short, it turns out he owns an estate agency here in Cornwall. I told him that I was looking for a small piece of land to buy and he mentioned that he knew of one that hadn't gone on the market yet. This one. Well, what do you think?'

'Think of what, exactly?'

'Of this as a place to build a house. As a home for you and Emma. You can't continue living where you are right now. And I know you haven't found somewhere to buy. So what about here? It's the perfect place to build a house.'

Abby touched him on the shoulder. She almost couldn't bear to destroy his excitement, but she had no choice.

'Mac, I couldn't possibly afford to buy this land, let alone build a house. It's a lovely idea, but completely out of the question.'

'I would bear the costs. After all, Emma is my daughter. You've met the financial costs of bringing her up on her own for years. Now it's my turn.'

Abby shook her head regretfully. 'I'm sorry, Mac. I couldn't possibly agree to it.'

His mouth tightened. 'Why not?'

'Don't you see? It's a wonderful, generous gesture, but I couldn't let us be beholden to you like that. It wouldn't be right.'

Mac's frown deepened. 'Beholden? Not right? Why don't you just come out with whatever it is you're trying to say?'

'Please understand, Mac. I've been independent all my life. I don't want to have to rely on anybody else. What happens if you meet someone you want to be with? Move away? Have a new family? What happens to us then? I'd never be able to meet the repayments on my own.' She shook her head. 'I'm sorry. I can't risk it.'

If it were possible, Mac's eyes turned an even darker blue. 'I have the right to make sure my daughter has as good a life as possible. You have no right to deny her because of some misplaced sense of pride. And what's more, I promise you, regardless of what happens in the future, I'll never abandon my child the way my father abandoned me.' His eyes narrowed. 'It is far more likely to be the other way around. You can up and leave with Emma any time you like, and I won't be able to stop you. How do you think that feels?'

Abby took a step towards him and touched him lightly on the arm. 'I wouldn't do that to Emma, or to you, Mac,' she said softly. 'Remember, I also know what it's like to grow up without a father. I would never deprive Emma of hers.'

Mac turned away and stood looking out to the horizon. This was a different side to Mac and her heart ached for him. But neither was she going to budge. He could be involved, she wanted him to be involved, but Emma was her responsibility and he had to understand that.

Mac swung around to face Abby. 'I want a DNA test,' he said abruptly.

Abby reeled. 'Why? I thought you believed me when I said you were Emma's father? Good grief, Mac, do you think I'm playing some kind of game here?'

He rubbed his face. 'I know you say now that you'll never take Em away from me, and I believe you mean it. But things change in life, Abby. I know that to my cost. People might mean to stick around, but in the end they don't.'

Abby started to protest but he cut her off. 'Besides, God forbid, what if something happened to you? What rights would I have then? At the moment, legally, you are her only blood relative. I wouldn't have a leg to stand on. A DNA test would prove I was the father to any court.'

What he was saying made sense, Abby admitted grudgingly. If she were in his shoes, would she take a chance that one day she might lose Emma? Absolutely not. She nodded.

'Okay. If, and only if, Emma agrees. The last thing I want is for her to think that you want the test for the wrong reasons. If you can persuade her, and if she's happy to have the test, I'll agree.'

The furrows between Mac's brow disappeared and he smiled. 'Thank you, Abby. That means a lot to me.'

They stood looking at each other for a long time. Mac took a step towards Abby, but before he could touch her, she turned away.

'Let's go home,' she said.

* * *

On the way back to her house, Abby thought about what Mac had said. Although she wanted Emma to have a relationship with a father who would be a permanent feature in her life, it felt as though everything was moving too fast. Mac wanted to be part of Emma's life and that was good. It would have broken Emma's heart if Mac had rejected her, but this… Wanting to have legal rights, wanting to contribute financially, it was more than Abby had anticipated. When she had told Mac about Emma, she had imagined a more casual relationship between father and daughter.

But now? He wanted more. And she couldn't blame him. And then there was this *thing* between her and Mac. Back then, she'd thought he was going to kiss her. And she'd wanted him to. But that would only make everything more complicated than it already was.

'Do you want to suggest the DNA test or shall I?' Mac asked.

'I think we should talk to her about it together,' Abby said. 'As soon as we get home.' She glanced across at him. 'She needs to know we're united about this, Mac.'

'At least we're agreed on something.' His expression was unreadable.

When they got back to the house, Mac suggested that they take a walk along the beach. Emma, as usual, was delighted to have any opportunity to spend time with her father. She particularly liked it when the three of them spent time together.

They stopped near some rocks and Abby poured hot chocolate from a flask she had brought.

'Em,' she started hesitantly. 'Mac and I have been talking.'

Emma looked at her warily. 'What about?'

'I think it's great that I've found you,' Mac said. 'As you know, I had no idea you existed until Abby told me. But now I want to make things more official.' He paused. 'I've got to kind of like having you as my daughter.'

A smile spread over Emma's face. 'And I kind of like having you as my father.' She threw herself at him and, wrapping her arms around him, squeezed him tightly.

The look in Mac's eyes made Abby catch her breath. The love for his daughter was there for anyone to see.

After a few minutes Emma released him and screwed up her eyes. 'How are things going to be more official? What do you mean?' She looked at Abby then at Mac. Her eyes lit up. 'Do you mean you two—?'

'No, Emma. You're way off there,' Abby interrupted quickly. Where on earth had Emma got that idea?

'I know it's not at all likely,' Mac said cautiously, 'but say anything happened to Abby, I'd want to have a legal claim on you. You know, make sure no one could take you away from me.'

Alarm flashed in Emma's eyes. 'There's nothing wrong with you, Mum, is there?' she said. 'You're not going to die or anything?'

Abby laughed. 'I have no intention of dying. At least, not for years and years. But, Emma, accidents do happen. What Mac is saying is that he's become very fond of you, and he wants everyone, particularly the courts, to recognise you as his daughter. Or rather him as your father. To do that you would both have to do a DNA test. Then if, and this is a big if, something happens to me, both Mac and I want to make sure you would get to stay with someone who loves you.'

Emma still looked anxious. Abby slid a glance at Mac. This was the last thing she wanted, Emma thinking they were hiding something from her.

Abby took Emma's hand in hers. 'I promise you, there is nothing wrong with me. If you don't want to have the test, that's fine. We'll find another way.'

'This test, is it like those they do in *CSI*?' Emma asked.

'Yes.'

'Will it hurt?'

'Not in the slightest. They'll take a swab from the inside of your mouth and do the same for Mac.'

Emma sat in silence for a little while.

'I don't mind, then. If you both think it's for the best.' She got to her feet and, finding a flat stone, turned to Mac. 'Can you make this skip on the water?' she asked. 'I can make it skip three times. Mum's record is four. Can you beat us?'

Abby and Mac shared a look of relief. Emma seemed reassured and what was even better, she was totally unconcerned about the test.

Mac took the stone from her hands. 'Four times, huh?' he said, grinning. 'I think I can do better than that.'

CHAPTER THIRTEEN

A FEW days later, Abby opened the door of her cottage to find Mac standing there. Her pulse stuttered disconcertingly. He was so damn good looking it just wasn't fair. But for once his easy confidence was absent. Instead, he looked ill at ease, almost embarrassed.

'Emma's out, I'm afraid,' she said. Anxiety rippled through her. He looked so serious. 'Is something wrong?'

'No,' Mac rushed to reassure her. 'It's just that I had an idea I wanted to run past you.'

Mac wanting to run something past her? That was a turn-up for the books.

'You'd better come in,' she said, standing aside to let him enter.

She signalled to him that he should sit, but Mac shook his head.

'Look, whatever it is, you'd better tell me.' Was this where he told her that the novelty of having a daughter was wearing off? Her heart rate upped another notch. If he let Emma down now, she'd throttle him.

'Remember you told me that Emma's birthday party had to be cancelled when nobody would come?'

Abby nodded. It had been almost the worst day of her life. It had been so cruel and so unbearable watching

Emma pretend it didn't matter. But Emma hadn't been able to hide the sobs coming from her bedroom later that evening. Abby had crept into bed with her daughter, holding her until the tears had subsided. That was when she had decided to leave London. She would never let her child be hurt like that again. Not as long as she had breath in her body.

'Well, I thought we should give her another party. Here. She's made friends now and perhaps it will take away some of the bad memories of London.'

Abby was so surprised she felt her jaw drop. It was the last thing she'd expected Mac to say. But she was touched and delighted and not a little ashamed. Once again, she had underestimated this man. As she looked at him her heart melted. He was a better man than he gave himself credit for.

'We could organise something really cool, like paint-ball or...I don't know...something else. We could arrange it all as a surprise.' Now that the words were out, there was no hiding his enthusiasm. 'I never had a party as a kid.' He smiled but he couldn't disguise the hurt in his eyes. 'I always wanted one, but my mother always refused. She said there was no way she was going to let a bunch of kids run riot in her house.'

'Me too,' Abby whispered. 'I would have given any-thing to be able to dress up in a party dress, just once. But my mum said parties weren't for the likes of us.'

They looked at each other and the world spun on its axis. Abby could hardly breathe. For a moment she thought he was going to pull her into his arms, but then he stepped back and let his arms to drop to his side.

What just happened there? Abby wondered. Her heart was racing as if she'd run up the highest hill in England. Every nerve cell in her body was zinging. Lord help her, she wanted him to have taken her in his arms. She wanted to lay her head against his chest, have his arms wrap around her, feel the pressure of his mouth against her. What was she thinking? Thinking that way spelled danger. He was so not the man for her. Why, then, did she feel this crushing sense of disappointment? Because she was in love with him. The realisation hit her like a ten-ton truck. She loved him and would do until the day she died.

'I think it's a great idea, Mac,' she said, turning away lest he read her discovery in her face. 'I can speak to the mums at the school, swear them to secrecy and get the invites out. We could organise it for the weekend. If we leave it any longer, someone's bound to give in to temptation and tell her. And I think the paintballing is a great idea. Emma's always wanted to have a go and the boys should enjoy it, too.' Hoping that she'd removed every trace of latent lust from her eyes, she turned back to him. 'I'm warning you, though, we'll both have to take part. You do know that, don't you?'

Mac grinned broadly. 'Why do you think I suggested it?' he said.

Emma was surprised but thrilled to find out about her party. Mac arrived before the partygoers and Emma flung herself at him, forgetting in her excitement to adopt the cool façade she had been trying to perfect lately.

'Isn't this the best idea?' she said. 'I can't wait for everyone to arrive so we can get started. Mum says she's going to join in, too.'

Mac looked at Abby over the top of Emma's head and grinned. 'I'm looking forward to seeing her moves,' he said.

Abby wagged a playful finger at him. 'Don't you underestimate me. I can run pretty fast when I have to.'

Emma's friends started to arrive, their laughter and shrieks of excitement filling the reception area. Mac had to shout above the clamour to make himself heard.

'Okay, guys. Before we get changed, we need to pick teams. Emma is captain of Team Arrows and, Simon, I believe you want to be captain of Team Blades. Since it's your party, Em, you get to pick first.'

Abby knew her daughter's every expression and she could see her hesitation as her eyes flicked between Abby and Mac. Abby's heart twisted painfully, sensing her torn loyalties. She wanted to choose Abby but also wanted to impress Mac. Was this how it was going to be from now on? She'd had her daughter all to herself for the past eleven years but now it was time to share her with someone else. Her father. Mac. The knot of jealousy felt alien to her but she had to remember this wasn't about her—it was about Emma.

Catching Emma's eye, she nodded her head slightly towards Mac. She caught the almost imperceptible flash of gratitude in her daughter's eyes as she selected Mac. Simon then chose Abby and the rest of the teams were quickly divided up.

Despite what she'd told Mac, Abby had no real idea what to expect. Obviously it had to do with firing balls of paint at each other and using various items around the course to hide behind to avoid being hit yourself. And taking the other team's flag.

When she emerged wearing her lurid green overall, she blushed under Mac's amused grin. She felt slightly ridiculous, holding her 'gun'. On the other hand, he looked the part in his blue overalls, like a dashing secret agent on a dangerous mission. The way he was looking at her warned her she was going to be his prime target. Abby felt a flutter of excitement—there was nothing she'd love better than to out-fox Mac. He was underestimating her if he thought she was Team Blade's weakest link! It was game on.

Fifteen minutes later Abby had to keep reminding herself it was only a game. The darkness, lit only sporadically by flashing lights and filled with atmospheric dry ice, heightened the tension and fun. Crouching behind a pillar, Abby paused to catch her breath. So far she'd managed to evade being shot, but so had Mac. Another flash of light and in that second she saw the top of his head behind a barrier. Abby crept forward, raising her gun slowly. Her finger tightened on the trigger and she stifled a giggle.

She didn't know how it happened but the next moment she was sprawled on her back with Mac's face inches from hers.

'Trying to sneak up on me, were you?' he growled into her ear. Abby could hear the triumph in his voice. She was distracted by the heat of his body on hers, his warm breath on her neck.

His eyes bored into hers. Her heart thumped against her ribs and she knew in that moment he was going to kiss her. Her lips parted involuntarily. At the very last moment, just before his mouth came down on hers, she wriggled out from underneath him. Despite being caught off guard, he moved much more quickly than she'd anticipated. Paint splattered from their respective guns until they were both covered from head to toe in myriad colours and laughing uncontrollably.

Grinning, Mac held out his hand. 'Truce?'

Abby took his proffered hand, only to let out a yelp of

surprise when he yanked her towards him. 'I believe you still owe me a kiss. And I intend to collect it...soon.'

It wasn't long before Emma's team triumphed, and after they had all cleaned up and changed they congregated in the café.

The children chattered happily about the game, arguing over their respective tactics.

Abby smiled at Mac, sitting opposite her at the table. 'Thanks for organising today. It's wonderful to see Emma looking so happy.'

'She's a fantastic kid. You have to take some of the credit for that.'

Abby glanced over at her daughter, her heart swelling with pride. 'Don't hurt her, Mac. I'll never forgive you if you do,' she said quietly. *And don't hurt me, she wanted to add.*

Mac shook his head. 'I've no intention of doing that.'

After they had cleaned up and the other children had left stuffed full of pizza and cake, Mac turned to Emma.

'The party isn't over yet,' he said. 'I've one more treat.'

Emma grinned at him. 'Tell me,' she implored.

'You have to come out to the car.' He led the way, a bemused Abby and Emma following in his footsteps.

'Close your eyes,' Mac told Emma. 'And no peeking.'

Emma did as she was told. Mac opened the boot of his Jeep and pulled out a board and something that looked like a kite. He placed them on the ground. 'Okay, you can open your eyes now, Emma.'

Emma's eyes grew wide. 'Is that what I think it is?'

'It's your very own kite-boarding stuff. In the spring, as soon as the weather is good enough, I'm going to teach you how to do it. You picked up windsurfing so quickly I'm sure we'll have you doing tricks with the kite board by the end of the summer.'

Emma turned to Mac and flung her arms around him. He picked her up and twirled her in the air. Abby's throat tightened. She knew this was Mac's way of telling them both he planned to stick around. When he deposited her back on the ground, Emma looked at him before hooking her arms into one of his and one of Abby's. 'This is the best day of my life,' she said.

Mac looked at Abby over the top of Emma's head.

'And mine,' he said quietly.

CHAPTER FOURTEEN

AS DECEMBER approached, winter began to tighten its grip. The wind was sharper and the days shorter. Emma and Mac still went mountain biking and Abby rejoiced to see her child grow ever more confident, although she still fretted until Emma had returned home in one piece. The DNA results hadn't come back yet, but Abby wasn't surprised. They had been told that it could take months.

Mac and Emma arrived back just before darkness fell. They were both spattered with mud and their cheeks were flushed from the cold.

'I'm going to beat you one of these days,' Emma teased Mac.

'I hope you're not letting her go too fast,' Abby warned Mac. 'The last thing I want is to be involved in the rescue of you two.'

'Oh, Mum, you worry too much,' Emma complained. 'Dad would never let anything happen to me.'

A chill ran up Abby's spine and as she caught Mac's eye she knew he, too, realised the import of Emma's words. She was calling him Dad. If there was any doubt in either of their minds, she knew there was none in Emma's.

'Run upstairs and shower and change out of your wet clothes,' Abby told Emma. 'I'll get supper on.'

Mac still looked in shock as Emma left the room.

'Dad!' he said. 'She called me Dad.'

'So she did. How does it feel?'

'It feels strange. Very strange. But good. Yes. Very good.'

'Would you like to stay for supper, too?' Abby asked.

Mac grinned. 'I don't even want to sit down. In case you haven't noticed, I'm filthy.'

Abby had to laugh. Mac's face was almost black with thick dust. Only his eyes, where he had been wearing his goggles, were mud free. Impulsively she leaned forward and wiped his cheek with her finger.

His hand caught hers and he looked down at her with a glint in his eye. Her breath caught in her throat.

'Careful, Abby,' he warned. 'Don't start something you can't finish.'

She pulled her hand away as if she'd been stung. They stood staring at each other.

'Tell you what,' Mac said. 'Why don't I go home, get cleaned up, and I'll organise supper for the three of us?'

'I thought you didn't cook.'

'Didn't you notice I said *organise*? I didn't say anything about cooking. There is a great Chinese a few minutes' walk away from me. That's what I had in mind.'

'Emma is going to the cinema with a friend,' Abby said, looking at her watch. 'The mother is coming to collect her in an hour.'

'In that case, why don't you come? You could feed Emma and then come over. By that time I'll have cleaned myself up. You've never seen my place.'

'I don't know, Mac. Is it wise?' They both knew what she was talking about.

Mac took a lock of her hair between his fingers. 'I promise you, you'll be safe,' he said. 'It's just two work colleagues, friends, spending time together.'

Safe? What did he mean, safe? The flash of disappointment was unexpected. Was he implying that she wasn't his type? Perhaps she had misread him? Flirting came as naturally as breathing to men like Mac. He probably wasn't even aware he was doing it. She really needed to remember that.

'Or did you have something less innocent in mind?' he said.

She flushed. Damn the man. It was as if he could read her thoughts.

'Of course not,' she said coolly. 'You and I both know that.'

'So that's sorted, then. I'll see you around eight. Don't worry, I'll let you get back in plenty of time to be here for Em.'

'Okay,' she agreed finally, knowing she was risking her heart. 'I'll be there at eight.'

Mac smiled to himself as he drove home. Abby was much more transparent than she realised. He could read every thought and emotion that flitted across her face. She just couldn't pretend. That was what he loved about her.

Good God. Where had that come from? No way was he in love with Abby. Okay, he found her attractive, well, more than attractive, sexy as hell, and she was brave and funny and good and loyal and, damn it—he was in love with her. The shock almost made him collide with a car coming in the opposite direction. He pulled over to his own side of the road and the car passed him with a blare of its horn.

No! This was crazy. It was simply that he lusted after her. She was a challenge. The first woman he had ever wanted that hadn't fallen into his arms. But he knew he was lying to himself. He was in love. For the first time. And with Abby Stevens, the woman who was the mother of his child. So to speak. This wasn't at all what he had planned. He didn't do love. He didn't do for ever.

Mac was in all kinds of trouble.

Abby knocked on the door, thinking for the umpteenth time that she should have phoned and made her excuses. Was she stark, raving mad? Every bone in her body was telling her that it was a mistake to be alone with Mac.

Just as she was thinking of turning tail, he opened the door. Her breath caught in her throat. What a difference from the mud-splattered man of earlier. He had showered and changed into a dazzlingly white short-sleeved shirt and black jeans. Her heart rate went into overdrive. He looked divine. So confident and self-assured.

'Abby!' He smiled at her as if he had been waiting just for this moment and her legs turned to jelly.

'Hello, Mac.' Damn it. She sounded breathless. She cleared her throat. 'I'm not late, am I?'

'Bang on time,' he said. 'Our food should be here shortly. Come on in.'

He stood aside to let her pass and she squeezed past him, terrified lest she brush up against him. She could almost feel the waves of magnetism emanating from him.

'Let me take your coat.'

She almost yelped as she felt his warm hands brushing the back of her neck as he helped her shrug out of her coat. Little goose-bumps sprang up all over her body.

He tossed her coat onto the sofa. 'Can I get you something to drink?'

'Some sparkling water would be nice.'

His flat was the opposite from her little house in every way possible. Where her home had cramped, if cosy rooms, his was modern and open plan, with floor-to-ceiling windows looking out over the sea. Where her home was cluttered with the everyday minutiae that living with a teenager brought, his was sparsely but expensively furnished with enormous white sofas and bleached floorboards. On one side of the room there was a small kitchen with white units and a black granite worktop. It was fitted with every conceivable appliance down to an in-built coffee maker, she noted enviously. Not that it looked used.

In front of the sofas, which were arranged to form an L-shape, was a modern gas fire that looked almost real.

As Mac was pouring her drink, she wandered over to the ceiling-height book shelves opposite the windows. She found herself intensely curious to see what he read. Apart from several well-thumbed copies of the classics, there were thrillers and medical textbooks. She found herself smiling. There were few clues here about Mac. Was that intentional?

'One sparkling water,' Mac said, holding out a glass.

As she took it from him their fingers brushed and once again she felt a zap of electricity run down her spine.

'What do you think?' Mac waved his glass at the room.

'I like it.' Taking a sip of her water, she walked to the window and took in the view. Beneath her the lights twinkled and the moon, as bright and full as she could remember seeing, lit up the sea, so that she could see the waves rolling onto the shore. The windows where she was standing were actually a set of double doors leading out onto a small balcony.

'You can hear the surf from outside on a quiet night,' Mac said, coming to stand behind her. He was close enough for her to catch a faint smell of soap. 'It's one of the reasons I bought it.'

'I've always fancied a place with a view,' Abby said. 'Who wouldn't? But at the same time just having my own place with Em is good enough for me.'

'You really love her, don't you?'

'It would kill me if anything happened to her.'

'Why have you never married, Abby?'

The question startled her. She whirled round, taken aback to find herself within inches of his broad chest. She lifted her eyes to his, trying to ignore the blood rushing in her ears. 'I never met anyone who wanted me enough to take on a child, I guess,' she said softly. Then she grinned. 'Actually, that's not the whole truth. I've never met anyone that I thought I could live with, let alone marry. And the older I get, the more used to having my independence I get. What about you?' she challenged. 'Have you never met anyone you wanted to marry?'

'Me?' Mac laughed. 'I'm not into marriage, I'm afraid. I can't see the point. Why get married only to tear each other apart? It also implies that there is only one person for each of us and I don't believe that either. Unlike swans, I don't think humans are meant to mate for life.'

'What about children?'

Mac looked thoughtful. 'Having children was something I thought I would never do. What was the point? I liked my life exactly the way it was. But now…'

'But now…?' Abby prompted.

'But now I find I like being a father.' He turned away. 'Emma's amazing. I'm proud to be her dad.' He turned back to Abby and grinned. 'I never thought I'd say that, let alone mean it. And I have you to thank.' He crossed over to where Abby was standing. 'Thank you for letting me share her.' He touched her gently on the cheek and tipped her face so that she was forced to look him in the eye. 'I've had some of the best days of my life since I got to know her…and you.'

Abby's breath caught in her throat. Her heart was hammering against her chest. Slowly he lowered his head and, tipping her chin, brought his mouth down on hers. Abby had never felt sensations like the ones that were rocketing around her body. His lips were warm and hard, demanding a response from her. His tongue flicked against her and spurts of heat ricocheted from the tips of her toes to the top of her head. Her body felt as if it were on fire.

She couldn't resist him if her life depended on it. She could do nothing except give in to the feelings that were zipping around her. Her body melted into his as if it belonged there.

He groaned and, dropping his hands to her hips, pulled her against him. She fitted there in the circle of his arms as if once they had been one, and she let her hands go around his neck as she gave in to her need.

Still kissing her, he lifted her into his arms as if she weighed nothing and carried her out of the sitting room and into his bedroom. He laid her gently on the bed and she looked at him, knowing what was going to happen yet powerless to stop it.

His eyes were dark, almost hazy, as he looked at her. Without taking his eyes from her, he slid his hands up her hips and, hooking the top of her tights with his thumbs, he began to unroll them slowly. She lifted her hips to help him. Inside she was a mass of confusion. What little part of her brain that could still think was shouting, No! Don't do this! But the far greater part was taken over by urgent need of her body. She knew she was helpless to deny him…or herself.

The only light in the room came from the lounge and the moon outside. It was dark enough to hide her shyness but light enough for her to read every nuance of his expression.

Once her tights were off he turned his attention to her blouse. He leaned over and dropped kisses in the hollow of her throat, across her collarbone, his hands all the while deftly undoing her buttons. He stopped kissing her as he drew the blouse apart. He was breathing hard as he looked down at her. Now she felt no embarrassment, no shyness, only wonder at the expression in his eyes.

Then she lifted her hips as he unbuttoned her skirt and let it drop to the floor.

'You are beautiful,' he said, his voice thick with desire.

She hated him being away from her even for a second and she pulled him back towards her. As he kissed her, she let her hands slide under his T-shirt, revelling in the feel of hard muscle under her fingertips. How could a man who was so toned be soft at the same time? she wondered as she lifted his T-shirt over his head. She pressed against him, feeling the hard warmth of his bare skin pressing against her. She wanted him so much, she didn't know if she could wait a minute longer to feel him, all of him against her, inside her.

A small moan escaped her lips as she searched for the button of his jeans, her fingers brushing the hair that travelled from his belly downwards.

This time it was him who was helping her as his jeans came off.

Then he stretched on the bed beside her. She blushed when she saw the extent of his desire for her.

He slipped a thumb inside the cup of her bra, teasing one nipple and then the other, until she didn't know how she could bear it.

Then his hand reached behind her, deftly unhooked her bra and her breasts sprang free.

He kissed her skin, running his tongue across each nipple. Her body was on fire. She couldn't wait any longer. She was going to explode.

'Please,' she whispered. 'I can't hold on...'

'Just a little longer,' he promised. 'But this time, our first time, I want to watch you.'

She shook her head from side to side. She wanted him inside her now. Moving with her. Filling this empty, aching void that she hadn't known, until now, existed.

'Shh,' he said. 'I promise you there will be time later.'

Giving in, she lay back, digging her fingers into his hair, curling her fingers tightly in an attempt to stop herself crying out as he inched his mouth downwards.

Dropping kisses on her belly, on the insides of her thighs, brushing his fingers gently between her legs. Then he removed her panties and just when she thought she couldn't bear the exquisite pain of her need any longer, he slipped his finger inside her. He raised his head and looked deeply into her eyes as she arched her body up to him. She couldn't help the cry that ripped from her throat as sensation after sensation rocked through her body. He was taking her somewhere she'd never been before, higher and higher, until at the top her body couldn't hold on any longer and she lost all sense of who she was.

Her head was still reeling as she clutched him to her. She needed him inside her, and greedily she pulled him on top of her, opening herself to him and using her hands to guide him inside her. They rocked together, more and more urgently, until triumphantly she heard him reach his climax, just seconds before she followed him.

They lay, breathing deeply, their bodies hot and entangled. She felt as if every cell in her body had merged with his. She had never known sex could be like this, a heady mix of the physical and emotional. His hands were brushing over her hair. Lightly touching her shoulder.

'My God, you're not nearly as prim and proper as you appear on the outside, are you?'

She blushed, but hearing the laughter in his voice she couldn't take offence.

'I haven't had many lovers,' she murmured.

He propped his head on his elbow as he looked down at her. 'I'm glad,' he said simply.

His hand trailed lazily over her neck and then onto her breasts and her breath began to quicken. 'I don't want to think of you being with anyone else,' he said possessively. 'I want you to be mine. Just mine.'

Her heart started its hammering again. She was surprised he couldn't feel it pounding against his hand as he continued to touch her body, searching for the spots that drove her wild. Didn't he realise that wherever he touched her drove her wild? Her last coherent thought as she succumbed once more to the relentless demands of his touch was that she loved him. Loved him, completely, irrevocably and for ever. Before she could help herself the words slipped out. 'I love you,' she whispered as he once more took possession of her, body and soul.

Mac lay listening to the gentle sound of Abby's breathing. Her hair was fanned out across his chest and he swore he could smell strawberries. It felt so right to have her curled up against him—right and peaceful.

As he began to drift off towards sleep, an image of Abby, Emma and himself came into his head. They were laughing together as they shared a meal around the table in Abby's kitchen. Abby and Emma were looking at him with such love and admiration it made him feel good. Better than he had felt in his life. But then he started. What had Abby said? She loved him. He knew women often said that in the throes of making love. They didn't necessarily mean it. He groaned quietly. But Abby wasn't any woman. She was strong and proud and honest. She wouldn't have said the words if she didn't mean them.

There was no chance of him falling asleep now. His mind was racing too fast for that. Gently he disentangled himself from Abby and eased himself out of bed. He wrapped a towel around his hips and crept out of the bedroom and into the sitting room. He opened the door to his small balcony and stepped outside into the cold air. Maybe it would knock some sense into him. He had been a crazy, selfish fool to let it get this far. He should have known better than to play with Abby. But he hadn't been able to help himself. Ever since she'd appeared back in his life, his need to take her to bed had been like an itch he'd needed to scratch. But he hadn't been thinking of her. What could he offer her? It was one thing to accept the responsibility of a child—there was nothing he could do about that, he had a duty towards Emma—but a relationship with Abby was out of the question. He hadn't changed his mind about not wanting commitment. Commitments brought trouble and pain. Commitments were not for him. Even if he loved her.

He heard the pad of feet behind him and two soft hands crept around his waist.

'What are you doing out here in the freezing cold?' Abby asked, laying her cheek against his back. Her silky hair was like a caress against his skin, and despite everything he had just been telling himself he wanted her there, always.

Suddenly she moved away from him and he felt it like a stab to his heart. He had to tell her what he felt before either of them got in any deeper.

'It can't be ten o'clock. Grief, Emma's due back at half past. I have to get home.' She had wrapped a sheet around her before coming onto the balcony and almost tripped over it in her haste to get back to her clothes in the bedroom. He smiled at her ungainly, faltering steps and had to force himself to stay where he was. If he touched her again, he'd be undone.

'My shoes—where are my shoes?' Abby's panicked voice came from the bedroom. She had slipped on her skirt and blouse and rammed her tights haphazardly into her bag.

'Hey, slow down. It'll only take you fifteen minutes to get home. Plenty of time.' He retrieved one of her high heels from under the sofa and the other from the floor halfway to the bedroom. 'Your shoes, milady,' he said.

She practically snatched them from his hands. 'It's

no laughing matter,' she said crossly. 'I've never not been there for Emma when she comes home. She'll be anxious. And anything could happen. There might be a fire. She could get trapped. Hurt herself and need me. What was I thinking, falling asleep?'

She put her shoes on and looked around feverishly. Mac picked up her coat from the arm of the sofa and held it out so she could slip her arms into it.

'C'mon, Abby. You know nothing's going to happen to her in the few minutes she'll be alone. It's just that you've been on too many rescues. That's why you're imagining the worst.'

She glared at him. 'Being a parent brings responsibility, too, Mac. And one of those responsibilities is protecting your child from any danger.'

Mac knew it was useless to argue. Besides, which would he rather? The woman who was mother to his child caring too much or caring too little? He groaned inwardly. Wasn't that the problem? Abby was the kind of woman who would always care too much. And he didn't want or deserve that.

He was aware of her lips brushing his, and then she was gone.

Happily, Emma hadn't got back by the time Abby brought her car to a screeching halt outside her little house. Everything was still in darkness. Mac was right. She had overreacted. But if anything should ever happen to Emma, she would simply die.

As she let herself in, she thought back over the evening. It had been the most exciting night of her life. A delicious thrill ran up her spine as she recalled how it had felt to be in his arms. She had never imagined that making love could be like that. Although she'd had lovers in her life before, neither of them had made her feel like that. Was it because she loved Mac? The thought frightened and excited her at the same time and she grew hot as she remembered how she hadn't been able to stop herself murmuring the truth to him.

She ran upstairs and switched on the shower. It would give her time to regain her composure before facing Emma. As she let the hot water stream over her body, she pushed aside the memory of Mac's hands. She could have sworn he wasn't immune to her. But then again, what did she really know about men?

He didn't say he loved you. The voice wouldn't go away. But that was okay. For the first time in her life she was going to throw caution to the wind and let life take her where it would. If there was one thing being with Mac had taught her, it was that life was nothing at all if you didn't take risks.

Nevertheless, she was still hurt and dismayed when over the next few days Mac was friendly but distant towards her. Although she hadn't expected protestations of undying love, neither had she expected to be treated like a one-night stand. Had she flung herself at him? Now that he had slept with her, was he no longer interested? He still spent time with Emma on a regular basis, but his invites no longer included her. It was becoming evident she had made a dreadful mistake. But one she could not regret. Making love with Mac, loving Mac, had made her feel alive. And if part of that was the dreadful pain of rejection she knew deep down that she accepted that, too. At least Emma had a father who loved and cherished her. That would have to do.

CHAPTER FIFTEEN

IT WAS another Saturday when Rebecca was on her own.
Josh had gone to work, telling her that he had loads of
paperwork to catch up on. Although he had promised to
be back soon after lunch, it was almost three and he still
hadn't returned. It was typical of Josh. In the four years
they had been married she had grown to accept that his
work would always take priority over her.

A few days earlier she had brought up the subject
of children again. Josh had refused to even discuss it
and they had argued. Since then they had been barely
speaking. Josh was spending more and more time at the
hospital and Rebecca had the distinct feeling that he was
avoiding her.

She packed a sandwich and a flask of coffee. Josh
hated hospital food. They could take their picnic and
despite the cold, maybe they could find a bench and sit
outside and talk. She blinked away the tears. When had
they last talked properly? She couldn't remember.

As she drove towards the hospital she suddenly felt
nervous. She could hardly blame Josh totally for the gulf
in their marriage. She could make more of an effort, take
an interest in his work, even if it did bore her senseless.
She would suggest they go into London for dinner, meet
up with old friends. It would be like it had been in the

beginning. Her spirits lifted. Perhaps they could still find their way back to each other and then if they did, Josh might agree to have children. She would make him see that a baby would make them happy again.

She turned into the hospital car park and searched for a parking place. Then she rooted around in the back seat of her car until she found the paper bag with the picnic. Once again she checked her make-up and her hair. Was that a frown line between her eyes? She shivered. Every day she was seeing signs that she was getting older.

She hopped out of the car and took a few steps towards the door of A & E. But then, to her left, sitting on a bench under a tree, she saw them. Josh and another woman. Like Josh, the other woman was wearing scrubs, and although her hair was pulled back in a ponytail and her face was devoid of make-up, she was still startlingly beautiful in the way only certain women could be. Rebecca felt a flash of envy. She knew she was beautiful, too, but she needed the help of make-up. She didn't have the natural beauty of the woman sitting next to Josh.

She was about to call out when she froze in her tracks. Josh threw back his head and laughed at something the woman had said. His arm was draped over the back of the bench, almost touching her shoulder. There was a familiarity about the gesture that spoke volumes. Rebecca couldn't tear her eyes away. When had she last heard Josh laugh? When had she last seen him looking so relaxed, as if he didn't have a care in the world? When had she last seen him look *happy*?

The woman raised her face to Josh's and smiled into his eyes. Rebecca's throat ached and she raised her hand to brush away the tears that stung her eyes. Slowly she backed away, terrified now lest they see her. Although she couldn't bear it, she knew. Knew with a certainty that rocked her soul. Josh was in love with this woman. Rebecca could see it in every line of his body, in the way it seemed as if she were something precious he had to protect.

Tears were blinding her as she groped her way back to the car. Whatever she'd had planned, whatever hopes she'd had for her and Josh making a go of their marriage, it was too late. If Josh loved this woman, he would be with her. He was too honest to continue with a marriage when he was in love with someone else. Anger was beginning to erode some of the pain. How could she have been so stupid not to have seen what was in front of her eyes? It wasn't work that was making Josh spend all these extra hours at the hospital, it was another woman.

Rebecca gripped the steering-wheel with numb hands. He would leave her. Maybe not today, or tomorrow, but soon. He would look after her financially, she knew that, but leave her he would. And all these years she had stayed with him—giving up her dream, her longing to have a baby, giving up her happy life in London to follow him here, to a place she knew she could never be happy—had been futile.

She turned the key in the ignition. She was damned if she was going to walk away with nothing. At the very least she would have a baby to love.

The telephone was ringing as Mac stepped in to his flat after playing squash. At first he didn't recognise the voice.

'Mac? Robert here.' Mac stood still. He had almost forgotten about the doctor in charge of doing the DNA test.

'Hello, Robert. How's it going? Have you news for me?' Too impatient for small talk, he cut to the chase. He knew it was ridiculous but suddenly he was nervous.

Robert cleared his throat. 'I do. You'll get a letter confirming the results tomorrow, as will the other party, but I thought as a professional courtesy I would ring you.'

Get on with it, Mac wanted to shout down the phone, but he held himself in check. Robert could have left him to find out by letter.

'And?'

'I'm not sure if it's good news or bad, but…'

If he could have reached down the telephone line and shaken Robert he would have done so. Why didn't the man just get on with confirming that Emma was his child? As soon as he had the proof, he would ring the lawyer and start the proceedings that would allow him to be named officially as Emma's father.

'The test is negative,' Robert said flatly. 'There is no way at all she could be your child.'

The breath came out of him like an explosion. He hadn't been even aware he had stopped breathing.

'What?' he managed. He couldn't have heard right.

'Emma Stevens is not your biological daughter. As I said, I have no idea whether this is good or bad news, but that is the result. A letter is on its way to her guardian.'

Mac felt the world tip. Emma was not his daughter. He couldn't believe it. Everything in him said she was. He couldn't love her the way he did if she wasn't his flesh and blood.

He was hardly aware of thanking Robert and re-placing the receiver. If it hadn't been mid-afternoon, he would have poured himself a stiff whisky.

Emma wasn't his child. Sara had either been lying or, he suspected, simply mistaken.

He was surprised at how devastated he felt at the news. What now? Would Abby stop him from seeing Emma? The thought made his stomach churn. Now he was about to lose her, he realised how much he had begun to enjoy the role of father.

And what about Emma? His heart ached for the little girl. She cared deeply about him. He knew that. How would she feel when she found out that he wasn't her father after all? He raked a hand through his hair. God, it was such a mess. Why hadn't he seen this coming? Why hadn't he reminded himself that there was always a possibility that the test would be negative?

But he knew the answer. Bit by bit he had fallen in love with the idea of being a father. He had enjoyed being around for Emma. Encouraging her to come out of her shell. All the things his father should have done for him, but hadn't. In some ways, he had been able to give Emma some of the childhood pleasures he'd never had, and it had healed something inside him.

Making up his mind, he picked up his jacket from where he'd flung it and was out of the door. He had to speak to Abby. She would know what to do.

Abby paced her small sitting room. Where was Emma? She'd promised she'd be back for lunch and it was now after one.

She picked up a magazine and attempted to read it, but there was no way she could concentrate. Emma knew Abby worried. She would have texted her had she been held up.

She had wheedled Abby into agreeing that she could go down to the beach with a friend from school. Simon was a local boy and knew the area well, so why was she worrying? They were going to go down to the beach and stop off for a burger. But Emma had promised she'd come home after that. Abby checked her watch for the hundredth time. Only five more minutes had passed, although it felt like a lot longer.

She almost jumped out of her skin when her mobile rang. She leaped on top of it. It was bound to be Emma, probably apologising for not being home, for forgetting the time.

And it was Emma. At least, she thought it was. The signal kept fading and all she could hear were muffled snatches of words.

'Em? Is that you? I can't hear you. Can you go somewhere where you can get a better signal?'

'No…stuck…help…'

Abby's blood ran cold. She could hardly make out the words but there was no mistaking the fear in Emma's voice.

'Em? Where are you?'

More static. Then three words that made her physically ill. 'Trapped…cave…tide…' Then all of a sudden Emma's voice came over clearly. 'Help us, Mum.'

Her daughter, her beloved Emma, was in trouble. Abby forced back the waves of terror that threatened to overwhelm her.

'Stay calm, Emma, and tell me where you are.'

'Cave…beach…hurt…'

'Are you hurt? God, Emma!'

But there was only more static on the end of the phone. 'Look, Emma, I don't know if you can hear me, but leave your phone on. I'll find you. I promise. Keep calm, I'm coming.'

'No time… Hurry—' And then the phone cut out.

Abby was almost sobbing with terror. She had to find Emma. But where to start?

For a second she couldn't think what to do, and then suddenly the door opened and he was there. Mac! Relief made her knees go weak.

'I knocked,' Mac started to apologise, but the expression on her face must have told him something terrible had happened. He was by her side in seconds, pulling her close. 'Breathe, Abby. That's it. Slow, deep breaths, and tell me what's happened.'

This was wasting time! She pushed him away.

'It's Em. She phoned. Just now. I couldn't hear properly. Just enough... Oh, my God. I have to go to her.'

Mac reached out for her and pulled her round to face him. His face had lost all colour and his eyes were as dark as ink.

'Tell me,' he said.

'She's trapped. And hurt. She needs us, Mac,' Abby moaned. 'Help me, find my baby. Our child. Please, Mac. You have to help me.'

'Listen to me.' He grabbed her by the shoulders. 'Look at me, Abby.'

She looked into his eyes. She saw fear and something else. Conviction.

'We're going to find our girl. Do you hear me? And she's going to be all right. But I need you to tell me everything.'

'She went to the beach with a boy from her class. Simon. That was almost three hours ago. She said she'd be back by one. She promised.' She took a gulp of air. Mac was right. Panicking now wouldn't help Emma. 'She phoned. The signal was bad. I could hardly hear her. All I could make out was that she was trapped. In a cave. And hurt.' She took a shuddering breath as terror returned. Her baby. Out there somewhere. Alone and scared.

Mac was already on his phone. 'I'm going to alert the rescue services. We need to get the coastguard and the other services out looking.' Abby paced as he spoke into the phone for a few minutes. All she could hear was Mac's side of the conversation, repeating what she had told him. When he finished the call, he looked grimmer than ever.

'What is it?' Abby asked. 'What did they say?'

'They said they'd mobilise a sea and air rescue,' Mac said. But Abby could tell there was something more. Something he wasn't telling her.

'Tell me everything they said.' She kept her voice level. 'I have a right to know.'

He hesitated.

'Please, Mac, tell me.'

'The tide is coming in,' he said. 'And it's higher than usual today. If they are trapped somewhere, it's only going to get worse.'

Abby cried out and sank to her knees. In a flash Mac was by her side. He lifted her into his arms and held her tight before placing her on the sofa.

'You stay here, Abby. In case Emma phones. Keep trying her mobile. I've got to go.'

Abby struggled to her feet. 'I'm coming, too.'

'It'll be best if you don't.'

'Don't even think of trying to stop me,' she said. She took a deep shuddering breath. 'I'll be okay. I promise. I won't panic and I won't get in the way. But I'm coming.'

Five minutes later they were prowling the cliffs above the beach front. Mac had managed to get hold of Simon's parents. They were also panic-stricken but had told them of a cave that Simon liked to explore. They told Mac that they had forbidden their son from going into the cave, but suspected that he, trying to impress his new friend, might have ignored their warnings. The cave was easily accessible when the tide was out but, depending on the size of the tide, could become filled with water, preventing escape. Instinctively Abby knew that this was where Emma was. At the very least they had nowhere else to try. When it arrived, the Royal Navy helicopter would keep searching from the air and the coastguard would search the shoreline.

As soon as Abby and Mac got the information about the cave, they ran towards the part of the beach where it was. Although Abby knew the tide was rising, she couldn't help a small cry when she saw that the beach had completely disappeared under the sea.

How would they get to the stranded children, and even if they did find them, how would they get them out?

'We need divers,' Mac was speaking into his mobile. 'The navy will have them. Get them down here immediately.'

Divers! If they needed divers to get to the children, they were in deep trouble. It would take time to get them here. And time was what they didn't have. With every minute, the tide was rising higher.

Mac ran into a shop selling gear for watersports. He returned a few minutes later with flippers. The kind divers used. 'I can move much faster with these. Try and get Emma again,' Mac said. 'Even if you can't hear her, she might be able to hear you. Tell her help is on the way. Try texting her, too. Sometimes a text will get through even if a call won't.' Uncaring of who might be watching, Mac stripped off his clothes until he was down to his boxers and T-shirt. Tossing his clothes to one side, he pulled on the flippers.

While he was doing that, Abby tried Emma's mobile again, despairing. She had tried every minute or two since she had got Emma's call, but it was hopeless. Her fingers fumbling with the tiny buttons, she sent a text.

Coming for you. Dad is here. Hold on. We love you.

As she pressed 'Send', Mac declared he was ready.

'We don't have time to wait for the rescue services. I'm going to go down there now. As soon as the Sea King gets here, make sure they know exactly which cave I'm searching. The coastguard, too. They'll have a pretty good idea of where the cave mouth is. The air ambulance is on its way with Lucy and Mike.'

He looked down at her and gently raised her chin, forcing her to look at him. 'I'm going to get her, Abby. I promise you. She'll be home safe with you soon.'

'Isn't it better to leave it to the Navy divers?' she had to ask.

Mac shook his head. 'She might be hurt. Or him. Or both. They may need medical attention. It has to be me.'

Abby nodded. Despite her terror, she knew Mac would do everything in his power to save their child, even if it meant sacrificing his own life. The thought of losing him, too, rocked her soul.

Just as he had done those weeks before, Mac disappeared over the side of the cliff. But this time the stakes were higher.

The water was freezing and murky. Mac forced himself to wait a minute or two to let the water settle. He had to be methodical and not let his impatience to get to Emma and her friend cloud his judgement. As he had hoped, after a few agonising seconds the water cleared and he was able to see the entrance to the cave. There was still a gap between the mouth of the cave and the sea, but Mac knew it wouldn't be long before that small opening disappeared.

He used his fins to propel himself towards the cave. The tide was so high. Would he be rescuing two corpses? No! Thinking like that did no one any good. He had to believe that Emma and her friend had found a high ledge to wait on.

He swam underwater towards the cave opening. After a few metres he stopped and raised his head to get his bearings. He was in a cave that stretched a metre above his head. It was almost completely dark inside and Mac had to strain to see anything. Damn it!

'Emma!' he shouted, his voice echoing in the semi-darkness. His heart plummeted when there was no reply. Had they got it completely wrong and were searching in the wrong spot? Or, even worse, was it too late?

He heard a noise coming from his right. He whirled round, trying frantically to make out in the gloom where the noise had come from. Then he saw them. Two small figures huddled together on a ledge. Relief coursed through him, to be replaced almost instantly by anxiety. They were still in desperate danger. The rising tide was lapping at their feet.

'I'm coming,' he yelled, frantically searching for another ledge. A higher one, where the tide couldn't reach. But there wasn't one. He had to get the children out. But how?

Quickly he swam towards the children.

'Hey, there,' he said softly. 'How're you doing?' He knew the children would be very frightened.

'Dad!' It was Emma's voice, Mac noted. Whatever injuries she might have, at least she was conscious. 'You found us. See, Simon? I told you my dad would find us. He rescues people all the time.'

The irony wasn't lost on Mac. The first time she really needed him was the day he'd found out that he wasn't her father. But that didn't change the way he felt. Not one iota. He couldn't love Emma any more if she were his biological child.

'Dad. Simon's hurt his leg. We think it's broken. That's why we couldn't get out. When the tide started coming in we managed to get up here, but we couldn't go any further.'

And you didn't think of leaving your friend and saving yourself? My brave, darling child. She was so much his and Abby's child, whatever the DNA test said.

Mac heaved himself out of the water and onto the ledge beside the children. There wasn't much space. A quick examination of Simon's leg told him Emma was right. It was broken. And not just broken—the boy had a compound fracture and was bleeding badly. The loss of blood, combined with the cold and fright, was having a bad effect on the young lad. He was shivering uncontrollably. They had to get him to hospital, and soon.

'I'm going to strap your leg as best I can,' he told the boy, 'and then I'm going to get you out of here, okay?' As he spoke he struggled out of his soaking wet T-shirt. It wasn't a great bandage, but it was all he had.

'I'm sorry, but this will hurt a little,' he told Simon. He straightened the leg as best he could before strapping it with his T-shirt.

'Emma, I'm going to have to take you out of here one at a time, do you understand? And I'm going to have to take Simon first. He's the one in need of help most urgently.'

It broke his heart to see the fear then resolve on Emma's face. She lifted her chin. 'That's okay,' she said. 'I can wait.'

He was so proud of her. Any other child would be crying, but not his Emma.

'Abby is waiting for you outside.'

He explained to Simon what he wanted him to do. 'Lie on your back and don't, whatever you do, try and fight me. I'm going to put my hands on either side of your head, and pull you out. As long as you don't panic, you'll be fine.' There was just a big enough gap between the top of the entrance to the cave and the water for him to make it out with the boy. But would there still be a gap by the time he returned?

Mac was facing the worst dilemma of his life. How could he leave Emma? What if he didn't make it back in time? How would he live without Emma? How would Abby live without the child she loved?

But if he had any chance of saving Emma, he had to act now.

'I'll be back as quick as I can,' he said. 'Hold on.'

He grasped Simon around the head and pulled him out of the cave, taking care not to let water splash in the boy's mouth. If the boy panicked now, it could be fatal for both of them. As he swam, his heart and soul was back in the cave.

He found the rock where Abby was still waiting. She had been joined by the crew of the air ambulance. Lucy and Mike were standing by, waiting to help him. From the corner of his eye he could see the lifeboat circling nearby. He knew they couldn't risk getting any closer. There was no sign of the Sea King. It must still be waiting for the divers.

'Where's Em?' Abby's face was white.

'She's still in the cave. I'm going back for her. I couldn't take her as well as Simon.'

Mac was helping Lucy and Mike carefully lift Simon out of the water and onto a stretcher. Before he could stop her, Abby jumped into the water and was swimming towards the entrance of the cave.

'No, Abby, wait!' he shouted, but either she couldn't hear him or she was ignoring him. She carried on swimming towards the cave.

Muttering a curse, Mac gave one final heave and his arms lightened as the injured boy was taken out of his arms. He plunged back into the water after Abby. Didn't she know that she, too, could drown? He could lose both the people he loved most in the world. The realisation cut through his fear. He loved Abby. He loved her more than his life itself. He had been running away from it but now, when he could lose her, he knew a life without her and Emma was no life at all.

The realisation added strength and soon he was back in the cave. By now there was no longer a gap between the top of the cave entrance and the cave and Mac had to take a deep gulp of air and swim underwater. His lungs were bursting as he once more emerged into the cave. To his horror he saw that the water was now up to Emma's waist, even though she was standing on the ledge. Abby was treading water nearby.

'Emma, we have to go now. You, too, Abby,' Mac said, trying to keep his voice even.

Emma was staring, her eyes wide with fear. 'I can't,' she said. 'I've hurt my arm.'

'Yes, you can, my love. Mac and I will each take one side of you. And we'll help you through. We won't let anything happen to you, I promise,' Abby said.

Mac marvelled at Abby. The fear was gone from her voice. It was steady and calm, as if she was suggesting a walk in the park.

'We'll be underwater for thirty seconds. But your mum and I will be on either side of you. All you have to do is keep as still as you can and let us pull you along. Can you do that?' he said.

'Yes,' Emma replied.

'Good girl. But we have to go now.' Mac slid back into the water. Abby held onto Emma's good arm as she slipped into the water and then she jumped in beside them. Mac's heart lurched. Getting through the channel, swimming against the incoming current, would be a challenge. But what choice did they have?

'Okay. On my count of three, we're all going to take a deep breath and then go under. Okay?'

Abby and Emma nodded.

'One, two, three,' Mac said, and then between them he and Abby had Emma. He gripped Emma around the waist, careful to avoid her injured arm. To his relief, the rising tide meant that the current wasn't as strong as it had been. But still he felt every second of the time they spent underwater. True to her word, Emma relaxed, letting them pull her along.

At last, when he thought Emma wouldn't be able to hold her breath any longer, they broke through into the fresh air. The three of them trod water, breathing in deep lungfuls of fresh, clean air, and then the lifeboat was beside them and men were dropping into the water, helping them lift Emma gently onto the boat.

As soon as they were all safely on board, the boat

sped off towards the shore. Over the top of Emma's head Mac and Abby shared a look. In Abby's eyes there was relief and gratitude and something else—love. Soon, when all this was over, he would tell her about the DNA test, but all that mattered right now was that he had his small precious family safe and well beside him.

CHAPTER SIXTEEN

'I WAS scared,' Emma said, 'but I remembered what Dad told me once and that helped me stay calm.' She was sitting on the hospital trolley. Her arm had been X-rayed and, as they'd expected, found to be broken. It had been put in a cast but the staff wanted to keep in her in overnight for observation. The bruise that was blossoming on her forehead suggested she had knocked her head, too.

'And what was that, darling?' Abby asked.

'He told me that panic kills more people than anything else. He said if you use your head, there is always a way out of most problems. So that's what I did.'

Abby slid a glance at Mac. Emma was more her father's daughter than she had realised. 'When Simon fell, I knew he had hurt his leg quite badly and I knew we couldn't walk out of the cave together. Not through the tide. So I climbed down to stay with him. But I had to get help. My mobile wasn't working. I could hear you, Mum. Some of the words, at least, but not everything. I didn't know for sure if you could hear me.

'I waded out, the tide wasn't so high then, and I waved my arms until I got someone's attention. Then I went back to stay with Simon.' Her voice trembled slightly. 'But on the way I fell over a rock that I couldn't see in the water and bumped my head. I think that's when I hurt my arm.'

'You were very brave. It must have been difficult to climb back up to Simon with only one arm.'

Why didn't you stay out of the cave once you got out? Abby wanted to ask. But she knew the answer. Her heart swelled with pride. Abby hadn't wanted to leave her friend alone and hurt by himself. As Mac had pointed out, she couldn't change her daughter's nature. And despite everything she had been through in the last hour or two, she wouldn't change her daughter for the world.

Eventually, Emma closed her eyes, the exhaustion and the excitement of the last few hours catching up with her.

Abby reached for Mac's hand as they watched her breathing deeply. To her surprise he didn't pull away. Instead, he brought her hand to his mouth and kissed each finger tenderly.

'My God, Abby. For a moment I thought I was going to lose you and Emma. Don't ever do anything like that to me again.' His voice was ragged.

'Don't want to have to train a new teammate?' she said lightly.

'I don't want to lose the woman I love,' Mac replied quietly.

Abby's heart kicked against her ribs. He'd said he loved her. Did he mean as a friend or a lover? She had to know. Silently she waited for him to go on.

'Two months ago I thought I was happy. I had a job I loved, a decent place to live where I could do the sports I enjoy whenever I wanted. It was a good life, a perfect life, until you walked into it.'

Abby couldn't stop her smile. He sounded almost

annoyed. But she knew his life had been empty of all that was important, even if he didn't.

'And then I found out I had a child. This child.' He bent over and kissed Emma gently on the cheek. 'At first I could hardly take it in. I didn't want it to be true. Emma would be nothing except a duty and while I knew I couldn't ignore my responsibilities, I never thought that she would become such an important part of my life. And as for you...' He sighed. 'You drove me insane almost from the moment I set eyes on you. Not just those cat eyes, or that mouth that just cries out to be kissed, or your body, which would make most women weep— those are the things that counted in my other life, but as I got to know you, I realised I was falling hard for you. And it frightened me.' He half smiled. 'That was a new one for me. I didn't think I was scared of anything but I was. I was scared of being in love.'

A warm glow was spreading upwards from her toes and surrounding her heart like a blanket. But she still couldn't be certain he was saying what she so desperately wanted to hear.

'I thought if I took you to bed, that would break the spell. But I was wrong. If anything, I wanted more. I wanted nights and nights with you. I couldn't imagine a time when I would no longer want you. Then you told me you loved me and that frightened me even more. What if I couldn't live up to your expectations of me? What if I let you—and Emma—down? What if I turned out to be like my father? I'd be dragging you and Em down with me. I couldn't do that. I tried to stay away from you, Abby. I wanted you to find someone else, even if the thought ripped me apart. And if it meant losing Emma, too, I knew the man you chose would be a good man. Someone who would love Emma the way she deserved.'

'Do you still believe that?' Abby clasped her hands together to stop herself from reaching out and pushing a wayward lock of hair out of his eyes. Didn't he know that she would never love another man as long as she lived?

'No. I don't. I came close to losing you and Emma today. I knew then that I couldn't let you go. I'm not strong enough to do that.'

Abby came and crouched by his side. Taking his hands in hers, she looked up into his eyes. 'You are the strongest man I know, Mac. In the truest sense of the word. You are not your father. And even if you were I would still take my chances with you. I would rather have a tempestuous life with you than one without you.'

He stood up abruptly, forcing her to drop her hands. 'But that's not all. The lab that took our DNA for testing called today. That's why I was on my way to see you.'

A tendril of fear curled around her heart. The look in Mac's eyes told her something was far from right.

He lowered his voice. 'Abby, Emma is not my child.'

'What?'

'Whatever Sara told you, Abby is not mine.'

Abby's head was reeling. 'But why did she say you were?' As soon as she said the words she guessed the truth. Sara probably hadn't been sure who the father was and that was why she hadn't wanted to give Abby a name at first. But when she'd known she was going to die, she'd given Abby the name of the man she would have liked most to be the father of her child, Mac. Perhaps in her heart she had harboured a dream that once her child was born, she would go to Mac and persuade him Emma was his. They would never know.

'Whoever the biological father of Emma is, it isn't me.'

The pain and disappointment in his eyes shook her.

What now? What would he do? There was no reason for him to continue with the relationship. He would walk out of Emma's life and what would that do to Emma?

'Emma's going to be devastated. She adores you. She's so proud to call you her father.'

Mac's jaw tightened. 'No prouder than I was to think she was my daughter. And I love her.' A small smile curled his lips. 'I never thought the day would come when I'd say that.' The smile faded from his eyes. 'I don't care what the test says. I don't care who the biological father is. Damn it, Abby, Emma is my daughter. I don't want to lose her.' He looked away. Emma was still sleeping peacefully.

He reached out and took Abby's hand and pulled her to her feet.

'Come with me. There's something I want to show you.'

'But, Emma... I don't want to leave her.'

'She'll be out for the count for an hour or two. We won't be that long. I'll ask them to bleep me the minute she wakes up.'

Abby hesitated.

'Please, Abby.'

She couldn't resist the appeal in his blue eyes. He was hurting.

She followed him out to the car park. He opened the door to his Jeep and helped her in.

'I don't suppose you're going to tell me where you're taking me?' she said.

He smiled at her and her heart cracked. She loved him so much it hurt. She would have given anything for Emma to be his child.

They drove in silence, turning onto the track where Mac had taken her a few weeks earlier. Abby was baffled. As they drove they passed diggers and lorries. There was obviously work going on.

Mac helped Abby out of the car.

'You and Emma are everything I wanted. I just didn't know it. I love you both.' He turned to Abby, pinning her with the intensity in his blue eyes. 'I'm in love with you, Abby. I'm not good at finding the words, but I know I couldn't bear to live without you. I want to wake up every morning with you beside me and I want yours to be the last face I see when I go to sleep. I want to live my life with you and Emma by my side. I want to have breakfast and dinner with you and Em, take you to Tiree to show you the place I grew up. The works.'

Abby's heart started to pound.

'I thought I could run from you. But I couldn't. I wouldn't let myself accept that I was falling for you.' He smiled sadly. 'Thinking I was a father was shock enough and even though it turned out to be the best thing that ever happened to me, I didn't know if I could commit myself to a wife. All I knew was that I didn't want to let you go.'

He gestured to the building site. 'When you refused to let me build this house for you, I thought I would build it anyway. I began to realise that I was putting down roots. Then, when I was discussing the plans with the architect, I saw the little sitting room with you in it, looking out to sea, a book in your hand. The garden where you would grow your roses. The kitchen where we would eat, the bedroom where I would fall asleep with you in my arms and the starlight shining in the window. Everywhere I looked, there you were. You and Emma. My family. My heart. My reason for living.'

He reached out and tipped her chin so she was looking into his eyes. 'Abby, I love you. I want you to marry me. I want you and Emma to be my family. I know she's not my biological child and that one day she might want to find her real father, but until then, could you love me enough to spend the rest of your life with me?'

A frisson of joy was spreading through Abby's body. Happiness swelled inside her. He loved her. But she had to be sure that this wasn't his way of hanging onto Emma.

'I'll never stop you seeing Em, whatever the results of the test say, and as long as she wants you in her life, which, knowing Em, is going to be for ever. You do know that, Mac?'

He glared at her. 'You don't think I'm saying all this simply because of Em, do you?' He smiled grimly. 'I love you. Heart and soul. For ever. I want babies with you, to grow old with you. To laugh with you. Argue, too, if it comes to that.' He pulled her into his arms. 'I love you, Abby Stevens. Will you get that into your stubborn head?'

The blood was singing through her veins. The way he was looking at her left no doubt in her mind. She brought her face up to his. 'For heaven's sake, how long do I have to wait for my fiancé to kiss me, then?'

And then he was kissing her as if he would never let her go, and she knew at last they had both found the place they were meant to be.

* * *

Emma was just waking up when they tiptoed back into her cubicle. One look at their faces must have told her something was up.

'Hey, what's going on with you two?' she asked.

Mac and Abby sat on the bed on either side of Emma, careful not to bump her injured arm.

'We have two things to tell you. Both are surprises. The first you're going to have to prepare yourself for, the second we think you'll like.'

Emma eyed them warily. Then she broke into a wide smile. 'I know what one of the surprises is,' she said. 'You two are getting married. Am I right?'

'You are. But how did you guess?' Abby said.

'Grown-ups can be so silly,' Emma said scornfully. 'I knew you were in love ages ago. Anybody, even a kid like me...' she slid Abby a mocking glance '...could see it a mile away. Even if you are old.'

Abby and Mac laughed. 'Hey, we're not that old,' Mac protested. 'There's still a few years before we get really ancient.'

'So you're okay with us getting married?' Abby asked.

There was no need for a reply. The smile that lit up Emma's face was all the answer Abby needed. 'I wished you would get married. Does that mean we'll all live together? For ever? Like a real family? I'll have my mum and my dad just like all the other children?'

Despite her happiness, Abby felt a chill. It was going to be a blow to Emma finding out Mac wasn't her biological father.

'Emma,' Mac said, taking her hand. 'I have something to tell you. But first I want you to know that I couldn't love you more than I do now.'

The smile left Emma's face. 'What's going on?' she whispered. She clutched Abby's hand again.

'Remember that test we had? To prove I was your dad?'

'When you and me went to the hospital?'

'Yes, that one.' He took a deep breath and Abby knew he was having difficulty finding the right words. 'It turns out that I'm not your father. At least, I never made you.'

'You mean it wasn't your sperm with my real mummy's eggs?'

Mac looked so shocked that Abby had to laugh. 'I've always told Emma the truth. And it seemed silly to wait until some other child gave her the wrong information. Emma knows how babies are made. At least,' she rushed on, in case Mac misunderstood, 'the biological basis.'

Emma frowned. 'I thought you said people made babies when they loved each other. But my real mum didn't even know who my father was.'

Oh, dear. Abby thought. This was going to take some explaining...

Luckily Mac stepped in. 'Your mum, Sara, was a kind, lovely person. But she was a little lonely. Sometimes people make babies because they want someone to love and look after. I think that's why Sara made you. Whoever your real father is, your mother made you out of love.'

'And you always have to remember that,' Abby said softly. 'She loved you more than anything in the world. So much she didn't want to share you.'

'But if Mac's not my real dad...' Emma's lip trembled and tears spilled down her cheek '...then we're not really a family.'

'Emma, look at me,' Mac said firmly. He waited until

Emma turned her blue eyes to his. Abby's throat tightened when she saw the trust there. 'You and Abby are my family. I love you both more than anything in the world. I want to be your dad for as long as you'll let me. I want to be the one who chases the boyfriends away, who picks you up from parties.' His voice softened. 'Who walks you up the aisle. We can carry on looking for your real dad, but if you let me, us…' he turned to Abby '…we want to adopt you, so you really belong to us. What do you say?'

Emma cuddled into Mac, snuggling deep into his arms. He stroked her hair, comforting her.

'I say yes,' Emma said. Then she pulled away and took hold of Abby's hand, too. 'So does that mean I can go to night-time parties now?'

EPILOGUE

ABBY stood by the window of her new home. In the sitting room, her mother and Mac's were chatting ninety to the dozen, each trying to outdo the other. Mac's mother had come down for the wedding and although she had grumbled about being away from Tiree almost constantly since she had got to Cornwall, Abby suspected she was pleased and touched that Mac had asked her to come to their wedding. Two more days then she'd be walking down the aisle with Mac, and she still couldn't believe it.

She felt his arm slip around her waist and she leaned against him, savouring the warmth and security of his embrace.

'Happy?' he whispered into her ear.

She nodded. Two more days and he'd be coming to live with her and Emma. He had refused to move in before, saying he wanted to wait until after they married. The house was everything he had told her it would be. Although enormous windows captured the view from every side, it was still cosy.

'You must come to Tiree to visit me,' Mac's mother was saying. 'I don't live in a grand house like this,' she sniffed, but Abby was beginning to realise that she didn't mean half of what she said, 'or in London, where all the fancy people live, but my house is good enough for me.'

'Your house is so sweet, Gran MacNeil,' Emma protested. 'I love it. Especially the chickens. And so is yours, Grandma Stevens,' she added hastily.

Abby smiled. Emma was ever the diplomat. Whatever differences the two older women had with their own children, there was no doubt they doted on their grandchild. Indeed, they spent all their time trying to compete for her affection.

Behind her, she heard Mac stifle a laugh. He had learned to be tolerant of both parents. 'At the very least,' he had told Abby, 'we both know how not to do it.'

Emma left the two old women to their bickering and came to stand next to Abby. She was to be bridesmaid at their wedding and was barely able to control her excitement about having a brother or sister to boss around in a few months' time. Mac reached across to pull her into the circle of his embrace.

'My two best girls,' he said. 'My daughter and my wife-to-be.' Mac and Abby had formally adopted Emma. His voice turned serious. 'Have I told you both that I consider myself to be the luckiest man alive?'

Emma giggled. 'Only all the time. You're so sad, Dad.'

He placed a proprietorial hand on Abby's stomach, where her body was just beginning to swell with her pregnancy.

'No, not that. Not any more.'

Abby raised her face to his. She never got over seeing her love reflected in his eyes.

'I have the best life,' Emma sighed happily.

'The best life. That's what we have. No one could be luckier.'

Together they watched as the sun melted into the sea.

LET'S TALK
Romance

For exclusive extracts, competitions
and special offers, find us online:

f facebook.com/millsandboon

⊙ @millsandboonuk

𝕐 @millsandboon

Or get in touch on 0844 844 1351*

For all the latest titles coming soon, visit
millsandboon.co.uk/nextmonth